IN THE DESERT
1873 – 1948

CANADA
WASHINGTON
IDAHO
OREGON
SCALE
0 20 40 60 Miles
Grand Coulee Dam
GRAND COULEE
COLUMBIA
SPOKANE RIVER
Spokane
Dry Falls
Wenatchee
COLUMBIA RIVER
YAKIMA RIVER
Moses Lake
SNAKE RIVER
Richland
Pasco
Kennewick
Wallula Landing
Walla Walla
Lewiston

Roll On, Columbia

ROLL ON, COLUMBIA

A Historical Novel

BOOK THREE

Into the Desert

BILL GULICK

UNIVERSITY PRESS OF COLORADO

International Standard Book Number 0-87081-472-9

Published by the
UNIVERSITY PRESS OF COLORADO
P.O. Box 849
Niwot, Colorado 80544

Cover painting: Norman Adams

Cover design & interior design and composition for Books 1–3:
Pauline Christensen • Longmont, Colorado

The University Press of Colorado is a cooperative publishing enterprise supported, in part, by Adams State College, Colorado State University, Fort Lewis College, Mesa State College, Metropolitan State College of Denver, University of Colorado, University of Northern Colorado, University of Southern Colorado, and Western State College of Colorado.

The paper used in this publication meets the minimum requirements of the American National Standard for Information Sciences—Permanence of Paper for Printed Library Materials. ANSI Z39.48-1984

Library of Congress Cataloging-in-Publication Data

Gulick, Bill, 1916–
Into the desert / by Bill Gulick.
p. cm. — (Roll on, Columbia : bk. 3)
ISBN 0-87081-472-9 (hardcover : alk. paper)
I. Title. II. Series: Gulick, Bill, 1916– Roll on, Columbia : bk. 3.
PS3557.U43I58 1998
813'.54—DC21 97-48795
CIP

10 9 8 7 6 5 4 3 2 1

Roll On, Columbia

Folk song by Woody Guthrie

Green Douglas firs, where the waters cut through,
Down her wild mountains and canyons she flew;
Canadian Northwest to the ocean so blue;
It's roll on, Columbia, roll on!
Roll on, Columbia, roll on!
Roll on, Columbia, roll on!
Your power is turning
Our darkness to dawn,
So roll on, Columbia, roll on!

Tom Jefferson's vision would not let him rest;
An empire he saw in the Pacific Northwest;
Sent Lewis and Clark and they did the rest;
So roll on, Columbia, roll on!
Roll on, Columbia, roll on!
Roll on, Columbia, roll on!
Your power is turning
Our darkness to dawn,
So roll on, Columbia, roll on!

At Bonneville now there are ships in the locks;
Waters have risen and cleared all the rocks;
Shiploads of plenty will steam past the docks;
It's roll on, Columbia, roll on!
Roll on, Columbia, roll on!
Roll on, Columbia, roll on!
Your power is turning
Our darkness to dawn,
So roll on, Columbia, roll on!

And on up the river is the Grand Coulee Dam;
The mightiest thing ever built by a man,
To run the great factories and water the land;
It's roll on, Columbia, roll on!
Roll on, Columbia, roll on!
Roll on, Columbia, roll on!
Your power is turning
Our darkness to dawn,
So roll on, Columbia, roll on!

Author's Note

In 1941, the Bonneville Power Administration paid folksinger Woody Guthrie $266.66 to spend a month writing twenty-six songs in praise of the development of government water and power projects. The ballad "Roll On, Columbia" was one of the songs he composed.

Used as background music to the twenty-minute documentary movie on the building of Grand Coulee Dam, it has been heard by millions of visitors to the site since that time, so it has proved to be a real bargain as a musical score.

Though I never met Woody Guthrie, I long have been an admirer of his songs. As I researched and wrote this book, I came to realize that we had a number of things in common. We both were raised in Oklahoma during the Dust Bowl and Depression years of the 1930s. I spent two years working for a private utility that was building electric lines to serve rural Oklahoma areas in need of power, flood control, navigation benefits, and irrigation water, just as he later worked for BPA, which was doing the same thing in the Pacific Northwest.

Called a "radical" in his day, all Woody Guthrie asked of the politicians was a job for a decent rate of pay. Coming to know construction workers as I did, I found them to be the salt of the earth and the strength of a nation in peace and war, just as he proclaimed them to be in his ballads.

Some fifty years ago I settled in the heart of the Columbia River watershed near its juncture with its largest tributary, the Snake. Since then, all my writings have dealt with some aspect of the past, present, and future of the two rivers. During these years, I have followed, reported on, and taken part in controversy as to what uses should be made of the waters of the legendary "River of the West."

In planning what probably will be my last book on the Columbia River, I decided that the best way to tell the story of what man has done to the river was from the viewpoint of five generations of white and Indian families whose fictional lives were closely entwined with the use and development of the Columbia from the establishment of Astoria in 1811 down to the present day. All other characters in the book are real.

Some twenty-five years ago in the introduction to my nonfiction book *Snake River Country*, I wrote: "Somewhere along the way I learned that a great river influences the lives of the people in its watershed just as surely as the acts of those people influence the life of the river. Without water, people die. Without people's concern, a river dies. Thus, this book …"

That statement still holds true today. So to all the river people I have known—both real and fictional—over the years, as well as to the memory of Woody Guthrie, this book is dedicated.

—Bill Gulick

Synopsis of Books One & Two

After his father drowns as the Astor supply ship *Tonquin* crosses the Columbia River Bar in 1811, sixteen-year-old seaman Ben Warren becomes the only American living at Fort Astoria. When the post is sold to the British in 1818, he decides to spend the rest of his life in the Pacific Northwest, though he is not interested in fur trading. Forming a partnership with a young Chinook Indian, Conco, they form a business of guiding ships across the dangerous bar. Under the Joint Occupancy Treaty in effect between the United States and Great Britain 1818–1846, citizens of both nations have equal access to the Oregon Country, whose eventual ownership will be decided by its residents.

In Hawaii, Ben meets Lolanee, the beautiful granddaughter of King Kamehameha, and promises to make her Queen of the Pacific Northwest if she will marry him and move into Hilltop House overlooking Astoria. This she does, though she finds her "kingdom" a primitive one. Meanwhile, Conco chooses as his mate a young Chinook girl, who is shocked when he makes her break tradition by not forcing the head of their first-born son into a press that will give it the slanted appearance that has long been a mark of royalty in the Chinook tribe.

Thus begins a dynasty of white and Indian families whose lives will be closely tied to the Columbia River for five generations.

When steam comes to the lower Columbia in 1836 with the British ship *Beaver*, Tommy, Ben's son, becomes a river captain, while Sitkum, Conco's son, assists him as engineer. Rivalry grows between the British Hudson's Bay Company and American emigrants, who are beginning to settle in the Willamette Valley. Tommy marries Freda Svenson, a young Swedish girl, and they file a land claim near Rooster Rock just downriver from the Lower Cascades.

News reaches Oregon that the Joint Occupancy Treaty ended in 1846 and that all the country south of the 49th parallel will become part of the United States. Steam-powered boats now dominate the lower Columbia and are beginning to be operated through the Cascades and into the desert sector of the river as far as the Snake.

Knowing that part of the river well, Tommy and Sitkum will play important roles in its development from 1847 to 1872. Later, their sons, Lars Warren and Alex Conley, will be involved in the events related in Book Two.

In late November 1847 Indians living near the Whitman Mission, terrified by an outbreak of disease that destroys half their tribe, kill Marcus and Narcissa Whitman in the Walla Walla Valley, along with twelve other whites, beginning a war that lasts for several years. Soon after peace comes and treaties are made assigning the Indians of the interior country to reservations, gold is discovered in the Snake River country, causing an influx of miners and increased traffic on the Columbia and Snake Rivers. At nine, Lars Warren joins his fourteen-year-old friend Willie Gray as the two boys work aboard a keelboat owned by William Gray, who is transporting supplies up the Columbia and Snake Rivers to the Idaho mines. Charting the Snake through Hell's Canyon, both boys become seasoned rivermen, destined to earn their captain's licenses before they are old enough to vote.

Meanwhile, Emil, Tommy's younger brother, follows the gold rush to California, becomes a lawyer, and meets a beautiful Spanish girl named Dolores. Marrying her and forming a business partnership with her brother Carlos, Emil moves north to Portland. Working as an eleven-year-old cabin boy aboard a river steamboat, Lars meets and falls in love with nine-year-old Daphne deBeachamp, whose mother, Lili, is bringing a bevy of ladies to the boomtown of Walla Walla, where she plans to establish a first class "Entertainment Parlor."

Fearful that his family might not accept his marriage to the daughter of a madam, Lars asks Emil to prepare the family for the news. Because it is now 1872 and only a year or two past Ben and Lolanee's fiftieth wedding anniversary, Emil arranges an "Anniversary Cruise" up the Columbia from its mouth to Lewiston, Idaho, 470 miles inland, covering three different sectors of the river, with the captain of each of the three boats—Ben, Tommy, and now Lars himself—a member of the Warren family.

As the cruise ends at the mouth of the Snake with everyone happy, seventy-nine-year-old Ben looks back on his long life, thinking of all the changes he has seen on the river and wondering what lies ahead for his grandson Lars in the desert sector of the upper Columbia.

Roll On, Columbia

1.

Even though her mother, Lili deBeauchamp, was known far and wide in the upriver country as the owner of the fanciest whorehouse in Walla Walla, the marriage of her beautiful, black-haired daughter, Daphne, to the handsome, yellow-haired young steamboat captain, Lars Warren, was the social event of the season. Conducted in the Catholic church by Father Patrick Flannigan, whose affection for the lady known as French Lil had become even warmer following her recent five-thousand-dollar contribution to the Church Building Fund, the wedding and the reception that followed in the next-door Parish Hall was attended by everybody who was anybody in the rapidly growing city.

All three living river captains in the Warren family were there with their wives, covering a long span of years in the history of the Columbia River from its mouth to the distant inland port of Lewiston, Idaho, 470 miles from the sea. Eldest of the clan was white-haired, seventy-nine-year-old Captain Benjamin Warren, whose father had drowned guiding the John Jacob Astor ship *Tonquin* in over the Columbia River Bar in the spring of 1811. With him was his still beautiful wife, Lolanee, the Hawaiian princess whom he had brought to America and promised to make Queen of the Pacific Northwest.

Also present was their oldest son, Captain Thomas Warren, who with his golden-haired Swedish wife, Freda, lived near Rooster Rock 125 miles up the Columbia just below the six-mile stretch of rapids called the Cascades. Coming up from Portland with his lovely Spanish wife, Dolores, was the youngest son, Emil Warren, the self-confessed landlubber of the family, whose only use for water was to float the boats of the Oregon Steam Navigation Company, which, largely through his efforts, had established a monopoly on the freight, passenger, and portage revenue on the Columbia, Willamette, and Snake Rivers.

Though not directly related to the Warren family, Carlos Ibanez, whose sister had married Emil Warren, and his flaxen-haired German bride, Hanna Lowehr, also were there. Born and raised a Catholic, Carlos had been forced to accept Hanna Lowehr's firm declaration that neither she nor their growing brood of children would convert to Catholicism from her Dutch-Reform-Congregational-Presbyterian faith. Carlos hoped that whatever heavenly scales weighed such matters would be balanced by the fact that Emil Warren was allowing his and Dolores's six children to be raised as good Catholics, while the new bridegroom, Captain Lars Warren, had promised that his and Daphne's children would become Catholics like their mother.

Following the wedding reception, Lars and Daphne spent the night in the bridal suite of Walla Walla's finest hotel, the Dacres. Next day, they were driven the thirty-two miles to Wallula Landing, where Lars's new command, the *Inland Queen*, was moored, in a luxurious Entertainment Parlor phaeton whose team of matched sorrel trotters was expertly handled by the huge, muscular Goliath Samson, personal bodyguard to French Lil and chief enforcer of decorum at her Entertainment Parlor, where ill-mannered behavior by male guests was frowned on and discouraged by whatever means were necessary. Despite his size, his touch on the reins of the team was as light, sensitive, and skillful as it was on the cello, drums, tambourine, and other musical instruments he played so well when called upon to do so.

By noon, they had traveled twenty miles, reaching the small settlement of ex–Hudson's Bay Company employees called Frenchtown. When they stopped in a grove of shade trees along the Touchet River to stretch their legs and eat the sumptuous picnic lunch prepared for them by the Dacres Hotel gourmet cook, Lars apologized to Daphne for the brevity of their honeymoon.

"I'm scheduled to take the *Inland Queen* downriver to Celilo this afternoon," he told her. "You'll go with me and share the captain's cabin, of course. Tomorrow, we'll make the run upriver to Lewiston. It won't be much of a honeymoon for you, I know, but it's the best I can give you for now."

"Oh, Lars, it will be wonderful!" Daphne exclaimed, her dark eyes sparkling. "When we first met, you were only a cabin boy, with Golly so suspicious of your intentions toward me he would have thrown you overboard if you'd done a thing out of line. Now you're captain of your own brand-new boat and he respects you as much as I do. Don't you, Golly?"

Not even Lili deBeauchamp herself would have dared take such liberties with Goliath Samson's name, but the dark-visaged giant was so fond of Daphne that he did not care *what* she called him, as long as she gave him a smile and a pleasant word now and then.

"Sure," he muttered between bites of his third ham-and-cheese-on-rye sandwich. "I like Lars fine now." After making what was for him a profound statement, he scowled at Lars and asked, "You two gonna live on the boat?"

"For the time being, we probably will. I've asked the Company to double the size of my cabin so that Daphne will be comfortable when we travel. Ashore, I've had the management of the Wallula Palace Hotel remodel the second floor so that we'll have decent living quarters there."

"That hotel ain't no palace, Lars, and Wallula sure ain't no place for a girl like Miss Daphne. Not with the teamster, sawmill, and railroad riffraff around, gettin' drunk, fightin', and raisin' a ruckus at all hours."

"Oh, pooh!" Daphne sniffed. "Working men don't scare me a bit. Mother taught me years ago that they never bother a real lady."

"You ain't never seen men as bad nor a town as rough as Wallula, Miss Daphne. Lars oughtn't to leave you alone there overnight. What you'd ought to do when he's gone is let me take you to Walla Walla, where you can stay with your mother."

"Fiddlesticks! I knew when I married Lars that I was marrying the river, too. He'll never be happy out of its sight—and neither will I. Wherever he says we should live, we will."

Spunky was the word for Daphne, Lars mused with a sudden rush of pride. "We won't be living at the hotel very long," he said. "While the railroad is being built, Wallula will be the center of activity along this section of the river. After it's finished and the workmen are gone, it will become a quieter, more civilized town, I'm sure. If you like, I'll build us a fine, big house overlooking the river there."

"From what I hear, the railroad might never *be* finished," Goliath Samson grunted gloomily. "People say old Doc Baker is running out of money again, with twenty more miles of railroad yet to be built."

"I know what people are saying, Golly," Lars said, shaking his head. "But Dr. Baker has managed to fool them all before. My guess is he'll find some way to get more financing and keep on building the railroad till it's finished."

Indeed, the outrageous, impractical project conceived by the cantankerous, crippled, forty-eight-year-old Dr. Dorsey Syng Baker had been pronounced dead so many times, yet still survived; it appeared to have the nine lives of the proverbial cat. A licensed physician who had graduated from Jefferson Medical College in Philadelphia in 1845, Dr. Baker had practiced in Des Moines, Iowa, for a couple of years, migrated to the Willamette Valley in 1848, then had forsaken the practice of medicine to engage in a number of business ventures. After marrying and fathering seven children, he had suffered an illness at the age of thirty-four that had crippled his left arm and leg. Refusing to recognize the fact that he would be physically handicapped for the rest of his life, he had moved his family to Walla Walla in 1858 and expanded his activities into farming, ranching, and the mercantile business.

Going into partnership with a friend named John Boyer, Dr. Baker found their store besieged by requests from wintering miners to keep pouches of gold dust in their big metal safe. Since the prospectors were glad to pay five dollars a month for the service, with the only record keeping required a tag on each sack noting the amount of gold dust in the pouch and its owner's name, the partners at first called their establishment the "Bank Place." As the town grew and demand developed for the services of a real bank, the partners applied for and received a charter for the first bank to be established in Washington Territory. From that day forward, the Baker-Boyer Bank, as it was named, boasted that it never had closed its doors on a business day nor lost a dollar of depositor money.

Though not a particularly religious man, Dr. Baker attributed his business success to the strict observance of two commandments: (1) never risk deposited funds in questionable ventures and (2) shun debt as you would the Devil.

As the gold boom in Idaho waned during the late 1860s, it became clear that the fertile, rolling hills and valleys of southeastern Washington Territory were producing a new kind of gold: wheat. Grown in such quantity that it became a glut on the local market, the high-quality grain soon was being exported to Portland, San Francisco, and Pacific Rim countries overseas, where it brought premium prices. Since the only means of transport was on boats owned by the Oregon Steam Navigation Company, the management of the O.S.N. was vitally interested in any project that would simplify transporting the sacked grain to the river landings where it could be taken aboard as revenue-earning cargo.

Following the Civil War, three railroad companies—the Union Pacific, the Great Northern, and the Northern Pacific—had promoted grandiose schemes to build transcontinental lines across the country. By 1869, only the Union Pacific had laid any track, but their line connecting Omaha to San Francisco was a long way from southeastern Washington's grain-growing district. In the Walla Walla area, farmers wanting to transport their wheat to market either had to make the long haul in their own wagons or pay professional teamsters as much as fifteen dollars a ton to take the sacked grain from their fields to the river landings.

"It costs us thirty-three cents a bushel to put our wheat aboard the riverboats," the exasperated farmers complained to Dr. Baker. "Adding freight charges to Portland, plus shipping costs along the coast or overseas, we have to pay close to a dollar a bushel in freight charges alone to get our wheat to market. Something's got to be done."

"I agree," Dr. Baker said testily. "Let's begin by getting a railroad company to give us a cost estimate on building a branch line from Walla Walla to Wallula Landing."

At that time, the nearest existing rail connection was with the Union Pacific at Kelton, Utah, six hundred miles away. Both the Great Northern and the Northern Pacific were lobbying Congress for forty-mile-wide grants of land across the continent against which they could issue bonds that would give them the millions of dollars they felt they would need before they could start laying track. If and when a transcontinental railroad passed through the Walla Walla area, it most likely would be the Northern Pacific. So it was that company Dr. Baker and the wheat-growing farmers pressured to give them a cost estimate of a feeder line from Walla Walla to Wallula Landing.

The news was not good. According to the Northern Pacific experts, thirty-two miles of narrow-gauge railroad would cost $673,000. Projected against anticipated freight revenue, which must be well under the rates charged by the Teamsters Association in order to attract business, there was simply no way the line could show a profit. Discouraged, the farmers gave up. But Dr. Baker did not.

"That's far too much," he snapped. "Give me a few days to do some figuring. I'm sure I can do better."

He did. Though he knew nothing about railroad-building, he had designed, supervised, or built with his own hands such things as sawmills, gristmills, houses, and barns. If made of wood, metal, or any combination thereof, he was confident that he could build a railroad or hire men with the necessary skills to build it for him. With his usual thoroughness, he figured out every detail of the project before calling together twenty-four of his farmer, banker, and business friends.

"According to my estimate, the railroad can be built for $330,000," he told them. "Half of what the Northern Pacific experts said it would cost. What I propose to do is form a company, with myself as president, that will sell stock and control every aspect of the project. That way, we can be sure that not a single dollar is wasted."

"How much stock must we sell?" John Boyer asked.

"We'll begin with $30,000, subscribed to, I hope, by the men in this room."

"Where will the other $300,000 come from?"

"A public bond issue, sold countywide. As I've worked out the figures, we can pay off the bonds at 8 percent interest in twelve years, with freight charges not to exceed eight dollars a ton. If we put the bond issue on the ballot this September, we can start work at once, cutting timbers for the rails in the mountains and floating them down the Yakima River to Wallula."

"Timbers?" a farmer asked in a puzzled voice. "You're gonna use wooden rails?"

"That's one of the cost-savers I've worked out, Ralph. Instead of iron rails, we'll use four-by-six fir stringers topped with three-eighths-by-two-inch strap iron on the straight stretches of track, with iron rail only on the curves."

"Will that work?"

"It's worked on the portage railroads at the Cascades and The Dalles. I don't know why it won't work here."

"Won't you need heavier locomotives here?"

"We'll see. What I plan to do after the bond issue passes is go east and see what the locomotive factories in Pittsburgh can build for us.

I'll get their price for thirty-pound rail, too, which we'll switch to later on. If it's too expensive in the United States, I'll check with mills in Wales, where I've heard there are good bargains."

The Walla Walla and Columbia River Railroad Company was incorporated during the spring of 1871, a year before Lars Warren was made captain of the new grain boat, *Inland Queen*. Soon, tales about "Doc Baker's Rawhide Railroad" that would become legend in the upriver country began to circulate. In order to save money on survey costs, one story went, Doc Baker hired an Irishman named Pat Puntry to determine the best grade across the hills and hollows between Walla Walla and Wallula. When the surveyor—who had a drinking problem—traded his instruments for booze, Doc Baker refused to replace them, forcing him to use a half-full bottle of whiskey for a transit level.

The grade Pat Puntry selected, railroad men reported later, was perfect.

Complaints about the quantity and quality of the food served in the Wallula boardinghouse where sawmill and railroad workmen ate were so loud and constant, rumor had it, that the laborers frequently threatened to go on strike. On one occasion, a story went, the cook was caught flavoring what was supposed to be duck soup by leading a live duck tied to a string through a pan of slightly salted warm water.

In order to save money, still another tale related, Doc Baker eliminated the cow-catcher on the locomotive he ordered from Pittsburgh, training a collie dog to walk along ahead of the locomotive, barking a warning to grazing livestock on the track. When a deaf or stubborn cow refused to move, the collie would raise his tail, to which a red flag was attached, in a signal for the train to stop.

Running short on strap iron, yet another story went, Doc Baker killed and skinned a bunch of scrawny cattle, cut rawhide strips—which *were* like iron—out of their pelts, then used the strips to top the rails. This worked fine until an unusually cold winter, which drove starving wolves down out of the Blue Mountains, with the ravenous animals eating what they welcomed as frozen beef jerky, causing the rails to fall apart.

Exaggerated as those stories undoubtedly were, the account of the "Bedbugs That Cost an Election" tale was true, for Lars later heard it from Will Baker himself. Concerned over the fate of the $300,000 bond issue, Dr. Baker embarked on a tour of the county ten days before the election, taking eleven-year-old Will along to drive the buggy as his father met and talked with businessmen whose votes he needed. In Dayton, thirty miles northeast of Walla Walla, the owner of a combined stage station, store, hotel, saloon, and eating house was a big, bluff, friendly man named Dewey Hollister.

"Everybody in the community liked Mr. Hollister," Will Baker told Lars. "Father knew if we got him on our side, he could influence a lot of votes. By bedtime, we were sure that he and all his friends were for us and would vote for the bonds. Then, during the night, things started crawling over us."

" 'Things'?"

"Bedbugs. Our bed, the sheets, the mattress, was full of them. So in the middle of the night, Father and I got up, went out to the barn behind the hotel where the stagecoach horses were kept, climbed up to the hay mow, and spent the rest of the night there. When we came into the eating house for breakfast the next morning, Mr. Hollister saw the sprigs of hay in our hair and asked Father why we had slept in the barn."

"And your father told him?"

"He sure did. Mr. Hollister got very mad, saying that if there were bugs in the bed, Father and I must have brought them there from somebody else's hotel. Father tried to calm him down, saying no harm had been done and we'd gotten a good night's sleep in the barn. But it didn't do any good. When the election was held a week later, the railroad bond issue lost by eighteen votes. Twenty-eight of the no votes were cast in Mr. Hollister's district."

Despite the bond issue defeat, Dr. Baker insisted on going ahead with plans to build the railroad. With his wife, Caroline, and their six-month-old daughter, Henrietta, he left for the East by stagecoach on December 4, 1871, headed for Kelton, Utah, where he planned to catch the train to Pittsburgh and New York. The nine days spent bucking snowdrifts, enduring near-zero cold, and putting up with the discomforts of overnight stops at stage stations with few amenities would later be described by Mrs. Baker as "a pleasure trip."

Conferring with the locomotive building company of Porter and Bell in Pittsburgh in late December, Dr. Baker signed a contract for the building of a seven-and-one-half-ton locomotive for $4,400, the shipping charges around the Horn and then up the Columbia River to Wallula Landing to be $1,424. Shortly afterwards, he ordered a second locomotive approximately the same size and price, one to be named *Walla Walla*, the other *Wallula*. Also ordered from the Pittsburgh company were several dozen sets of iron trucks and wheels to be fitted to wooden flatcars built at the site. Delivery was promised in early summer 1872, by which time Dr. Baker planned to have a dozen or so miles of track completed from Wallula eastward so that the railroad could start earning money.

Going to New York, where he hoped to sell stock in the railroad to eastern bankers, he found them friendly and interested, but too cautious to invest at the present time, for several railroads much larger than his were rumored to be rushing toward financial disaster. Pricing thirty-pound rail, he found that the best he could do in the United States was seventy-one dollars a ton, with freight charges to Portland of an additional ten dollars, raising the total price to eighty-one dollars a ton. Since eastern bankers would extend him no credit, the price must be paid in gold—which he did not have.

Checking with British factory representatives in New York City, he got a much more friendly reception and price. Thirty-pound rail cast in Wales and shipped from Liverpool would cost him forty-four dollars a ton, to which an added twelve dollars' freight and fourteen dollars' duty would bring the total to seventy dollars, a savings of eleven dollars a ton.

As to the terms of payment, that would be no problem, the British representative assured him, for England was used to "making liberal terms to customers in the far-off colonies of Her Majesty's Empire." Ten percent down, say, 20 on delivery, and the rest spread over a period of five years at 12 percent interest? Would that be satisfactory, old boy?

Repressing his impulse to tell the representative that Washington Territory was no longer a British colony, Dr. Baker said the terms would be fine.

When he returned home in the spring of 1872, building of the Walla Walla and Columbia River Railroad resumed in earnest.

Now in late May 1873, twelve miles of track had been laid between Wallula Landing and Frenchtown, over which the two locomotives, the locally built flatcars, and the single passenger car completed to date were making regular runs. Maybe *runs* was not the right word, Lars mused as he and Daphne got back into the phaeton and resumed their journey to Wallula. That was too fast a pace to describe the gait of the narrow-gauge train. Because the strap iron topping the wooden rails now and then came loose as the train passed over it, a "snakehead" occasionally pierced the floor of a car, causing the passengers to panic and the train to stop. Because of the slow speed of the train, no passengers ever were injured, but the experience was disconcerting.

In the desert-like region of low rainfall east of Wallula, sand drifts often buried the tracks, causing derailments. Like the snakeheads, these were not great problems, for with the help of crowbars, fenceposts, and muscle power supplied by the backs of the train crew, passengers, or passersby on the nearby road, the light engine and cars could easily be lifted back on the rails. On one occasion, when a husky young pedestrian headed for Wallula came over and did yeoman work helping lift the train back onto its track, the conductor offered him a free ride the rest of the way as a reward for his services.

"No thanks, I'll walk," he replied. "I'm in a hurry."

Slow though its trains were, when the Walla Walla and Columbia River Railroad offered to carry sacked wheat over its twelve miles of completed track for half the rate the Teamsters Association was charging, it acquired most of the business, for the Oregon Steam and Navigation Company shrewdly agreed to accept the grain at the end of track as if it were being loaded aboard the boats themselves. To the cries of "Foul!" by the teamsters, Emil Warren, the O.S.N. attorney who had formulated the policy, merely smiled and replied, "All we've done is declare the Touchet a navigable river, which moves our loading dock twelve miles east. Be grateful for the wear and tear we're saving you on your wagons."

Reaching Wallula in mid-afternoon, where the *Inland Queen* was waiting with steam up after being brought down the Snake and Columbia from Lewiston by First Mate Herb Blalock and Chief Engineer Alex Conley, Lars gave Daphne a brief tour of the living quarters prepared for them on the second floor of the Wallula Palace Hotel. Insisting that his employer, Lili deBeauchamp, had ordered him to inspect those quarters and report back to her, Goliath Samson went along, grumbling his disapproval of everything he saw.

To begin with, he complained, Miss Daphne would have to cross the bleak, cheerless, dingy lobby to get to the stairway leading up to the second floor, subjecting herself to the lecherous stares of the desk clerk, the men lounging in the lobby, and the drunks coming out of the adjacent bar. Upstairs, the suite in which she and her husband would live occupied only a quarter of the floor, comprising a sitting room, a bedroom, a small kitchen, and an even smaller bathroom, while the other three-quarters of the floor was broken into crib-like rooms in which almost any kind of activity could and probably would go on.

"It just ain't no place for a lady, Lars. I'm gonna have to tell Miss Lili that."

"Don't you dare, Golly!" Daphne flared. "If you do, I'll never speak to you again!"

Looking like he had been pole-axed, the big bodyguard flushed and mumbled, "I'm just tryin' to look after you, Miss Daphne."

"I know you are. But that's my husband's job now. He's perfectly capable of handling it."

"I know he is. But—"

"A woman's touch is all these rooms need. Give me a few weeks, I'll have them looking like a real home."

"All right, Miss Daphne, I promise I won't say nothin' bad to your mother. But just to make sure nobody's botherin' you, I'll come down from Walla Walla and look in on you now and then. Okay?"

Standing on tiptoe and pecking him lightly on the cheek, Daphne laughed and said, "You're sweet, Golly! Come see me anytime."

2.

By the second week in June, Captain Lars Warren, his bride Daphne, and the *Inland Queen* had made half a dozen trips up the Snake to Lewiston, then back downriver to Wallula and Celilo Landing, carrying light loads of passengers and full cargoes of sacked grain that had accumulated at the landings after being hauled there from farmers' fields in Teamsters Association wagons. Granaries along the river were pretty well emptied of last year's wheat now, making room for the bountiful harvest that would begin coming in toward the end of the month and continue all summer long, giving the *Inland Queen* and other O.S.N. boats plenty of cargo to carry for months to come.

The normal schedule at this time of year was to take two days going upriver from Wallula to Lewiston, overnight there, spend two days coming down the Snake and loading a full cargo of sacked wheat en route, make an afternoon stop at Wallula Landing, then run on down to Celilo for the night, with an early departure upriver-bound scheduled for shortly after dawn the next morning. Today as Lars slowed engines, drifted downstream from the Wallula dock, and then turned the bow back into the current and gently worked his boat toward the landing, he was pleased to see a smaller stern-wheeler, the *Explorer*, already tied up there, with his longtime friend, Captain William Polk Gray, waving a greeting to him from the upper deck just outside the pilot house.

"Ahoy, Lars! Kill any big rattlesnakes this trip?"

"Nary a one, Willie! They don't grow 'em like they used to!"

Standing beside him in the pilot house, Daphne asked curiously, "What's this about killing rattlesnakes?"

"Years ago, Willie Gray and I worked for his father, taking a sailing barge up the Snake to Lewiston. Willie was fourteen years old, while I was only nine. Going ashore on a sandbar to tie a winch-line to a snag, I nearly stepped on the granddaddy of all rattlers. When Willie yelled a warning, I jumped ten feet high. By the time I hit the ground, he'd killed the snake with a shovel."

Shading her eyes as she peered across at the tall, spare man with the neatly trimmed black beard and the sharp blue eyes who was waving at them from the bridge of the adjacent boat, Daphne nodded in sudden recognition.

"Oh, yes! Captain Gray! He came to our wedding, didn't he?"

"He certainly did. He's a good friend and one of the best O.S.N. captains on the river."

Daphne's eyes twinkled. "Present company excepted?"

"That goes without saying. But you can say it anyway."

Going ashore, Lars and Daphne took Captain Gray to their quarters in the Wallula Palace Hotel for coffee while the *Inland Queen* was reloading before heading on downriver to Celilo. As she served, Daphne apologized for having no sweetbreads to go with the coffee.

"We've spent so little time here, I've yet to stock a proper pantry and kitchen. But before long, I will."

"If your coffee is a fair sample of your cooking, Mrs. Warren," Captain Gray said gallantly, "I'll look forward to that day."

"What a flatterer you are!" She gave him an appraising look. "Lars tells me your father named you William Polk Gray in honor of the man who was President of the United States at the time you were born."

"That's right. Then wished he hadn't."

"Why?"

"My father was a man of strong political opinions, ma'am. When I was born, Great Britain and the United States were arguing over which country should own the Pacific Northwest, which they were sharing under the Joint Occupancy Treaty. James Knox Polk campaigned on the promise that if he got elected, he would claim everything as far north as Russian Alaska under the motto 'Fifty-Four-Forty or Fight!' My father agreed with him. After getting elected, President Polk settled with Great Britain for the 49th parallel, which is a long way south of Alaska."

"Leaving you stuck with the name."

"Right. Which didn't bother me until I got old enough to understand what my father was saying when he got into political arguments with other men. His face would get red as fire, his eyes would flash, and he'd yell: 'I named my son Polk after that weak-willed, soft-spined jellyfish of a man. Now every time I look at the boy I get so mad I want to wring his neck.' "

Daphne giggled. "You knew he didn't mean it, of course."

"On the contrary, ma'am, it scared me so bad I'd run off and hide till my mother came and told me he'd calmed down."

Knowing that the *Explorer* was a specially equipped boat often leased by the Oregon Steam Navigation Company to the U.S. Army Corps of Engineers, which frequently employed Willie Gray to do river-improvement survey work for them, Lars asked Gray if he were involved in a Corps project now. Willie nodded.

"Matter of fact, I am. So is the O.S.N. As you might expect, your Uncle Emil is in it, too. He's authorized me to ask you and your chief engineer, Alex Conley, to help me."

"To do what?"

"Assess the navigability of the Columbia River from its juncture with the Snake north to the Canadian border. Both the Corps and the Company want the upper river mapped, its rapids and hazards charted, and an estimate made of how much it will cost to make the river navigable to Canada."

As a workboat, Lars knew, the *Explorer* was equipped with twin boilers, dual engines, a split stern-wheel, triple rudders, fore and aft power capstans, sturdy spars on either side by which the boat could "grasshopper" up through the rapids, and an internally cross-braced bow built to take a lot of abuse.

She also carried steam-driven rock drills, explosives, and experts who knew how to use them to blast rock obstructions in the channel. So far as the three hundred miles of Columbia River north of the Snake to the Canadian border was concerned, they had been little traveled by steamboats, Lars knew, for most of that stretch of river ran through bleak, empty, barren country whose volcanic outcroppings were so ugly and forbidding that it was called "scablands." Still, since exploring a little-known section of river was bound to be an exciting experience, Lars welcomed the opportunity to go along.

"Sure, I'll be glad to go with you," he said. He looked inquiringly at Daphne. "While I'm gone, would you like to go up to Walla Walla and visit your mother?"

Daphne shook her head. "What I really would like, dear, is to spend some time here making this place more livable. There are dozens of things I've got to do."

"How long will we be gone?" Lars asked Captain Gray.

"A week or so."

"Well, there's no reason why Herb can't handle the *Inland Queen.* But you say you want Alex, too. What can he do that your own engineer can't?"

"It's not what Alex can do, Lars. It's what he is."

"You want him because he's an Indian?"

"That's right."

Lars got up. "Let's go down to the landing and tell Herb and Alex about their new assignments. On the way, you can explain to me what kind of cockamamie scheme you and Uncle Emil have cooked up."

To begin with, Captain Gray said as they left the apartment, went down the stairs, and headed for the boat dock, both the government and the Oregon Steam Navigation Company wanted to avoid trouble with the Indians, if at all possible. Following the Whitman Massacre in 1847, the Cayuse War had spread misery over the inland country for two years. After the Stevens Treaties in 1855 established reservations for most of the upriver tribes, trespasses by white miners and retaliation by the Yakimas and other dissident natives resulted in the 1856–58 Yakima War, costing many Indian and white lives, mandating the closure of all the lands east of the Cascades to white settlement for three years, and eventually costing the United States government six million dollars.

"Since neither the O.S.N. nor the government wants anything from the Indians except free passage for steamboats up the Columbia, your Uncle Emil persuaded the Corps to give me five thousand dollars' worth of presents to pass out among the tribes who control crucial passages on the upper Columbia. To bargain with them, I need an interpreter who knows the language and the chiefs."

"Then Alex is your man—if he'll cooperate."

"Why shouldn't he? He works for the O.S.N., doesn't he? His family and yours have been friends for years. As I got the story from Emil, it was your grandfather who persuaded the Chinook Indians to give up their practice of head-flattening."

"You seem to have gotten a lot of family history from Uncle Emil," Lars said wryly, shaking his head. "Most of it wrong. When Grandfather Warren came to the mouth of the Columbia with the Astor party in 1811, Chief Concomly of the Chinook tribe was the most powerful Indian leader in the Pacific Northeast. If he had not been friendly, the Astorians would not have survived."

"He was one-eyed, I understand, with a flattened head."

"One-eyed, yes. A flattened head, no. Among the Chinooks, a cone-shaped head was a mark of distinction and royal blood. The board tied to an infant's skull shortly after birth made the head pointed, not flat."

"Didn't it squash the brain?"

"Not at all. Chief Concomly and all his descendants were very bright people. The Chinooks knew the lower Columbia River and its bar better than the best white navigators did. During the thirty years Concomly, his son Conco, and Grandfather Warren worked as bar pilots, they never lost a ship."

"It was Conco's son, Sitkum, who became the first Chinook baby not to have his head flattened, Emil tells me. He says the practice was abandoned because of your grandfather's influence on Conco."

"The way Grandfather Warren told the story," Lars said, "Conco wanted his firstborn son to look as normal as possible, so that when he grew up he could become a part of the white man's world. Which is what Sitkum did."

"From what your father told me, he and Sitkum have been working together since the days of the old Hudson's Bay Company ship *Beaver*, back in '36. But why did Sitkum move so far upriver?"

"Both he and my father were steamboat men. When sternwheelers came upriver, so did they."

"Sitkum's wife is a Yakima woman, I understand."

"That's right. She belongs to the Klickitat band, horse Indians who roam over the bunchgrass country northwest of the Columbia. Some of her relatives are Wanapums, river Indians who live in the Priest Rapids area. Do you plan to take a steamboat through there?"

"If it can be done, yes."

"Then you'll have to deal with the Dreamer Prophet, Smowhala. Maybe Alex can help you there ..."

Although his father, Sitkum—whose name meant "half size" or "little one"—was a full-blood Chinook Indian, Alex Conley knew much less about his father's side of the family than he did about his mother's. Among her people, she told him, it was the custom during the long, cold, snowy winter months for the old men with good memories to relate "grandfather tales" to the children, so that the youngsters would become familiar with the history and traditions of the tribe.

But his Chinook father had told him few such tales. When questioned by his curious son, Sitkum grudgingly admitted that his grandfather, Conco, and his great-grandfather, Chief Concomly, had lived in a village near the mouth of the Columbia River. It was true, Sitkum said, that the Chinooks were a seafaring people who not only crossed the tumultuous bar at the mouth of the river in sixty-foot-long cedar canoes, but traveled far to the north up the coast to the Strait of Juan de Fuca, Vancouver Island, and Puget Sound. It was also true, he admitted when pressed, that in olden times unenlightened mothers in the tribe strapped boards to their babies' heads until they took on a cone-like shape, misnamed as "head-flattening" by white people. But the custom had been abandoned years ago, and the great village in which he and his ancestors had been born had vanished into oblivion.

Now twenty-three years old, Alex was aware of the fact that he was the first male member of the family to bear the surname "Conley," which his father had adopted a year before he had been born. In the Yakima tongue, his mother's name was *Ka-e-mox-nith*, which meant "Spotted Fawn" in English. Though his father refused to talk about it, his mother told him that the decision to take a "white" name had been made by Sitkum during the Cayuse War, when angry Oregon Volunteer soldiers had headed upriver from the Willamette Valley vowing to avenge the victims of the Whitman Massacre.

"Captain Tommy Warren told your father that if he wanted to work on the river he must keep his hair cut short, wear his Oregon Steam Navigation Company uniform at all times, and live as much like a white man as he could. I did not like it, but I agreed it was the only thing to do."

"Why did he pick the name 'Alex Conley'?"

"His father's name was 'Conco,' his grandfather's 'Concomly.' Among the white fur traders at Astoria, 'Alexander' was a common name, so when you were born, he chose it for you."

"Why is he so ashamed of his Chinook ancestors?"

"Probably because most white people look down on lower Columbia River tribes as diseased, dirty 'Siwashes' who are full of lice and fleas, live on fish, and are too lazy to work. He refuses to be identified with that kind of Indian."

On several occasions as a child, Alex had heard his father and mother engage in heated arguments during which his father would declare that he would not permit the members of his family to "Go back to the blanket." By this, Alex eventually learned, his father meant that he would not let his family live in lodges on the Yakima Reservation, even though Spotted Fawn was an enrolled member of the tribe. Building a four-room frame house on a deeded lot at Wishram on the north side of the Columbia, just a few miles below Celilo Falls, Sitkum insisted that his family live like white people, even though they were on Indian land.

Just as Tommy Warren never had known how his childhood Indian friend, Sitkum, had acquired his skill with steam engines, neither could Lars Warren explain how that same skill had been passed on to Alex Conley. Like Sitkum, Alex had been taught to read, write, and do sums, so had acquired the basic knowledge needed to read and understand an instruction book explaining how a steam engine worked. But beyond that he possessed the keen, observing, practical eye of a water-oriented Indian, whose ancestors from time immemorial had been in tune with the environment in which they lived.

In olden times, Sitkum had once told his son in a rare revelation of his Chinook past, each village had its *hyas tyee* canoe designer, a skilled craftsman whose blueprints were in his head, who chose the proper hundred-foot cedar tree to be felled, supervised the chiseling, burning, and shaping of its interior, the pitch of its bow and stern, and every tiny detail of its construction until it became the perfect seagoing canoe his mind had planned it to be. For generation after generation before the white man came to the Pacific Northwest, Sitkum said, the *hyas tyee* master canoe makers had practiced their craft. After the Spanish, the British, the Russians, and the Americans came to call along the Northwest Coast in their sailing ships, it had taken very little time for the lines seen and liked by the *hyas tyee* canoe designers in the white man's vessels to appear in the native-made cedar canoes.

So far as Sitkum was concerned, learning how a steam engine

propelled a ship was merely an extension of the skills long used by the *hyas tyee* canoe designers.

Truth was, as chief engineer on the *Inland Queen*, Alex Conley loved his work and was good at it. When aboard a steamboat, he was comfortable in the white man's world. But ashore there were times when he yearned to learn more about his Indian heritage.

Because he was so far removed from his father's roots on the lower Columbia, he had become more and more intrigued with the "grandmother tales" his mother, Spotted Fawn, had told him as a child. Even though white missionary teachers on the Yakima Reservation had made persistent efforts to wipe out what they regarded as heathen, superstitious beliefs, the fourteen related bands which the 1855 Stevens Treaty had melded together as the Yakima Nation still shared a rich spiritual life. When the bands met in powwows or "first-food" festivals at places removed from the Fort Simcoe Reservation grounds, they practiced their rituals with great reverence.

According to the *shamans* (holy persons) and the *tewats* (medicine men), the Indian world had been made by *Speelyi*, a mischievous, trickster spirit of the animal world identified as Coyote. Continually feuding with him were Beaver, Fox, Magpie, Crow, Bear, and a host of other animal spirits. In addition to these mythical figures were North, East, South, and West wind spirits, whose constant struggles for dominance caused the changing seasons. During the long nights in the winter lodges, it was the custom for the grandfathers to tell tales of great feats of hunting, warfare, and long trips to the buffalo country far to the east along the headwaters of the Missouri River. Interspersed with these were grandmother tales of the nefarious doings of *Speelyi* and his rivals.

As a child, Alex had been awed by the grandfather tales of warfare and buffalo hunts told by elderly men. But what really made him squirm and giggle with delight were the grandmother tales told by the women among his mother's people. By long custom, the teller of such tales lapsed into a special kind of language as she acted out each story, using an ancient, colorful dialect which made her voice squeak like a mouse, caw like a crow, roar like a bear, hiss like a snake, and imitate whichever character she was pretending to be. Though his father, Sitkum, called this sort of thing ridiculous and refused to listen to either the winter tale-telling or the spring and summer story sessions, he could not prevent Spotted Fawn, who was a strong-willed woman, from going to them and taking the children along.

For years as Alex was growing up, he had enjoyed the expeditions into the world of his mother's people, for they were great fun and a welcome change from learning the skills needed to become a steamboat engineer.

Hearing about the Dreamer Prophet, Smowhala, and the new hope he was inspiring among his people, Alex had become curious about the Dreamer faith, so he had gone to the Priest Rapids village in which the mystic ceremonies were taking place in order to see for himself what was happening. Given an insight into a spiritual world he never knew existed, he became fascinated with the Wanapums and Smowhala, the Dreamer Prophet. Only now was he beginning to understand the meaning of scenes he had witnessed and words he had heard as a child …

"It is evil, evil!" the Old One chanted, swaying his stooped, withered body back and forth as he squatted on a glistening black basaltic rock overlooking the rushing river. "Oh, *Nami Piap* [Creator], forgive them, for they know not what they do. They are taking *nasau* [spring salmon] and eating them greedily, forgetting that the first-come fish are for you. My Above Brother, they do not remember the dark days of long ago. When I warn them that the black days will come again, they laugh. Oh, Watcher in the Sky, be merciful to them, even though they do not give you the thanks you deserve."

The first time his mother had taken him to the great fishery at Priest Rapids, Alex had been just six years old. It was early spring. Though the sun shone brightly, the chill of winter still lay over the land. All along the eleven miles of rapids where the channel of the Chiawana (Columbia) River narrowed so that the great runs of fish migrating to their spawning beds in Canada must swim near rocks where they could easily be caught, the Wanapums and related tribes were harvesting their traditional food bounty.

Hundreds of gleaming fifty-pound fish were being impaled on spears and lifted out of the swirling waters. Others were being ensnared in cigar-shaped traps made of willow withes. Many more were being taken in nets woven of strong-fibered roots, weighted down with round stone sinkers, then lifted out of the deep pools by the combined efforts of half a dozen men.

Here at the home of the Wanapums (River People), spirits ran high, for winter was over, spring was at hand, and the time of long fasting was done. Among the Wanapums, there should have been a feeling of contentment and rejoicing, with prayers of thanks rising from the throats of the *shamans* and the *tewats* to the sky where the good spirits dwelled in gratitude for the gift of food. But no one was praying. In the heart of the Old One, there was a great sadness, for he knew that the people had lost their way and would suffer for it.

Over the cooking fires of the Wanapum village on the sandy flats near the river, the women were laughing and chattering merrily as they stripped thick slabs off the big fish, impaled the meat on sharpened slivers of green wood, then hung the oily, gleaming red flesh at an angle to the fire so that the tasty flesh soon would be broiled. Fat dripped from the fish, spattering the hot coals below, sending out a tantalizing odor of the food soon to be eaten. Irritated by the laughter of the women, the Old One shook his deer-hoof rattles and began another chant, oblivious to the curious gaze of the child who had crept near like a timid mouse and now was absorbing his every word.

Closing his red-rimmed, burning eyes, which had been nearly blinded by age, the glare of sunlight reflected off water, wind-driven sands of summer, and snows of winter, the Old One cried to the uncaring sky, "Soon I shall not be able to see Wasotas [Saddle Mountain]. Soon my people will carry me up the bluff and bury me beneath the broken rubble of rocks. I fear my ghost will roam forever up and down the river because *Nami Piap* is angry."

Now sensing the presence of the child and his hunger for knowledge, the Old One opened his eyes, lowered his gaze, and spoke in a voice full of love.

"Little One, you are growing up in a new world. The centuries are for the young. Soon you will go out and find your guardian spirit. Perhaps it will be strong enough to help you show the people how to live after their thousand years of uneasy death."

When Alex later asked his mother what the Old One had meant, Spotted Fawn explained that it was a custom among her people for a boy to go on his *Wyakin* quest between his ninth and twelfth birthdays, climbing alone to an isolated spot high in a mountain wilderness, where he would wait, meditate, and pray until the Sky Spirit sent down a messenger who would give him the rules by which he would be guided for the rest of his life. As to what the Old One said about a thousand years of uneasy death, he, like all prophets and holy men, was speaking in the special language such persons used, Spotted Fawn said, in which past, present, and future often were blended into one.

When Alex asked his father when he would be permitted to go on his *Wyakin* quest, Sitkum snorted and said, "Never, if I have anything to say about it. That kind of nonsense is for blanket Indians, not for you. The only guardian spirit you'll need is the ability to read and write, with common sense enough to keep your boiler pressure at a safe level and your engine bearings properly oiled so they won't seize up."

Truth was, as he grew older and began to work with his father on the O.S.N. Company boats, Alex Conley found life on the river in the white man's world much more satisfying than any mode of living he had observed in the world of "Blanket Indians." Riding horses, hunting buffalo, or making war against tribes living east of the Continental Divide did not appeal to him in the least. Though he enjoyed going on root-digging, berry-picking, and tule-reed-gathering expeditions with his mother and her people, it was the association with other boys and girls he liked, rather than the harvests themselves. But he still was fascinated by the early spring trips to Priest Rapids, where he listened with growing interest and understanding to the Old One's rambling chants and tales of olden times.

"As *Ahn* [Sun] stands in the sky as my witness, Little One, remember well what I say. The time is coming when I must go back into the earth, whose dust lives forever. We live, we die, and, like the grass and trees, renew ourselves from the soft clods of the graves. Stones crumble and decay, faiths grow old and are forgotten, but new beliefs are born. The faith of our villages is dust now, but it will grow again. Again the people will learn how to sing the sacred songs that in olden times filled their baskets with food."

"They *sang* for their food?" Alex asked incredulously.

"Indeed, they did," the Old One replied. "After *Nami Piap* had punished the people with a thousand years of fire and ashes, he created a new race called the Wanapums, sending *Anhyi* into the sky to sit still all the time and warm the world. There was no darkness and no winter, just spring and summer. No one worked to get food and everyone was happy. They played and slept, their bellies full of strength. No one worried about the winter and the stinging cold. No one hungered or grew lean. It was just like the old days, when *Speelyi* roamed the river."

"How did they sing for their food?"

"By following the sacred ritual taught them by the Head Man, who was holy. When the people were hungry, they would gather in their longhouse, sitting cross-legged on their mats. Closing their eyes, they would sing the sacred words as the Head Man taught them to do. Seven times they would sing. When they opened their eyes, the longhouse would be full of baskets of food."

"Why did they stop doing that?"

Because they lost their way, the Old One answered. For many years, the people lived happy and content, without knowledge of wrongdoing or evil, until their leader died. They sorrowed for him, wailing so long that they forgot everything but their selfish grief. They even forgot the words of the food-bringing songs.

"This caused *Nami Piap* to become angry," the Old One said. "To punish them, he sent *Anh* to hide behind the mountain. Then darkness came and a bitter, cold wind blew across the land. The people shivered in their lodges, their hearts sick with fear. Many died of starvation. Others wandered off into the darkness and were lost."

When only a handful were left on the Sacred Island, the Old One continued, a young man who remembered the past and could see into the future called the people together. "We have forgotten the sacred song that brings food," he said. "We have remembered only false things of little worth. Let us try to recall the holy words of the food-bringing song."

This proved a difficult thing to do. Huddling in the darkness, the people closed their eyes and tried to sing. Word by word, bit by bit, they pieced the song together, while the young man led them. Seven times they sang in the cold darkness, then, as they finished, the great, terrible voice of *Nami Piap* thundered, "You have forgotten me! You have forsaken the holy ways! That was wrong and I cannot forgive you. But because you are my people, I will not let you perish. You will live, but not in the easy ways you have known.

"Sun will warm you again, but only part of the time. He will go away, but he will return each morning. I will give you Moon and Star to watch over you by night. No more will I send food to your houses.

You must work to get your food; those who do not will die. You will suffer. Remember that I am the Power who gives you food and makes it possible for you to find it."

"On this island I will put food for all," said the great voice of *Nami Piap*. "There will be times of cold and times of warmth; therefore, you must learn a new way of life. Every seventh time Sun visits you, dance and sing. When the food grows each spring, hold a feast of thanksgiving, sharing the new roots and the first salmon, because everything that grows must be shared.

"Dance and sing so I may know you are remembering. Never taste the first food without doing that. Do not force me to take Sun away again, because if you do, you will forever wander in darkness and dampness where there are only snakes and frogs to eat."

In order to fulfill his promises, the Old One said, *Nami Piap* then asked all living things to volunteer to give themselves to the people. *Nasau*, the big spring salmon, was first. *Choos*, water, was second. Third was *Skolkol*, the bulb root; fourth, *Yamish*, the deer; fifth, *Weohono*, the huckleberry, and so on down through a long list of things needed by the people to live.

"As a final reward if the people would live in the ancient ways, dance the old dances, and sing the old songs," the Old One concluded, "*Nami Piap* made them the best promise of all."

"What was that?"

"Someday, he promised, he would send them another holy man, who would teach them what they must do to bring back olden times, when there was no evil in the world and food was given them."

"Do you think that day will ever come?"

"Yes, I do, Little One. It already has come. The name of the holy man is Smowhala, the Dreamer."

3.

SINCE THE COMPLETION of Doc Baker's narrow-gauge railroad from Wallula Landing to Frenchtown, the Teamsters Association and the men who made their living driving freight wagons from the farmers' fields in the Walla Walla Valley to the O.S.N. Company loading docks on the Columbia River had fallen on bad times. Because the haul now was a third shorter than it formerly had been, with the O.S.N. accepting sacked grain at Frenchtown as if it were being loaded aboard the downriver-bound grain boats, the Teamsters Association had to drop its fifteen-dollars-a-ton rate to under ten dollars in order to compete.

The shorter haul meant that a third fewer teamsters were needed to do the work, so they must find other employment, none of which paid as well as their driving jobs. Mostly, this other work consisted of lifting the hundred-pound sacks of grain out of the wagons, loading them aboard railroad flatcars, then riding the cars to Wallula Landing, where the sacks must be transferred to the cargo decks of the riverboats. Priding themselves on their skill at handling teams of draft horses pulling heavy loads, the laid-off teamsters regarded this dollar-a-day work as beneath their dignity, for all it required was a strong back. Still, since it was the only work available, most of the unemployed teamsters took it.

"What we'd ought to do," Coot Woodley told his friend Jake Putzer as they lounged atop the grain sacks of a flatcar headed for Wallula after an exhausting morning of loading sacked grain aboard the train, "is make them dumb-ass officers we elected to run the Teamsters Association call a strike."

"Against who?"

"The goddam farmers, the goddam railroad, and the goddam steamboat company, that's who. We'll bring them greedy bastards that are makin' money off us workin' men to their knees."

"Last meeting we had in the Union Hall, Coot, you made a motion to do just that. But it got voted down two to one."

"Sure, by the guys who're workin' and don't give a damn for those of us who ain't."

"Well, you can bet they won't vote to strike 'long as they've got jobs."

Badly hung over after a night of carousing in Walla Walla, during which they had made the rounds of the saloons and whorehouses, both men were in a foul mood, their dispositions soured even more by the morning's strenuous labor, the bumpy train ride under a blazing sun to Wallula, then several hours more work in the stifling heat, dust, and bad air of the cargo deck of the *Inland Queen* as they off-loaded the hundred-pound sacks of grain from the flatcars to the boat.

Pausing to mop his sweating face, Coot Woodley eyed the two uniformed officers of the boats moored at the landing as they escorted the lovely, black-haired, recent bride of Captain Lars Warren along the sandy path leading from the landing to the Wallula Palace Hotel. Beside him, Jake Putzer leered and grunted, "Good lookin' piece, ain't she?"

"Yeah. And barely broken in."

"Think you'd like to break her in some more?"

"Sure. But what I'd like to do even more is get even with that big bouncer who throwed us out of French Lil's last night," Coot growled. "We weren't doin' the girls no harm."

"How could we? The prices the whores charge at French Lil's, we couldn't afford to take them to bed. All we was tryin' to do was mooch some free drinks and a Dutch lunch. Least, I *think* that was what we was tryin' to do. I was purty drunk by then."

"So was I," Coot muttered. "But drunk or not, Goliath Samson had no call to boot us down the stairs like he did. If he'd asked us nice and polite to leave, we'd of left."

"Big as he is, nice polite ain't his style. We should of had better sense than to barge in."

"Aw, who is French Lil to put on airs? She still runs a whorehouse."

"D'ya suppose she's taught her daughter any whore tricks?" Jake speculated. "Like how to do it five ways for five dollars?"

"I dunno. But I'd sure like to find out."

Getting the last sacks of grain transferred from the flatcars to the cargo deck of the *Inland Queen* after another hour's labor, the two men walked up to the hotel, where they had rented a cubbyhole of a room for the night for fifty cents, bought a nickel mug of beer apiece in the bar off the lobby, then carried their drinks, sausages, hard-boiled eggs, slices of rye bread, and dill pickles from the free lunch table out to the porch, where they sat down to cool off while they drank and ate.

Apparently a switch in skippers had been made aboard the *Inland Queen*, for as the boat cast off her lines and pulled out into the river, Captain Warren remained ashore, raising his right hand to the bill of his cap in a farewell salute to the officer in the pilot house. Soon after the big cargo boat cleared the dock, Captain Warren embraced his wife, who had come down to the landing with him and the other O.S.N. skipper. Waving, Daphne Warren watched as the two men boarded the *Explorer* and made preparations to get under way. Noting that no passengers or cargo were aboard the smaller stern-wheeler, Coot asked the tall, skinny hotel clerk, who had come out on the porch, who its captain was and where it was bound.

"That's Captain William Gray in the pilot house," the clerk said. "He's working for the Corps of Engineers on a river-mapping survey to find out how far up the Columbia steamboats can go."

"Why is Lars Warren with him?"

"He and Captain Gray are old friends. They're also taking along the chief engineer of the *Inland Queen*, Alex Conley, because he's a full-blood Indian with relatives living near Priest Rapids. That's in case they have to dicker with Smowhala, the Dreamer, over river-passage rights."

"Why should white people give a damn about the rights of dirty, good-for-nothing Indians?" Coot sneered as he watched Daphne Warren return to the hotel, cross the porch and the lobby, and go upstairs.

"Beats me. Maybe to head off another Indian-white war."

By dark a few hours later, both Coot Woodley and Jake Putzer were very drunk. They were also very broke, having spent all their hard-earned wages on ten-cent shots of bad bar whisky washed down with nickel mugs of not much better beer. In the noisy, smoke-filled, foul-smelling atmosphere of the Wallula Palace Hotel bar, they had managed to cash in a few friendship tabs with several Teamsters Association drivers who had been lucky enough to get jobs at the nearby sawmill, where railroad ties and four-by-six stringers were being cut and transported to flatcars headed east to the end of track for Doc Baker's still-building railroad. But after cadging a couple of drinks off friends they hoped would help them get driving jobs for the sawmill, Coot made the mistake of loudly bragging, "By God, I'm a better driver than any teamster in this room! Any son-of-a-bitch doubts that, I'll whip his butt right here and now!"

Unfortunately, Jake Putzer had the bad judgment to back up his friend's boast, saying he'd take on any man left standing after Coot got done. In the ensuing brawl, the two men were roughed up considerably, then ejected from the bar and told to go up to their room and sleep it off.

Staggering across the lobby under the disapproving scowl of the desk clerk, Coot Woodley and Jake Putzer managed to find the stairs, climbed up to the second floor by hauling themselves hand over hand along the railing, then started to turn right toward their room at the far end of the hall. But before doing so, Coot Woodley stopped.

"Jus' a minute, Jake. I got a great idea."

"Like what?"

"Like why don't we pay a visit to Daphne, French Lil's daughter?"

"What for?"

"So she can tell us what whore tricks her mother's taught her. Like how to do it five ways for five dollars."

"I ain't sure that's a good idea, Coot. She's married to Lars Warren—"

"He's gone up the river for a week. She prob'ly misses him somethin' terrible. We could take his place."

"D'ya really think she'd take us on?"

"We won't know unless we ask."

"What if the desk clerk hears us pounding on her door?"

"Hell, Jake, we won't pound," Coot whispered hoarsely. "We'll just tap, real quiet like. When she asks who us who we are, we'll tell her we're old friends of French Lil, who used to give it to us five ways for five dollars."

"She never did that, Coot," Jake muttered drunkenly. "Least not to me."

"But Daphne don't know that, Jake! C'mon, let's have some fun! Even if she won't open the door, we'll scare the pants off her. She'll scream bloody murder, then run to her mother in Walla Walla. Which'll teach French Lil not to mess with us."

"Well, since you put it that way—"

Turning left down the hall and moving as quietly as they could, the two men paused in front of the door to the corner apartment. When his soft rap brought no response, Coot knocked more sharply. After a moment, he heard a woman's voice respond.

"Who's there?"

"A friend of your mother, honey-pie."

"What's your name?"

"Faith, an' I'm Father Patrick Flannigan, darlin'," Coot answered, with a broad smirk and a wink at Jake, "bringin' greetings from your mother."

"You don't sound like Father Flannigan to me."

"I've got a bad cold, dearie. Open the door. Then you can show me how your mother taught you to do it five ways for five dollars."

Overcome with a spasm of laughter at his friend's sense of humor and his comical imitation of an Irish brogue, Jake Putzer was half doubled over and holding his sides when the door suddenly swung open. As he looked up, up, and up, he was horrified to see that the huge figure filling the doorway was that of French Lil's big bodyguard, Goliath Samson.

"What did you say?"

Frozen with terror, Coot Woodley seemed to be having a memory problem. Finally, he muttered, "'Scuse me. Seem to of got the wrong room." He turned to flee, but ran into Jake Putzer, who had been too surprised to move. Reaching out with his big hands, Goliath gathered both their shirt fronts up under their chins, lifted them clear off the floor as if they were rag dollars rather than husky men, then cracked their heads with a *thunk* that sounded like ripe watermelons being dropped on concrete.

Carrying the two unconscious men along the hall to the head of the stairs, he gave them a heave, then watched with a satisfied look on his face as they tumbled, slid, and bounced down to the floor of the lobby, while the tall, skinny desk clerk stared in amazement. Daphne Warren came out of the room, put a hand on his arm, and asked in a puzzled tone of voice, "What was that all about, Golly?"

"Just a coupla drunks, Miss Daphne. Seem to have knocked on the wrong door."

"Well, I didn't think the man sounded like Father Flannigan. Why would he say what he did?"

Though his employer, Lili deBeauchamp, had agreed with Goliath Samson's plea that she let him go down to Wallula every few weeks and make sure her daughter was getting along all right in her new surroundings, it had been pure coincidence that had placed him in the Wallula Palace Hotel just in time to let Miss Daphne serve him the first supper she had cooked for a guest in her newly furnished kitchen. A fine meal it had been, too, with dessert just served in the form of a cheese-topped slice of apple pie when the drunken intruders had pounded on what they correctly claimed was the wrong door.

"Don't worry about it, Miss Daphne," Goliath said, escorting her back into the apartment. "Livin' in a hotel like this, people do make mistakes. I'll have a word with the desk clerk before I leave, askin' him to make sure it don't happen again."

4.

ABOARD the *Explorer* as the boat steamed toward Priest Rapids seventy-three miles up the Columbia, Willie Gray, Lars Warren, and Alex Conley knew they were going where no river steamer ever had gone before. Back in 1865, when the O.S.N. Company had tried to reduce his five-hundred-dollar-a-month salary, Captain Leonard White had quit in a huff, followed a gold boom in the Arrow Lakes region of Canada to the upper Columbia, and built his own steamboat, the *Forty-Nine,* there.

"From what I heard," Willie Gray told Lars Warren, "it wasn't the river that beat Len White, it was the fact that the gold strike petered out."

"He did his steamboating up in Canada, I understand," Lars said.

"That's right. He launched the *Forty-Nine* at the Little Dalles, just sixteen miles south of the border, ran it up through the Arrow Lakes for a hundred miles or so, then steamed on north into the Canadian Rockies until he ran out of water. But the passenger and freight revenue just wasn't there. After a couple of years, he gave up, sold the boat, and came back to the United States."

The stress of fighting ice floes, lining through rapids, and fending off creditors had taken a heavy toll on Captain White's health, Willie Gray said. After losing his boat, he worked in San Francisco and in Portland for a few years, then died in the spring of 1870. Since he had proved that the freight and passenger revenue of the Canadian sector of the upper Columbia was insufficient to support a boat, the only piece of river left to be tested for both navigability and traffic potential was the two hundred miles of the Columbia between the mouth of the Snake and the 49th parallel.

"From what we've seen so far," Lars said as he gazed out across the bleak, barren, sand and lava wasteland lying above either shore, "this is not the kind of country white settlers will file land claims on very soon. The only thing it seems to grow is sagebrush."

"Seems a shame to waste such a fine stretch of river on it," Willie Gray said, nodding in agreement. "A man couldn't ask for better steamboat water than this."

Broad, deep, and with few rocks in its channel, the Columbia indeed was a placid river in this sector, traversing a wide, empty land. A few miles above the mouth of the Snake, its course changed from north to west. Four miles farther on, it turned north again, receiving the waters of a much smaller river flowing in from the west, the Yakima. Though the vegetation growing along the banks in this area gave no indication of it, Lars knew that the higher reaches of the Yakima River along the eastern slope of the Cascades were covered with magnificent stands of Douglas fir, ponderosa pine, and western larch, all growing on federally owned land. It was from this region that Doc Baker was getting the logs for the cross-ties and stringers for his railroad.

"He signed a contract with the government allowing him to cut all the trees he wants off federal lands for five cents per thousand board feet," Lars said.

"How does he get the logs to Wallula?"

"He's had crews in the mountains felling trees all winter and spring. When the snow melts and the river rises, the logs are floated down the Yakima at the peak of high water. The timing has to be just right or lots of logs will be left stranded when the river level falls."

Eyeing the sandbar stretching diagonally across the mouth of the Yakima as the *Explorer* steamed past, Captain Gray nodded. "That I can believe. Come late summer, the Yakima won't be carrying enough water to float a two-by-four, let alone a log."

An hour before sunset, the *Explorer* pulled into a quiet eddy below a sloping lava bluff on the east side of the river, having made by Captain Gray's reckoning fifty-eight miles since leaving Wallula. Tying up there for the night, the fires under the boilers were banked, the cook prepared supper for the officers and crew, and then, as the warm early summer twilight fell, Willie Gray and Lars Warren questioned Alex Conley about what problems they might expect to encounter next day with Smowhala, the Dreamer Prophet, when they reached his village at Priest Rapids twenty miles on up the river.

"All he wants is to be left alone," Alex said reluctantly, for this was not a subject he liked to talk about.

"Will he be hostile?"

"No. He doesn't believe in violence. But he won't be friendly either."

"Have you seen the rapids?"

"Many times. There are seven of them in all, covering an eleven-mile stretch of river. Only three of them are bad, though in all of them the water is swift and the rock ledges dangerous."

"Will we need to use grasshopper spars or the line?" Lars asked.

"In some spots, we may. What I suggest we do is tie up downstream from the last rapid, go ashore, then walk the bank of the river the whole eleven miles, making a chart of the rocks, ledges, channels, and fast water. Along the way, we can visit the half dozen or so Wanapum villages, talk to the people, and tell them what we plan to do."

Captain Gray nodded. "Giving them presents for letting our boat go upriver later, I suppose."

"I'd be careful about trying to buy their friendship, Captain Gray," Alex said, shaking his head. "The women will appreciate a few gifts like pots, pans, knives, and blankets. But Smowhala himself has said time and again that he'll never take as much as a grain of wheat or a single bead from a *Suyupo*."

"Which means 'white man,' I understand."

"That's his polite term," Alex said with a wry smile. "Usually, he calls whites '*Upsuch*,' which means 'Greedy Ones.' "

"How old a man is he?" Lars asked

"Forty to fifty, I would say. Nobody knows for sure. From some of the stories he's told his people, he's lived many lives and has died and been reborn many times, so he may be as old as the *Chiawana* itself."

"I hear he's a hunchback," Captain Gray said.

"That's true. He was born that way, I'm told. He walks slightly stooped over and squints up at people with his head twisted to one side. From the time he was a child, he's been different, a born *shaman*."

"I heard he had a terrible fight with Chief Moses, who thought he'd killed him and thrown him into the river, only to have him come back to life."

Uncomfortable about being drawn into a subject he did not like to discuss, Alex nodded. According to a legend long circulated among the Wanapums, Chief Homli, who lived in the Wallula area to the south, and Chief Moses, whose domain was in the coulee country of the *Chiawana* to the north, had gotten jealous of Smowhala's growing influence over the River People. Chief Homli's constant harassment had pushed Smowhala and the Wanapums north into the territory of Chief Moses, who deliberately picked a quarrel with the *shaman.* Attacking Smowhala and beating him so severely that all signs of life left his body, Chief Moses tossed what he thought was his corpse into a dugout canoe, pushed it out into the river, and watched it drift away, sure that he had gotten rid of his hated rival.

But Smowhala had not died. According to an account that later gained wide circulation, after the canoe had drifted a hundred or so miles down the *Chiawana,* the Above One plucked Smowhala's battered body out of the dugout, then took it on a year-long journey during which the flesh healed and the spirit was reborn. Distilled from knowledge gained in Brigham Young's Mormon country far to the southeast, in *Wovoka's* Paiute country to the south, and in many other strange and distant lands where his spirit wandered for at least a year, the Dreamer faith was born. Returning to his people in the Priest Rapids area as its Prophet, Smowhala began preaching it to all who would listen.

"Return to the old tribal ways," he pleaded eloquently. "Stay free of the soldiers and the reservation Indians. Do not recognize Kamiakin as Head Chief of the Yakimas nor any of the thirteen subchiefs of the related bands brought together and called a nation under the terms of the treaty.

"Do not live with other tribes or let your blood be thinned by breeding with them or the whites, for then the Indian in you will die out and there will be no full-bloods left among you. Do not cut your hair or give up your braids. If you remain pure and keep the faith of your ancestors, the day will come when the Greedy Ones will go back where they came from, when all the animals and all the Indians that have ever lived and died on the earth will come back to life. Then the paradise we once knew will return."

Like his father, Sitkum, Alex Conley certainly did not want to go back to being a "blanket Indian." But the spiritual mysticism of the Dream Maker, as Smowhala sometimes was called, had a strong appeal. For example, there was good reason to believe his claim that he could understand *Speelyi* (Coyote) and *Ahah* (Crow) and could communicate with them in a spirit tongue that no other human being could understand.

When death hovered over a village, *Speelyi* would howl, informing Smowhala that a certain individual was doomed. Smowhala could predict the exact day that the first salmon would appear in the river, where the first tender roots of spring could be found, and where *yamish* (Elk) would bed down so that he could be killed when the village needed food.

Even more mysterious was his ability to foretell when earthquakes would shake the land, and when the sun or the moon would be extinguished for a time and a blanket of darkness would cover the earth. In urging the Wanapums to locate their villages where neither Chief Homli, Chief Moses, nor the Greedy Ones could molest them, Smowhala made some dire prophecies that the Wanapums found difficult to believe.

"In time to come," Smowhala told the River People, "the *Suyapos* will ride in big canoes that belch fire. In the seasons ahead the *Upsuch* will ride over the land in carriages that run on rails harder than wood, with a smoking monster pulling them. In days far ahead, the Greedy Ones will build dams that will close the *Chiawana* to salmon, so that the fish will come no more.

"But that will not happen for a long while. At Priest Rapids, we will find fish, firewood, and peace. In our time and for many long years to come, there is nothing the *Suyapos* will want at Priest Rapids, so we may be permitted to live out our lives there unmolested. If we go back to the ways of our ancestors, the good days will come again."

Unlike white people, Smowhala and the Wanapums divided the year into six seasons rather than four. Instead of winter, spring, summer, and fall, the River People named their six seasons according to a formula given Smowhala by *Wowshuxkluh*, the realistic little wooden bird whose carved image was so sacred that it was kept in a small box in the Prophet's lodge and taken out only on special occasions. Having been allowed to see it while attending the "Sun-turns-around" ceremony marking the beginning of the Wanapum year, Alex knew that its back and wings were black striped with white, its underside orange. Its eyes were represented by large brass tacks. A sprig of real feathers attached to the carving formed the tail. A bird seen in this area only in late spring, it bore a close resemblance to a colored painting he had seen of a bird called "Bullock's oriole."

Whatever its species, *Wowshuxkluh* had promised to call to the fish, to the roots, and to the animals when the sun started its return trip north to warm the land of the Wanapums, telling them it was time to begin their journey. Smowhala said the Sacred Bird decreed, "*Yehku Keelah* is the name of the first period. It is then that we must hold the old, religious dances, which will continue for three days and two nights.

"*Tzinbuk* is the second period. It is then that the Sacred Bird will call to the salmon.

"The third is *Ahah Mi,* the Crows Coming period.

"The fourth period, *Hish Hish*, is named for the small insects such as mosquitoes and gnats which come at this time.

"*Shihtash*, the fifth period, is Time to Move out to the Root Digging Places.

"The sixth and final period is *Yakahtash*, Fall Fishing and Hunting Time, which continues until cold weather comes and the Wanapum year begins again."

Wowshuxkluh would commence talking on the shortest day of the year, Smowhala said, and continue until late summer. After the final food of the year, huckleberries—*weohno*—ripened and were ready for harvest, the Sacred Bird would fall asleep until it was time for him to waken and start talking again.

Reaching a favorable moorage in quiet water downriver from the lower end of Priest Rapids the next day, Captain Gray tied off the *Explorer*; then he, Lars, and Alex went ashore to pay their respects to the Dreamer Prophet. There was no mistaking Smowhala's dwelling, for it was by far the biggest lodge in the village, measuring, Lars guessed, twenty-five feet in width by seventy-five feet in length. Though he knew that Indian dwelling places ranged from skin to mat to brush shelters, most of those he had seen in the Columbia and Snake River country had been round, no more than ten or twelve feet in diameter, containing only a single family. But Smowhala's lodge was large enough to serve as a shelter or meeting place for up to a hundred people.

"How do the Wanapums raise that kind of lodge?" he asked Alex.

"Quite simply. After the entrance is set to the east, poles are placed on each side for whatever length is needed, with the far end being closed when the structure is long enough. Whether the covering is of scraped hides, panels of tule reed mats, or squares of canvas does not matter. The placing of the poles is the same. The dwellings are weatherproof and warm. I've seen longhouses two hundred feet long, serving as a meeting place for a whole village."

"Does Smowhala have a large family?"

"The last I heard, he had ten wives, but only one son and one daughter. He loved the daughter, who was eleven years old, so much that he refused to tell anybody her name, for fear that the evil spirits would come and take her away from him. But his precaution failed. A year ago, she took sick and died in spite of all the horses he gave the *tewats* to save her. Her loss hit him so hard, they say, that he lay down and died on her grave, in an effort to join her."

"He *died?*"

"That's what his people believed. For three days and nights he lay beside his daughter on the pile of rocks where her corpse had been placed, not moving or breathing. Then one day he revived and walked back down the hill into the village, bringing a message from the spirit world. It was not yet his time to die, the Above One had told him. He must go back to his people and continue preaching the Dreamer faith until his prophecies came true."

Though Lars wanted to ask Alex if he believed in the Dreamer religion, he did not, for he knew that it was the Indian way to respect all spiritual beliefs, whether a person agreed with them or not. On the north side of the longhouse, Lars noticed as they approached, a small square was enclosed by a fence made of whitewashed driftwood. In the center of this square, a tall pole had been erected, from which flew a multicolored flag. This was Smowhala's personal flag, Alex said, then explained its meaning as the Prophet earlier had done for him.

"This is my flag," Smowhala said. "It represents the world. God told me to look after my people—all are my people. There are four ways in the world—north and south and east and west. I have been all those ways. This is the center. I live here. The red spot is my heart; everybody can see it. The yellow grass grows everywhere around this place. The green mountains are far away all around the world. There is only water beyond—saltwater. The blue is the sky and the star is the North Star. That star never changes, it is always in the same place.

"I keep my heart on that star—I never change."

When Lars asked if Smowhala and his Dreamer cult tried to keep their rites secret from white people, Alex shook his head.

"Anyone is welcome to their services. Before they begin their meetings, a boy carrying a bell walks around outside the fence, while the people chant an invitation to come in. When everyone is inside the longhouse, the women stand in rows of twelve, their arms crossed, their hands extended, and the tips of their fingers touching their shoulders. They keep time to the ringing of the bells and the beating of the drums as they dance the *Washani* sacred dance and sing the sacred Dreamer songs, tapping their feet on the packed dirt floor, which has been covered with fresh clean sand. Then Smowhala preaches."

"What does he say?"

"Whatever fits the occasion. For instance, I attended a meeting a year or so ago when Major MacMurray, an army officer, came to visit the Wanapums and explain to them why they should either move to the Yakima Reservation and become government wards or file land claims under the Homestead Act, as they were entitled to do."

Major MacMurray did this, Alex said, by using a checkerboard, saying that the black squares in the surrounding country belonged to the railroad and that all the white squares were available for homestead claims by either Indians or whites. While Smowhala and the River People listened respectfully, the officer urged them to file land claims. When he had finished, he asked for Smowhala's thoughts on the matter.

"I do not like the new law," the Prophet said, after long silence. "It is against nature." He then went on to relate the history of the world since its creation, as he knew it:

> Once the world was all water and God lived alone. He was lonesome and he had no place to put his foot, so he scratched sand from the bottom and he made rocks and he made trees and he made a man and the man was winged and could go anywhere.
>
> The man was lonesome and God made a woman. They ate fish from the water and God made the deer and other animals and he sent the man to hunt and told the woman to cook the meat and dress the skins.
>
> Many more men and women grew up and they lived on the banks of the Great River whose waters were full of salmon. There were so many people that the stronger ones sometimes oppressed the weak and drove them from the best fisheries. They fought and nearly all were killed.

God was very angry, and he took away their wings and commanded that the lands and fisheries should be common to all who lived upon them. The lands were never to be marked off or divided. God said he was the Father and the Earth was the Mother of mankind; that nature was the law; that the animals and fish and plants obeyed nature and that man only was sinful. This is the old law.

After a while, when God is ready, he will drive away all the people except those who have obeyed the laws.

Those who cut up lands or sign papers for land will be defrauded of their rights and will be punished by God's anger.

You ask me to plough the ground? Shall I take a knife and tear my Mother's bosom? Then when I die, she will not take me to her bosom to rest.

You ask me to dig for stone. Shall I dig under her skin for her bones? Then when I die I cannot enter her body to be born again.

You ask me to cut grass and make hay and sell it and be rich like white men, but how dare I cut off my Mother's hair?

It is a bad law and my people cannot obey it. I want my people to stay with me here. All the dead men will come to life again; their spirits will come to their bodies again. We must wait here in the home of our fathers and be ready to meet them in the bosom of our Mother.

A while later, another military officer, Captain Huggins, reported an interesting encounter he had had with Smowhala while leading a company of dragoons in the area. In search of two mules that had strayed from camp, Captain Huggins decided to visit the Oracle of Priest Rapids. When he and his troopers rode into the village, Smowhala came out of his lodge and greeted him cordially. Captain Huggins later described the meeting.

"*Nika* Smowhala—I am Smowhala," the short, stooped, somewhat obese, middle-aged Indian said in a rather soft voice. "You want to see me?"

"Yes. I am looking for a pair of lost mules."

"You did not come to see me about the land?" Smowhala asked hopefully.

"What land? I have nothing to do with land."

"I and my people live on a little piece of land here at Priest Rapids," Smowhala said, looking disappointed. "Some white men want to take it away from us. The white man has plenty of land. I knew an Indian who went to Washington and he passed for days through good uncultivated land east of the mountains. Beyond the great sea some men have big tracts fenced in just to keep a few deer and grouse. Nobody interferes with them. Yet white men come from these very countries and say the Indian must not keep his land because he hunts over it instead of plowing it. I will not plow my land. If I did, it would not protect me. Joseph's people had good fields and gardens, but they were driven away."

What the Prophet was referring to, Captain Huggins knew, was Chief Joseph and the Wallowa band of Nez Perces, which by treaty had been given a reservation in northeast Oregon, only to have the settlers, the state, and the federal government threaten to take it away from them, forcing them to be confined with the rest of the Nez Perce tribe on a much smaller reserve in Idaho Territory east of Snake River.

The same thing was happening to Sitting Bull and the Sioux Indians a thousand miles to the east in Dakota Country, Captain Huggins knew, where the sacred Black Hills region—promised to remain the property of the Sioux tribe forever—had been taken from them because white men had discovered gold in the area. Because tensions were high between Indians and whites all over the West, with the Army cast in the uneasy role of peacemaker or enforcer of government edicts, the situation was touchy.

"But Smowhala," the captain said, "the country is filling up with white people and their herds. The game is nearly all gone. Would it not be better for your young men to learn how to work?"

"My young men will never work," Smowhala answered. "Men who work cannot dream. Wisdom comes to us in dreams."

"You say that wisdom comes in dreams," Captain Huggins said, "and that men who work cannot dream. Yet the white man, who works, knows many things of which the Indian is ignorant."

"His wisdom is that of his own mind and thoughts," Smowhala said. "Such wisdom is poor and weak."

"What is the wisdom of which you speak?"

"Each one must learn his own wisdom. It cannot be taught in words."

"Can it only be learned in dreams?"

"Much also may be learned by singing and dancing with the Dreamer at night. You have the wisdom of your race. Be content."

"It is said that you teach some great and wonderful deliverance is coming to the Indians and that they will be wealthy and powerful as in the past."

"Yes, this is true. If the Indians will listen to the messages that come to them, they will be given help by the Above One."

"What will the nature of this help be?"

"I cannot say. But it will be sudden and powerful."

"How do you know that your messages are true and that help will come?"

"How do I know spring will come?" Smowhala answered patiently. "Because it is now fall. We must have help from a stronger power if we are to exist. Without it our case is hopeless. Therefore, it is sure to come. Do the white teachers believe what they teach?"

"Who can read the heart of another? Some of them admit they do not believe what they teach. But they say good comes from teaching it." After a silence, Captain Huggins voiced the question he long had wanted to ask. "Is it true, Smowhala, that you hate all white men?"

"No, it is not true. But the whites have caused my people great suffering."

"Talking with you has been good, Smowhala," Captain Huggins said as he prepared to leave. "I hope you will be my friend. As a token of friendship, I give you a present of two good blankets."

Though the Dreamer Prophet merely glanced at the proffered gift without any indication of interest, one of the young men standing nearby hastily snatched up the blankets. Smowhala did shake hands with the captain before they parted, saying,

"If they tell you Smowhala hates all white people, do not believe them. As a token of my friendship, I promise you this. Your mules will return."

Two days later, they did …

Meeting with Smowhala now, Captain William Gray, Lars Warren, and Alex Conley were treated with the wary, cordial reserve the Dreamer Prophet used when dealing with white men he assumed wanted something from him. As Captain Gray spoke politely in English of their plan to walk the length of the rapids, descend them in an Indian canoe manned by natives who knew their hazards, then attempt to take the stern-wheeler *Explorer* through them and as far up the Columbia as a riverboat could go, Alex translated what Gray was saying into the Yakima tongue. Like many intelligent tribal leaders,

Smowhala understood English well enough and was able to communicate with white men in that language when forced to do so. But as a matter of courtesy and better understanding he preferred to have an interpreter present who would put the white man's words into his own tongue.

"Tell him that before we take the steamboat upriver, we will give his people ample warning, so that they can pull their nets out of the pools where they are fishing," Captain Gray said. "Tell him that we will not disturb any part of his land. Say that we want his friendship and have brought gifts for him and his people."

After telling Smowhala this in the Yakima tongue, then listening carefully to the measured words of his reply in the same language, Alex said, "He says *Speelyi,* the Coyote Spirit who made the Earth, put the *Chiawana* in this country to be used by all people, whether red or white. He says in an Indian village just above Priest Rapids lives a *Suyapo* called 'Old Pierre' who used to work for the Hudson's Bay Company and knows the rapids better than any other man. It would be wise to hire him as a guide, he says, and have him supply an Indian crew."

"We'll do that," Gray said. "We thank him for his good advice."

"As for gifts, he says, he will accept nothing for himself," Alex continued. "But his people may do as they wish. This is the Wanapum way."

Leaving the longhouse, Willie and Lars discussed how best to explore and chart the eleven miles of Priest Rapids. For them, this would not be a new kind of adventure. Their experience exploring big-river rapids went back to their 1859 employment by the senior William Gray taking a sail- and oar-propelled freight barge up the Columbia and Snake when Willie Polk was just fourteen years old and Lars Warren only nine.

"As far as I'm concerned," Willie said, "we'll save ourselves a lot of trouble and time if we just hike up the river to wherever Old Pierre lives, then pay him to get us a crew of Indian boatmen and a dugout canoe. Agreed, Lars?"

"Except for the hiking part," Lars said, nodding. "Why walk if we can ride horses?"

"Where will we get the horses?"

"That will be no problem," Alex said. "The Indian villages are full of horses. I can rent all we'll need cheap."

“Good. Let’s get at it today. You line up the horses, Alex, spreading gifts around where you think they’ll do the most good. We’ll pack up some instruments, charting materials, camping gear, and enough food for a couple of days, then head up the river. Be sure and get me a horse with a level deck and a comfortable pilot house. I’m not much of a rider.”

5.

LARS'S INSISTENCE that they rent Indian horses and ride rather than walk upriver to wherever it was Old Pierre lived turned out to be good advice, for instead of the distance being just a little over eleven miles, as they had expected, it actually was seventy-five. To Smowhala and the Wanapums, Alex explained without apology for the misunderstanding, distance and travel time were relative matters, for they were never in a hurry. Instead of taking only half a day to get there, three days were required before the old French-Canadian boatman who was said to know the Columbia River from Priest Rapids to its source in the Canadian Rockies better than any man alive could be located.

Though Willie Gray complained about being rump-sprung from the pounding given him by his not very comfortable Indian horse, he did admit that the more miles of the Columbia they inspected by land, the more river they would be able to chart by water coming down.

When they made camp the first evening adjacent to a prominent outcropping of lava in the middle of the river called "Victoria Rock," Willie asked Lars why the landmark had been given a British name.

"Because it looks like Queen Victoria, I suppose."

"You mean she's short, squat, and ugly?"

"That I wouldn't know, Willie. But they do say that once she takes a stand, she's hard to move."

"Pa thinks it's un-American for Britishers to name mountains, rivers, and rocks in the Oregon Country, when we ended up owning it."

"From what you've told me about his feelings for President Polk, there are some Americans he doesn't like either."

"Pa hates all politicians, Lars. Matter of fact, he's writing his own history of Oregon. He says since he came west in 1836 and helped make the country, he's got a right to tell what really happened."

"Speaking of history," Lars said, "I've got a good notion that this boatman we're looking for, Old Pierre, made some in his day."

"In what way?"

"He was a man-eater."

"A *what?*"

"A cannibal. When he and the *voyageurs* he was traveling with lost their canoe on the upper Columbia and tried to walk back to Fort Colville, only one man survived—him. He ate the others."

"Where did you hear that?"

Picking up a well-worn book on the history of the Columbia which he had brought along, Lars showed it to Willie and Alex. "My grandfather, Benjamin Warren, came out with the Astor party when it first settled at the mouth of the Columbia in 1812. Alexander Ross, who wrote *Fur Hunters of the Far West*, was also a member of the party and my grandfather's close friend. Later, Ross was put in charge of Fort Okanogan on the upper Columbia, an Astor Company trading post, then Fort Walla Walla, whose ruins are near Wallula. He tells the story in his book. Would you like to hear it?"

Both Willie and Alex said they would. This was the grisly tale Alexander Ross related:

> At a distance of seventy miles from Boat Encampment there is a very bad system of rapids, known to the *voyageurs* as the *Dalles des Morts*. They are about two miles long from end to end. Many a poor fellow has closed his earthly career by entrusting himself to their treacherous waters, and a number of solitary graves are here to be seen, and names of victims never found are carved on the surrounding rocks.
>
> Along this portion of the river there occurred in the year 1817 one of those terrible episodes of frontier life, at the thought of which the heart turns sick. On the 16th of April of this year, a party of twenty-three men left Fort George, now Astoria, to ascend the Columbia and cross the Rocky Mountains by the Athabasca Pass. On the 27th of May they arrived at the mouth of the Portage River, or Boat Encampment, after the most severe labors and exposure in dragging their canoes up the rapids and making their way along the rocky shores.
>
> Seven men of the party were so weak, sick, and worn out, that they were unable to proceed across the mountains, so they were given the best canoe and sent back down the river to Spokane House. After leaving the Rocky Mountains they went rapidly down the river until the *Dalles des Morts* were reached. Here, in passing their boat over the rapids by a line, it was caught in a whirlpool, the line snapped, and the

boat and all its contents of provisions, blankets, &c, was irrevocably lost.

Here the poor fellows found themselves utterly destitute, and at a season of the year when it was impossible to procure any wild fruit or roots. The continual rising of the water completely inundated the beach, which compelled them to force their way through a dense forest, rendered almost impervious by a thick growth of prickly underbrush. Their only nourishment was water. On the third day, Macon died, and his surviving comrades, though unconscious how soon they might be called on to follow him, divided his remains into equal parts, on which they subsisted for several days.

From the sore and swollen state of their feet, their daily progress did not exceed two or three miles. Holmes, the tailor, shortly followed Macon, and they continued for some time to sustain life on his emaciated body. In a little while of the seven men only two remained alive, Dubois and La Pierre. La Pierre was subsequently found on the borders of the Upper Lake of the Columbia by two Indians who were coasting it in a canoe. They took him on board and to Kettle Falls, from whence he was conducted to Spokane House.

He stated that after the death of the fifth man of the party, Dubois and he continued for some days at the spot where he had ended his sufferings, and on quitting it they loaded themselves with as much of his flesh as they could carry; that with this they succeeded in reaching the Upper Lake, around the shores of which they wandered for some time in search of Indians; that their horrid food at last became exhausted, and they were again reduced to the prospect of starvation; that on the second night after their last meal, he (La Pierre) observed something suspicious in the conduct of Dubois, which induced him to be on his guard; and that shortly after they had lain down for the night, and while he feigned sleep, he observed Dubois cautiously opening his clasp knife, with which he sprang on him, and inflicted on his hand the blow which was evidently intended for his neck.

A silent and desperate conflict followed, in which, after severe struggling, La Pierre succeeded in wresting the knife from his antagonist, and having no other resources left, he was obliged in self-defense to cut Dubois's throat, and that a few days afterward he was discovered by the Indians as above mentioned.

After Lars had finished reading the account, both Willie Gray and Alex Conley were silent for a time. Then Willie shook his head and said softly, "What a terrible story!"

"Men will do terrible things," Alex said, "when they're trying to stay alive."

"I've heard of white people eating their dead," Willie said. "Like the Donner party did when it got caught by an early winter blizzard in the high Sierras back in 1847. Or the Otter party after it was attacked by Bannocks in eastern Oregon in 1860. In both cases, the survivors turned cannibal. But this is the first I've heard of French-Canadian *voyageurs* eating their own kind."

"Among my people," Alex said, "there are grandfather tales of cannibalism handed down in the form of verbal myths. Which may be a good reason for not having a written language like the *Suyapos* do."

"The name of the boatman recommended to us by Smowhala," Lars said, "is Pierre Agare. He's said to be the last of the Iroquois *voyageurs* brought out by the Hudson's Bay Company from Montreal, so I assume he's the survivor Alexander Ross wrote about."

Alex nodded. "I'm sure he is. I met him at Fort Colville a year ago. He would be in his late seventies now, still hale and hearty in spite of being almost deaf, nearly blind, and just about out of teeth. He's outlived several Indian wives, I'm told, and has more sons and grandsons than he can count."

"Do you suppose we can talk him into getting us a canoe, a crew of paddlers, and guiding us down the river?" Willie asked.

"Money is the only kind of talk he'll listen to, Captain. He's got dollar-marks for eyeballs."

Finding the man named Pierre Agare living in a sprawling, ramshackle log cabin on the east side of the Columbia a few miles upstream from a turbulent stretch of water called Rock Island Rapids, Captain William Gray bargained with the rawboned, stooped-shouldered, cantankerous French-Canadian for two hours next morning before reaching an agreement.

"*Oui, M'sieu*, for 'wan hundred dollar' a day, I will supply a *très bien bateau*," Old Pierre said at last. "How beeg? It will be thirty feet long, four feet wide, an' two feet deep, *M'sieu*. This you must onnerstan', *mon capitan*, is ze smallest *bateau* that weel carry your baggage, the three men in your party, myself, and the four paddlers it will take to handle it in the wild waters we will be passing through."

"So we're agreed," Willie Gray said. "One hundred dollars a day ..."

"In gold, *M'sieu*."

"In gold—"

"For me and ze *bateaux*. For each paddler, of course, dere will be an extra charge of ten dollar' a day—also in gold. Zey will need lots of food, *M'sieu,* for paddling is very hard work. Plus a ration of rum for all of us at the end of each day to warm our bellies and blood …"

With the financial details settled at long last, Old Pierre selected four paddlers from among the sons or grandsons who were living in skin tepees and driftwood shacks adjacent to his cabin. At least Willie assumed they were direct descendants, for their names were Big Pierre, Little Pierre, Pen-waw (which Alex said meant "Pierre" in the local Indian tongue), and a stray named Joseph. All the paddlers were swarthy, black-eyed, well-muscled men, just as Old Pierre himself must have been in his younger days. Watching them load the bateau under the critical eye of Old Pierre, Willie Gray grumbled to Alex Conley, "Bad as his teeth are these days, Old Pierre will have to gum us to death if he turns cannibal. But those paddlers of his look mean enough to take mighty big bites, should they get hungry. Which d'ye suppose they prefer—white meat or dark?"

"Let's hope we don't find out."

Whatever seeing, hearing, or chewing infirmities he suffered, it was clear that Old Pierre knew exactly what he was doing when it came to running a river in a native canoe. His station would be standing at the steering oar in the stern of the craft. Directly ahead of him where he could act as an interpreter if need be, Alex Conley would sit cross-legged in the bottom of the canoe, facing forward, holding a sounding pole with which he would measure the depth and test the condition of the bottom of the channel.

Stowed amidships under tautly lashed canvas tarpaulins was the party's supply of food, drink, blankets, surveying instruments, and camping gear which they wanted to keep dry. Also seated facing forward and using the relatively level surface of the canvas-covered supplies as a work table, Lars Warren would record distances, chart rocks and hazards, and map the river in as much detail as possible.

The four paddlers would sit facing backwards at oarlocks on alternate sides, so that they could see the steersman and carry out his commands, ready to pull ahead or back water as ordered. In the bow of the boat, Old Pierre grudgingly permitted Captain William Gray to kneel, sit, or stand, as he wished, so that he could read and memorize the river for future reference. When Willie insisted on carrying aboard a sturdy six-foot-long pole with which he would attempt to prevent the canoe from crashing against a rock Old Pierre might not know was there, the half-blind, nearly deaf old *voyageur* snorted contemptuously, "*M'sieu*, such a rock does not exist. Even if I cannot see it or hear the water striking against it, I will feel its presence long before we are in danger of striking it. But if you want to try steering ze boat from ze bow wit' your little stick, go ahead. When you slip and fall overboard, I weel tip my cap as we pass, say *Adieu et bon voyage.*"

Either out of respect for Old Pierre's knowledge of the river or in recognition of the fact that it was useless to argue with a person so hard of hearing, Willie did not bother to point out that from the age of nine to the present day he had never encountered a rapid in the Columbia or Snake River system that he could not swim.

As the lines securing the *bateau* to the bank were cast off and the boat pulled out into the river, several of the women being left behind in the village cried, wailed, and howled in such apparent anguish that Lars began to think they all believed that the crew of the boat was doomed to perish in the waters ahead. Indeed, he himself felt the power of the river as never before, for it was running in full early summer flood. Icy snowmelt water coming off mountain glaciers upstream were frigid to his hand, and the rumble of the rapids had an increasingly ominous tone. Instead of having the comfortable buffer of a two-hundred-foot-long, forty-foot-high, steam-powered stern-wheeler between his feet and the surface of the river, he now was sitting down in the trough of the channel itself, his chilled bottom only a board's thickness removed from a cold dunking. Instead of being in control of his fate, he was at the mercy of a nearly blind and deaf old boatman and his savage crew, who might or might not know what they were doing.

Unable to make sense of the raucous bantering going back and forth between the wailing women on the bank, the half-blood paddlers, and Old Pierre, Lars asked Alex if he had any idea what they were saying.

"The women are calling him all kinds of names," Alex answered, "saying he's a stupid, evil old man, hell-bent on drowning their husbands or sons. Apparently, only one of the paddlers has ever gone down this stretch of river before. They say he's going to make them all widows. He laughs at them and says as long as the paddlers do what he tells them to, they'll be safe. If not, they can drown, for all he cares. He says he'll be glad to take the widows into his bed."

"The randy old goat!" Willie exclaimed.

"Is Rock Island Rapids a bad one?" Lars asked Alex.

"It can be, he says. Once, years ago, when he ran it in an overloaded Hudson's Bay Company canoe, the *bourgeois* in charge of the party refused to take his advice as to which channel to run, picked the wrong one, split the canoe on a rock, and drowned eight of the sixteen men aboard—including the *bourgeois* himself."

"I hope Old Pierre remembers which channel to take today," Willie said. "And can see well enough to find it."

"He hasn't drowned yet, he says. He doesn't intend to drown now."

Despite his outwardly cavalier attitude toward the hazards of the river, it became apparent that Old Pierre was basically a cautious man. As the river narrowed and the current quickened a mile upstream from Rock Island Rapids, he steered the *bateau* into an eddy on the east bank, ordered fore and aft lines secured around black boulders lying above the high-water mark, then invited Captain Gray, Lars, and Alex ashore with him for the purpose of making a careful inspection of the dangers ahead. Taking his clipboard and pencil along, Lars spent the next two hours drawing a detailed sketch of Rock Island Rapids as they examined it foot by foot.

This was the final draft of the sketch he drew.

Returning to the *bateau* after the inspection had been completed, Willie, Lars, and Alex resumed their positions aboard, while Old Pierre harangued the four half-blood paddlers in their own tongue as he gave them detailed instructions as to what he expected them to do. His first order seemed to be for them to strip off all their superfluous clothing, for each man took off his jacket, shirt, trousers, and moccasins, leaving their dark, muscular bodies clad only in skimpy, dirt-stained, gray-white loincloths. To keep the hair out of their eyes, each man pushed his braids and forelock up under a bright-colored handkerchief, which he then tied tightly around his head.

"Looks like they're getting ready to take a swim," Lars murmured apprehensively to Alex.

"Either that or they plan to work up a sweat," Alex grunted.

In addition to long oars extended from locks on alternate sides of the boat, each paddler placed beside his feet a shorter paddle and a stout pole with which he could fend off rocks, if need be. As the fore and aft lines were cast off and Old Pierre steered the *bateau* out into the strong current of the river, the veteran *voyageur* startled Lars by throwing back his head and letting out a bloodcurdling howl.

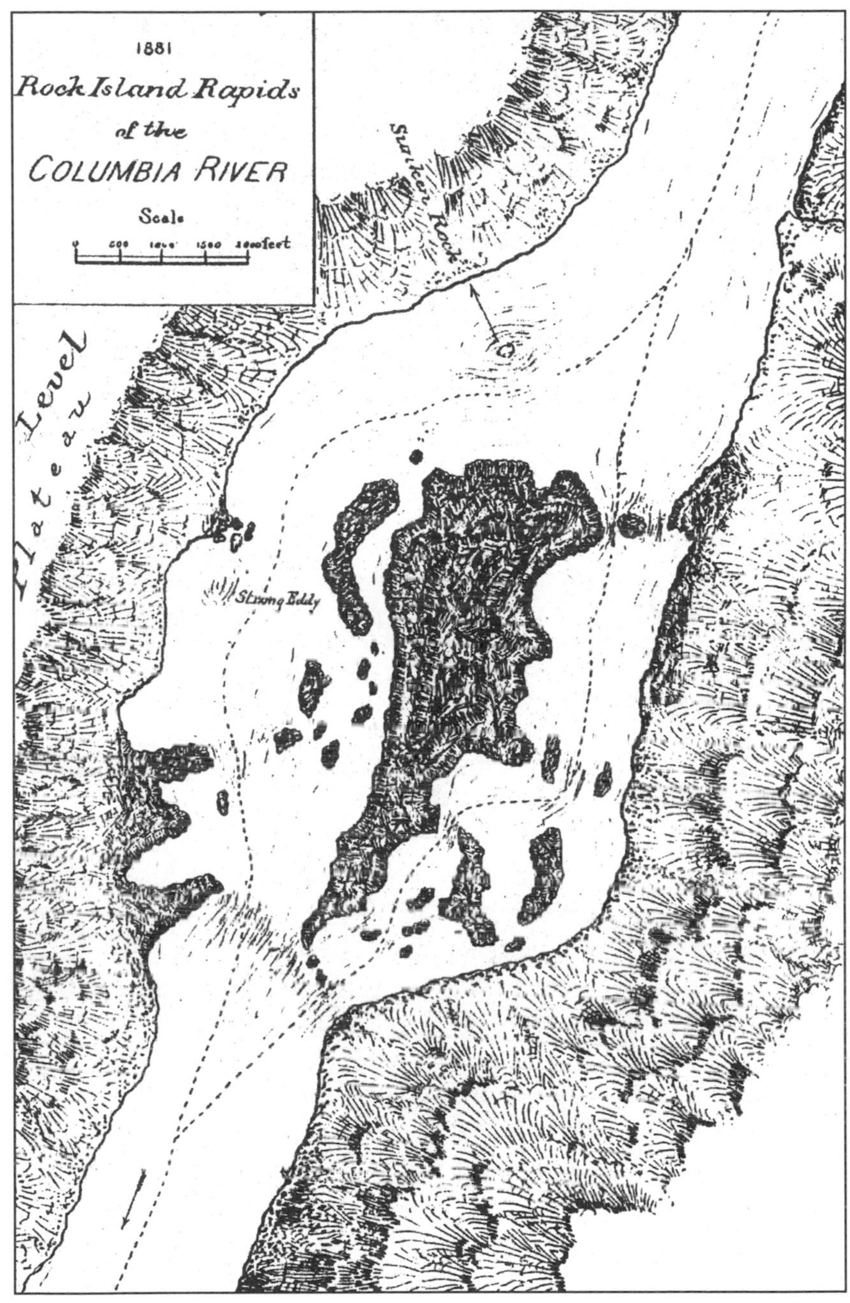

SEN. EX. DOC. No. / 86, 1st SESS, 47th CONG.

"Klosche nanitch! Sagahalie Tyee skookum chuck! Chako, chako!"

As the four half-blood paddlers bent to their oars with long, powerful strokes that increased the speed of the already swiftly moving *bateau* toward the rapid, they began chanting in unison, *"Klosche nanitch! Sagahalie Tyee skookum chuck! Chako, chako!"* Bewildered, Lars shouted at Alex, "What are they saying?"

"It loses something in the translation," Alex cried, cupping his hands around his mouth to make himself heard. "But roughly they're yelling, *'Look out, God of the Big River Rapids! Here we come!'* "

From his experience making downriver runs through rapids aboard a stern-wheeler, Lars knew the importance of traveling faster than the current did in order to maintain steerageway. But until now he had not realized that the same principle might hold true in a dugout canoe. Well into the speeding race of the upper reach of the rapids now, the *bateau* was traveling so fast that Lars shuddered at the thought of striking one of the huge black rocks that were passing by on either side. Still, Old Pierre and the half-blood paddlers continued to shout, *"Klosche nanitch!"*

"Saghalie Tyee skookum chuck!"

"Chako, chako!"

Directly behind him, Lars realized, Alex had risen to his knees, seized his shoulders, and was screaming in his ear, "*Chako, chako!* Look out, big rapids! Here we come!"

Caught up in the excitement of the moment, Lars found that he was shouting, too, while in the bow of the *bateau* his longtime friend from boyhood river-running days, Willie Gray, was thumping the end of his stout stick against the bottom of the boat in rhythm with the cries of the paddlers and the shouts of his friends behind him. As the dugout canoe pitched down into the trough and then rose up to split the crest of each wave, great surges of icy water broke over the men in the boat, drenching them to the skin. But they all were too intent on the dangerous passage to notice.

Directly ahead loomed an immense black rock toward which the boat was being carried at tremendous speed. Did Old Pierre see it? Lars wondered. Half-blind as he was, probably not. In the bow of the canoe, Willie Gray had become aware of it, too. But even as he turned to gesture and shout a warning, he lost his balance, and saved himself from falling overboard into the raging waters by letting go of his stick, dropping to his knees, and grabbing the boat's sides with both hands. As Lars turned to shout a warning to the steersman, Old Pierre gave an abrupt hand-signal to the paddlers. Their reaction was instantaneous.

With one pair taking two deep pulls on the right-hand oars, the other pair pushing strong back-water thrusts on the left-hand oars, then Old Pierre adding a quick sideways stroke with the steering oar, the rock that a moment ago had appeared to be directly ahead suddenly was passing an arm's length away on the right-hand side.

Old Pierre issued another command. Again, the paddlers responded instantly. With the deep-thrust oars bending like willows, the *bateau* spun around for two complete turns in the eddy into which Old Pierre had steered it. Then it broke clear and was heading downriver again.

Engulfed now in the tumbling, roaring waters of the main channel of the rapids, which extended, as Lars later mapped them, through just under a mile of wild water, the *bateau* experienced no difficulty in staying afloat, though it gave its passengers an extremely rough ride. Reaching a quiet stretch of river just below the rapids where a sandy beach on the right-hand shore offered a good camping spot, Old Pierre steered the canoe to the bank, and the thoroughly soaked, chilled passengers and crew went ashore. Though several hours of daylight still remained, Captain Gray agreed with Old Pierre that a good day's work had been done and they might as well camp here.

"D'ye remember enough of what you saw to draw a good chart of the rapids?" he asked Lars.

"I think so. As soon as my hands thaw out, I'll make a rough sketch, then check it with you, Alex, and Old Pierre before I fill in the details."

"I'll appreciate that, Lars. From what I've seen today, I suspect Rock Island Rapids may be more of an obstacle to navigation than Priest Rapids. If O.S.N. Company boats can't get through, we'll have to write off developing traffic on the upper river."

After camp had been made, a fire built, and everyone changed into dry clothes, Lars set up a drawing table and laid out a rough sketch of the area to be mapped, using a scale of two thousand feet to the inch. After setting down what Willie, Alex, and he himself had seen of Rock Island Rapids, he conferred with Old Pierre, who not only had taken the boat through them under today's conditions but possessed an intimate knowledge of what the rapids were like at all seasons of the year. Even though the ancient *voyageur*'s eyesight was so bad he could barely see the mapping sheet and his hearing so poor that Lars doubted he heard much of the questions he was asked, he understood so exactly what was wanted of him that all Lars had to do was set the information down as it was given to him. This was the gist of what Old Pierre said:

> There are two channels, *M'sieu,* the east and west. We used the west channel today. At this stage of water, I am sure that a good, powerful steamer, properly handled, could go up it. In extreme low water, the west channel becomes nearly dry, thus is unnavigable. The west channel is considerably wider than the east one, and is quite straight except at the lower end, where it is made crooked by dangerous rocks just beneath the surface.
>
> The east channel is deeper, *M'sieu,* and is the better one in low water. In extremely high water, it also is better, though in ordinary floodwater like today, the west channel is the best for boats.

Looking over Lars's shoulder as he sketched and listened to Old Pierre's description of varying water conditions, Willie Gray nodded, then said, "Looks to me like the west channel would be the best bet for year-round navigation. We'll need to blast out a few rocks, of course, which'll take time, money, and a work order from the Corps of Engineers."

"About blasting rocks, I know nothing," Old Pierre said with an indifferent shrug. "In my day, we took the rivers, the mountains, the country, and the people as we found them. Why try to change what *le bon Dieu* made?"

"There's another possibility," Captain Gray went on, proving himself to be as hard of hearing in his own way as Old Pierre was in his. "We could build a boat-railroad around the rapids on the west bank, which is flat and fairly low. That would cost a lot of money, but the Corps can get an appropriation from Congress if we can show it's feasible. Be sure and note that possibility on your map ..."

Next morning after the party embarked in the *bateau* and continued its journey down the river, the current for ten miles or so was much quieter, the channel wider, and the hazards to navigation in the form of rock ledges and protruding boulders so few that Willie Gray, from his vantage point standing in the bow of the boat, called back to Lars only now and then, "There's one we'll have to blast, Lars. Mark it on your chart."

Recording the hazards to navigation visible at this stage of water, Lars knew that neither Willie nor he ever would put their complete trust in a chart of the river, when their boat's safety was concerned. Even though frequently employed by the Corps of Engineers to survey, inspect, and blast clear a channel to a specified depth, Willie Gray had declared time and again that any pilot who trusted a Corps chart of a river was bound to rip open the bottom of his boat sooner or later. Sure, a chart showing where safe water was supposed to be could be helpful. But in full spring flood a powerful river current could pick up rocks of any size, carry them downstream like bottle corks, then drop them capriciously right in the middle of what a week before had been designated on a chart as a safe channel. All a chart did was give a pilot a notion of how a certain stretch of river *ought* to look. Any change noted by his sharp eye meant trouble.

Seen now from the river where before they had been riding on land, the immensity of this bleak desert country was awesome. Rising precipitously above the eastern shore, sheer brown lava bluffs which Lars estimated to be at least two thousand feet high defined the course of the river. Back from the west shore, the rise was more gradual, though of equal height, with the hazy range of the ten-thousand-foot-high Cascades dimly seen in the far distance.

As they approached the landmark called "Victoria Rock," Lars made a hasty sketch of it, which he would later improve by adding the *bateau* itself, its passengers and crew, an eagle in flight, and a couple of Indian tepees in the distance ahead on the left-hand shore. Examining first the rock, then the sketch, Willie Gray pronounced his critical judgment.

"When you first see it, that rock does resemble Queen Victoria. Close up, it looks like a Greek goddess, the Egyptian sphinx, or maybe even Cleopatra. But I still say it ought to have an American name."

"How about Eagle Nest Rock?"

"Yeah, that'd do fine. Looks to me like it does have an eagle's nest on top."

Rising one hundred feet above the river to the left of the main channel, the flat top of the columnar, black basaltic formation was crowned with a large, brushy nest constructed by a pair of eagles. It

Victoria Rock

had been there for a number of years, Alex said. Since male and female eagles mated for life, the same pair probably had lived there and raised a brood of eaglets each year for a long while. A romantically inclined writer might call it "A Crown to the Goddess of the Columbia," Lars reflected, but he was content to give it the more prosaic name of "Eagle Nest Rock."

"Do the Yakimas or the Wanapums kill eagles to get feathers for their headdresses?" he asked Alex.

"No, neither tribe made fancy headdresses until they got horses, crossed the mountains to the buffalo country, and began trading with the Blackfeet, Crow, and Sioux," Alex said, shaking his head. "Even those tribes seldom killed eagles for their feathers. Instead, a brave would climb up to a nest when the eagle was gone, conceal himself under some brush until the bird returned, then reach up and pull a feather out of its tail without hurting anything but its dignity."

"Wouldn't the eagle attack?"

"Its first reaction was surprise, I'm told, which would make it fly away. Then it would get mad, come back to the nest, and look for the man who'd stolen the feather. But by then—if he was smart—he'd be gone."

For half a dozen miles downstream from Victoria Rock the Columbia flowed quietly through a starkly dramatic country bordered on either side by high basaltic bluffs. During past eons in the mountain-building period, lava flows had poured down from the peaks to the west, leaving deposits in every conceivable shape lying stacked horizontally like cordwood, standing vertically like barkless trees, or curling in twisted piles helter-skelter across the ground, forming niches, grottos, and fantastic formations of all shapes.

But these marvels just above water level were nothing, Old Pierre said, compared to "ze giant tree of stone" deposited in a coulee a thousand feet above the river when *Le Grand Lac du Bonneville* burst its dam and caused the Great Flood ten thousand years ago.

"Wait a minute, Pierre!" Willie Gray protested in a loud enough voice to get through the old *voyageur*'s shield of deafness. "Is this our Captain Bonneville you're talking about?"

"It is a name I have heard, *Capitan.* Who he belongs to, I do not know."

"Well, there was an American Army officer named Benjamin Bonneville who took a leave of absence and brought a party of trappers out to the Oregon Country a few years before my father got here. Later, he was put in charge of Fort Vancouver about the time Washington Territory was organized. But I never heard of a lake or a dam being named after him, let alone the one you say broke ten thousand years ago and deposited a petrified tree a thousand feet above today's river level."

"This is a story that I have been told, *M'sieu,*" Pierre answered with a shrug. "What you Americans call a tall tale, a legend, a pulling of ze long bow."

"Like a myth," Lars said.

"Or what my people call a grandfather tale," Alex said. "As a matter of fact, I've heard it, too."

"I have seen ze stone tree," Old Pierre insisted. "If you wish, I can show you where it lies today."

"How did it get there?"

"When ze dam broke, it was still a wooden tree, so it floated there. When ze water went down, it stayed, then turned to stone."

"How did Lake Bonneville get its name?"

In his days as a *voyageur* with the Hudson's Bay Company, Old Pierre said, the petrified tree lying half-buried in a sand-drifted coulee a thousand feet higher than the river level had been a landmark since the earliest days. The Indians of the area claimed it had been deposited there centuries before when the channel of the river was at that height. A *bourgeois* well versed in geology had told Pierre that this was just one more link in a chain of evidence that proved that in the not too distant past the Columbia had been a river of such magnificent proportions that the present-day stream was a rivulet in comparison. Other physical pieces of geological evidence were the terraces ranging from fifty to five hundred feet in height containing deposits of gravel of different ages wherever concave bluffs bordering the present-day river channel occurred.

Though neither Lars nor Willie had seen the fifty-mile-long gash called "Grand Coulee" or the three-mile-wide scar named "Dry Falls" over which a river of tremendous proportions had poured when the Ice Age ended and the dam broke ten thousand years ago, both men realized that in this country such things could happen.

"One of these days," Lars said, "I'd like to spend a week or two exploring the coulee country with a geologist who can explain what happened ages ago."

Still suffering from the aches and pains acquired during the seventy-five-mile ride north in search of Old Pierre, Willie winced and shook his head.

"Count me out on a horseback trip, friend. Until they fill Grand Coulee with enough water to float a stern-wheeler, I'll just cruise the Columbia River where it flows today."

6.

A FEW MILES BELOW VICTORIA ROCK the party passed the mouth of a low, sandy wash coming in from the northeast which Old Pierre called Moses Coulee. Four miles farther on, the tranquillity of the river was broken for several hundred yards by a moderately rough expanse of water named Gualquil Rapids, which offered no great obstacle to a stern-wheeler. For the next seven or eight miles the river was perfectly smooth, with the Indian paddlers lifting their oars and letting the *bateau* float along unaided, while Old Pierre used his steering oar only now and then to keep the boat in the center of the current.

Passing a small stream called Crab Creek and elevations of land named Saddle Mountain and Sentinel Bluffs, the party followed a wide bend of the river first to the east, then back again to the south through a country composed of sandy, gravelly, worthless soil, fit only for scattered tufts of bunchgrass and low clumps of sagebrush.

For the next five or six miles the river was wide, deep, and sluggish in the early afternoon heat of the summer day, looking more like a lake than a river. The dead water was caused, Lars supposed, by the damming effect of the eleven miles of obstructions in the Priest Rapids sector. Agreeing with Lars's suggestion that camp be made a mile or two upstream from the rapids so that they could be inspected and charted before being run in the *bateau*, Captain William Gray told Old Pierre to find a favorable slack-water spot along the east shore where the canoe could put in for the night.

With several hours of daylight still remaining after camp had been made, Old Pierre bridled at the request that he walk the length of the rapids with Willie, Lars, and Alex, pointing out in detail the hazards of each one so that Lars could note them on his chart.

"*Mon Dieu, Capitan*, my poor old legs will barely carry me from ze boat to ze shore. Even if I could walk so far, my eyesight is bad, so I would see very little."

"You saw well enough to steer us through some mighty bad rapids today," Willie said sharply.

"Zat is different, *M'sieu.* I did not have to see zose rapids. I could feel them. Also, I have run ze river so many times I remember every rapid on it *parfaitement.*"

"If that's the case," Lars said, "could you describe the eleven miles of white water we'll be going through tomorrow well enough for me to sketch the rapids on my chart?"

Nodding vigorously, Old Pierre tipped another generous portion of rum from the jug Captain Gray had provided as part of the agreement into his cup, took a big swallow, closed his eyes, then said,

"Zat will be easy, *M'sieu.* Just tell me when you are ready to write down what I say …"

Checking the information given him by Old Pierre that afternoon against the actuality of running the eleven miles of rapids the next day, Lars was amazed by its accuracy. This was what he recorded and later experienced:

> The *first ripple* of the system of Priest Rapids is a slight one as far as the swiftness is concerned; the water, however, is shallow, flowing over immense boulders and jagged rocks, which were plainly visible from the boat and at a variety of depths below the surface. Near the left bank many of these rocks come above the water, and the whirls plainly told that many others were just below the surface. Our course lay about the middle of the stream, and the sounding pole would indicate one instant perhaps a depth of three or four feet, the next ten or twelve, and the next five or six. Through this portion of the river a steamer could go now in safety after finding and knowing a thoroughly good channel.
>
> The *second rapid* is about as bad a place as there is on the whole river. All about, the bedrock points and islands rise up in ugly, black, jagged masses, threatening destruction to anything that touches them. The bottom, as in the first ripple, is composed of huge boulders and rocks, and the water flows swiftly over this dangerous bottom and these outcropping rocks with a depth of only three or four feet. The fall here is considerable; we passed over one fall of at least three feet.
>
> A steamer could not ascend this rapid without the use of a line, and even then the greatest care would be necessary. A smooth stretch of water then followed, and we came to the *third rapid,* which was swift and shallow, with considerable bedrock jutting up near both shores. The bed of the river at this rapid is the same as it has been all along, composed of large boulders.

For about five and a half miles now the river is quiet and slow, with rocks scattered about here and there, generally in clusters. The water is so shallow that we were able to see the bottom for a great part of the way, and is from twelve to twenty feet in depth. The *fourth rapid* is in this stretch of water, but is very mild in character and presents no obstruction.

We now come to a very bad portion of the river, consisting of the three lower rapids of Priest Rapids. We are able to tell from the preparations by Old Pierre and his crew that considerable danger lies along the *fifth rapid*, in which the water is very turbulent, boiling and roaring a great deal. This boiling and foaming is not, however, necessarily attended with great swiftness of current, for in this ripple we did not move as fast as in some others which appeared much more quiet. In fact, the tumbling over the uneven bottom which causes the agitation tends to check the velocity considerably.

The long, irregular mass near the right bank which lies along the fifth rapid continues on down the river for about two and a half miles, with only an occasional break.

A little below the fifth rapid we come to where the main channel is divided into two by another long, irregular, jagged mass of the same black basaltic rock, thrown along almost in the center of the river. We choose the right-hand channel of the two, and, after swiftly passing a few ugly-looking projecting points, we find ourselves in the *sixth rapid*, shooting with the speed of a race-horse down through the canal-like channel between these two long rock islands. For about a mile we tore along with the united speed of the raging torrent and our yelling Indian oarsmen. The channel seemed to have plenty of water, but is quite narrow, being about sixty to eighty feet wide. We went through it at the rate of about twenty miles an hour.

The left-hand channel is the one better suited to purposes of navigation, I believe. It is crookeder and the water is not so swift as in the straight-away one through which we came.

Emerging from the canal-like sixth rapid, Old Pierre threw the boat to the left to avoid some bad-looking water dead ahead, and, after a little further tumbling and rolling about in the *seventh rapid*, we emerged with a shout of joy from the eleven miles of Priest Rapids. We all know now that our dangers are passed, and thank God for allowing us to safely come through all the rapids.

We soon make for shore, and camp on the right bank, having made during the morning, about eighteen miles.

Well satisfied with the work Old Pierre and his half-blood oarsmen had done for the river exploration party, Captain William Polk Gray paid them in gold for three days' labor, gave them what remained of the food and rum supply, then took them aboard the

Explorer, which was moored nearby, where the boat's cook prepared and served them a good meal after first being warned by Captain Gray of their tremendous appetites.

"In the days when Hudson's Bay Company brigades crossed Canada from Montreal to the lower Columbia," he told the cook, "the usual ration of meat was seven pounds per man each day. Don't let them go away hungry."

While waiting for the meal to be cooked and served, Lars utilized the time to draw a sketch of the upper Columbia River from just above Rock Island to its source as described to him by Pierre Agare. It did not surprise him to learn that when Captain Leonard White had built and launched his stern-wheeler *Forty-Nine* back in 1865, Old Pierre had been aboard during its maiden voyage from just south of the Canadian border to as far upriver as the gold-boom region. Among other geographical oddities of the Columbia, Old Pierre described the curious fact that in the area called Skookumchuck Prairie, the river began an elongated oval, first flowing north for 150 miles, circling west around the end of a mountain range, then flowing south again to eventually pass within a short distance of where it had flowed north three hundred river miles ago. There, Old Pierre said, a flat, open prairie only two miles wide separated the north- and south-flowing portions of the Columbia River.

"When I told zis to Captain White," Pierre said with a chuckle, "he got very excited. I must take him to ze place, he said, so dat he could see if it would be possible to dig a canal across ze short neck of land, take a boat through it, and save three hundred river miles on ze trip from Montreal to ze lower Columbia."

"That sounds like Len White," Willie said. "He concocted more wild schemes than an Indian dog has fleas. Did you take him to the place?"

"*Non, M'sieu.* He was too busy carrying miners and freight to ze Arrow Lakes gold-strike to get that far upriver. Like all Americans, he was a *pelton*—a crazy man—always wanting to change what *le bon Dieu* made."

As soon as Pierre Agare and his boatmen had washed down a prodigious meal with enough rum to intoxicate ordinary mortals, they said farewell, cast off the lines of the *bateau*, and began the return trip to their village. After they had gone, Willie Gray, Lars Warren, and

Alex Conley spent several hours discussing what they had learned during the past week's exploration of the Columbia River from the mouth of the Snake to above Rock Island Rapids.

"What we're talking about here is roughly a hundred and thirty miles of barely navigable river running through desert country as bleak and empty as God ever made," Willie said. "So far as I'm concerned, it would be a waste of Corps money and O.S.N. Company time to do the rock-blasting and channel work that will have to be done before steamboats can go upriver on a regular schedule. Do you gentlemen agree?"

"I sure do," Alex said. "Right now, the only people living along this stretch of the Columbia are Indians, who have no use for steamboats."

"If I were asked to make a prediction," Lars said contemplatively, "I would say that the lower end of Priest Rapids is as far up the Columbia as the O.S.N. Company ought to go at the present time. But when this part of the country begins to attract white settlers in ten to twenty years, I imagine a town of considerable importance will be developed in the area, which has a lot going for it."

"Such as?"

"Water power, for one thing. A low dam and a wheel just below Priest Rapids would provide lots of free power for a flour mill and a sawmill. The Yakima River, which comes into the Columbia a few miles downstream, grows fine timber in the mountains of its upper valley, has fertile soil that will produce all kinds of crops, and has access to roads leading south to The Dalles and west to Puget Sound. As we've seen, there's good steamboat water from here to the mouth of the Snake and beyond, which means that for all practical purposes the inland country below here has water-level access to the sea. Those are important assets."

"I'm inclined to agree," Willie said. "But for now, we've done the job we were paid to do. Tomorrow morning, we'll head downriver."

Pleasant as steaming down the wide, deep, tranquil river was the next day, the scenery on either shore held little of interest. Their course during the forenoon lay nearly due east, then, where the Columbia swung south again, vertical chalk-white bluffs from one to six hundred feet in height bordered the river for a distance of ten miles or so. During the day Lars noted nineteen lodges of Indians Alex said were Wanapums or relatives engaged in fishing and drying salmon.

Except for an occasional sandy island below the mouth of an incoming river, where the course of the boat must be kept to the deeper water of the adjacent channel, there were no impediments to navigation. After pulling into shore and making camp six miles above the mouth of the Yakima that afternoon, the boat got under way at an early hour the next morning. Even though the low-water period of mid-summer had not yet come, the shallowness of the Yakima and the extensive sandbars near its mouth made it clear that it would not be navigable to steamboats for a long enough period of the year to warrant establishing regular traffic on it.

Passing the mouth of the Snake at ten o'clock next morning, Willie Gray told Lars that in his opinion a person could look farther and see less in this part of the country than anywhere else in the West. So far as the bleak, dreary wasteland adjacent to the juncture of the Snake with the Columbia was concerned, Lars admitted it was not very appealing. Except for the two rivers, nothing but sagebrush and sand drifts were in sight. A person could scan the horizon for mile after mile without seeing a tree. The heat through the summer was excessive, high winds prevailed much of the time, and sand blew into everything.

"By the glare of the sun and the flying sands," Captain William Clark had complained in his journal on October 18, 1805, "one's eyes are in a continual state of winking, blinking, and torment. The Indians of this part of the country are very much afflicted with sore eyes, which they ascribe to the glare of the sun on the desert and rivers and the prevailing sand-bearing winds ..."

Truth was, Lars said, he was more interested in the rivers than the land through which they flowed.

"If the men in the Warren family had wanted to be farmers, Willie, they would have settled in the Willamette Valley. But only Uncle Emil did—and even he makes his living from the river. So long as water flows downhill and steamboats run, so will I."

7.

Though both Daphne Warren and the manager of the Wallula Palace Hotel tried to downplay the unpleasant incident of the two drunken male intruders that had occurred during his absence, assuring Lars that such a thing would never happen again, the very fact that it had happened once spurred him into drawing up plans for a home of their own. Buying an acre lot atop a rise of land overlooking the river and arranging financing with the Baker-Boyer Bank in Walla Walla, he put carpenters and other skilled craftsmen to work building a comfortable two-story frame house topped by a cupola-observatory patterned after what in New England was called a "widow's walk."

It was not nearly as spacious or well equipped as the third-floor observatory at his grandparents' Hilltop House overlooking Astoria and the lower Columbia, where a nineteen-power telescope mounted on a 360-degree swivel gave a spectacular view of the Columbia River Bar and the Pacific Ocean far out to sea. But the sweeping view of the mile-wide river flowing down from the north, its final swing westward toward the sea between the darkly looming basaltic bluffs of Wallula Gap, and the majestic river beyond, on whose shimmering surface a constant traffic of O.S.N. Company stern-wheelers passed to and fro, was stunning.

"I don't like the term 'widow's walk'," Daphne complained the first time she looked at the plans and asked Lars what the rounded structure atop the house was called. "Certainly, I don't intend to walk around up there, worrying about your boat being wrecked and my becoming a widow."

"I know you don't. But steamboats do have accidents, Daphne—like going aground, being holed by snags, and exploding boilers."

"What if they do? Climbing up to the top of the house and looking out over the river because your boat is running late won't do you, me, or the boat any good."

"Tell you what we'll do," Lars said with a laugh. "We'll call it the 'Crow's Nest.'"

Truth was, in a company as well run as the O.S.N., accidents of any kind were a rare occurrence, though now and then they did happen. Like the wreck of the *Yakima* two months ago, when an engine bearing failed, causing a sudden loss of power just upstream from John Day Rapids. A fairly new boat, the *Yakima* was two hundred feet long, could carry five hundred passengers and five hundred tons of freight, and was the pride of the grain fleet running from Celilo Landing to Lewiston.

Like all the stern-wheelers on the upper Columbia, she was long and narrow, with a shallow draft, a sleek handsome appearance, and a well-earned reputation for speed. On one memorable trip, she set a record between Celilo and Lewiston when she made the 260-mile upriver run against a strong spring current in forty-one hours and thirty-five minutes.

Well built and powerful though she was, her designer had never anticipated that the boat would be forced to drift through a rapid sideways without power. When she did, she soon hung up on submerged rocks; then, pounded by surges of current striking her broadside, toppled over and went under. Fortunately, her well-trained crew put the ample lifeboats carried aboard to good use, transporting all the passengers and crew safely ashore, though a full cargo of sacked wheat was a total loss. In his attempt to explain to Daphne why the boat had broken up so quickly, Lars found himself involved in technicalities that she could not understand.

"A riverboat is built different from an oceangoing steamship," he said. "For instance, it has a flat bottom and practically no keel."

"What's a keel?"

"The long, lengthwise beam on the bottom that keeps a vessel stable. A five hundred ton stern-wheeler like the *Yakima*, which had a flat bottom and a shallow keel, draws only three feet of water, while an oceangoing steamer the same size has a much deeper keel, which makes it draw at least fifteen feet. By its very design, the ocean steamer is much less likely to break up when it's wrecked, while the stern-wheeler, with a flat bottom and very little keel, is given whatever rigidity it has by an arrangement of a king post, fore and aft hogging posts, and chains."

"What are hogging posts?"

Though Lars was beginning to realize it was hopeless, he tried to simplify the subject for his bride by taking a pencil and paper and drawing her a diagram.

"In contrast to an ocean steamer, which is fairly rigid, a sternwheeler is very flexible. If it didn't have something to hold it together, it would be like—well, like a fat lady putting on a formal gown without first getting into a corset."

"Lars! That's silly!"

"On the contrary, it's rather apt. You see, in the middle of a sternwheeler there's a tall king post, with two or more shorter hogging posts set on each side forward to the bow and backward to the stern. Chains are run from the deck of the boat up over the hogging posts to the king post so that when they're tightened—as they have to be from time to time—the boat is pulled snugly together, just like the fat lady being laced into her corset, so that she'll look nice and trim in her gown."

Daphne giggled. "I can't wait to tell Mother this!"

"Well, your mother certainly is trim enough," Lars said, flushing. "Don't you say I called her fat."

"You're special to her, Lars. You know that. She likes you so much she's going to help us furnish our new house. To begin with, she's giving us her Marie Antoinette bed."

"I didn't know she had one."

"That's because you've never been in her bedroom," Daphne said with a smile. "It's truly a magnificent bed, Lars. You'll love it, I know."

"I'm not sure I want your mother to give us such a personal piece of furniture, Daphne."

"Oh, pooh! Don't be such a stick-in-the-mud! If we don't take it, we'll hurt her feelings. She's just dying for us to give her a grandchild, you know. I imagine she thinks a big, bouncy bed will speed things along."

"Did she actually say that?"

"No. But I suspect that's what she's thinking. Anyhow, I told her we're working on it as hard as we can ..."

In the Portland headquarters of the Oregon Steam Navigation Company, Emil Warren, as attorney for the corporation, was accustomed to responding to the requests of President John C. Ainsworth for documentation of ongoing projects with alacrity and a minimum of questions. So when Ainsworth asked him that rainy January morning to search the blueprint cabinet for sheets of a proposed project Emil thought the O.S.N. Company had abandoned several years ago—a railroad line from Portland to Salt Lake by way of Walla Walla—he found the prints and gave them to the company president without comment.

After perusing them briefly, Ainsworth nodded his head, smiled, and said, "Yes, these will do fine." Glancing up as Emil started to leave the office, he added, "One more thing, Emil."

"Yes?"

"I'm expecting a visit from Dr. Dorsey Syng Baker, the Walla Walla banker and railroad-builder. You know him, of course."

"Yes, Sir, I do."

"I understand that the narrow-gauge railroad he's been building from Wallula Landing to Walla Walla the past couple of years has come to a halt because of a shortage of funds. The end of track is now at Whitman Station, ten miles west of town. He needs a hundred thousand dollars to finish it."

"Is the O.S.N. Company thinking of furnishing it?"

"Only if we can buy into the project on our own terms. But dealing with Doc Baker is like trying to pick up a porcupine with your bare hands. It's hard to get a proper hold without bloodying your fingers. So I may try to run a bluff."

"How can I help?"

"To begin with, I want you to find some excuse to come into my office after he's been here ten minutes or so. Hopefully, I'll have him softened up by then so that he'll be receptive to my terms. All you need to do, Emil, is confirm whatever I say—in an offhand sort of way."

"He won't be easily fooled, John. As long as you've dealt with him, you should know that by now."

"I do, Emil. Still, I'm going to try."

When Dorsey Syng Baker came in an hour or so later, Emil greeted him cordially, inquired about the state of his family's health, the weather, and business conditions in Walla Walla, then told him John Ainsworth was expecting him in his private office. A stooped, thin, nearly bald man with a flowing white beard and piercing blue eyes, Dr. Dorsey Baker looked preoccupied as always, merely nodding and wasting no words on social amenities before going into the office and closing the door behind him. After ten minutes had passed, Emil did as instructed, first tapping discreetly on the door of the president's office, then, when invited to enter, doing so.

"Sorry to interrupt," he said, "but I need to check a contract in your file."

"Help yourself, Emil," John Ainsworth said amiably. "You know Dr. Baker, don't you?"

"Yes, Sir. We spoke a few minutes ago in the outer office."

"I've been showing him these blueprints we had made a couple of years ago when we were discussing a deal with the Union Pacific on building a railroad from Portland to connect with their transcontinental line in the Salt Lake area. He says the project is news to him."

"I imagine it would be. We did not publicize our plans."

"I told him we weren't sure what route we would take beyond the big bend of the Columbia at Wallula Gap, but were seriously considering going through Walla Walla. He tells me he's already built twenty-two miles of narrow gauge railroad along that route, though for the time being his project has come to a halt because of a shortage of money."

Dr. Baker's eyes snapped as he interrupted sharply, "I did not say that, John. What I said was that cold winter weather has forced a temporary construction halt during which I plan to make a subscription drive in order to sell enough shares of stock to ensure the railroad's completion by the end of the year."

"Well, whatever the reason, nothing is happening at the moment. While we're on the subject, Emil, have you had any response from the Union Pacific to the latest proposal we made them?"

"No, I haven't."

"As I recall, we offered to exchange our right-of-way along the south side of the Columbia River between Portland and Umatilla for a substantial number of shares of Union Pacific stock and a seat on the Board of Directors, didn't we?"

"That was the gist of the proposal, yes."

"To which they replied that they would take our offer under advisement?"

As Emil most definitely recalled, the Union Pacific's reply had used the words "preposterous" and "unacceptable" several times, though buried deep within the verbiage of their letter the polite phrase "take under advisement" probably had been included.

"Something to that effect, yes."

"What I've suggested to Dr. Baker is that if we can sweeten the deal by including his little narrow-gauge railroad, which is yet to be completed, we might be willing to go back to Union Pacific and re-open negotiations. Do you think that's possible?"

Before Emil could frame a reply, Dr. Baker snapped, "Don't waste your breath, Emil. As I've said time and again, I do not intend for ownership and control of the Walla Walla & Columbia River Railroad to get out of my hands."

"But if you lack funds—" Ainsworth began.

"I'll raise them, John. One way or another, I'll get the money I need on my own terms."

"You won't consider borrowing a hundred thousand dollars at 10 percent interest from the O.S.N. Company in exchange for a mortgage against 51 percent of your stock and a seat on the Board of Directors?"

"Not for a minute! In order to raise the money to build my railroad so far, I have mortgaged my home, my land, my cattle, and all the assets I possess—including my good name—as well as putting past, present, and future freight revenue into construction costs and rolling stock. But I will not risk the money of depositors in my bank nor will I turn over the running of my railroad to anyone outside my immediate family. That is final, John."

"Then I'm afraid I can't help you, Dorsey, much as I'd like to."

Getting stiffly out of his chair, Dr. Baker limped to the door, opened it, then turned and shook a threatening finger at Ainsworth.

"So be it, John. But you're going to regret this day. I'll make you two predictions, here and now, with Emil Warren as my witness."

"Yes?"

"First, I'll finish my railroad in time to carry next summer's wheat harvest from the Walla Walla Valley to your loading dock at Wallula."

"I hope you do, Dorsey. We can use the business."

"Second, once my railroad is completed, it will make so much money that the Oregon Steam Navigation Company will try to buy it from me within five years. When they do, my asking price will make you faint."

"Just out of curiosity, Dorsey, what will your asking price be?"

"One million dollars. Not a penny less. Good day, gentlemen."

After the door slammed shut, both John Ainsworth and Emil Warren were silent for a time. Then Ainsworth shook his head and murmured, "I believe he meant it, Emil."

"He did, John. So much for your bluff ..."

Through his brother, Tommy, and his nephew, Lars, both of whom saw Doc Baker at close range during his return trip upriver, Emil Warren followed the fortunes of the banker–railroad-builder with considerable interest during the ensuing year. Whether or not Dr. Baker believed that the O.S.N. Company planned to go into the railroad business with or without the Union Pacific as a partner, his actions during and after the cold two-day journey home made it clear that he intended to finish the final ten miles of track-laying just as he had promised to do.

Taking the early morning boat from Portland to the Lower Cascades, the portage train around the rapids, then the *Onconta*, with Captain Tommy Warren in command, from the Upper Cascades to The Dalles, Doc Baker barely acknowledged his long friendship with Tommy by a curt nod, then spent the four hours of the run sitting alone in a deck chair set in the lee of the main cabin, protected from the cold, drizzling rain by a heavy overcoat, muffler, and black western-style hat. From the way he stared bleakly into the gray haze astern, he made it clear that he wished to talk to no one.

"I told the steward to take him a mug of coffee," Tommy told Emil later, "and invite him to come up to the pilot house where it was dry and warm. After making sure the coffee was free, he accepted it. But he declined my invitation to the pilot house, telling the steward he had some important thinking to do, and wanted to be alone."

After spending the night in The Dalles at the Umatilla House, where he rented the cheapest room the hotel offered, eating a frugal supper that evening and a skimpy breakfast next morning, he caught the train for the fourteen-mile portage to Celilo Landing, where he boarded the *Inland Queen*, with Captain Lars Warren in command. When Lars, who greatly appreciated the loan and repayment terms he and Daphne had been given by the Baker-Boyer Bank for their recently completed house in Wallula, invited Dr. Baker up to the pilot house to share warmth and coffee, the invitation was accepted. But neither the new house nor the much appreciated loan remained the subject of conversation for very long.

"You're an ambitious young man, Captain Warren," Dr. Baker said bluntly. "I understand the Oregon Steam Navigation Company pays you very well."

"Yes, Sir. As I stated on the loan application, my current salary is three hundred fifty dollars a month."

"You recently got married, I'm told. You bought an expensive lot and have built a fine house in Wallula. May I ask if you have considered any other long-term investments?"

"Well, Dr. Baker," Lars said a bit sheepishly, "my wife and I are planning to have a baby."

"When?"

"We don't know yet, Sir. But we're setting aside a portion of my salary every month to get ready for it."

"A commendable thing to do," Dr. Baker said with an approving nod. "But a baby was not the kind of long-term investment I had in mind."

"What did you have in mind, Sir?"

"Shares of stock in my railroad. If it's as successful as I think it will be, the stock will triple in value within five years."

"Could I invest as little as five hundred dollars, Sir, with payments of fifty dollars a month?"

"You certainly can."

"Then I'll do it, Dr. Baker. It's in my interest to see your railroad succeed. Do I need to sign anything?"

"Your word is enough, Captain Warren. I'll deduct the monthly payments from your bank account and send you the stock certificate when it's paid for."

Later, when Lars told his father and uncle what he had done, both of them invested in five hundred dollars' worth of stock themselves. Emil said with a chuckle, "Might as well get a piece of the profit from that million-dollar sale Doc Baker says he's going to make to the O.S.N. Company five years from now."

Leaving the boat at Wallula, Dr. Baker joined a dozen other passengers in the "hearse," as the square, enclosed car attached to the string of flatcars behind the puffing *Walla Walla* as the little Pony engine was called, riding with them the twenty-two miles to the end of track at Whitman Station ten miles west of Walla Walla. Though most of the occupants of the car appreciated the rosy glow of heat thrown out by the coal-burning cast-iron stove at the front of the car, Doc Baker complained it was far hotter than it needed to be, a waste of expensive fuel, and unhealthy for robust men who soon must bundle up again when they went outdoors.

At Whitman Station, where his twenty-one-year-old son Frank awaited the train with a buggy in which they would make the ten-mile drive into town, Doc Baker shoved the young man over to the left-hand side of the seat, saying curtly, "You don't drive fast enough to suit me."

After slapping the team of winter-shaggy sorrels into a brisk trot with a badly worn buggy whip, the last foot of which was missing, he responded to Frank's suggestion that they buy a new one with a negative grunt.

"Can't afford a new one right now. This one works well enough."

"But, father, it's been broken for a year."

" 'Waste not, want not,' Son. We've got a railroad to build."

As the oldest son in the Baker family, Frank knew better than to argue with his father. Like Frank himself, his two younger brothers, Henry, now seventeen, and Will, fifteen, had been taught that the most important things in life were education, frugality, and work. Born just before the family moved to Walla Walla from the Willamette Valley in 1860, the youngest son had been the victim of an unaccustomed bit of whimsy by his father, who, in recognition of the move, had insisted that the new baby be christened "Walla Walla Willie." When his wife expressed misgivings, saying, "Don't you think he'll be teased about his name?", Doc Baker shrugged.

"If he's teased, he can fight."

Six years younger than Frank, Walla Walla Willie had borne his unusual name with humor, good grace, and, when the teasing went too far, had defended it with his fists. Now fifteen and giving promise of becoming as shrewd and levelheaded in business matters as his oldest brother and father were, he recently had begun to use the more conventional name "W. William Baker." Even his once-whimsical father now admitted the name was more suitable for a young man destined to become a banker, though within the family it was usually shortened to "Will."

During the cold drive home, Frank Baker could see that his father was deeply troubled, though it was not until the next day that he was told the details of the refusal of financing by the O.S.N. Company. Having been put on the Board of Directors on his twenty-first birthday, Frank attended the board meeting that morning in the office at the rear of the bank. Also present were Dr. Baker's partner, John Boyer, Civil Engineer Sewell Truax, and merchant Bill Green, all of whom were board members and investors in the railroad. As they sat around the plain pine table, they were attentive to Dr. Baker's words, "In our last meeting, gentlemen," he said, "we discussed the matter of issuing stock for sale to raise funds for quick completion of the line. Now I want to propose that we make this offer at once, and on very liberal terms—so liberal that we can expect them to attract investors without delay. Speed is essential now. We must have more funds at once."

"Is there some special reason for speeding up?" Sewell Truax asked.

"Yes. A new line is about to be put in from Portland to Walla Walla. The O.S.N. Company has decided to go into the railroad business."

A stunned silence during which the board members exchanged looks of shock fell over the room.

"Sooner or later," Dr. Baker went on, "we'll have to make a choice—compete or sell. Because of our limited capital, the fact is clear that when that time comes, our aim should be to sell at a profit. In order to do that, we must have our line completed and equipped with first-class rolling stock. No more 'rawhide.' No more makeshifts. It will have to be a going concern."

There was another silence. Then Bill Green said, "It looks rather gloomy, Doctor."

"Gloomy!" Baker snorted. "It's not gloomy. It's a challenge! Gentlemen, we're engaged in giving the community what it wants and needs. Even now, before our line is finished, the improvement in transportation has started a boom in wheat. Look at the shipments we're loading. Look at the way farmers are breaking new land for seeding. Are we going to sneak off now with our tails between our legs just because of some competition? No, by George! We deserve to win this fight and we're going to win it!"

To a man, the assembled directors applauded.

What he proposed to do, Dr. Baker said, was call a mass meeting of the farmers, businessmen, and townspeople interested in seeing the railroad completed and ask them to buy enough stock to give the company the money it needed to finish the line in a timely manner.

"I am not what you would call a popular man," he said with a grim smile. "Now that there is a possibility of another railroad being built, there will be some people wanting to see me fail. But we must try. Are we all agreed?"

When the directors said they were, Dr. Baker announced a mass meeting to be held in the district schoolhouse in a week's time. When the evening came, more than three hundred people filled the seats and stood around the walls. When they were assembled, Dr. Baker rose and addressed the crowd.

"Gentlemen, I am sure we are agreed that a prompt completion of the railroad will be of general benefit. The directors of my company have authorized me to make an offer of stock to the citizens of the Walla Walla Valley on a fair and equitable basis—namely, seventy-five thousand dollars' worth of stock in the Walla Walla & Columbia River Railroad Company at its original cost, with the guarantee that within one year of the date of full payment, the railroad will be completed, equipped, and running."

Folding the paper from which he had been reading, he sat down. During the long silence that followed, men exchanged glances, some smiling and nodding their heads in agreement, others scowling and shaking their heads in disapproval. John Boyer got to his feet.

"Gentlemen, it seems to me that the Doctor's offer should be considered favorably. Since he has carried nearly all the burden and risk through the initial stages, with the soundness of the investment well demonstrated by now, it seems to me that the terms of his offer are fair and generous."

"You call it generous to ask for seventy-five thousand dollars?" a man in the back of the room shouted.

John Boyer smiled and sat down without answering. Sigmund Schwabacher, a respected local businessman, got to his feet.

"Dr. Baker," he said briskly, "may I ask on what basis the need for seventy-five thousand dollars is computed? According to your original estimate, this final ten miles of construction, including a terminal station, would require considerably over one hundred thousand dollars. How will the difference be made up?"

"With the railroad's current freight revenue from Whitman Station to Wallula," Dr. Baker answered, holding up a sheaf of papers. "I have an exact calculation of that revenue on these sheets, if you would care to examine them."

"If the estimated revenue falls off—on account of competition, say—what good will your guarantee be?"

From the way the prominent vessel in his father's right temple pulsed noticeably, Frank Baker, who clearly saw it from his front-row seat, knew that his father was having difficulty controlling his temper. Since Dr. Baker had suffered a partially disabling stroke twenty years ago, had endured a lesser stroke three years ago, and had bluntly predicted that when the third stroke occurred—as it inevitably would—it would kill him, Frank silently prayed that his father not have it now.

"As I said before, Mr. Schwabacher," Dr. Baker answered in a calm, measured voice, "if the citizens accept my offer, the road will be completed within one year."

Apparently satisfied, Mr. Schwabacher nodded and sat down.

"Since your company is already making twenty-five thousand dollars' profit a year," a skeptical member of the crowd shouted, "you aren't exactly headed over the hill to the poorhouse, are you?"

"Yeah," another cried. "With that kind of income, what do you need our money for?"

"Gentlemen, you're missing the point he's been trying to make," John Boyer said patiently. "What Dr. Baker is saying is that by practicing strict economy and cutting construction costs to an absolute minimum, he believes he can plough current freight revenue back into the project at a rate that will allow him to complete the railroad in a year's time."

As the general discussion broke down into a disorganized hubbub of argument across the crowded room, someone called out to Almos Reynolds, a farmer, millwright, and longtime businessman known for his levelheadedness.

"What's your opinion, Reynolds?"

"Well," Mr. Reynolds said, getting slowly to his feet. "I don't mean to be antagonistic to the offer. I'm a good friend of Dr. Baker's and I respect his business judgment. But, frankly, I think it's too much to expect to raise seventy-five thousand dollars in the community at this time. To most of us, that's a lot of money."

"You bet it is!" a man cried.

"What I suggest we do," Reynolds continued, "is form a committee that will take the offer under advisement, consider it from every angle, then report back to this body with its recommendation."

"An excellent idea," agreed B. L. Sharpstein, a local attorney whom everyone respected. "If you will serve as its chairman, Almos, I'll be glad to act as its secretary and serve on the committee with you."

Following an expression of approval by a majority of the men present, a committee of seven farmers and businessmen was selected, directed to study the offer, then make its recommendation in writing in ten days' time. As the meeting broke up and Frank Baker moved with his father toward the door, Almos Reynolds edged through the crowd to Dr. Baker's side, touched his elbow, and said, "Sorry if I disappointed you, Doctor. Under the circumstances, it was the best I could do."

"I know, Almos. We'll just have to wait and hope for the best."

8.

On a cold late January evening a week later, Almos Reynolds called at the Baker home just after supper. Greeting him at the door, Frank took his coat, hat, and gloves, placed them on the entryway hall tree, then escorted him to his father's study. For some time he could hear the murmur of the two men's voices behind the closed door but could not make out what they were saying. Presently Reynolds left, his face as solemn as Dr. Baker's as they shook hands and parted. When the visitor had gone, Dr. Baker motioned Frank into the study, where the first thing the young man noticed was a letter lying on the desk.

"What did the committee say?" he blurted to his father.

"They rejected my offer," Dr. Baker said grimly. "They turned me down."

"Oh, Father!"

"In my opinion, they've made a very foolish decision—one they'll someday regret."

"I just bet they will!"

"But they did make a counterproposal. Instead of buying seventy-five thousand dollars' worth of stock, they've offered to raise a subsidy of twenty-five thousand dollars, on the condition that I'll complete the railroad within a year's time."

"A subsidy? That sounds pretty good."

"No, it's not good at all," Dr. Baker answered somberly, shaking his head. "In the first place, twenty-five thousand dollars is only a third of what we need. In the second place, taking the subsidy will place me under an obligation to them that I'm reluctant to accept."

"What sort of an obligation?"

"To give them a voice in the way I operate my railroad, even though I still own a majority of the stock. That's their purpose, of course. But I deeply resent their crude attempt to put me under their thumb."

"Are you going to turn them down?"

Again, Frank saw the vein in his father's temple throb. Pounding his clenched fist on the desk, Dr. Baker exclaimed, "I won't be dictated to, by George! Just let them try!" Leaning back in his chair, he closed his eyes for a moment, took several deep breaths, then, becoming more composed, opened his eyes and said, "I want to think this through before I make a final decision. Goodnight, Son. I'll talk to you in the morning."

The lamp in the study was still burning when Frank went to bed a few hours later, but however late his father may have stayed up thinking the matter through, he arose at six and was at the breakfast table when Frank came down the next morning. As soon as breakfast was over, he said curtly, "Hitch up, Son. We're driving out to Whitman Station where Major Truax is working today. I want to talk things over with him. You might as well listen to what he has to say."

Because he was in a hurry, Dr. Baker again insisted on doing the driving. As a former surveyor with the Corps of Engineers, Sewell Truax had done excellent work selecting a route and grade for the railroad, had bought a substantial number of shares of stock in the enterprise, and was a member of the Board of Directors. As the buggy careened and jolted over the frozen ruts of the uneven road, Frank questioned his father.

"Have you decided what to do about the subsidy offer?"

"Yes. We'll have to accept it."

"How will you make up the difference?"

"That's what I want to talk to Truax about. I'm hoping he can suggest possible further cuts I may have overlooked. The difference will have to come out of my own pocket."

"How about the bank? If the railroad is bound to succeed, wouldn't an investment in its stock be good for the depositors?"

"Whether it would be or not," Dr. Baker answered sharply, "I have no right to use my depositors' money in my own undertakings. But one way or another I'm going to match that subsidy by liquidating everything I own, postponing all possible purchases, putting current freight revenues into construction costs as they arise, and selling additional shares of stock to the few friends I have left who believe in me and the railroad. The job is going to get done one way or another. I'm counting on Major Truax to help me do it."

A week before Easter that year, Daphne Warren made her mother, Lili deBeauchamp, extremely happy and her husband, Lars, glow with pride by announcing that she was pregnant. According to the best calculation she could make, she told Lars, the blessed event would occur around the first of November. Not wanting her to be alone any more than necessary, Lars arranged his schedule through the spring and summer so that he was absent from their new home overlooking Wallula as few nights as possible.

"Going upriver, I'll have to overnight in Lewiston," he told Daphne. "But coming down, I'll drop off at Wallula, then let Herb Blalock take the *Queen* on down to Celilo. He'll make an early morning start there next day, then pick me up here in early afternoon for the upriver run to Lewiston."

"Why make such fuss over me?" Daphne protested. "I've never felt better in my life."

"Because I want to be with you as much as I can to make sure you don't overdo."

"You mean I mustn't chop wood or perform acrobatics—which I've never done anyway and don't intend to start doing now?"

"I know you'll behave sensibly, Daphne. Still, I want to be with you as much as I can."

For some years now the fertile grain-growing region of southeastern Washington Territory had been producing far more wheat than its scant population could consume, so the prosperity of its farmers depended on getting their grain to market down the Columbia to Portland, Puget Sound, and overseas. All along the 140 miles of the Snake River from its mouth to Lewiston, farmers in the Palouse Hills region were increasing their plantings and getting fantastic yields, some going as high as one hundred bushels to the acre. Every few miles along both sides of the Snake, warehouses at river level were overflowing with hundred-pound sacks of wheat awaiting shipment downriver.

In addition to the *Colonel Wright*, which had been the first sternwheeler to operate between Celilo and Lewiston, and the recently completed *Inland Queen*, other boats such as the *Spokane*, the *Harvest Queen*, and the *Annie Faxon* were in the process of being built at Celilo and would join the grain fleet on the upper river soon after Doc Baker finished building his railroad. Because of the abundant grain harvest from its beginning in late June through July and August, the cargoes of sacked wheat carried aboard O.S.N. Company boats would keep them busy all through summer, fall, and winter, barely emptying the river-landing warehouses in time to make room for the new harvest.

Mile by tedious mile during the summer, Doc Baker kept his railroad building toward Walla Walla. With the beginning of harvest, every westbound string of flatcars pulled by the puffing little *Wallula* or *Walla Walla* was laden with towering rows of sacked wheat, while the eastbound string of flats drawn by the same laboring locomotives was loaded down with ties, hardware, and iron rails, which, because of the heavy, growing traffic, now were being laid to replace the wooden stringers. What Doc Baker was using for money to pay the workmen and material-suppliers, no one could say; but somehow he kept the project going.

When Lars insisted that Daphne be checked by Dr. Walter Lyman to make sure her pregnancy was progressing normally, she took the train to the end of track six miles west of Walla Walla in late July, where Goliath Samson met her with the phaeton and drove her on into town. After visiting with her mother for a week, she returned to Wallula, telling her husband that Dr. Lyman had assured her she had nothing to worry about.

"He gave you a careful examination?"

"No, not really. He just felt my abdomen, looked at my face, said my color was good, and asked me about my appetite. When I told him I had a yen for dill pickles and peach ice cream three times a week, he said that was a sure sign the baby would be a boy. Mother gave him a cigar and a couple of drinks for his fee and sent him on his way rejoicing."

"That doesn't sound like much of an examination to me."

"It wasn't. But Mah Chen gave me a very thorough going-over."

"The fat old Chinese lady who's worked as your mother's cook ever since she came to Walla Walla?" Lars exclaimed incredulously. "What does she know about having babies?"

"Just about all there is to know, Mother says. In China, she was trained as a doctor in a system of medicine she says goes back four thousand years. She's been taking care of Mother's girls for a long time, giving them herbs and powders to treat them when they're sick, keeping them from having babies when they don't want to, or helping them when they do. Mother says she trusts Mah Chen a lot more than she does an old fuddy-duddy like Dr. Lyman, who may be good at setting broken legs and digging out bullets but doesn't know beans about having babies."

Sweet, demure, and innocent though Daphne appeared to be, Lars knew that her mother had taught her a tough, no-nonsense practicality that enabled her to face the facts of life without flinching. With trains running to and from the end of track and Walla Walla each day, she could keep in close touch with her mother while Lars was gone, being assured of help if she needed it.

Though the expected baby was not due for two more weeks, Lars found when he reached Wallula on a downriver stop in mid-October that the Chinese woman, Mah Chen, had moved in and taken over the household. From this day forward until the birth took place, she made it clear, she would be in charge of the cooking, the cleaning, and every detail of his and Daphne's daily routine, with no deviation from the rules she laid down permitted. When he made a token protest, telling Daphne that he was the master of this house and he resented being ordered around by a fat Chinese servant, Daphne laughed and told him to relax.

"Resent her orders all you like, dear, so long as you do as you're told. She won't pay the slightest attention to a thing you do or say."

Despite all the difficulties Doc Baker had encountered in building his thirty-two miles of narrow-gauge railroad, the Walla Walla & Columbia River Railroad was completed as promised before the end of the year. Designating October 23, 1875, as official opening day, he invited as many members of the community as could get into the "Hearse," which still was the single passenger car the line could afford, and aboard a dozen empty flatcars provided with benches as seats, to be his guests in an all-day round-trip excursion scheduled to leave the downtown station at nine o'clock in the morning.

Since by now the company owned two dozen flatcars, a second section pulled by the *Wallula* could have been used to accommodate the large number of eager passengers unable to find seats on the first section. But with local warehouses still bulging with unshipped sacked wheat and a downriver-bound steamboat in need of cargo due to stop at Wallula Landing in early afternoon, Doc Baker made sure that the second train would be loaded with paying freight.

Coming upriver from Portland to take part in the celebration were the president and chief attorney for the Oregon Steam Navigation Company, John Ainsworth and Emil Warren. When he had stopped by to pay his respects to Lars and Daphne before going on to Walla Walla the afternoon before, Emil had complimented Daphne on how well she looked, then told her she must be pleased with her fine new house.

"It's certainly big and roomy," he said.

"Just like me!" Daphne exclaimed. "But I can't wait for *my* roomer to move out. I'm sick and tired of carrying her around."

"You think it will be a girl?" Emil asked.

"That's what Mah Chen said when she checked my pulse. In China, she says, a good pulseologist can diagnose all kinds of illnesses and predict the sex of babies long before they're born just by feeling a person's pulse."

"Dr. Lyman says it's going to be a boy," Lars said. "He based his prediction on Daphne's yen for dill pickles and peach ice cream."

"Well, it's nice to know you're being scientific about this," Emil said dryly. "Since Dolores and I have had three boys and three girls without getting any predictions at all, we've learned to take whatever the good Lord gives us and let it go at that."

Next morning in Walla Walla, Frank Baker was assigned the task of making sure that the members of the Board of Directors of the railroad, the principal stockholders, the committee representing the providers of the subsidy, and the two officials of the Oregon Steam Navigation Company were shown to their seats in the "Hearse," while Doc Baker went from flatcar to flatcar, seeing to it that the ladies and their gentlemen escorts were comfortable on their benches. Fortunately, the late Indian Summer day was cloudless and warm, making the shade of parasols and wide-brimmed hats welcome and adding color to what promised to be a gay, festive day.

A few minutes after nine, the whistle squealed, steam hissed, and the drive wheels of the little Pony engine began to turn as the train got under way. Joining the other dignitaries in the passenger car, Dr. Baker's eyes glowed with pride as he accepted the praise of his invited guests.

"Well, Doctor, you've won," Ainsworth said genially. "I congratulate you."

"Thank you, John. I don't consider the war won by any means—only the first battle. What your railroad will do to mine once you build it remains to be seen."

Giving Emil Warren, who was seated nearby, a quizzical look, Ainsworth asked, "Shall I tell him?"

"Might as well, John. He's bound to find out sooner or later."

"Find out what?" Doc Baker asked with a scowl.

Ainsworth smiled as he laid a hand on the Doctor's arm. "We've given up our plan to build a competing railroad."

"You have?"

"There were too many uncertainties, not the least of which was the failure of the Union Pacific to make a firm commitment. They kept hoping you would go bankrupt, figuring once you did we could buy you out for ten cents on the dollar."

"I told you I would finish it."

"I know you did. I should have believed you. Instead, I tried to run a bluff, guessing that when I showed you the prints of a project that had never gotten beyond the talking stage, you'd fold and toss in your hand. But you didn't. You turned out to be a better poker player than I was."

"That's not a good analogy, John. I never play cards."

"In any case, you won and I lost. From now on, the O.S.N. Company will stick to steamboating."

Reaching Wallula just before noon, the excursion section drawn by the *Walla Walla* pulled into the passing track so that the section of flatcars carrying the paying freight could move on down to the loading dock where the *Inland Queen* was moored. On the sandy flats near the mouth of the Walla Walla River, which here joined the Columbia, tables and chairs had been set up in the shade of a grove of cottonwood trees planted years ago by the Hudson's Bay Company when the site had been an important fur-trading post. In appreciation for the large volume of freight revenue produced for its steamboats in this part of the interior country, the Oregon Steam Navigation Company had paid for a picnic lunch prepared and served by the staff of the Wallula Palace Hotel.

Because Daphne's time was so close, Lars had told her mother, who was closing her Entertainment Parlor in Walla Walla for the day so that she and her employees could join the excursion, he and his wife would not try to make the trip but would join the party for the picnic lunch. Puzzled by their unexplained absence, Lili deBeauchamp was about to send Goliath Samson up to their house on the hill when her extremely upset son-in-law came running through the grove of trees, shouting loudly, "Dr. Baker! Where are you? Dr. Baker, I need you!"

Breaking off his conversation with Almos Reynolds and Sewell Truax, Dr. Baker doffed his hat, waved it to show Lars where he was in the milling crowd, then, as the young man rushed up to him, said sharply, "Here I am, Captain Warren. What are you so excited about?"

"My wife! She's having a baby!"

"Is she alone?"

"Oh, no! She's got an old Chinese woman with her who's supposed to know all about babies. But she ran me out of the house."

"Your wife ran you out of your own house?"

"No—Mah Chen did. She said if I didn't get out of the bedroom, she'd take a broom to me and run me out of the house. And she did!"

"Mah Chen knows what she's doing, Lars," Lili deBeauchamp said soothingly. "She's brought a lot of babies into the world."

"Well, I'm not going to let a fat old Chinese cook take charge of *my* baby's birth when there's a white doctor available. Please, Dr. Baker! Come up to the house with me and make sure my wife is all right."

Though Dorsey Syng Baker was a licensed physician and had practiced medicine for a time, he was not in active practice now. Like most doctors of his day, he seldom was present to assist women in having babies, leaving that task to midwives or women who had given birth to children of their own. But since he was here and Lars had appealed to him for help, he felt he must oblige.

"Very well, Captain Warren. Take me to your lady. I'll see what needs to be done."

Joining the procession following Dr. Baker and Lars Warren through the grove of cottonwood trees and up the hill to the big new house overlooking the river were Lili deBeauchamp, Goliath Samson, and Emil Warren. Well acquainted as Emil was with the fierce loyalty of Chinese *amahs* to their charges, he doubted that even this group of people could intimidate Mah Chen, if she chose to pick up her broom and keep *them* out of the house.

But she did not. Instead, as they climbed the steps of the front porch, went into the living room, and paused at the foot of the stairs, she came out of the master bedroom above carrying a small, cloth-wrapped bundle in her arms. When Lars bounded up the stairs two at a time and attempted to see what was inside the bundle, she gave him a peek at a red, wrinkled face, a pair of tightly closed eyes, and a wide open mouth, which suddenly emitted a surprisingly loud squawl.

"You got nice little girl, Captain Warren. She velly pretty."

"Is Daphne all right?"

"She do fine. You can go in and see her now. But you no stay long."

Moving down the stairs as Lars went into the bedroom, Mah Chen placed the swaddled newborn baby in Lili's welcoming arms with a beaming smile.

"You be grandma now, Miss Lili."

"How wonderful, Mah Chen! That's what I've long wanted to be!"

Mah Chen gave Dr. Baker a puzzled look. "Why you come here? You think somebody sick?"

"Blessed if I know why I'm here, Mah Chen. You seem to have things well in hand." Turning to Emil, he snorted, "C'mon, let's get back to the picnic. I want to make a speech and try to sell some stock."

Brushing aside Daphne's half-joking apology for not giving birth to a boy that someday would grow up to become a steamboat captain, thus carrying on the Warren family tradition, Lars agreed with her suggestion that the girl-child be given a name honoring both their mothers. Because Americans always butchered the pronunciation of foreign names, her first name would be "Lily" instead of "Lili"; her middle name "Frieda" instead of "Freda." But both grandmothers would be remembered.

"By the time she grows up," Lars said, "this part of the country may be so crisscrossed by railroads that steamboats will be outmoded and we won't need captains anymore."

"Oh, Lars! You'd be lost without the river."

"Yes, I suppose I would be. But times change, Daphne. When I look back on what's taken place on the Columbia since Grandfather Warren came out with the Astor party sixty-five years ago, I have to wonder what will happen to this country in our children's lifetime."

"Well, whatever happens, dear, I'm sure I'll have more babies. Some of them are bound to be boys. If the country is going to be full of railroads, maybe one of our sons will grow up to be president of the company. Then we'll get free passes to ride in style wherever we go."

9.

In his speech following the picnic lunch, Doc Baker began by saying, "Ladies and gentlemen, I am no speaker. I just do practical things. I might say, though, that soon we will have a railroad we can be proud of in every respect. Two very fine, modern locomotives will soon be on their way, which we plan to christen the *Blue Mountain* and the *Mountain Queen.* A good passenger coach is under construction locally, and we are pricing first-class coaches in the East, with a view to placing an order soon.

"We expect to have thirty or forty new freight cars before long. As you probably know, all the wooden rails now are replaced with iron, so the thought of 'snakeheads' need cause you no more uneasiness. I think I may say that without any doubt our railroad will be on a par with any narrow-gauge line in America.

"I trust you have enjoyed today's excursion. As soon as I have accommodated all those of you who wish to buy shares of stock in what is going to be the most profitable railroad in the Pacific Northwest, we will get aboard the train and begin the return trip."

Loud, enthusiastic applause broke out following Doc Baker's speech, then he turned over the dozen or so potential stock-buyers to his son, Frank, while he walked down to the boat landing with John Ainsworth and Emil Warren, who were about to board the *Inland Queen* for their return trip to Portland. As Ainsworth shook hands, he smiled.

"You should be very happy, Doctor. Every one in the community seems to be proud of you."

"Today, yes. The fault-finding may start tomorrow."

"Over what?"

"That remains to be seen. But I'm sure there will be something."

"Well, let me know if you need any help. I'll be glad to do what I can."

Because the completed railroad had reduced freight rates charged by the teamsters from twelve dollars a ton to six, Walla Walla businessmen and farmers remained pleased and happy during the remainder of the year. When the railroad made a further rate reduction to five dollars a ton, the shippers should have been pleased even more. But since all the revenue was being reinvested in new engines, rolling stock, and improvements to the line, no dividends had yet been paid. Aware of the fact that Doc Baker himself owned 75 percent of the stock, the citizens' committee that had supplied the twenty-five-thousand-dollar subsidy and the people who had invested in shares of stock in anticipation of receiving substantial, immediate returns began to grumble.

"Look at all the money Doc Baker is taking in."

"Yeah, where is it going, for God's sake?"

"Into his own pocket, likely. Where else?"

In farming communities all over the West, these days, a populist philosophy encouraging the establishment of local collectives called "granges" was springing up, the theory behind it being that by combining the buying power of the people, the price of goods and services could be brought down drastically, with the profits then distributed among the members. As a beginning, the local Grange had supplied the twenty-five-thousand-dollar subsidy for the railroad, had established a cooperative blacksmith shop in the area, and now was demanding that Doc Baker and the Board of Directors for the Walla Walla & Columbia River Railroad show their appreciation for its patronage by a further reduction of the freight rates from five dollars to four.

Like many communities in the Pacific Northwest, which had been settled by a roughly equal mix of North and South supporters during and after the Civil War, Walla Walla boasted two newspapers, the *Union* and the *Statesman*. Taking opposite sides on every issue, the former usually supported what its publisher called "Private Enterprise," while the latter backed what it called "Working People." As might be expected, neither found any virtue in the other's philosophy.

On his way to a board meeting on a bright early spring morning, Doc Baker encountered a friendly banker rival, Levi Ankeny, who asked, "Seen the *Statesman* this morning?"

"No, I seldom read it. I read the *Union*."

"So do I usually. But when I heard the editor of the *Statesman* had written an article and published a poem titled 'The Railroad and the People,' I bought a copy and read it. It's quite a piece of work, Doctor. He makes you out to be a first-class villain."

"Does he indeed!" Dr. Baker snorted.

Levi Ankeny grinned and handed him the paper. "Read it, Doctor. You may want to frame it and hang it on the wall of your office. Or you might find a use for it in your outhouse."

Present at the board meeting were John Boyer, Major Sewell Truax, William Green, Dr. Dorsey Baker, and his son Frank. Scanning the *Statesman* article, which the other board members said they already had read, before the meeting began, Doc Baker found it to be a shrill diatribe deploring the profits the railroad was raking in and a blunt demand that the freight rates be lowered.

"You're one of the biggest farmers in the valley, Doctor," William Green said. "Do you belong to the Grange?"

"No," Doc Baker snapped. "I don't like the way they do business."

"They've set up their own blacksmith shop, you know," Major Truax said. "A communal, nonprofit affair, aimed at cutting their equipment repair and horseshoeing costs. The independent blacksmiths are up in arms."

"They should be. I've yet to meet a farmer who could shoe his own horse."

"According to the *Statesman*, the Grange members are circulating a petition demanding that the railroad lower its rates or risk losing their business."

"Where would they take it?"

"Back to the Teamsters, they say."

"Who were charging them twelve dollars a ton before the railroad was completed," Doc Baker said, "not to mention taking three times longer to make the haul between Walla Walla and Wallula and ruining the wagon road we built because the Teamsters, the farmers, and the county refused to spend any money maintaining it."

"That's all true, Doctor," John Boyer said. "But facts have no bearing on their complaints. What the Grange members plan to do, the *Statesman* says, is ask the county to spend tax money repairing the wagon road, insist that the Teamsters lower their rates to make them competitive with ours, and petition the territorial and federal governments to pass legislation regulating the freight rates railroads can charge."

"All of which will happen the day pigs learn how to fly," Doc Baker snorted. Following the general laughter, he rapped on the table and declared, "The meeting will come to order. Please read the minutes, Frank."

By the time the next board meeting convened two weeks later, the petition circulated by the Grange had been signed by a substantial number of local farmers and merchants, published in both Walla Walla newspapers, and discussed in several open meetings. Couched in legal terms and filled with the appropriate number of *Whereases* and *Be It Resolveds*, two of the main points of the petition were that the railroad was supposed to be a public service and that it had been subsidized by a substantial contribution of money provided by members of the Grange.

"I knew it!" Doc Baker exclaimed. "The minute that twenty-five-thousand-dollar subsidy was offered, I knew it meant trouble! But there's no way we can change it now. The question is, what are we going to do?"

After some discussion, it was agreed that the detailed financial statement of the Walla Walla & Columbia River Railroad, which had been prepared for the stockholders on January 9, 1876, should be given to the petitioning Grange members and be published in both newspapers, along with President Dorsey Baker's detailed reply to all the demands made by the complainants. His explanation would point out: First, the eighteen-cents-per-bushel rate was already low enough to enable farmers to ship at a profit. Second, up until now and into the foreseeable future, all the company's net revenue was committed to being invested in the purchase of new rolling stock and improvements in the line. Third, no dividends had yet been paid to the stockholders, nor was it likely that any could be declared for some time. When the road did begin to show a profit, the stockholders who had invested their money and taken all the risks certainly would be entitled to a commensurate return on their investment. Therefore, the freight rates would not be lowered at this time.

In response to Dr. Baker's well-reasoned explanation of the railroad's position, a committee of Grange members demanded and got a meeting with him, at which they eloquently expressed their outrage in not-so-reasonable terms.

To begin with, they questioned his statement that the eighteen-cents-per-bushel freight rate was low enough.

"Your railroad between here and Wallula, where we put our sacked wheat aboard O.S.N. Company boats, is only thirty-two miles long, Doctor," one farmer complained. "Once it gets aboard the boat, it has two hundred miles to travel to Portland, plus another hundred miles to Astoria, with a fourteen-mile rail portage between Celilo and The Dalles, then another six-mile rail portage around the Cascades. That means the grain sacks have to be loaded, unloaded, then loaded again seven times before the wheat is shipped overseas. Still, the O.S.N. Company charges us the same rate your railroad does—eighteen cents a bushel. Does that sound fair to you?"

"My stockholders and I invested $330,000 in building our thirty-two miles of railroad," Doc Baker replied dryly. "The O.S.N. Company did not have to build themselves a river."

"Well, then, what is this nonsense about 'commensurate returns to the stockholders'?" another farmer protested. "You own 75 percent of the stock, don't you? The only stockholder you're really concerned about is yourself."

"Are you saying I'm not entitled to make a fair return on my investment?" Doc Baker asked coldly.

"Not when it comes out of *our* pockets. After all, we did give your railroad a subsidy."

"Which amounted to less than 8 percent of its total cost," Doc Baker snapped. "Admittedly, your contribution came at a time when it was badly needed. But it does not give you the right to dictate how the railroad should be run."

"That's a mighty selfish attitude to take, Dr. Baker. Speaking as chairman for the rate-adjustment committee of the Grange, I must inform you—"

"Speaking as president of the railroad," Dr. Baker interrupted curtly, "I say you are entitled to your opinion; I am entitled to mine. My opinion is that the Company would be foolish to accede to your request. That's final."

"But, Dr. Baker—"

"Until the Grange learns how to run a blacksmith shop, Sir, it has no business telling me how to run a railroad. Good day, gentlemen."

When Doc Baker reported the discussion to the board members at the next meeting, they agreed that his answer had been right. But in view of the animosity that was building up in the Grange, John Boyer suggested that the board offer the possibility of a rate adjustment in the future.

"By the end of the year, when we've finished paying for new equipment, I believe we should review this whole question again. We all know how rapidly revenue has been increasing. Once we're relieved of the heaviest expenditures, profits will be high—I might say fantastically high. Certainly we should do all we can for the public good. Perhaps by the end of the year we could reduce freight rates and declare a dividend at the same time. That would please everybody."

"You're right, John," William Green said. "Bad feeling is building up in the community. We ought to do something to tone it down."

Doc Baker disagreed. "You gentlemen don't seem to realize that we may not have more than three or four years before we'll be forced to sell the railroad. Where would we be then, I'd like to know, if we've been giving away our profits?"

"In my opinion," William Green said stubbornly, "we'll be asking for trouble unless we do something for the people who put up the subsidy—"

"Don't talk to me about the subsidy!" Doc Baker bristled. "That was just a smart trick by the Grange members designed to give them a chance to dictate to us. I've no patience with talk about the subsidy."

After the board meeting had adjourned and Doc Baker and his son Frank were not around, the three other board members, John Boyer, William Green, and Sewall Truax, held an informal session away from the bank. All were agreed that some sort of action was required now.

"I don't think we ought to wait a year before taking a stand on this matter," Green said. "I think we ought to use our majority vote on the board to reduce freight rates immediately. People are beginning to look on Dr. Baker as an enemy of the community. I don't like the way feeling against him is building up."

"Neither do I," John Boyer said. "Still, I hate to oppose him. What do you think, Major?"

"I guess I'm a sentimental old fool," Truax said, shaking his head, "but I can't bring myself to disagree with that man. I keep remembering the years we worked together building the railroad. Day after day, I've seen him out there fighting dust, sand storms, sleet, labor, and construction problems that would have made an ordinary man throw up his hands and quit.

"I've seen him come into camp night after night long after dark so dog-tired he couldn't walk another step. But he'd be up next morning before any member of the work crew, wrestling with problems that had all of us beat. Somehow, after all that, I've got to support him—even if he's wrong."

"Maybe if we tried to reason with him," Green said tentatively, "we could get him to go along with us—"

"He's too stubborn to listen to reason, Bill. You should know that. All we can do is bring the matter to a vote, then vote him down."

"His son Frank will back him, of course," Green said. "But if the three of us stick together, we can make him do things our way."

"Which I don't like at all," Truax said. "For the time being, let's wait and see if the Grange members carry out their threat to boycott the railroad. If they do, we can consider taking action then."

With the coming of summer and a new bumper crop of wheat to be moved, neither Doc Baker nor the Grange had budged from their position. In fact, as president of the company, Doc Baker had raised the grain-shipment rate from five to five-fifty in order to pay for the newly arrived locomotives, whose delivered cost had been greater than anticipated. Feeling that he was taunting the Grange and daring it to act, it did so, declaring that from this day on, all the sacked wheat owned by its members would be transported from Walla Walla to Wallula Landing in wagons driven by the farmers themselves or in those owned by the Teamsters Association.

Getting the County to appropriate five thousand dollars in tax money to make repairs on the road and the Teamsters to lower their rates to eight dollars a ton, the Grange boasted it had won a great victory, which soon would force the railroad to lower its rates or go bankrupt. In this emergency, the three directors who favored a rate revision felt compelled to call a meeting and express their feelings in Doc Baker's presence. William Green was the first to speak.

"Dr. Baker, I honestly believe that this war has gone too far. I've expressed my opinion to other members of the board, two of whom agree with me. We may have justice on our side, but in my opinion we're butting our heads against a stone wall. So I'm making the motion that we go along with the request of the Grange and lower the freight rates to four dollars."

A silence lay over the room for some time. Squirming uncomfortably, Frank Baker, who was taking the minutes, said nothing, his pencil poised to record the name of the board member who would second the motion, if one should choose to do so. Without a flicker of emotion showing on his face, Doc Baker stared first at Green, then at John Boyer, and finally at Sewell Truax. At last, he demanded, "Well?"

Turning to exchange looks with John Boyer, Major Truax sighed and shook his head.

"Sorry, John. I can't second the motion. If you do, I'll vote against it."

"Thanks for taking me off the hook, Major," Boyer said, a ghost of a smile touching his face. "I can't vote against him either."

"Well, gentlemen," Doc Baker said gruffly, getting to his feet and taking his hat off the rack in the corner of the room, "if there's no further business, we may as well adjourn."

John Boyer overtook him as he went through the bank, saying, "Dorsey, I hope you understand that Bill Green wasn't turning against you."

"Of course, of course!" Doc Baker said impatiently. "Just an honest difference of opinion."

"You do realize we have a problem? If the farmers won't give us their business—"

"We'll have to take measures to make them change their minds, won't we? Which is just what I intend to do."

"How?"

"To begin with, I'm taking the next downriverboat to Portland. I want to talk with John Ainsworth."

"What can he do?"

"Plenty, if he really wants to help as he promised me he'd do. I'll let you know when I get back from Portland."

Because shipments of grain from the Walla Walla Valley had fallen off drastically since Grange members had begun their boycott of the railroad and switched their patronage to the Teamsters, the Oregon

Steam Navigation Company was well aware of what was going on, John Ainsworth told Doc Baker when the two men met in his Portland office a few days later. But until now, he had not realized the seriousness of the dispute.

"Seems to me the Grange is cutting off its nose to spite its face. There's no way the farmers can pay the Teamsters eight dollars a ton for making a slow wagon haul that your railroad will do for five-fifty in much less time. Are they stupid or stubborn?"

"A little of both, I'm afraid. But if your company will help me, I've got a plan that will bring them to their senses."

"What do you have in mind?"

Doc Baker told him. As Captain Ainsworth listened, the beginnings of a smile lifted the corners of his mouth, then, as Doc Baker finished, expanded into a delighted laugh.

"Why not? If the Populists have their way politically, Doctor, one of these days they'll pass some laws that will spoil the games men like you and me like to play. But until that time comes, we might as well enjoy ourselves. Publish the notice under my name. You have my word that the O.S.N. Company will support you."

A few days after Doc Baker's return to Walla Walla, the following announcement was published in both papers and posted on the Wallula Landing wharf:

NOTICE TO SHIPPERS

Effective immediately: In accordance with special contracts with the Walla Walla & Columbia River Railroad Company and because of recently increased demands on shipping facilities, the Oregon Steam Navigation Company will give priority to preferred freight. Only such freight as is consigned to the above railroad for shipment to the Wallula Landing is classified as preferred freight.

(Signed) *J. C. Ainsworth*, Pres.
Oregon Steam Navigation Co.

Obeying instructions to the letter, Captain Lars Warren and all other O.S.N. Company employees refused to accept, load, or even permit to be stored on Company property a single sack of grain brought to the landing in Teamsters Association wagons or those driven by Grange members themselves. Stony-faced under the storm of abuse rained upon them by Teamsters and Grangers, Lars and his fellow workers strictly followed the rules given them from on high.

"Under current policy, only preferred freight is being accepted for shipment on O.S.N. Company boats."

"When will freight that's not 'preferred' be accepted?" the Teamsters and Grangers demanded.

"When we have room for it."

"When will that be?"

"Can't say."

Since the only warehouses that could shelter the grain from the weather were owned by either the railroad or the steamboat company, all the sacks of wheat brought down to the landing by the Teamsters or the Grangers had to be stacked outside, where the grain would dry out and lose weight under the scorching summer sun or soak up moisture, gain weight, and begin to sprout when the fall rains began—both conditions that would downgrade the quality of the wheat and cost the farmers money in the marketplace. Meanwhile, sacks of grain carried by the railroad were either being stored under protective warehouse roofs or being quickly transferred to downriver-bound boats.

Within two months' time, the trains from Walla Walla to Wallula Landing were carrying a full capacity of sacked grain, while the Teamsters Association's and the Grangers' wagons were being seen no more. In fact, business got so good that in early fall Doc Baker proposed to the Board of Directors that the question of a rate adjustment be reexamined. When the directors had done so, the proposal he made passed unanimously. As a result, the following advertisement appeared in both Walla Walla papers on October 21, 1876:

FREIGHT & PASSENGER RATES OF THE

Walla Walla & Columbia River Railroad Company

On and after this date, freight will be received for transmission from our Depots at the following rates:

RATES ON DOWN FREIGHT

(Per Ton Weight, on Board)

GRAIN, FLOUR, BACON & LARD

From Walla Walla to Wallula $4.00
From Walla Walla to Whitman $1.00
From Whitman to Wallula $3.75

The freight rate war was over.

10.

Though wrecks and boiler explosions on the Columbia and Snake were hazards known and feared by Lars Warren and other O.S.N. Company captains, the worst disaster yet to occur on the upper river involved not a boat but a scow working on a Corps of Engineers project. Planning to improve the channel at the upper end of Umatilla Rapids by blasting out some rocks that were a danger to navigation in that sector of river, the terrific explosion aboard the scow—which killed thirteen men instantly and seriously injured half a dozen more—was witnessed by the surveyor in charge of the operation, W. F. Bassett, who, by a strange set of circumstances, happened to be riding a horse along the adjacent shoreline when the blast occurred.

> One of Mr. Bassett's duties (the *Walla Walla Statesman* reported a few days later) was to measure the rocks which were situated in the channel and thus enable the men employed to remove obstructions and blast with the greatest advantage. He also casually inspected in person the work done in behalf of the government.
>
> WHAT HE SAW OF IT
>
> Last Wednesday morning—the day on which the explosion occurred—Mr. Bassett left Umatilla quite early for the purpose of measuring some of the rocks to be blasted, and likewise to inspect some of the work already accomplished. From Umatilla up to the upper rapids, where the men were engaged, is about five miles. This distance was traveled by Mr. Bassett on horseback. He reached the rapids quite early in the forenoon, and after completing his work started to return to Umatilla.
>
> The scow was anchored near the middle of the river, and a small boat was used in conveying Mr. Bassett to and from the shore. He left the scow on the morning of the fatal disaster about 8:30 o'clock, and was taken ashore in a skiff, manned by two men—Mosier and Snooks. Reaching the shore in safety Mr. Bassett mounted his horse and started back to Umatilla, leaving Mosier and Snooks at the landing putting

aboard some gas pipes, flour and other articles which were to be conveyed to the scow.

Mr. Bassett had gained the upper bank and was traveling rapidly toward town when, about three-quarters of a mile distant from the scow, he reached a high, clear spot commanding a fine view of the river for a long way, up and down. He was riding ahead and happened to be looking at the scow, as he was taking in, with one sweep of his eye, the broad expanse of river and landscape, when suddenly the air above the boat was darkened with a thick, black cloud of smoke. Through the smoke he could indistinctly discern what appeared to be pieces of plank, shattered timber, and mangled portions of human bodies, being hurled to a great height. The idea of an explosion flashed through his mind, and Mr. Bassett instantly reined his horse, and turned his face toward the scow.

Just as he turned, the report of the explosion reached him. It was louder than any clap of thunder he ever had heard—stunning and deafening him for an instant. Scarcely had thirty seconds elapsed before the dense cloud of smoke began slowly to float upward, leaving a clear space between its lower edge and the surface of the water. This enabled him to see the fragments of the wreck which, by that time, began to rain down for a considerable time around where the scow had been moored.

Comprehending the fearful situation of affairs, and knowing that assistance would be required to save those who were wounded, Mr. Bassett turned his horse's head towards the point where he had just left Mosier and Snooks with the skiff. It seems that these men had nearly completed loading the skiff, and were about to push off for the scow, when the explosion occurred. They immediately threw out what was in the skiff and started for the scene of the disaster, rowing with might and main.

Before Bassett had proceeded far he saw the skiff making for the wreck, and knowing that it would be useless for him to go any further, stopped. By this time the smoke had all cleared away and a portion of the hull of the scow could be seen floating down on the current, and also large quantities of the debris from the wreck. For some moments no sign of human life was visible, and Bassett concluded that every soul aboard the scow had met his fate. But while he was looking eagerly in the direction of the scene, he observed one man struggling in the water, and immediately after saw him climb up on the wreck. Just then he saw another man clamber on to the wreck, and an instant later a third, whom the two others assisted up.

Meantime, Mosier and Snooks were urging their boat forward toward the wreck to render all the assistance in their power. At the moment the explosion occurred, the scow broke from her mooring and was borne down the current. Working arrangements aboard the scow, Bassett later explained, consisted of a platform extending twelve or fifteen feet out over the water, which had been built at the stern of the craft. On this platform the men stood while working the drills and preparing to lower the blasting charge into its proper place.

Three strong hawsers were attached to the bow of the boat. One hawser extended directly forward of the bow and was firmly anchored higher up the stream. Two other strong ropes were attached to the bow on each side and fastened out some distance each way. These ropes were for the purpose of holding the scow steady against the swift current, and preventing it from shifting from side to side, and likewise to enable the men to draw the boat up and down as the occasion rendered necessary.

When the rock had been perforated with the drills at a certain point, the blast prepared, lowered, and the fuse ignited, the scow was always drawn some distance upstream—sufficiently far as to be out of danger's reach—until the charge exploded. This was always done by means of a capstan, around which the central hawser was wound. After the blast went off, the scow would be lowered again to the same place and operations resumed. From the time the fuse was ignited until the explosion occurred was usually five to ten minutes, which afforded ample time to get the boat out of the way.

Nineteen Men

Were employed about the boat, but at the time of the explosion Mosier and Snooks were ashore, leaving 17 men aboard. Of that number only four have escaped—McGinnis, Finneron, Russell and Gray. Beyond the possibility of reasonable doubt, thirteen unfortunate human beings were hurled into eternity without a moment's warning. McGinnis states that the water-blast had been lowered, the fuse ignited, and a number of men were at the capstan heaving ahead, when the fatal occurrence transpired. Mike Connolly, who was the foreman of the men in the scow, had just entered the cabin. McGinnis says he remembers to have seen him standing in the door of the cabin, giving some orders to the men who were working at the capstan. Suddenly he saw Connolly going up into the air, and cannot recollect anything more until he found himself struggling in the water. McGinnis, Russell, Gray and Finneron were all standing on the platform at the rear of the scow at the time. How far into the air they were blown is not known but McGinnis states that a sufficient time elapsed in making the aerial flight to allow the scow to float its full length. The instant the explosion took place the boat was torn loose from the hawsers and was carried down on the current.

The persons mentioned started on their upward tour from the stern, and when they struck the water the bow of the boat was only a few yards below. McGinnis was the first person whom Bassett saw clamber up on the wreck. Gray was picked up by the men in the skiff, clinging to a fragment of the wreck, and was thus saved. He was very badly injured and his recovery is extremely doubtful. One arm is broken, a portion of the heel blown away, gashes inflicted on the back of his neck and cheek, by flying fragments of the wreck, and other portions of his body bruised. The other three men are more or less bruised, but their injuries are not considered serious. Soon after the explosion the men were taken from the wreck and conveyed ashore.

At Umatilla

Mr. Bassett finding he could be of no service, concluded it would be best for him to go to Umatilla and inform them of the disaster. The wrecked hull soon drifted down over the middle rapids, and Bassett, supposing there might be some of the helpless victims still clinging to it, thought it would be a wise plan to hurry down to Umatilla and get a number of boats out to render what assistance was possible. He accordingly galloped toward the town, anxious to get there before the wreck could float down. Mr. Stone, one of the contractors, Mr. Tabor, the government employee, and Capt. Coe, were all stopping at the hotel in Umatilla when the explosion took place. The report was very loud, and the violent concussion shook every building in the place. These men knew that some accident had happened, and started for the rapids without delay. They were met by Mr. Bassett about a mile above town, who told them what had happened. They continued on, and Bassett came to Umatilla and got several boats to look for victims. Soon after the wrecked hull floated down, and also large quantities of debris. On looking in the hull only the body of McCabe was found. He was the cook on board the scow. His body was horribly mangled. An effort was made to draw the wreck to the shore, but the current was so strong that it was unsuccessful and had to be abandoned. The force of the explosion was terrific.

About 75 pounds of the explosive compound was on board the scow. The cabin was literally blown to atoms. Scarcely a fragment of it could be found. Most of the unfortunate men on board must have been torn into hundreds of pieces. Some idea of the terrible force may be had when it is stated that not even the beds, blankets, clothing and other light articles could be found. Not even fragments of the victims' hats could be discovered. These articles are all light, and would undoubtedly have floated. A small piece of a blanket was discovered after the explosion, but it was riddled into shreds by the concussion. One of the men who escaped says he saw a number of the heavy drills going up through the air. These and other heavy articles must have struck the men in their ascent and torn them frightfully. There was about 400 pounds of giant powder stored on the shore opposite where the scow was moored, and the wonder is that the concussion did not cause that quantity to explode.

The shock and report was felt and heard for a long distance in all

> directions. The report was distinctly heard above Wallula—a distance of 25 miles. The total loss to the contractors in the way of scow, tools, appliances, loss of time and etc., will be in the vicinity of *$3,000*. Work has necessarily been suspended owing to the disaster. An effort will be made to obtain an extension of time in which to complete the work. We are unable at present to state when operations will be resumed.

In late November 1876, Lars Warren learned that his father, Captain Tommy Warren, senior O.S.N. company pilot on The Dalles–to–Portland sector of the Columbia, had just missed being involved in another disaster, the wreck of the *Daisy Ainsworth*, pride of the middle-river fleet. Though too charitable of his fellow officers to say so, his father's later description of the accident indicated that if Tommy himself had been in the pilot house the night the wreck happened, the boat would not have been lost.

"Ordinarily, Captain John McNulty and I substitute for each other on runs between The Dalles and Portland when either of us has put in too many hours at the wheel," Tommy told Lars. "But since this was a night cattle run, with no passengers aboard, neither Captain McNulty nor I saw any reason why First Mate Martin Spelling couldn't handle it."

Built and launched at The Dalles in the spring of 1873, the elegant *Daisy Ainsworth* had been named in honor of the youngest daughter of O.S.N. Company President John C. Ainsworth, who had taken the wheel himself, with his daughter at his side, when the boat made its first trial run. Designed by master builder John Holland, the "Daisy," as she fondly was called, was truly a palace boat, boasting all the luxuries of the day. Cabin and stateroom floors were covered with deep-pile Brussels carpets. Silver plate adorned dining saloon tables and sideboards; crystal chandeliers glittered with cheerful candlelight.

After making her usual daylight run from the Upper Cascades to The Dalles with a full complement of passengers under Captain McNulty's command, on November 22, 1876, the *Daisy Ainsworth* was turned over to First Mate Martin Spelling, who was instructed to convert her into a cattle boat. Never a man to decline a paying cargo, the sharp-penciled local freight manager of the O.S.N. Company had accepted a shipment of 210 live beef cattle to be transported from The Dalles downriver to the Upper Cascades Landing on the Washington shore, a forty-five-mile trip that would take five or six hours.

"The boat usually scheduled for the night run was the *Idaho*,"

Tommy told Lars. "But she was too small to handle that many cattle, so the *Daisy Ainsworth* was pressed into service."

The late November weather had turned stormy, with snow squalls blowing through the Gorge. No moon shone to relieve the darkness. Looking down on the messy cattle-loading process as the nervous, bawling animals were driven aboard the freight deck, First Mate Martin Spelling watched critically from the pilot house high above, around which curtains had been drawn on three sides in order to shield the pilot's eyes from ambient sidelights that might interfere with his night vision directly ahead. A thin, stooped man in his late forties, First Mate Spelling was a sober, conscientious officer who knew the river almost as well as Captains John McNulty and Tommy Warren did, with no blemishes on his record.

When the loading had been completed, Spelling reached for the speaking tube and whistled to the engine room, cautioning Engineer William Doran to stand by, pulling the whistle cord in a signal to the deckhands to cast off fore and aft lines as the heavily laden *Daisy Ainsworth* prepared to pull out into the darkness-shrouded river. The proposed range markers and light buoys which the Corps of Engineers planned to install as aids to navigation had not yet been put in place, so only small circles of fitfully burning coal-oil running lights framed the outline of the boat. But First Mate Spelling knew the forty-five miles of broad, cliff-lined river ahead as well as he knew the lines in the palms of his hands. Furthermore, he remembered the exact location of shore lamps gleaming on docks, landings, warehouses, and commercial buildings in the infrequent settlements along both the Oregon and Washington shores. Like all experienced river pilots, he knew how to take a fix on the position of his boat by blowing a few blasts with the steam whistle, then listening intently to returning echoes a few seconds later, giving him a reading on his whereabouts as precise as a sighting of a headland or a cliff top on a brilliant, sunny day.

After two hours of blind running through the snow-laced dark at medium speed, the *Daisy* passed Crates Point on the Oregon side of the river. Acting Captain Spelling put the wheel hard over, angling directly across to the Washington channel in order to avoid the sandbar opposite Cayuse Rock. With the wind howling up the Gorge against the boat's bow, the big stern-wheeler drove on into a nasty chop whose whitecapped waves were beginning to smoke with streaks of foam. Passing long, low Memaloose Island, where the river Indians had for untold generations placed their dead on raised platforms to await their journey to the spirit land, the boat skirted Mosier Rocks, then threaded her way through the treacherous channel between Eighteen Mile Island and the Oregon shore. Since it was now past midnight, the settlements of Hood River, on the Oregon shore, and White Salmon and Underwood, on the Washington shore, showed few lights for their occupants had gone to bed hours ago.

Knowing that he was near the end of his run, Captain Spelling called for half-speed as he stared intently into the darkness ahead, his eyes seeking the wharf lantern marking the end of the dock at the Upper Cascades, just upstream from which was a broad, low, gravel bank where the restless cattle, which had begun lowing nervously at the blast of the whistle over their heads, would be driven ashore. Having taken a bearing on a landing light on the Oregon shore directly across from which he knew the Upper Cascades wharf to be, Spelling was puzzled that the lantern he sought had not yet come into sight. A feeling that something was wrong came over him. Intermittently through the snow squalls, he now could see a light blinking ahead, but it appeared to be at least a quarter-mile upstream from where it *ought* to be. The echoes bouncing back from the boat's whistle sounded wrong, too. And was that low roaring sound he was hearing being made by rapids where he was positive no thundering white water existed?

Even as he reached for the speaking tube to order the engines stopped and reversed, the *Daisy Ainsworth* struck an underwater reef with a shuddering crash. Pitched forward against the wheel, Spelling realized too late that the boat was half a mile downriver from where he thought it to be, that the unyielding shoal of rocks upon which the craft had struck lay only three hundred feet upstream from the powerful rapid called the Upper Cascades, and that the pride of the middle-river fleet had broken her back in a mortal blow from which she could not recover.

"By putting out bow and stern anchors, he managed to hold her steady in the stream for a while," Tommy told Lars. "But in the confusion the cattle stampeded, broke down the railings, and went overboard. Only a few of them managed to swim to shore."

As the boat settled on the reef, her main hog chains broke immediately, with some of the smaller ones snapping soon after.

Discovering when daylight came that what Spelling had taken to be a wharf light on the Oregon shore actually had been a lantern on a scow loaded with wood, which that afternoon had anchored a mile downstream from the permanent wharf, the crew aboard the *Daisy Ainsworth* found her situation precarious as the boat perched on underwater rocks only three hundred feet upstream from the falls.

During the day, salvage experts employed by the O.S.N. Company and the Corps of Engineers brought a large work-barge downriver from The Dalles, from which they managed to get long lines on the wreck, holding it in place while her cabin, saloon furnishings, and engines could be removed and later installed on other boats. As the most expensive stern-wheeler ever built for the middle-river run, the hull and its equipment had cost sixty-thousand dollars, the engines twenty-five-thousand dollars more.

"Insurance will cover part of the loss, of course," Tommy told Lars, "but the Company will pay for that later in the form of increased rates."

"How is Martin Spelling taking it?" Lars asked.

"Badly, I'm afraid. Given the circumstances, it's the kind of accident that could have happened to even the best of pilots. But he insists on taking all the blame."

Indeed, even though John Ainsworth spoke no word of criticism and assigned him a first mate's berth on the lower river run a couple of weeks later, Martin Spelling fell ill after working a month or so and was put on paid sick leave until he recovered. But he never did. Grief-stricken, broken in spirit as well as health, he died a few months later.

"Tuberculosis," said the medical report. But his rivermen friends knew that Martin Spelling had died from a broken heart.

11.

THOUGH PEACE between whites and Indians had prevailed in the inland country for the past twenty years, all it took to panic settlers living along the Snake and Columbia Rivers was a rumor of a hostile incident anywhere in the West, for such an event always inspired newspaper editors to publish alarming tales of mayhem and murder. The strange thing about these grossly overdrawn tales, Lars Warren noticed, was that people living in river settlements invariably accepted the wildest accounts as gospel truth, so long as the bloodshed occurred in communities well removed from their own, while at home they continued to associate with the local Indians on the best of terms.

Having survived a number of Indian war alarms, Emil Warren cynically noted the close connection between scare stories and the state of the local economy.

"When times are good, white merchants and settlers get along fine with their red brethren," he told Lars. "But when the price of hay falls and business needs a shot in the arm, there's nothing like a good Indian scare to boost sales to the military posts and encourage the politicians to beg for funds to defend hearth and home."

Indeed, ever since the end of the Civil War, funding of military posts built to protect emigration along the Oregon Trail and guard isolated settlements in the Pacific Northwest against Indian attack had dwindled alarmingly. With all the formerly hostile Indian tribes now placed within the boundaries of reservations, the need for military posts such as Fort Walla Walla, Fort Lapwai, and Fort Spokane was of such little importance to the budget-makers in Congress that they were seriously considering phasing them out.

This past summer, that attitude had changed dramatically when General Custer had gotten himself and 267 of his soldiers killed by the Sioux in the Battle of the Little Bighorn in southeastern Montana.

By an odd coincidence, two days before the "Custer Massacre" of June 25, 1876, the killing of a Nez Perce Indian by a white man in the Wallowa Valley 125 miles southeast of Walla Walla had brought that region to the brink of war.

The way Lars Warren heard the story, a white settler named A.B. Findley discovered that some of his horses were missing. Enlisting the aid of a neighbor, Wells McNall, who was helping him with the summer work, he attempted to track them down. Findley, whose ranch was not far from the Nez Perce summer village called "Indian Town," was an honest, conscientious, sensitive man, well liked and respected by the Indians who knew him as well as by his white neighbors. In contrast, McNall was quick-tempered and had an intense dislike for Indians.

Since white settlers shod their horses while Indians did not, distinguishing hoofprints was no problem. The trail led north, over a low height of land separating the drainage of the Wallowa River from that of the Chesnimnus. On June 23, the two men followed that trail into the camp of a small group of Nez Perces who were hunting deer in the Whiskey Creek area.

Though neither the missing horses nor the Indians were in the camp, it was apparent that the members of the hunting party had not gone far, for their rifles were leaning against a tree; presumably, they had been placed there to relieve the hunters of their weight while they took packhorses to pick up several deer they had just killed nearby. Wanting to question the Indians about the missing horses and not sure what their attitude would be, the two white men decided to take possession of the rifles until they had consulted with the red men.

When the five Nez Perce hunters returned to camp with their laden packhorses, they were surprised and alarmed to find their rifles in possession of the whites. One of them, a strong, muscular, proud man named *Wil-lot-yah*, demanded belligerently, "Why you take our guns?"

"We want to ask you some questions," Findley said patiently. "Three of my horses are missing. The tracks led here—"

"Goddam, I didn't steal no horses! Give me back my gun."

"Mind your mouth, you greasy bastard!" McNall snarled. "Them tracks was as plain as day. They led right to your camp, where we lost 'em when they got mixed up with the tracks of your horses. We want to know what you done with 'em."

"Nothing, I tell you! We didn't steal them and we done nothing wrong! Give me back my gun!"

"Go to hell! We want to know what you done with them horses."

Angrily, *Wil-lot-yah* moved forward, lunging toward the rifle, which Wells McNall had leaned against the trunk of a tree, shielded behind his body. Both men seized the gun, wrestling for its control. Hoping to stop the struggle before either of them got hurt, Findley raised a large-caliber buffalo gun he was carrying and pointed it at them.

"Stop it! Hear me—stop it!"

Getting his finger through the trigger guard of the Indian's rifle, McNall fired the weapon. Singed along the calf and foot, *Wil-lot-yah* let out a howl of rage and redoubled his efforts to wrest the rifle out of his adversary's hands. A small, wiry man, and outweighed by thirty pounds, McNall felt himself being overpowered. In desperation, he shouted, "He's going to kill me, Fin! For God's sake, shoot him!"

In a reflexive action which he did not even realize he was taking, Findley pulled the trigger. Struck squarely in the chest by the huge ball, the Nez Perce hunter was killed instantly. Stunned by what had happened, the four other Indians turned on their heels and fled.

"My God!" Findley muttered hoarsely, staring down at the body at his feet. "What have I done?"

"You shot a red son-of-a-bitch who was about to kill me!" McNall exclaimed. He looked nervously around. "We'd better get out of here and tell our people what happened. When Chief Joseph hears about this, he's bound to go on the warpath."

But for a time at least, the Wallowa Nez Perces took no hostile action. Since the main body of the Indians had not yet arrived in the valley from their winter home in the depths of the Big Canyon of the Snake, the "massing of the settlers for defensive purposes," as the local papers reported, consisted only of a few of them spending the night at the McNall cabin, then riding down to the Indian camp the next day to see what had happened. The Indians had gone, taking the body of the impetuous young hunter, *Wil-lot-yah*, with them for burial near their winter village. Ironically, two of the missing horses turned up near the Findley ranch a couple of days later. Adding to the irony was the fact that A.B. Findley, a deeply religious man, was so stricken by what he had done that he offered to give himself up to the Nez Perces for trial and punishment under their laws, though his white neighbors would not permit this.

The whites censured him not for the killing itself but for fear that his act might incite the angry Indians to take revenge upon their households. The greatest irony of all was that the Nez Perces, knowing Findley to be a good man and their friend, placed no blame on him for the killing, putting the fault where it rightfully belonged—on Wells McNall, who had seized the rifle of the young Nez Perce, grappled with him, cursed him, fired the first shot, and then called for Findley to shoot him.

When bands of Nez Perces began arriving in the valley that summer, they were not as friendly as they had been in previous years. Instead of visiting the white settlers as before, they set up targets and did a lot of riding back and forth on their warhorses, hanging under their necks and shooting at a full run, a show-off stunt they had learned from the Sioux which no warrior who cared about accuracy and the conservation of ammunition would dream of using in battle. At night they frequently held war dances.

Toward the end of August, Chief Joseph arrived. By then Findley had become so conscience-stricken over what he had done that he swore he would never shoot the needle gun again—and never did. Shortly after making camp in Indian Town, Chief Joseph came to the Findley ranch for a visit one late afternoon. Preparing the evening meal, Mrs. Findley happened to look out the open door toward the children who were playing in the yard. She saw an Indian approach on a spotted horse, halt, and dismount. Alarmed, she hurried out into the yard, then stopped as she saw the children run to the Indian, throw their arms around his legs, and greet him with laughter.

"Well, I do declare!" she exclaimed, smiling. "How are you, Joseph?"

"Your children grow big and strong. You must feed them well."

"They eat like starving bears. How is your family?"

"Healthy and hungry, too. Is your husband home?"

"No, but he soon will be. Can you stay for supper?"

"That would please me."

"Then I'll go in and finish getting it ready."

"Good. I'll stay out here and talk to the children."

"If they pester you too much, shoo them away. They can be an awful nuisance."

Chief Joseph laughed good-humoredly. "Not to me, Mrs. Findley. My village is full of children. They don't bother me at all."

When her husband came home and found Chief Joseph there, he was nervous at first, Mrs. Findley noticed, but the Nez Perce leader's calm manner and quiet dignity soon put him at ease. When supper was over, he looked at her and said, "Take the children outside, please. Joseph and I must talk."

"Come, children. We'll go for a walk."

After a silence, Findley said, "You heard what happened?"

"Yes. Now I want to hear it from you."

As simply, honestly, and frankly as he knew how, Findley told him about discovering the three horses missing, asking Wells McNall to help him track them down, and following their trail to the hunters' camp. He related taking possession of the Indians' rifles so that no violence would occur when they were questioned about the horses, how the act had been misunderstood by *Wil-lot-yah*, the struggle that had ensued, how he had tried to stop it, and how he had shot the Nez Perce without really meaning to do so. At that point, Joseph raised a hand and stopped him.

"Did McNall curse *Wil-lot-yah?*"

"Yes. As I recall, he did."

"He asked the Spirit God to make you shoot him?"

"He begged me to shoot him, best I can remember. Without meaning to, I did. So I'm the one responsible for the killing."

Brooding for some moments upon what he had been told, Chief Joseph at last shook his head. "You speak with a straight tongue, for this is the way the hunters who were in the party have told the story to me. In my view, you are not to blame. The white man Wells McNall is the real murderer."

Since there was no way McNall could be brought to trial and because Chief Joseph refused to accuse Findley, the matter ended there. Truth was, Joseph and his small, peaceful band of Nez Perces were faced with a much bigger problem. For years now they had been resisting the efforts of white authorities to move them from the Oregon area granted them by the Treaty of 1855 to a much smaller reservation across the Snake River in Idaho. When, in late May 1877, the federal government ordered the band to move to the Lapwai Reservation or be put there by force, Joseph reluctantly began to move his people and all their earthly possessions across the raging waters of the Snake River in the depths of the Big Canyon. While camped within one day's travel of the reservation boundary, two of his young men—taunted beyond endurance by past indignities inflicted upon them by callous white men—took blood vengeance against their tormentors.

What history would call the "Nez Perce War" ensued.

Though the conflict never touched the Columbia and Snake River sectors upon which the Oregon Steam Navigation Company ran its boats, the transportation boom stimulated by the war lasted much longer than the conflict itself. Troops, supplies, newspaper correspondents, Army officers, and politicians of all kinds filled the cargo and passenger decks of upriverboats for the next two years. Rumors of uprisings by tribes such as the Wanapums, led by Smowhala the Dreamer Prophet, or the Columbias, led by Chief Moses, inspired numerous newspaper editorials demanding that the state, territorial, or federal government supply arms and money with which to equip volunteer companies of militia prepared to fight pitched battles against hordes of bloodthirsty savages in order to protect their communities.

On one occasion, Lars Warren found himself pressed into service as a naval commander when the stern-wheeler *Spokane*, which had just been launched and turned over to him at Celilo Landing, was converted into a gunboat on which he was forced to serve.

It happened in this manner: Inspired by the heroic, futile war waged by the Nez Perces against federal troops for three months in 1877, a group of dissident Bannock Indians left their reservation in southwestern Idaho Territory in the summer of 1878 and rode west across the Blue Mountains into Oregon. Gathering on the south bank of the Columbia near Umatilla, they made plans to cross the river into the land of the Yakimas, to whom they were related. Alarmed newspaper writers claimed that the Bannocks were planning to join forces with three thousand fierce Yakima warriors, who regional newspaper editors declared were ready to help them in a war of extermination against the whites. In order to counteract this threat, the military commandant at Fort Walla Walla was appealed to for aid.

"The Yakimas ain't about to go to war against the United States," Alex Conley told Lars when the rumor first began to circulate. "They've got better sense than that."

"You don't think they'll help the Bannocks?"

"No way. The last thing they want is another war. This is all newspaper talk."

Even so, the Pacific Northwest Army District commander, General Frank Wheaton, felt it prudent to order a contingent from the 2nd Infantry, which was stationed at Fort Walla Walla, to go aboard a gunboat that would patrol the Columbia River between Umatilla and

Celilo to prevent a crossing by hostile forces. Since the Army had no gunboats in the area, it commandeered the *Spokane*, placed nineteen regulars and forty-two volunteers aboard, and armed them with a Gatling gun, a small howitzer, and rifles. Not sure whether he had been drafted into the Army, Navy, or Marines, Captain Lars Warren watched in amazement as a spit-and-polish young lieutenant named Hughes supervised a crusty Irish sergeant named O'Brien in the distribution of two hundred sacks of flour around the upper deck where presumably they would protect the boat's defenders against attack.

Much to his surprise, the gunboat did see some action one day, which was dutifully reported by the "war correspondent" assigned to cover the story, then later printed with banner headlines in the regional newspapers:

> Thirteen miles below Umatilla yesterday morning, it was observed that the Bannocks had swum three hundred horses to the Washington side and were attempting to get another two hundred over. The *Spokane* rounded to and fired, frightening off the Indians on the north bank. Troops landed to pursue them and to gather up abandoned livestock.
>
> Later in the day a few miles downstream at Thanksgiving Island near Arlington, the Spokane surprised another band of Indians attempting a crossing. The volunteers and soldiers bombarded both sides of the river, driving off the braves. A fleet of canoes on the south bank was destroyed and more horses were brought aboard the sternwheeler.
>
> Her mission accomplished, the *Spokane* returned to Umatilla, sullenly watched from the river bank by the chastened Indians.

Whether the dissident Indians were properly impressed with the might of the military forces thrown against them or simply got tired of war, no one could say. But after a few more minor engagements in which little damage was done to either side, the Bannocks returned to their reservation and the war was declared over.

Because Lars Warren never was sure which branch of the service he had been drafted into and had suffered no wounds more serious than ringing eardrums, he did not apply for a medal or a pension.

But in times to come, grandfather tales told in the lodges of the river Indians would magnify "The Day the Gunboat Roared" into a major legend.

12.

Thanks to the Walla Walla & Columbia River Railroad, the years between 1874 and 1879 were a time of great prosperity for the farmers of the Walla Walla Valley. Wheat and flour exports increased tenfold. According to one economic expert, Dr. Dorsey Syng Baker's thirty-two miles of narrow-gauge track during that period of time was the most highly profitable transportation system on the North American continent.

Although his profits still caused grumblings among the shippers, no further open warfare over railroad rates developed, for the farmers and merchants knew that the valley's prosperity was owed to the railroad.

The directors of the company had decided to bide their time before reopening the rates issue. Finally, it was Doc Baker himself who proposed that the rates be reduced. But he took this step only when he found himself financially set for his next and final venture.

The phrase "commensurate returns," which he had used in rejecting the petition from the Grange, had involved some long-range planning.

"Our company has only a short time in which to make an overall profit on our investment," he explained at a meeting of the Board of Directors. "Serious competition may crop up at any time, either in the form of a regionally financed line or one affiliated with a transcontinental company."

"By regional, I assume you mean the O.S.N. Company," John Boyer said, "while nationally the Union Pacific or the Northern Pacific might try to compete."

"Exactly. Right now the O.S.N. Company is rolling in money because of its highly profitable steamboat business. But if the big railroad companies decide to build a line across the Cascades to Puget

Sound or down the Columbia to Portland, they could drive both us and the O.S.N. Company into bankruptcy."

"What do you suggest we do?"

"Make a deal with the O.S.N. Company. With the board's approval, I'd like to go down to Portland and talk to Captain Ainsworth about combining our resources."

Given the board's blessing, Doc Baker traveled to Portland in February 1878, where he asked John Ainsworth, "Would you like to buy my railroad?"

"The last time we mentioned that subject," Ainsworth said with a wry smile, "you put a million-dollar price tag on your line. Has your asking price come down?"

"No. It's gone up. My price now is a million and a half."

Conferring with the other directors, President Ainsworth learned that their position was the same as his. Even though Doc Baker owned a fine, profitable railroad, the Oregon Steam Navigation Company felt it should stick to the steamboat business.

"We're making good money, Dorsey. We own all the boats on the river, as well as the portages and most of the landings. So for all practical purposes, we own the river itself."

"I differ with you there, John."

"Well, however you feel, Dorsey, we've decided that our best policy is to sit tight and wait. When the transcontinental railroad does come, we'll simply sell out for a lump sum, then retire and live on our accrued profits."

"If you have any by then."

"Don't worry, we will. In any event, the directors have instructed me to decline your offer."

"Very well. Then I'll choose my other alternative."

"Which is?"

"To go into the steamboat business myself."

"Oh, come now, Doctor! You're talking nonsense!"

"No, I'm not, John. Just because you own all the steamboats, the portages, and most of the landings, you think you own the river. You don't. The company that owns the *approaches* to the river, where all the freight of the inland country is generated, owns the river. I happen to own the most important approach east of the Cascades."

"That's true. But you have no boats."

"I can build them, John. If you don't buy my railroad, I will."

"The O.S.N. Company still controls the portages. What if we refuse to transship your freight?"

Doc Baker's smile was bleak. "I've been in touch with some powerful friends back in Washington, D.C., about that possibility. The Columbia is a federally regulated river on whose free navigation the government has spent a lot of money. As you well know, John, the Oregon Steam Navigation Company has been the chief beneficiary of those improvements. My friends back east tell me that the government would consider any threat by your company to restrict public use of the portages as a very selfish act, for which you would pay dearly."

Passing on Doc Baker's threats to the O.S.N. Company Board of Directors at a hastily called meeting that afternoon, President Ainsworth immediately was asked the question "Is he bluffing?"

"He never plays poker, he tells me. And from what I know of him, he never makes empty threats."

"But to build a fleet of steamboats—"

"Why not? His railroad and rolling stock are paid for and bringing in more freight revenue than our boats do in the upper river country. So far as getting the federal government to crack down on our monopoly of the portages, every politician living east of the Cascades or around Puget Sound would be only too happy to pass regulatory laws that would break our backs."

"What's your opinion, Emil?" one of the board members asked the senior O.S.N. Company attorney, who was present at the meeting. "Should we stick to our decision to stay out of the railroad business, then try to compete with Dr. Baker if he follows through on his threat to build boats? Or should we buy him out?"

"Why not compromise?" Emil Warren said after a few moments of thought. "These past few years, we've seen how shaky financing a transcontinental railroad can be. Both the Union Pacific and the Northern Pacific have been dragged into bankruptcy lawsuits by disgruntled stockholders. But Dr. Baker has proved he knows how to run a profitable railroad, just as we've proved we know how to run a successful steamboat line."

"That's true."

"He's asking a million-and-a-half, John says. Suppose we offered him somewhat less for a majority interest in his company, then let him and his staff run it until the Union or Northern Pacific gets ready to move into the Pacific Northwest? We can reorganize and call ourselves the Oregon Steam & Rail Navigation Company."

"We already own right-of-way along the south bank of the Columbia between Wallula and Portland," another director commented, nodding approvingly. "We could quietly begin to acquire right-of-way on the north bank, too."

"We certainly could," Emil said. "While we're at it, we'll buy easements along all the water-level routes on both sides of the Snake between Lewiston and the Columbia. This will put us in a real position of power when the big railroad companies try to deal with us."

Requesting and obtaining from Doc Baker a few days' time in which to put a deal on paper, the Board of Directors finalized an offer which satisfied all parties concerned. For the sum of $1,200,000, six-sevenths of the capital stock of the Walla Walla & Columbia River Railroad was transferred to the Oregon Steam & Rail Navigation Company, while Dr. Baker retained a one-seventh interest. After the contracts had been signed, Captain Ainsworth shook hands with Doc Baker and then burst into a great, irrepressible laugh.

"You ornery old son-of-a-gun. I guess I should have let that shipper boycott ruin you while I had the chance!"

Under the terms of the agreement, the Baker Railroad would maintain its identity and operate the line for the time being. Its board would be composed of John Ainsworth, William S. Ladd, and T. S. Peabody, the Wallula agent for the O.S.&R.N. Company, while Dr. Baker would continue as president, with his son, Frank, acting as vice-president, secretary, and treasurer.

Shortly thereafter, John Ainsworth made an announcement. "Because of the increasing grain shipments now being generated in the Walla Walla Valley, we are building what is designed to be the biggest, best, and finest steamboat ever to be launched on the upper river. It will be named after the builder of the Rawhide Railroad—who also happens to be my good friend and the stubbornest man in Washington Territory—Dorsey Syng Baker."

13.

MOST OF THE RESIDENTS of Wallula Landing agreed that fat, bumbling, dimwitted Bunky Burger was usually so drunk by the time the sun went down that he had trouble distinguishing fact from fancy. Even so, they admitted that Bunky always told the truth about any event he saw—or thought he saw. Usually, when something spectacular happened, other people were present who would give their account of the event, against which Bunky's garbled, inarticulate, cockeyed story could be compared.

But as fate would have it, Bunky Burger chanced to be the sole witness to what would pass into legend as the most spectacular episode in the history of Doc Baker's Rawhide Railroad.

This episode was the suicide by drowning of the Pony engine, *Wallula*. It happened in this manner: Soon after Dr. Baker sold his narrow-gauge railroad to the Oregon Steam & Rail Navigation Company, the decision was made to widen the track to standard gauge; purchase new, more powerful locomotives to replace the tiny *Walla Walla* and *Wallula;* and merge the Company with financier Henry Villard's Northern Pacific, which, backed by $35 million in paper assets, was in the process of building a transcontinental line westward from Minneapolis–St. Paul through Spokane, then down the Snake and Columbia to Portland.

Working as a day laborer on the track-widening project, Bunky found that it consisted of laying a third rail a foot or so outside the second rail of the narrow-gauge track so that the wheels of the older locomotives and flatcars could run on the older tracks until the wider gauge was in place. Beginning at the railroad yard in Walla Walla, then proceeding thirty-two miles west to the turnaround and unloading incline at Wallula Landing, this method made it possible for construction of the new gauge and destruction of the old to go on at the same time.

With his usual frugality, Dr. Baker had managed to find a buyer for the two narrow-gauge locomotives and strings of flatcars—a logging company in western Oregon—to whom all the outmoded equipment except the Pony engine, *Wallula*, had been sold and shipped prior to the memorable night on which the locomotive decided to drown itself rather than be carried off into the tall timber of the Siskiyou Mountains.

Exactly how Bunky Burger happened to be in a position where he alone witnessed the swan dive of the *Wallula* he could not say. This was not an unusual circumstance, for by ten o'clock of a hot summer night, Bunky's mind and memory usually were so hazed by drink that he could not recall why he happened to be anyplace. The important fact was, he was where he happened to be at that particular time, and thus had an unimpeded view of what he thought he saw, which could not be contradicted by any other witness.

As he later testified, what he thought he saw was this: The little Pony engine, *Wallula*, being parked on a flat stretch of narrow-gauge track two hundred yards from the river in the warm darkness, panted like a tired, winded old man who has just walked a long way. Soon after the engine stopped, its engineer, whom Bunky knew as Mac, and its fireman, Pat, climbed down out of the cab and headed up the hill toward the Wallula Palace Bar where, Bunky guessed, they would have a few cold beers. Which struck Bunky as a sensible thing to do, for the day had been very hot, firing the engine must have raised a tremendous thirst, and their day's work was done.

Having already consumed half a dozen beers himself, with a fresh one in his hand, Bunky was content to remain seated on a stack of railroad ties fifty feet away from the panting Pony engine, which to Bunky looked like it could use a few cold beers itself. From the talk he had heard on the job, the *Wallula* was scheduled to be fired up one last time tomorrow morning, then would chug slowly down the incline and be taken aboard the freight deck of the *Inland Queen*, which was due to arrive at ten o'clock downriver-bound for Celilo.

How did the little engine feel about leaving home? Bunky wondered. Would it like working in the woods? Would it miss seeing and whistling at all the cows, horses, sheep, dogs, coyotes, and people it had come to know during the years it had carried passengers and freight between Walla Walla and the steamboat landing? Would the high trestles, steep grades, and frequent curves of the Siskiyou country make it nervous and afraid it might slip and fall off the rain-slicked track? Or did little Pony engines even *have* feelings?

Musing on these questions as he took another swallow of beer, Bunky heard—or *thought* he heard—two short toots of the *Wallula*'s whistle, a signal that it was about to move. Ordinarily, it was the engineer or the fireman who pulled the cord that activated the whistle. But as Bunky recalled—or *thought* he recalled—both Mac and Pat had climbed down out of the cab a few minutes ago and gone up the hill to the Wallula Palace Bar to have themselves a few beers.

Still, he had heard the whistle toot.

The next thing he heard—or *thought* he heard—was the hiss of steam, the squeal of drive wheels, and the clank of the drawbar being engaged. The little engine began to move. Slowly, at first, then, following a metallic clashing of gears, the locomotive slammed into what Bunky supposed Mac or Pat would call "full-throttle balling the jack."

This struck Bunky as very strange. What was the little engine's hurry? Beyond the short stretch of level track on which the *Wallula* now was parked, the incline leading down to the steamboat landing was steep and rather short. Furthermore, a derail device was clamped to the river end of the track in order to prevent a runaway flatcar or engine from rolling into the river when no steamboat was anchored there. And the *Inland Queen* was not due to dock for another twelve hours.

Nevertheless, the little Pony engine *Wallula* was headed down the incline toward the unoccupied landing as fast as it could go.

Because Bunky's experience working on the railroad had not included witnessing what happens when a runaway locomotive going down a steep incline hits a derail device, he watched with considerable interest as what might be called an "irresistible force" met an "immovable object," wondering what would happen. Curiously enough, what happened was a kind of Mexican standoff in which neither the irresistible force nor the immovable object won or lost.

Instead, without budging an inch, the immovable object deflected the irresistible force up and out over the dark surface of the river in as graceful a swan dive as Bunky had ever seen a little Pony engine make. As the locomotive struck the water, its boiler fire was extinguished with a massive hiss, then it sank out of sight into deep water, leaving only a large, spreading circle on the surface for a time to show where it had vanished.

Interesting, Bunky mused as he took another swallow of beer. *Very interesting indeed.*

How long an interval of time passed between the *Wallula*'s swan dive into the river and Mac and Pat's return to the spot where they had left the engine parked, Bunky could not say. But he had finished the beer by then, had let the empty bottle fall to the ground, and had closed his eyes and taken a little nap. Next thing he knew, Mac had grabbed him by one shoulder, Pat by the other, and they were shaking him, shouting angrily.

"Where'd it go, Bunky?"

"What'd you do with it, Bunky?"

Even when cold sober, Bunky often found it difficult to describe events he had witnessed—or *thought* he had witnessed—in a way people could understand. When roused from a nap with seven bottles of beer in him, he found it impossible to say anything that made sense. The best he could do was pantomime what he *thought* he had seen happen.

Reaching up to pull an imaginary whistle cord, he went *toot-toot* to illustrate what the little Pony engine had said when it gave warning it was about to move. Puffing out his cheeks, he went *hiss-hiss* to show the sound it had made as it fed steam to its drive wheels. Doing a *clank-clank* and a *chug-chug*, he audibly demonstrated the sounds it had made as it got under way. To conclude the explanation, he extended his arms over his head, put his hands together, then pantomimed the arc of a swan dive as the speeding locomotive struck the derail, vaulted into the air, then descended with a final hiss beneath the dark surface of the river.

At first, Mac and Pat did not seem to believe him. But faced with the indisputable facts that (1) the locomotive was gone, and (2) Bunky never lied about what he *thought* he saw, the bewildered engineer and fireman went back to the Wallula Palace Bar; organized a search party equipped with pine-knot torches, long poles, and rowboats; and soon located the spot where the *Wallula* had made its dive, identifying it beyond all doubt by a pair of Mac's gloves, Pat's lunch box, and half a dozen loose sticks of cordwood that had been in the cab and now were floating on the surface of the river.

"Blamed old engine was gettin' mighty cranky," Mac muttered as he tried to explain the loss of the *Wallula* to the Oregon Rail & Navigation Company agent, Clem Purdy. "If I told Doc Baker once, I told him a dozen times that them drive-wheel brake shoes were wearin' out and ought to be replaced. But he was too tight to spend the money."

"Drawbar's shot, too," Pat agreed. "Bump it the wrong way, it'd slip into gear on its own 'fore you knew it and the fool engine would start to roll."

"So it could of took off by itself, just like Bunky claimed it did," Mac added, nodding in agreement.

"Well, now, that may be true," Clem Purdy said, scratching his head in puzzlement. "But how did it blow its own whistle?"

"What's a toot or two to Bunky, Clem? With a few beers in his belly, he's apt to hear a whole brass band."

Probing around by torchlight thirty feet offshore, the search party soon located the exact position of the sunken locomotive, finding it lying in the dark brown silt deposited in quiet water just downstream from the mouth of the Walla Walla River, sitting upright, with its bell-shaped smokestack ten feet underwater. When the *Inland Queen* arrived from Lewiston at ten o'clock the next morning, already well laden with a cargo of sacked wheat collected at landings along the 140-mile length of the Snake River, it had no trouble steering clear of the sunken locomotive as it docked. After being told what had happened, Captain Lars Warren rejected the suggestion that he try to raise the locomotive and bring it aboard.

"That's a job for a salvage boat, not for the *Queen*," he told Agent Purdy. "Make a report to the company, Clem. Maybe insurance will cover it."

Since Doc Baker considered insurance a form of gambling, in which pastime he never indulged, there turned out to be no insurance on the rolling stock of the Rawhide Railroad. So the locomotive that had drowned itself rather than leave home remained in its watery grave while buyer and seller bickered over the question of legal ownership. When the Siskiyou Logging Company, which had bought it, demanded that five hundred dollars be deducted from the sales contract price because of nondelivery, Emil Warren countered with the claim that delivery to the river had been made as promised. The fact that it had been made twelve hours before the boat arrived was an accident over which the seller had no control. However, as a goodwill gesture, his company would knock one hundred dollars off the total due under the contract.

Since both parties conceded that the little Pony engine was not in the best of shape the night it took its swan dive, the $250 figure finally agreed on settled the matter once and for all. Meanwhile, as the level of the river fell in early autumn, a portion of the *Wallula*'s smokestack emerged above the surface of the water, causing boats docking at Wallula Landing to veer a few feet upstream in order to avoid fouling their stern-wheels. Learning that the cost of raising the locomotive would far exceed its salvage value, Emil Warren tried to persuade the Corps of Engineers to declare it a hazard to navigation and remove it at government expense. But the request was denied, a Corps official curtly saying, "You put it there; you fish it out."

Because converting from narrow to standard gauge and expanding loading facilities at Wallula Landing required extensive rebuilding anyway, the Oregon Rail & Navigation Company, which was being taken over by the Northern Pacific, found it easier to build a new dock and rail incline a hundred feet to the north of the little Pony engine's watery grave where it would not be a hazard to navigation no matter what the level of the river.

In times to come, the vivid account of its swan dive into the river as related by Bunky Burger would grow into a legend far more imaginative than anything he could have dreamed up. On several occasions during the lifetimes of Captain Lars Warren, his children, and his grandchildren, projects to raise the locomotive were proposed and then abandoned because of physical or funding difficulties. To this day, the little Pony engine *Wallula* lies buried in the dark brown silt near the juncture of the Walla Walla River with the Columbia where it makes its big bend westward toward the Pacific Ocean ...

A frequent traveler between Wallula and Lewiston and a major shipper of sacked wheat from his warehouses along the Snake River, Sewell Truax long had been Lars Warren's financial adviser and friend. A muscular, firm-jawed man in his early fifties, whose close-cropped black hair was just beginning to be speckled with gray, he was continually seeking ways to make money in the upriver country, then did his best to persuade Lars to invest in the projects with him.

Graduating from Norwich University in Vermont with a degree as a civil engineer in 1850, Truax had done survey work in New

England for a while, then caught Oregon fever and come west with a wagon train to the Willamette Valley in 1853. Working as a U.S. deputy surveyor in the Rouge River country until an Indian uprising in 1855, he enlisted in the local militia as a volunteer. When the Civil War started in 1861, he entered the service of the United States as captain of Company D, 1st Oregon Cavalry, soon reaching the rank of major.

For a time during the 1860s, he was in command at Fort Walla Walla in Washington Territory, then at Fort Lapwai, in Idaho Territory. At the end of the Civil War, he resigned his commission and went back to his chosen profession, civil engineering. During the building of Dr. Baker's railroad, he acted as superintendent of construction through its crucial years, using his sharp pencil and critical judgment to keep down costs, which pleased Dr. Baker so much that he was made vice-president of the company.

Following its merger with the O.R.&N. Company, Major Truax sold his stock in the Rawhide Railroad and turned his shrewd engineering mind to other moneymaking projects. Acquiring several parcels of valuable land along both sides of the Snake River between its mouth and Lewiston, he homesteaded or bought out the lapsed rights to grain-producing fields on the rolling plateau back away from the river, then built storage warehouses on strategically located sandbars on the river itself, where stern-wheelers could pull in and load sacked wheat.

Like other progressive landowners in this part of the country, he had been quick to utilize such modern agricultural inventions as gang-plows, discs, harrows, and harvesters pulled by thirty-six-animal spans of horses or mules, with the wheat then being threshed by giant steam-powered separators. Because yields as high as one hundred bushels to the acre were becoming commonplace all over what was known as the Palouse Hills Country, the crying need of the growers now was to reduce freight rates to the point where they could make a reasonable profit.

"As matters are now," Major Truax told Lars as he stood beside the young captain in the pilot house of the *Inland Queen*, "we farmers pay as much to get our wheat hauled from the fields down to the boat landings just two thousand vertical feet below as we do in freight charges to Portland. We can't put up with that much longer."

Slowing the boat's stern-wheel as he nosed the *Queen* in toward the sandbar landing below the Truax warehouse, Lars let his gaze roam upward along the steep slash of narrow, twisting, treacherous wagon road along which heavily laden grain wagons must make their way in order to bring their loads down to river level. For 140 miles along both sides of the Snake River, he knew, local farmers were forced to survey, build, and maintain river access roads themselves, for county funds were not available.

Furthermore, grain-hauling in this country was a risky business. In many places, the rate of descent was so steep that rough-locks of chains or logs must be placed behind the rear wheels of the wagons to act as brakes. Professional teamsters skilled enough to do the job charged exorbitant wages. Fall rains, winter snows, and spring torrents eroded and gullied the roads so badly that they had to be repaired and regraded each year.

"So what's your solution?" Lars asked.

"It's simply a matter of putting the law of gravity to work," Major Truax answered. "There has to be a way to dump the wheat into slides, chutes, or tubes and then let it slide down on its own. Mark my word, Lars, the man who invents and patents such a system will make a fortune."

"You're working on it, I take it?"

"You bet I am. When I get it perfected, I'll let you know."

By the time the next harvest season rolled around, Major Sewell Truax had invented, patented, and installed a means of transporting wheat from an unloading station on the heights down to his warehouse landing on the sandbar where the O.R.&N. Company boats loaded cargo. On paper, the system looked like it ought to work.

What Truax had done, Lars learned, was construct a closed wooden chute four inches square and thirty-two hundred feet long extending from the heights to the river below. After opening the one-hundred-pound burlap sacks in which the wheat was hauled from the field to the unloading station, the grain was discharged onto a screen, which removed coarse foreign substances, then allowed to fall into the buckets of an overshot wheel, supplying the impetus to turn the wheel just as water would do. From the wheel, the grain was discharged into the chute, then started on its way down to the river level two thousand feet below.

But from the beginning, there were problems. First, the slightest amount of moisture in the wheat caused blockages that were difficult to clear. Second, since the chute was not vented, a troublesome vacuum was created, causing an uneven flow. Third—and most serious—the rate of descent was so steep that the friction heated the grain to the point that by the time it reached river level it was charred black.

When one wag suggested that the charcoal-colored wheat be sacked and exported to countries that baked black bread, Sewell Truax was not amused. Doggedly, he went back to his drawing board.

For several weeks following the first failure, he spent long hours in his river-level warehouse office sketching changes aimed at solving the grain-chute problems. One of the experiments he tried was taking the top board off the chute in order to eliminate the vacuum. This it did. But it also caused much of the grain to be lost over the sides of the chute. That which did reach the bottom was still charred black.

In an attempt to eliminate the friction factor, Truax tried lining the bottom of the chute with glass. This helped some, but when he installed sheets of glass experimentally in a three-hundred-foot section, he found that aligning the pieces just right so that there would be no seams between the joints required far more skilled labor than he could afford, while the vacuum problem remained unsolved.

Persisting in his efforts, he finally was well enough satisfied with the modifications he had made and tried on a small scale to have the entire thirty-two-hundred feet of the chute torn apart and rebuilt.

"This time, I think I've got it," he told Lars after the *Inland Queen* had made her lines fast to the warehouse loading dock, with a dozen or so skeptical farmers on hand to witness the critical trial. "The key was baffles and vents. I put one of each into the chute at intervals of one hundred feet. Here, I'll show you on this sketch—"

"Later," Lars broke in, holding up a restraining hand. "Once you've demonstrated it does work, I'll let you explain it to me. Right now, I just want to make sure a deckhand with a water hose is standing by to put out any fires started by hot grain."

Major Truax had been right. This time, the grain chute worked perfectly. Not only did the wheat slide down without a single blockage or interruption, it stayed cool and retained its natural golden color, with the baffles and vents at hundred-foot intervals serving the dual purpose of slowing the rate of its descent and cleansing it of all impurities such as dirt and chaff.

Forming a company in which Truax, Lars, and Emil Warren were majority stockholders, five grain chutes were built from the bluff tops down to the river landings along the lower Snake during the next few years, paying excellent royalties to the owners, dividends to the investors, and saving regional farmers considerable money in hauling charges, while at the same time bringing the O.R.&N. Company increased revenue in downriver freight.

Though the Truax Grain Chute was protected by patent from being copied by competitors, the law-of-gravity principle Major Truax had used was free and available for any enterprising inventor clever enough to find a new and different way to use it. The most ingenious and successful system put into operation during the next few years in the lower Snake River country was the Mayview Tramway.

Conceived, built, and operated as a community project by a group of farmers with no formal training as engineers, the cable-car tram was an adaptation of the way ore had been moved for years in the nearby mining country of western Idaho and eastern Oregon. Located on a level plateau two thousand feet above river level, a grain storage yard served as an unloading area for farm wagons. Six feeder tracks branched out from the nearby brakehouse, which contained the big wooden drums and metal shoes used to control the speed of the cars as they moved down the steep grade toward river level. After being taken from the farm wagons, the hundred-pound sacks of wheat were stacked five deep alongside the tracks, on which large tram cars were parked.

Each sack was hand-loaded by a crew of strong, well-muscled men, each of whom soon developed a knack for snatching a sack, turning, placing, and balancing the load in each car. During the fifty-one years that the Mayview Cable Car Tramway operated successfully, one particular early-day sack-loader—a man named John L. Morrison—became legendary for his skill, endurance, and strength.

"Can you believe," Lars asked his uncle, Emil Warren, after hearing an account of John Morrison's feat from a farmer who had witnessed it, "that the man is so strong and durable he's paid double wages—seven dollars a day instead of three-fifty—for doing the work of two men in the same ten-hour shift?"

"If it were me," Emil said wryly, "I imagine my output would be about a sack an hour. How many does he load?"

"His record, they say, is thirty-seven hundred sacks in a single shift. At a hundred pounds per sack, that figures out to be one hundred eighty-five tons."

When first put into operation, the normal load for a cable car was forty-five sacks of barley or thirty-five sacks of wheat, the difference caused by the fact that, while the sacks used were the same size, barley was bulkier so it weighed less. Running on narrow-gauge rails similar to those first used on Doc Baker's road, the cable cars on which the grain was transported up and down the hill ran on three tracks as far as what was called "the passing place," then on four parallel passing tracks designed so that downward- and upward-bound cars could get by one another. Beyond this midpoint spot, a single track led in each direction.

At the bottom of the hill, the cable cars ran out onto a turntable where they entered the warehouse, which was also used as a storage shed. While workmen there unloaded the sacked grain from one car, other laborers on the bluff above were busy loading a car there. When the car at the bottom was empty and the one at the top full, a signal flag was waved at river level, then the brakeman in the loading station at the top of the hill carefully let the full car begin its cautious descent down the steep slope, which action automatically started the empty car upward toward the passing place. The time required for a loaded car to descend from the bluff top to the river level normally was three minutes. As the ascending and descending cars approached each other, they tripped an automatic switching device, which caused them to swerve aside as they passed at the midpoint of the hill.

Pulled by a stranded steel cable five-eighths inches in diameter and 4,800 feet long which ran from the brakehouse at the top to the turntable below, with a car attached to each end, the tracks for the tramway were supported on trestles and timbers anchored into the side of the bluff. With typical farmer ingenuity, when the builders noted a seepage a few feet below the top of the hill, they dug it out to expose a substantial spring whose water could be used for cooling purposes in the brakehouse, if only a means could be devised to raise it to that level. That means was soon found in the form of a hydraulic ram, whose basic principle, as most dryland farmers knew, was that the weight of seven gallons of water falling one foot had the power to lift one gallon one foot. With a reservoir on the heights behind which water lifted by the ram was stored, its contents were used both to quench the thirst of the workmen on a hot summer day and to cool the huge friction brakes of the tram.

When moving the three thousand or more sacks a day from the heights down to river level during the peak weeks of the harvest season, the giant wooden brake wheel often became so hot that only the frequent use of water kept it from burning up. As water was splashed onto the hot metal shoes and wooden brake drum, clouds of steam rose into the air and banshee-like screams of protest pierced the eardrums. In the first stage of operation, the brake had been only a single wheel around which wooden shoes strengthened with iron were fitted. Attached to the shoes were iron straps which pulled the shoes together in a squeeze around the brake drum when the brake lever was set. This primitive arrangement was quickly abandoned when it was blamed for the deaths of two workmen during the first year of the tramway's operation.

As Lars heard the story, the accident happened in this manner: In late afternoon of a blisteringly hot day, the last load had just been placed in the car at the top of the hill. Two men, William Bly and Harry Johnson, working at the warehouse at river level, decided to ride the empty car up and go to a dance at Pomeroy that night. As Jim Parker, the brakeman, released the lever to allow the loaded car to start downward, the lever caught in the open position. Try as he might, he could not pull it back into place. Completely out of control, the car ran wild, gaining momentum with every foot it traveled.

As the heavily laden car fell like a meteor from outer space toward the river landing two thousand feet below, it pulled the empty car and the two captive passengers upward at the same rate. At the passing place, the ascending and descending got by each other without colliding, but for the two trapped workmen who had hitched a ride, there was no escape.

When their car crashed into the brakehouse at tremendous speed, both men were killed instantly.

Following this tragedy, Lars heard, a new braking system was devised for the Mayview Tramway, utilizing two wheels and a double wrap of cable. Even so, there was grim truth in the saying then current in occupations where heavy materials were moved by tramways, endless belts, or other mechanical means: "What kind of safety devices do they have? Why, mostly, friend, all they got is a man with a loud voice. When he sees an accident about to happen, he just rares back and yells: 'Look out!' "

14.

Ever since the Chief Joseph War had reached its tragic end with the surrender of the fleeing Nez Perces and their imprisonment in what the Indians called *Eekish Pah*—the "hot country" of Oklahoma—Captain Lars Warren had found his chief engineer, Alex Conley, reluctant to talk about his relatives and friends. A mixture of Chinook, a coastal tribe, and Yakima, an inland tribe, Alex had conflicting loyalties, Lars knew, insofar as the native leaders in this part of the country were concerned.

For Smowhala, the gentle Dreamer Prophet, Alex had a deep respect. But he was too much a part of the white man's world himself to live the simple, spiritual way Smowhala's doctrine required. Chief Moses, who called himself head chief of the Columbia tribe, Alex viewed as part politician and part fraud, a crafty schemer willing to play both ends against the middle in order to achieve his goals. The attitude held by Chief Moses toward the Nez Perce War was a perfect example of Moses's conviction that he could get more out of the government by talk than by violence.

In a time and place where settlers living in isolated homes in the eastern part of Washington Territory panicked at every rumor of a threatened Indian attack, Chief Moses built up a great deal of goodwill by playing the role of an Indian leader who consistently advocated peace. Following the well-circulated dispatches of white correspondents who were covering the Nez Perce War and recording one victory after another of Indian warriors over supposedly well-trained federal troops, few white people living in the upper Columbia River region doubted what would happen if Chief Moses decided to turn the thousands of warriors supposedly under his command loose against the white community in support of Joseph and his gallant followers.

Blood would flow ankle-deep in every hollow.

Well aware of this fact, Chief Moses never once threatened to support Chief Joseph and his people by going to war. Instead, he repeated time and again, "I have kept the peace. I tell the young men they must not go to war. I will not let them kill innocent white women and children."

To make sure his message reached the right places, he had letters written and telegrams sent to important people such as Father James Wilbur, Yakima Indian agent; Governor John McGraw of Washington Territory; and General Oliver Otis Howard, commander of federal troops pursuing the Joseph band. In each and every case, local and regional newspapers picked up and printed the dispatches as reassuring, front-page news for worried readers, "Chief Moses says he will keep the peace."

Typical of his letters was one he sent General Howard shortly after the end of the Nez Perce War:

> I, Moses, chief, want you to know what my *tum-tum* (heart) is in regard to my tribe and the whites. Almost every day reports come to me that soldiers from Walla Walla are coming to take me away from this part of the country. My people are excited and I want to know from you the truth, so that I can tell them, and keep everything quiet once more among us. Since the last war (the Nez Perce) we have had up here rumors that I am going to fight if the soldiers come. This makes my heart sick. I have said I will not fight and I say it to you again ... I am getting old and I do not want to see my blood shed on my part of the country. Chief Joseph wanted me and my people to help him. His orders were many. I told him, "No, never!" I watched my people faithfully during the war and kept them at home.

Though the Colville Reservation was established by Executive Order in 1872, Chief Moses refused to go either to it or to the Yakima Reservation, as he was being urged to do. Instead, he and the widely scattered Columbia bands for which he was the principal spokesman continued to live and roam across the upper Okanogan and Columbia River country, professing peace but a threat for war. As a reward for controlling his people, Chief Moses at last got what he wanted—an invitation in 1879 to travel to the nation's capital in Washington City to meet with the Great White Father, President Rutherford B. Hayes.

Between Lewiston on the Snake and Celilo on the Columbia, Captain Lars Warren had the dubious honor of playing host to Chief Moses and his retinue aboard the *Inland Queen*, as the party—which was traveling in style at government expense—made its way by boat downriver to Portland, then by oceangoing ship to San Francisco. Spending a couple of nights there, the chiefs were taken to the theater, where, before a full-house audience, they appeared onstage in costume to thrill the crowd with a glimpse of real live Indians in all their pagan glory. A born actor, Chief Moses made such an impression that more than one reporter suggested he should join the troupe of Buffalo Bill Cody, who was starring in his own production, *Knight of the Plains*, in another jam-packed San Francisco theater just a few blocks away.

But Chief Moses had more important things to do at the moment. Journeying with his delegation overland via the Union Pacific to Washington, he signed a paper with proper ceremony giving him and the tribes he represented a reservation of their own.

And a huge reservation it was, running north from the juncture of the Chelan and Columbia Rivers to Canada, bordered by the Okanogan River on the east and the crest of the Cascades on the west, exceeding in size even the Yakima Reservation, which until then had been the largest Indian reservation in Washington Territory. Placed on what was first called the Moses and then the Columbia Reservation were the Wenatchees, Entiats, Chelans, Methows, Okanogans, and any other regional bands wishing to live there. So far as Moses himself was concerned, he felt he was also chief of bands living on the Colville Reservation to the east, such as the San Poils, Nespelems, and Colvilles, though *their* chiefs disputed his claims.

By this time, the tragic remnants of Chief Joseph's defeated Nez Perces had been transported to Indian Territory in what would become eastern Oklahoma, where their plight as exiles had begun to raise a great deal of sympathy among religious people and the eastern press. Consummate politician that he was, Moses talked to Joseph—who also visited Washington City in the spring of 1879—and they agreed to merge their pleas for justice in appeals to their mutual friend, General Howard, to eastern religious leaders, and to the national press.

From the first establishment of the reservation system, it had been government policy to put all the bands living in a certain area together in close proximity to one another on a single reservation, whether they got along with one another or not. In the white world, Lars told Alex, this would be equivalent to merging towns, counties, or congressional districts regardless of the wishes of the residents, with no overall authority to enforce local or regional laws. Add the fact that

Moses had been granted a one thousand dollar annuity, while salaries paid to some of the other headmen ranged downward to five hundred dollars, one hundred dollars, or in some cases nothing at all; the causes of dissension were numerous indeed.

Often the politically appointed agents in charge of the reservations were lazy, greedy, or downright dishonest. For example, the white man in charge of the Colville agency at first claimed that the annuity due Chief Moses was to be just a house worth one thousand dollars, not cash. When he could not make that stick and Moses insisted that he be given the annuity in twenty-dollar gold pieces, the agent grudgingly cashed the government check but withheld five twenty-dollar gold pieces for handling the transaction. When after much foot-dragging a house was built for Moses, it was so ramshackle that its worth was closer to one hundred dollars than the required one thousand dollars.

As a child playing with boats and fooling around in shallow water at the river's edge near their Rooster Rock cabin, Lars Warren often had heard his mother accuse his father of remembering the dates of explosions, wrecks, or other steamboat disasters far better than he recalled his own children's births. Admitting the truth of this, Captain Tommy Warren would smile fondly at Freda, then give her the same answer his father, Captain Benjamin Warren, had given Lolanee when accused of the same crime.

"It's just human nature, dear, to remember disasters more clearly than happy events. When you have a baby, it's always a happy time for me."

"What a prevaricator you are!" Freda exclaimed. "Can you tell me what year Lars was born?"

"That's easy—1850." Frowning thoughtfully, he added, "As I recall, that was the year Dad and a group of his Astoria friends built the double-ended paddle-wheeler *Columbia*. What a clunker that was!"

"Lars or the boat?"

"Freda! You know I meant the boat."

"Well, at least you got the year right. Now tell me the month and day."

"Why, it must have been around the Fourth of July. I distinctly recall hearing how people lining the banks of the Willamette River shot off a lot of fireworks when the *Columbia* poked her blunt front end into the mouth of the river after working herself off the mudflats downstream."

"You're close, darling," Freda admitted grudgingly. "Lars was born July 6. But there were no fireworks at Rooster Rock."

Because their own child, Lily Frieda Warren, had been born on the day Doc Baker's Rawhide Railroad celebrated its completion to Wallula, October 23, 1875, Lars had no difficulty remembering their first baby's birthday. But he did admit that since then, special happenings on the river such as wrecks, explosions, and the launching of new boats often were dates more vividly engraved on his mind than birthdays.

In order to fulfill the need for the transport of grain and passengers down the Snake and Columbia, the O.S.N. Company by 1878 built and launched seven big steamboats: the *Harvest Queen*, *John Gates*, *Spokane*, and *Annie Faxon* at Celilo; the *Mountain Queen* and *R. R. Thompson* at The Dalles; and the *Wide West* at Portland.

Slated to run on the upper river between Celilo and Lewiston, the *Harvest Queen* was a veritable palace of a boat, in Lars's opinion, the finest and fastest stern-wheeler on the upper river. After acting as a guest pilot from Wallula to Lewiston on her maiden trip, Lars gave Daphne such a rapturous description of the new boat's virtues and capabilities that a wife less used to having a steamboat captain for a husband would have thought he had found a new lady love.

"She's two hundred feet long, with a thirty-seven foot beam and a seven-and-half-foot-deep hold. She can carry five hundred tons of freight, has luxury quarters for a hundred cabin passengers, with dining and bar facilities for twice that number. Under a full head of steam, she can do thirty miles an hour. She has a shallow enough draft to navigate the Snake all the way up to Lewiston in most stages of water and can be docked at all the river landings for easy loading. She's a real beauty of a boat."

"Is she going to be yours?"

"No, I'm scheduled to stay with the *Inland Queen*," Lars said with a frown. "But the Company did ask me to go along with the new captain on his first run up to Lewiston and back to teach him the river."

"Who is the new captain?"

"A young fellow named Jim Troup."

"How young?"

"Only twenty-three. Why the O.S.N. Company would give such an expensive new boat to a still-wet-behind-the-ears officer like him, is beyond me."

"Oh, my goodness!" Daphne exclaimed, throwing up her hands in mock horror. "He is young, isn't he? How old were you when you got your captain's rating?"

"Twenty-one. But I'd been on the river since I was nine."

"Maybe he started young, too."

"Well, from what I saw of him running up to Lewiston and back, he does seem capable enough," Lars said grudgingly. "I suppose he'll be all right."

"It was nice of him to let you take Lily along. She's never happier than when she's on a boat."

"I know."

"She told me she had a wonderful time. She claims you let her steer the boat. Is that true?"

"More or less," Lars said, nodding. "Coming downriver just below Palouse Rapid, she was in the pilot house with Captain Troup and me, bright-eyed and curious as always. When Captain Troup, who was quite taken with her, asked if she would like to steer the boat, she said she certainly would. He got a stool, lifted her up to the wheel, and told her she was the pilot now. He'd say, 'Two spokes to port, Madam Pilot, if you please. Steady as she goes. Look sharp, now! Bring her three spokes to starboard.' "

"I'll bet she loved that!"

"She certainly did. It's amazing how strong and sure-handed she is for a five-year-old, Daphne. When he told her two spokes to port or three spokes to starboard, that's exactly what she gave him. And she held the boat right on course until he ordered a change."

"Don't tell me we're going to have a female steamboat captain in the Warren family!"

"I'm afraid the O.S.N. Company is not quite ready for that, dear. But she does love being on the river."

Though there now were enough boats on the Snake and Columbia to handle the grain and passengers being moved downriver, the captains and crews of the newly launched craft were keeping a wary eye on a mode of transportation that could greatly affect their livelihood, if and when it became a reality—the railroads. In February 1878, Dr. Baker sold six-sevenths of his stock in his narrow-gauge line to the Oregon

Steam Navigation Company, with himself remaining as president. A year later, in May 1879, he sold his remaining stock to Henry Villard, who had bought the O.S.N. Company and was beginning his spectacular career as a transportation king.

For a time, Dr. Baker remained as president and began building a branch line from Whitman Station south into Oregon by way of a new town named Weston, apparently planning to take the rails on across the Blue Mountains to make a connection in Utah with the Union Pacific in the Salt Lake area. But after completing only twelve miles, Dr. Baker, whose health was failing even as his banking business was booming, decided he had had enough. Selling his remaining stock to Henry Villard, he went out of the railroad business—still ahead of the game.

Unlike Doc Baker, who never gambled, Henry Villard played the empire-building game with million-dollar chips. A man of vision and purpose, his grand scheme was to establish a great commercial kingdom in the Pacific Northwest by building a network of rail, river, and ocean steamer lines that would bring in new settlers by the hundreds of thousands. For a while, every hand he played was a winner.

First, he realized, he must control access to the region, which meant the Columbia River. By building along its banks, he would be in a position to meet and beat any westward-bound railroad, whether it be the Northern Pacific, now struggling across Montana, or the so-called Oregon Short Line, proposed from Salt Lake northwest across Idaho, the Snake River, and the Blue Mountains.

Like Doc Baker, Villard at first favored the three-foot narrow gauge, which was practical and cheap; he ordered grading to begin for such a line along the Columbia from Wallula to Celilo. Because the fourteen-mile portage road from Celilo Falls to The Dalles and the six-mile portage track around the Cascades were also narrow-gauge and had been acquired by his purchase of the O.S.N. Company, he knew they would be compatible with the line being laid west along the Columbia from Wallula. But there was a flaw in that plan, which he quickly saw.

Both the Northern Pacific and Union Pacific were standard gauge—four feet eight inches—which would require a transfer of freight between the cars of their lines and his. This would be a major obstacle, he knew, discouraging through movements of freight. Very likely, either or both companies would be encouraged to build their own lines along routes he could not control. For example, the Northern Pacific might build across the Grand Coulee country and the Cascades directly to Puget Sound, as Everett, Seattle, and Tacoma were urging it to do. Or the Oregon Pacific, which had formed a company headquartered in the Willamette Valley, might strike a deal with the Union Pacific, bypass the Columbia River route, build east across the Oregon Cascades and high desert country, then effect a meeting with the Union Pacific somewhere around Olds Ferry.

Not wanting to risk that, Villard changed his plans, ordering the right-of-way survey crew to widen the grade and prepare for the laying of standard-gauge rail. With his usual luck, the financier guessed right on both scores, managing by some fancy financial footwork to stay a step ahead of the wolf pack of promoters trying to bring him down. By 1883 he had joined his now standard-gauge Columbia River line upriver from Portland to Wallula to the Northern Pacific, which had built southwest from Montana to Spokane, and with the Oregon Short Line built by the Union Pacific to Snake River, across the Blue Mountains, and down to the south bank of the Columbia at Umatilla Landing.

For the time being, at least, the transportation empire being created by Henry Villard had two transcontinental connections.

Anticipating the completion of rail lines along the Columbia and Snake, Villard instructed Emil Warren, who was now acting as chief of operations for the steamboat branch of the O.R.&N. Company, "to effect a redistribution of carriers" along the river route between Lewiston and Portland.

"We've got too many boats on the upper river," Villard said. "Unless we move them to where they're needed on the middle and lower sectors of the river, we'll have choke points at the portages that will make our farmer-shippers scream. See to it, will you."

As Emil had quickly learned, humorless, short-tempered, blunt-spoken Henry Villard never softened an order with a question mark. Move the boats, he said. How they were to be moved was Emil's problem.

With its five hundred-ton carrying capacity, the *Harvest Queen*, which had been making the run from Celilo to Lewiston for three years, was first on the list of boats to be moved from the upper to the middle river. By now, Captain James W. Troup, though only twenty-six years old, knew the hazards of the run almost as well as Lars himself did. Even so, he was quick to take advantage of Emil's suggestion that he seek Lars's advice as to how a stern-wheeler should be handled when being steered downstream over thundering waterfalls and dangerous rock-strewn rapids.

"Emil tells me that between you, your father, and Captain William Polk Gray you know every rock in the river by its first name."

"We've kissed a few," Lars said with a laugh. "But we try not to sit too long on their laps."

"You charted the upper Snake twenty-five miles above the mouth of the Salmon in 1862, I understand. And you were first mate on the *Shoshone* when Captain Sebastian Miller brought her down through the Big Canyon in '70."

"That's right."

"How does a man prepare for taking a boat through that kind of water?"

In the course of several sessions during the next few weeks, Lars told Captain Troup what he had learned about running wild water. The first lesson was that it was useless to fight the power of the current when moving downriver. Unless your stern-wheel was turning at full speed to give you steerageway, you had no rudder control in a forward direction. With the wheel turning full speed astern, you could get enough lateral steerageway to keep your boat in the main channel, where the water was deeper, but if a sharp rock jutting above the surface split the main channel in two, it became a by-guess and by-God gamble as to which was the best chute to take, with only a few seconds to make up your mind.

"So far as I know," Lars said, "no one has ever tried to take a steamboat over Celilo Falls and down through The Dalles Rapids before. Further downriver, a boat went over the Cascades by accident back in '58. It was called the *Venture*."

"Did it survive?"

"Oddly enough, it did. Here's what happened."

Built by R. R. Thompson and Laurence Coe, who were captains and stockholders in the O.S.N. Company, the *Venture* had been launched just above the Upper Cascades; it was to be put in service on the same middle river run to The Dalles on which Lars's father,

Captain Tommy Warren, and his Chinook Indian friend, Sitkum, were serving as pilot and engineer aboard the *Mary*. Two years earlier, when surprised by an early morning Indian attack at Bradford's Store with cold boilers, Sitkum had managed to borrow enough hot coals from the cook's stove to begin a fire which, fed with everything aboard that would burn, gave Tommy enough steam to cast off and steer the boat out into the river, though for a few minutes it was touch and go as to whether the *Mary* had enough power to resist the pull of the rapids downstream as she angled across the river and out of range of hostile fire.

"As Dad has told the story to me," Lars said, "he had to lie on his back in the pilot house and work the wheel with his feet while a wounded young deckhand named Johnny Chance shouted directions to him from the shelter of the port rail. It was a close call, he said. But they made it."

Even with that example of the river's power to go by and no Indian attack to hurry the *Venture* on her way, Captains Thompson and Coe, with forty passengers aboard for the trial trip, pulled out from the Upper Cascades dock before the *Venture*'s boilers could supply the engine with a full head of steam. Sucked into the rapids and completely out of control, she went over the turbulent boil of the Upper Cascades, a fall of five feet, stern first; bounced merrily along through three miles of white, surging, rock-strewn water; stayed upright as she tumbled over the four-foot-high falls of the Middle Cascades; then tossed and heaved through three more miles of angry water until finally lurching over the five-foot drop of the Lower Cascades. Striking a rock ledge just under the surface of the quiet water there, she stranded until her passengers and crew were rescued by a sailing schooner.

"The only person lost," Lars said, "was a man who panicked and dove overboard when the *Venture* went down the first waterfall. Apparently he thought he could swim better than the boat could. His body was never found."

"Well, that's one mistake I'll never make," Captain Troup said, shaking his head. "When I go over the falls, I want all the wood and iron the boat's got between me and the water. I'm not much of a swimmer."

Called "Celilo" by the local Indians and "Tumwater Falls" by the lower river tribes, the great Columbia River fishery was a series of chutes, channels, and tumbling rapids that extended some fourteen miles from its head to its foot. In Lars's opinion, the *Lewis and Clark Journals* had described it best:

> The first pitch of this falls is 20 feet perpendicular, (William Clark wrote), then passing thro' a narrow channel for 1 mile to a rapid of about 8 feet fall below which the water has no perceptible fall but verry rapid. Capt. Lewis and three men crossed the river and on the opposite Side to view the falls which he had not yet taken a full view of. At 9:00 A.M. I set out with the party and proceeded on down a rapid Stream of about 400 yards wide. At 2 1/2 miles the river widened into a large bason to the Stard. Side on which there is five lodges of Indians. here a tremendious black rock Presented itself high and Steep appearing to choke up the river; nor could I see where the water passed further than the current was drawn with great velocity to the Lard. Side of this rock at which place I heard a great roreing. I landed at the Lodges and the natives went with me to the top of this rock which makes from the Stard. Side, from the top of which I could see the dificuelties we had to pass for several miles below; at this place the water of this great river is compressed into a channel between two rocks not exceeding *forty-five* yards wide and continues for 1/4 of a mile when it again widens to 200 yards and continues this width for about 2 miles when it is again intersepted by rocks. The whole of the Current of this great river must at all Stages pass thro' this narrow channel of 45 yards wide.

Above and below this fourteen-mile section of turbulent river, the Columbia was half a mile wide and relatively tranquil, Clark wrote, but here—where the river literally turned on edge—he estimated its current to be thirty miles per hour.

The description of Celilo Falls by William Clark had been written in late October, Lars knew, when the volume of water in the river was at its lowest point and the twenty-foot vertical falls higher than at any other time of year. During the peak spring runoff in late May, snowmelt over the headwaters of the Snake and Columbia supplied such a tremendous volume of water that Celilo Falls and the fourteen miles of rapids immediately downstream leveled out into a broad, tumbling, roaring chute of white water on the surface of which any object that floated was impelled downriver at breakneck speed.

"Ideally, late May would be the best time to take the *Harvest Queen* down to the middle river," Lars told Captain Troup. "Can you wait until then?"

"I'm afraid not. Emil says Mr. Villard wants the middle riverboats in place by the first of March. I told him if we get some heavy rains and a sizable runoff in late winter, as we usually do, I'd be willing to give it a try."

Busy on his Celilo-Lewiston run, Lars saw the rains come and the runoff begin in late January 1881. He heard that Captain Troup had decided to make the dangerous run in early February. As a matter of curiosity and an opportunity to gain more river-running experience, Lars would have been glad to go along, if invited, but was not in the least surprised that an invitation to be a guest pilot was not forthcoming. At best, a veteran captain such as Jim Troup needed no advice when running a river; at worst, the O.R.N. Company would not risk losing two seasoned steamboat captains in a single accident if a disaster did occur.

Since this was the first time a big stern-wheeler ever had been taken over Celilo Falls and down through what Lewis and Clark called the "Long Narrows," details of the run of the *Harvest Queen* soon became part of the legend of the river.

Leaving Celilo Landing a quarter-mile above the falls the morning of February 4, 1881, the *Queen* carried a large load of pitch-filled cordwood for the boiler furnaces, as well as a good supply of dimension lumber for repairs and bracing. Four carpenters, three mechanics, and half a dozen deckhands were aboard, in case emergency repairs must be made. Though the maximum October drop of twenty feet at the main falls had been smoothed out by runoff to six, plunging over the brink, Captain Troup told Lars, was like landing on concrete after dropping off a building.

"When she struck the water below the falls, both her rudders were ripped away. More than half the slats in the stern-wheel were so badly damaged the wheel fouled before we could stop the engines."

Lurching sideways completely out of control, the *Harvest Queen* broke a drive rod on her starboard engine, slewed across the channel into a rock, knocked a gaping hole in her hull, and filled two below-decks compartments with water. As she glanced off the rock, she shot across a sharp lava reef and smashed away a large section of her bow housing.

"I ordered an anchor dropped," Captain Troup said, "but the rush of the current parted the chain. Fortunately, the crew managed to rig a kedge, which held till the engineer could get the engine running on pillow blocks. With it working, we limped into an eddy where we could secure lines ashore, tie up, and make repairs."

The patching process took a week. With the worst of the hazards behind him now, Captain Troup resumed his record-setting trip through the turbulent waters of the Big and Little Dalles, at last reaching the broad, tranquil sector of the middle river on which the *Harvest Queen* was slated to serve.

Though running a big river steamer down both Celilo Falls and Cascades Rapids, as later was done by Captain James Troup and other pilots, never became a routine event without danger or risk, it did develop into something of an exact scientific operation which only a few qualified river captains were allowed to perform. One of the best of these practitioners was Captain John McNulty, who, a year after Captain Troup's run, set a record that would never be equaled.

Built at The Dalles in 1878 for the middle river run, the elegant *R. R. Thompson* was a big, luxurious boat designed to serve passengers who insisted on the best accommodations. Two hundred and fifteen feet in length with a thirty-eight-foot beam and a large freight deck, the *Thompson* boasted nicely fitted-out passenger facilities and a ladies' cabin furnished with quality carpeting, plush settees, and polished wood-paneled walls. Though not the fastest boat on the river, she was built for comfort and was described by travel agents of the day as a "palace boat" with the "finest cuisine afloat."

For four years, she proved herself to be the most popular boat on the middle river. But the 1882 completion of the south bank railroad east from Portland to Umatilla spelled doom for the luxury steamboat fleet, so one by one the stern-wheelers were brought down over the Cascades to the lower river.

By all odds, the rapids-running trip of the *R. R. Thompson* provided the most excitement. On June 3, 1882, under the command of Captain John McNulty, she left The Dalles at six-thirty in the morning. Running at full speed to the Upper Cascades, she reached the landing there in 121 minutes. This was an average of twenty-three miles an hour, quite respectable for a stern-wheeler designed for comfort and luxury rather than speed.

Pausing only briefly to survey the route ahead and alert the chief engineer that he intended to take the boat through the rapids as fast as it would go, Captain McNulty pointed the *Thompson*'s bow into the boiling current and rang for full speed ahead. Because the river was running in early summer flood, the rocks, ledges, and other navigational hazards were buried under heaving mountains of foam. Tearing through the twisting six miles of rapids in six minutes and forty seconds, the *Thompson*'s speed for the run was just under sixty miles an hour.

That record would never be matched.

A week later, when Captain James Troup was asked to bring another O.R.N. Company boat, the *Mountain Queen*, down through the Cascades Rapids, a locomotive pulling half a dozen passenger-filled cars along the south bank track was given a running start so that it could attempt to keep up with the speeding steamer. Even though the boat's time of eleven minutes was much slower than the run of the *Thompson*, the locomotive lost the race by three hundred yards.

Still later, in 1888, Captain Troup again was in the pilot house when the *Hassalo* made a serious attempt to beat the record set by the *R. R. Thompson*. Running the Cascades in late summer when the water was low, the channel narrow, and the rocks more dangerous, Captain Troup took the boat through the six-mile run in a flat seven minutes, only twenty seconds short of the record set by the *R. R. Thompson*.

15.

"When a railroad bridges a river," Captain Tommy Warren told Lars gloomily, "it's time for us to look for another line of work. Our day is done."

By 1885, two bridges had been completed across Snake River, one at Ainsworth, just above its juncture with the Columbia, and another at Riparia, halfway between its mouth and Lewiston. The Oregon Rail & Navigation Company, which had maintained its separate identity, did not go out of the steamboat business in the upper river country. But it came perilously close. Instead of constructing solid, low-level spans across the Snake, which would have blocked upstream navigation to Lewiston permanently, the railroads put in place swing-spans, which could be opened to permit the passage of steamboats and then closed for travel by trains.

How Emil Warren managed to persuade Henry Villard to keep a few stern-wheelers such as the *Inland Queen*, the *Annie Faxon*, the *Spokane*, and the *John Gates* on the Celilo-Lewiston run even after the completion of the rail lines and their bridges, Lars Warren did not know. It was fortunate he did, for on this stretch of river it soon was proved that the railroads could not replace water transport for either passengers or freight.

So far as passengers traveling west from Salt Lake were concerned, the change of trains at Umatilla could be endured if the traveler were headed for Spokane and points east. But if he were going to Lewiston, traveling on a clean, well-appointed stern-wheeler with an excellent dining room and bar, as well as a comfortable stateroom, was much more pleasant than riding on a jolting, cinder-choked, smelly day coach.

As for the movement of freight, wheat farmers in the Walla Walla Valley and the Palouse Hills found the railroads to be long on promise but short on fulfillment. Though a freight train could move wheat to market well enough when it got the empty cars to the right place at the right time, the two needs seldom were met. To their great annoyance, the farmer-shippers often found their sacks of grain piled in twelve-foot-high, quarter-mile-long rows at the railroad sidings, waiting in the sun, wind, and weather for the trains to haul them downriver to Portland. Since the farmer received no payment for his crop until it reached the marketplace, he was not happy with the delay.

As a consequence, every downriver-bound boat was laden with all the sacked wheat it could carry, with the farmer-shippers paying premium rates to put it aboard. Howls of protest from the inland country carried down the Snake and Columbia, through the Gorge, and were heard loud and clear in the Portland office of the O.R.N. Company by Emil Warren.

"We need more railroad cars in the Snake River country, Mr. Villard," Emil said. "And more boats."

"I know! I know! Bringing so many boats downriver was a mistake. I admit that. Fix it."

"Boats don't run rapids upriver, Sir."

"So build new ones where we need them. I'll see what I can do about getting more railroad cars."

What really was needed so far as transport on the Columbia River was concerned, Emil pointed out, was implementation of an "Open River" policy by the federal government, an improvement long advocated by the farmers and businessmen living east of the mountains. Since this would mean building locks and canals around both the Cascades and Celilo Falls, the project was so vast it could be undertaken only by the federal government. Busy with railroad-building at the moment, Henry Villard refused to get involved in it. "It's too political for me," he told Emil. "But if you want to develop it, go ahead."

"The first thing we'll need to do," Emil said, "is start the process by getting one foot in the door. Maybe a modest appropriation for a feasibility study by the Corps of Engineers would be the way to begin. I'll take a couple of Oregon congressmen to dinner ..."

In late May 1885, Lars Warren received a notice from the Portland office of the O.R.N. Company that Chief Joseph and his exiled band of Nez Perces were returning to the Pacific Northwest. They could be expected to arrive at Wallula Junction by rail within the week. As government wards, they were being escorted by federal troops, so he was instructed to give them special treatment.

Lately, regional newspapers had been filled with stories dealing with their plight—some sympathetic to them as innocent, long-suffering people, who had been greatly abused; others, as a band of bloodthirsty, murdering savages who still had not been punished enough for the crimes they had committed.

"Even their relatives who took no part in the war are bitter against them," Alex Conley told Lars. "They claim Chief Joseph and his band are responsible for all the misery brought to the Nez Perces who stayed on the reservation, so they deserve to suffer for what they've done."

"How many people are being returned?"

"Three hundred or so. Some will go back to the reservation in Idaho, I understand. The rest will go to the Moses Reservation."

"Who decides which individuals go where?"

"The Indian agent, I suppose."

According to tales told by the Indian grapevine, Alex said, the personal invitation to Chief Joseph from Chief Moses to come and live in his country had been crucial in obtaining government permission for the return of the exiles. Once the decision had been made, the question arose: How will the whites who lost relatives, friends, and property during the war react to having the Indian dissidents as neighbors again? Since Joseph had been given so much publicity, he was regarded as the worst criminal, with indictments against him in many communities.

Still hoping to go back to the Wallowa area and sure that if he went to Lapwai he would lose all chances of returning to his ancestral homeland, Chief Joseph accepted the invitation from his friend Chief Moses to go to the Colville Reservation. He and the other warriors against whom feeling ran high in Idaho would go to Colville, while the Indians with relatives and friends on the Lapwai reserve would go there, hoping that their family ties would protect them from white vengeance.

Dr. W. H. Faulkner, a physician and special agent for the U.S. Indian office, was put in charge of the transfer. Though he was sympathetic toward the Indians, he proved to be just as impatient as General Howard had been eight years earlier when it came to setting a deadline for their move.

"Faulkner arrived at the Agency May 5 to find the Indians not yet ready to depart," a reporter wrote. "Agent Scott judged it would take two weeks before they could possibly dispose of their stock. In spite of this, the doctor told Joseph he expected his people to leave Friday May 21, ready or not, and make preparations accordingly. The Nez Perces were thus forced to dispose of their animals quickly and cheaply."

A few days before departure, Dr. Faulkner did permit the Nez Perces to take time off from their preparations to visit the graves of relatives who had died during the stay of the exiles in this unhealthy land. One of Chief Joseph's daughters was among those who had succumbed to the diseases that had reduced the tribe's numbers by more than one-half while in exile.

"Before daybreak on May 21 the Indians were awakened and put to tearing down the tipis before starting over the prairie for Arkansas City, where they would board a train," the reporter wrote. "A fine mist began falling. Then came rain, which drizzled steadily through the day. There was not room enough in the wagons, so the men plodded in the mud. Women walked with their men all the twenty-five miles made that day."

Reaching Arkansas City, Kansas, at midnight the second day, the sodden, weary refugees were loaded into the "emigrant sleeping cars" of the Atchison, Topeka and Santa Fe Railroad the next morning. Joining them were a number of bewildered children who had been attending the Chilloco Indian School, some of whom had been so frightened at the prospect of riding on a train that they had tried to hide under their beds at the boarding school. Yellow Bull, who had not expected the children to be released, was so overwhelmed with joy that he rushed up with tears in his eyes to thank Dr. Faulkner.

The journey took five days. Reaching McPherson, Kansas, at nine o'clock the first night, the 35,000 pounds of baggage and the three hundred Indians were transferred to a Union Pacific train.

"The doctor was aware of what seemed to be a thousand curious folks crowding around for a glimpse of Joseph and his Indians. By midnight, they were ready to roll out on the Union Pacific through Denver, Colorado, and Cheyenne, Wyoming, to Pocatello, Idaho."

The trip was not an easy one. For rations the Indians carried 2,000 pounds of hard bread, 160 pounds of sugar, 2,498 pounds of precooked beef, and 140 pounds of coffee, prepared during various stops when the travelers could get off the train, build a fire outside, and brew it.

At Pocatello, railroad officials started making preparations to divide the train, sending the Indians bound for the Colville Reservation north to Butte, then west to Spokane over the Utah Northern and Northern Pacific lines. Those headed for Lapwai would take the Union Pacific northwest to Wallula Junction. While the route to be taken mattered little to most of the returning exiles, Chief Joseph must have known that the first ran through the country of their bitter enemies, the Bannocks, crossing their retreat trail just a few miles west of the Camas Meadows site where the Nez Perces had inflicted a stinging defeat on General Howard and his Bannock allies, while the second led to the former site of the long-vanished trading post named after their tribe, Fort Nez Perces, now called Wallula, a Nez Perce word meaning "mouth of the waters."

Dr. Faulkner refused to let the railroad crew divide the train, saying that his orders were to take the entire band through to Wallula Junction before separating it. Going into the telegraph office and wiring the Indian Bureau for further instructions at seven o'clock that evening, he was joined by Captain Frank D. Baldwin, Fifth Infantry, who was serving as judge advocate on General Miles's staff.

"A lot of white people in Idaho and Montana are after Joseph's scalp," he warned Dr. Faulkner. "I urge you to keep your Indians together and move them on as fast as possible."

"Won't the Army protect them?"

"We'll certainly try. But feeling against Joseph and his people has been mounting steadily in this part of the country. Already a dozen indictments for murder have been issued against Joseph. A United States marshal will be in Pocatello tomorrow morning, I've been told, prepared to serve a warrant that will put Joseph behind bars."

"Surely he can't do that!"

"Legally, no. But he may try. My advice to you, Sir, is to keep your Indians moving."

As a crowd of increasingly hostile people began gathering around the train, Dr. Faulkner was more fearful than Chief Joseph, who remained stoically calm. Deciding to take Captain Baldwin's advice, Dr. Faulkner got railroad agent Morse to agree to take all the Indians together as far as Wallula Junction. Without waiting for an answer to his telegram to the Indian Bureau, the doctor ordered the train to roll early the next morning.

After crossing the flat, sage-covered plains of southern Idaho

Territory at the breathtaking speed of forty miles an hour; picking up a company of 3rd Infantry, commanded by Captain Dempsey, as protection en route at Fort Boise; making the long, twisting climb over northeastern Oregon's Blue Mountains within sight of the south slope of Chief Joseph's beloved Wallowa Mountains; winding down the western side of the Blues through the Umatilla Indian Reservation; then turning north to the Columbia and Washington Territory; the well-traveled Indians reached Wallula Junction on May 27, 1885.

Waiting for them there was Charles E. Monteith, agent in charge of the Lapwai Reservation, whose administration for the past several years had been turned over to the Presbyterian church in the hope that a religious order would be less corrupt and better able to educate the Indians than the graft-filled military regime which formerly had been in charge of the reserve.

Although Lars and Daphne Warren had a formal nodding acquaintance with Charles Monteith, who was a lay worker in the Presbyterian church, they had not invited him to stay in their home following his arrival in Wallula the day before. A generation ago, the competition be tween Catholics and Presbyterians for Indian souls had been one of the causes of the Whitman Massacre, Lars had been told. While the conflict between the two religions was less openly bitter now, ecumenical peace had not yet filtered down to the level where a good Catholic family could be expected to house a rigid Presbyterian under its roof when there was a commercial hotel such as the Wallula Palace available.

After talking to several of his refugee friends among the Nez Perces, Alex Conley told Lars that the Indians took it for granted that the returning band would be divided.

"Agent Monteith will decide which are good or bad Indians by making them answer just one question."

"What's that?"

"Do you want to go to Lapwai and be Christian or go to Colville and be yourself?"

"I'm not sure I understand that."

"That's how Chief Joseph's nephew, Yellow Wolf, put it to me. What it means is that the returning Nez Perces who will agree to cut their hair, give up their horses, and accept the Presbyterian religion will be permitted to go to the Lapwai Reservation. Those who keep their braids, their horses, and their beliefs in the old, heathen ways must go to the Colville Reservation."

Only seventeen years old when the war began, Yellow Wolf had proved himself to be an outstanding fighter during the conflict. Since then, he had become Chief Joseph's most loyal follower, taking the place of *Ollokut*, Chief Joseph's younger warrior brother, who had been called "leader of the young men" until killed during the final battle.

Though no written instructions to that effect were ever publicized, Yellow Wolf apparently had it right, Alex said, for the Nez Perces chosen to go to the Lapwai Reservation in Idaho were all part of the Christian group, while those selected to go with Joseph to Colville belonged to the wild band. The Colville contingent was slated to travel by train to Ainsworth, Riparia, and Spokane, from which city they would go by wagon west to the Moses Reservation. The Indians headed for Lapwai would be taken aboard the *Inland Queen*, then transported up the Snake to Lewiston.

After breakfast the next morning, the three hundred returned Nez Perce exiles assembled on the sandy flat just above the river, listening with hushed, respectful attention as Chief Joseph addressed them for what they knew would be the last time. Though Lars could not understand the words of Chief Joseph's brief farewell to the relatives and friends he might never see again, Alex translated them for him.

"I am not going back to my home country in the Land of the Winding Waters," Joseph said quietly. "Someday I hope to do so, for that is where the bones of my father and mother lie buried. Instead, I am going to the land of my brother, Chief Moses. There, he promises me, I may live in peace. If I go to the Lapwai Reservation now, my own people may fight me. I do not want that to happen. I have had enough of war. Goodbye, my people. Go home in peace. Let no more blood be shed in our land."

After the train carrying the band headed for Colville pulled out, the contingent bound for Lapwai on the *Inland Queen* filed aboard under the stern, watchful eye of Agent Charles Monteith. Standing in the pilot house beside Lars, Daphne Warren held the hand of their four-year-old daughter, Sara Jane, a worried frown on her face as she gazed down at the slim figure of their nine-year-old daughter, Lily, whose gleaming, golden hair stood out in sharp contrast to the heads of the black-haired Indians shuffling aboard in single file. In her newly created role of assistant purser, she was checking them off one by one on a form attached to the clipboard in her hand.

"Do you really have to take Lily along on this trip, Lars?" Daphne asked petulantly. "Making her associate with these sad, miserable people will depress her terribly."

"She'd be hurt if I didn't take her along, Daphne. As a member of the crew, she knows it's her duty to go."

"Oh, Lars, that's just a title you gave her as an excuse to let her ride on the boat! How can she be a crew member when she's only nine years old?"

"I was drawing a crew member's pay when I went up the Snake at the same age, dear. I earned my pay. So will she."

Feeling a small hand tugging at his, Lars stooped, picked up Sara Jane, and held her so that she could see what was going on below. In contrast to Lily, who was blue-eyed and blonde—like Lars and his mother, Freda—Sara Jane had black hair and eyes—like her mother, Daphne, and grandmother, Lili. Apparently destined to grow up with a more conventional interest in dolls and feminine things than her older sister, Lily, who cared only for engines, steamboats, and objects in the masculine world of her father, Sara Jane gave her mother far fewer causes for concern than Lily did.

"Sooner or later, you've got to tell Lily that her dream of becoming a steamboat captain is just that—a dream," Daphne said firmly. "Since she's not a boy, she's got to stop acting like one."

"I have told her, dear. Many times. The problem is convincing her."

"Well, you've just got to bring her to her senses."

"The last time I told her, I suggested she give serious consideration to the fact that her parents, the Oregon Rail & Navigation Company, and the good Lord who created her all agree that being a steamboat captain is not an acceptable job for a lady."

"What was her answer to that?"

"She said her parents and the Oregon Rail & Navigation Company may be against lady steamboat captains. But until she hears otherwise from God, she doesn't believe that He objects."

Kissing his wife and youngest daughter goodbye and then sending them ashore, Lars ordered the lines cast off and took the *Inland Queen* out into the river. Truth to tell, he mused, Lily was proving to be as quick a learner in the ways of a river as he had been when forced to swim every rapid in the Snake with Willie Gray twenty-five years ago. A wiry, well-muscled, nimble girl, Lily was eager to learn all there was to know about running a boat in all kinds of water. From the engine room to the freight deck to the fore and aft docking lines to the pilot house and the wheel, she had observed, imitated, and helped in all the tasks that needed doing from the first day she had come aboard. Instead of regarding her as a pest who must be treated well because she was the captain's daughter, every officer and crew member aboard the *Inland Queen* looked on Lily Warren as their protegé and pet.

While the boat was laying to at the mouth of the Snake eleven miles up the Columbia, waiting for the Ainsworth swing-span bridge to open, Lily climbed up to the pilot house, knocked on the door as she had been taught to do, then entered when Lars invited her in.

"Here's a copy of the passenger list, Sir. It's been checked and approved by Mr. Monteith and Purser Wykoff."

"The numbers are all I'm interested in, Lily. Can you give them to me?"

"Yes, Sir. Ninety-two adults, twelve children, and fourteen infants have come aboard. They are carrying their own rations, Mr. Monteith says, so we won't have to feed them."

"Very good, Lily. That's a fine report."

As the bridge swung open and the *Inland Queen* began to churn its way against the current of the Snake, Lily gazed down with concern at the mass of listless, travel-weary Indians huddled in apathetic groups on the deck below, her bright blue eyes warm with sympathy.

"What awful things did those people do, Father, that they should be made to suffer so?"

"Well, to begin with, they objected to being put on a reservation ..."

"Didn't they want to live with their own people?"

"They *were* living with their own people in the Wallowa country, Lily. They wanted to stay there. But when trouble broke out between Indians and whites in other parts of the West, the federal government told the Wallowa Nez Perces it could take better care of them if they moved to the Lapwai Reservation in Idaho."

"But they wouldn't go?"

"They started to go. Even though Chief Joseph hated to leave the Wallowa country, he was too intelligent a leader to involve his people in a war they could not win. But when his band was only a day's travel from the reservation, a few rash young bucks killed some white men for what they thought was just cause. In retaliation, a company of federal troops attacked the Indians in White Bird Canyon, got badly whipped, and a long, brutal war began."

"How long ago did this happen?"

"The war began in June and ended in early October 1877. The survivors were taken to the Indian Nations down in Oklahoma, where they've been held as prisoners ever since. Over half of them died of malaria and other diseases, I've been told, for the Nations is not a healthy country for mountain-bred Indians."

Her eyes sad and brooding as she stared down at the ragged, blanket-wrapped figures on the deck below, Lily shook her head in bewilderment. "Why did our government do such a terrible thing, Father? I thought it was supposed to protect people."

"They're Indians, Lily. For some government officials, that's reason enough to mistreat them."

"It's wrong, Father! Alex is an Indian. He's one of your best friends and the nicest person I know."

"He's a civilized Indian, Lily, who's doing his best to live like a white man. Chief Joseph and his people are wild Indians, who want to live free."

"Why should that make a difference in the way the government treats them?"

"I don't know. But it does."

"Why?"

Patting his daughter on the shoulder, Lars said gently, "That's a question I can't answer, Lily. Being an Indian and well acquainted with Chief Joseph, maybe Alex can. Why don't you run down and have a talk with him?"

Though she was too considerate of Alex Conley's feelings to ask him why he was trying to live like a civilized Indian while Chief Joseph and his band of Nez Perces were not, Lily did question him as to his reasons for wanting to become an engineer on a white man's boat. Now in his mid-thirties, clean-shaven, his black hair cut short, proudly wearing the blue serge uniform of the O.R.&N. Company with the gold-braid emblem of crossed oil cans shining on the left sleeve, Chief Engineer Alex Conley bore little resemblance to the bedraggled, listless Nez Perce refugees lounging on the lower deck. Removing his cap and holding it on his lap as he sat beside Lily Warren on a bench just outside the open door of the engine room at the stern of the boat, where he could hear and quickly respond to a missed beat, he gave her questions grave, thoughtful attention.

"Why did I become an engineer, Lily? Because my father was one. He taught the skills of his trade to me."

"His name is Sitkum, isn't it?"

"That's right. He became an engineer on Captain Tommy Warren's boat, just as I later did on the boat of your father, Captain Lars Warren."

"Did your father learn to be an engineer from his father?"

"No, Lily. When his father—whose name was Conco—was young, there were no steamboats on the lower Columbia. There were only sailing ships. In those days, it was a tradition among my grandfather's people, the Chinook Indians, to meet ships out to sea beyond the mouth of the Columbia River and pilot them in across the bar. That was how your great-grandfather, Captain Benjamin Warren, and my grandfather, Conco, met and became friends."

"I've heard that they were the first bar pilots on the lower Columbia. Father is very proud of that."

"So am I. We should both be proud, too, Lily, that my father and your grandfather served as assistant engineer and second mate aboard the *Beaver*, which was the first steamboat on the lower Columbia back in 1836."

"Since almost all the men in the Warren family have been sailing ship or riverboat captains," Lily said pensively, "I can understand how they could change from sail to steam when the time came. But for you and your father, becoming an engineer on a riverboat must have been something entirely new and hard to learn. I don't know how you managed to do it so quickly and so well."

"It was the most natural thing in the world to us," Alex said with a smile. "You see, it was what our *tah-mah-na-wis* told us to do."

"Your what?"

"*Tah-mah-na-wis* is an Indian word, Lily, whose meaning is hard to explain. Fate, destiny, magic, guardian spirit, a quiet voice inside a person telling him: 'This is what you must do.' When it speaks, we listen."

"Is it ever wrong?"

"Never, Lily. But if a person does not heed it, he will be unhappy the rest of his life."

"Can a woman have a *tah-mah-na-wis?*"

"Certainly. Why do you ask?"

Giving Alex a quick sidelong glance, then turning her gaze back to the white-water wake being churned up by the threshing stern-wheel, Lily gave a despondent sigh.

"Because I think I've got one. But don't tell Father I told you about it. Promise?"

"I promise, Lily. What is it telling you to do?"

"It's saying loud and clear that when I grow up I've got to be a steamboat captain, even though my father, mother, the Oregon Rail & Navigation Company, and maybe even God agree that I won't be allowed to be one. What do I say to my *tah-mah-na-wis* about that?"

"Nothing," Alex said gently. "Just listen to what it says to you ..."

Meanwhile, the Chief Joseph band of refugees continued on by train to Spokane Falls, Alex learned later from the Indian grapevine, then went by wagons sixty-five miles west to Fort Spokane, which was adjacent to the Colville Reservation. In the group were 120 adults, including Chief Joseph and Yellow Bull, who was second in command; sixteen children; and fourteen infants.

Fearing a loss of business because of his presence in the area, merchants in the town of Colville, just outside the reservation, called Joseph a "large, fat-faced, scheming cruel-looking cuss" and members of his band "thieves, murderers, and demons," subscribing to the theory that "the very best Indians are those planted beneath the roses."

From his behavior under extremely trying circumstances during the past month, it was doubtful that Dr. Faulkner would have agreed with that indictment of his wards. Officially, his responsibility had ended when the exiles reached Spokane Falls. However, he was so concerned for the Indians, many of whom were ill, that he traveled along with them to Fort Spokane and personally delivered the sick to the post surgeon.

Chief Joseph's band had come home, too.

16.

THROUGH ALEX CONLEY and the Indian grapevine, Lars Warren followed the fortunes of the returned exiles in their new home on the upper Columbia River with considerable interest. A strange friendship existed between Moses and Joseph, Alex told him. Some ten years older than Joseph, Chief Moses was officially recognized as the leader of five Salish tribes: the Wenatchees, Entiats, Chelans, Methows, and Okanogans. He also claimed he was head chief of the San Poils, Nespelems, and Colvilles, though certain leaders among those tribes—such as the badly crippled San Poil chief Skolaskin—violently rejected his authority.

First established by Executive Order in 1872, with its boundaries modified in 1879, 1880, and again in 1884, the Colville Reservation lay between the Columbia and Okanogan Rivers, extending north to the Canadian line. It was a large reserve, with plenty of good water, grass, and timber. Eventually, fragments of seventeen tribes of Plateau Indians were placed on the reservation. Chief Moses was their principal spokesman.

Though circumstances dictated that they be friends, Joseph and Moses had totally different personalities. Joseph was soft-spoken and dignified, drank nothing stronger than sugared coffee, and was content with two wives. Moses was loud and talkative, loved his toddy, and usually had at least five wives. On one occasion when asked how many children he had, he thought for a few moments, then shook his head and admitted he had lost track.

When a Catholic priest sent word to him that he must put aside all but one of his wives, Moses asked Agent Gwydir if the priest had a wife. Gwydir told him that the priest was not allowed to have a wife. Moses thought that over, then said, "Tell the Blackrobe that I will give him one of my wives if he will keep his mouth shut."

At first the Nez Perces were placed across the Columbia from Fort

Spokane, so that they could be protected from the soldiers, who, it was feared, would ravish the women, and from Moses, whose drinking and gambling habits would do them no good.

Poorly clad, badly sheltered, and provided with insufficient food, the returned exiles were confronted with the hostility of the San Poils, into whose living space they had intruded. Calling Moses's and Joseph's people "murderers and horse thieves," Skolaskin launched such a violent attack on the government for placing the Nez Perces in San Poil territory that Joseph asked that he and his people be permitted to move fifty miles west to the Nespelem valley.

Moses was delighted with the decision. But when Joseph and 132 Nez Perces rode into their valley, the Nespelems greeted them with unconcealed hostility. As had happened in Indian Territory down in Oklahoma, the Nez Perces once again were being imposed upon a band of Indians who did not want to share their living space with strangers. Because indifferent agents let two years pass before supplying seed grain and farming tools, they were wholly dependent upon the federal government for rations. Some of the impoverished exiles desperately tried to replace the horses they had been forced to sell in Indian Territory by betting blankets issued them for warmth against Nespelem ponies in gambling games.

Even if they had wanted to become farmers—which they did not—they would have found it impossible. What tillable land existed in the area already was occupied by the Nespelems, who refused to share it. In an effort to keep the Nez Perces at home and force them to farm land they did not have with tools that had not yet arrived, the agent issued an order requiring all Indians to have permits before leaving the reservation—an order completely ignored by the Nez Perces. Yet so dependent had they become upon the government for food that when several of them went to Lapwai for an extended visit with relatives, Chief Joseph sent his nephew, Yellow Wolf, with a message urging them to come back to Nespelem in time to get their share of a beef issue.

Now past sixty and the most senior of the Oregon Rail & Navigation pilots, Captain Tommy Warren—who had gloomily told his son, Captain Lars Warren, that when railroads bridged a river or built lines along its banks the days of steamboat men were done—had reason to modify that prediction during the bitter-cold month of January 1886. The cause of his attitude change was his being asked to assist Captain Kenneth Manning, master of the iron-hulled side-wheeler *Olympian*, in the rescue of the passengers on a snowbound train which had become marooned in the Columbia Gorge near Hood River.

"When Henry Villard makes a mistake," Emil Warren told Tommy in the Portland office of the O.R.& N. Company before asking him to participate in the rescue effort, "it's never a small one. For two years those iron-hulled boats he had built back in Delaware and put in service on the West Coast have been white elephants. Now maybe one of them can redeem herself."

The two craft conceived by Villard in what most steamboat men declared a complete lapse of common sense were the *Olympian* and her sister ship, the *Alaskan*. Both were iron-hulled side-wheelers of magnificent proportions. The *Olympian* was 262 feet long and 40 feet wide, while the *Alaskan* was 14 feet longer. The *Olympian* arrived in Puget Sound in 1884, Emil told Tommy, and was put in service on the Tacoma-Victoria run under the Oregon Rail & Navigation Company flag.

"She's really something to write home about, Tommy. She's got incandescent lights, mahogany tables in a 200-foot-long main saloon, plush furniture, and the finest Wilton velvet carpet money can buy. Each of her fifty staterooms is fitted with polished mirrors and ornate washstands. Some of the staterooms have brass bedsteads instead of berths.

"She's rated at 1,400 tons; her dining saloon seats 130 people; she has fancy glass chandeliers and an ebony trimmed grand staircase. She looks elegant and expensive—and she is."

"She lost money on Puget Sound, I take it?"

"Tons of it. So Mr. Villard told me to bring her down to the Columbia and see what I could do with her here. Since she draws nine feet of water, the only place I could put her in service was on the Portland-Astoria run. She hasn't lost quite as much money there—still, she's dropped a bundle. Now we're hoping she can give the O.R.& N. Company some positive publicity by saving the passengers on a snowbound train."

On January 22, a massive blizzard had struck the Gorge just west of Hood River, paralyzing both rail and boat traffic. Because of unusually low temperatures earlier in the month, the Columbia River had been frozen over solid from bank to bank during the past two weeks, making the river impassable to wooden-hulled boats. Massive drifts of snow now covered the O.R.&N. tracks along the south bank rail line, bringing all traffic to a standstill.

Upon reaching Hood River two mornings ago, the westbound Pacific Express had been halted and ordered to remain there while means were sought to rescue her passengers and those expected on the following trains.

"Captain Manning has plenty of experience piloting the *Olympian*," Emil told Tommy. "But he doesn't know the river between Portland and Hood River nearly as well as you do. With his boat's iron hull and power, she ought to be able to break through the ice if you can guide her into a channel more than nine feet deep so she won't run aground."

"That I can do."

Since it was past noon on the cold, cloudy, late January day before Tommy went aboard the boat and it got under way from the Portland dock, darkness was falling by the time the *Olympian* had moved down the Willamette River to its mouth, then turned east and started fighting its way up the ice-choked channel of the Columbia. Tying up for the night just below Vancouver, the *Olympian* resumed its rescue attempt at seven-thirty the next morning, finding the river frozen over so solidly from its surface to its bottom that it was forced to act like a gigantic chisel, ramming its sharp, iron-clad bow into the unyielding pack ice time and again until its forward progress was halted, backing up, then charging and forcing itself atop the ice until its weight broke it apart and opened a narrow channel up which it could steam.

As they stood in the pilot house while the big metal buckets of the side-wheels churned fragmented chunks of ice astern with a deafening din, Captain Kenneth Manning shouted to Captain Tommy Warren, "It's like chopping up blocks for an icehouse with a fourteen hundred-ton wedge! How far upriver do we have to go?"

"Forty miles!" Tommy yelled back. "Do you think she'll hold together that long?"

"God knows! But we'll keep trying till she rams her way through or falls apart!"

Hour by hour, the big iron-hulled *Olympian* made slow progress, the chopping action of her side-wheel buckets breaking up the floes so that the sluggish current could carry the shards of ice downstream.

Ten miles above Vancouver, the boat nearly met disaster when a huge section of what appeared to be a solid sheet of river ice suddenly broke loose and started floating downstream, taking the boat with it.

"It was like the whole surface length of the Gorge had given way," Tommy told Emil later, "with the boat caught in the middle, leaving her helpless. For nearly an hour and a half she was carried back downriver until she was thrown into an eddy below the sandbar upstream from Vancouver, where she lodged against solid ice."

Though both bow and stern anchors were put out, they failed to hold, with the eddy itself finally keeping the boat in place, where it remained during the night. By morning, the bulk of the loosened ice floe had moved on downriver to such an extent that Captain Manning judged it safe to try again.

By mid-afternoon, the *Olympian* had managed to buck her way through ice jams at Fisher's Landing, Rooster Rock, and Cape Horn. By evening, she had made it to Dodson's Fish Wheel Landing, four miles below Bonneville, which was where the Lower Cascades Rapids began. Learning that a short distance upstream, ice was piled up twenty feet above the surface of the river, Tommy told Captain Manning it was useless to attempt going any farther.

"We're about ten miles west of where the train is stalled," he said. "One way or another, the marooned passengers will have to find their way to us. There's no way we can go to them."

"The railroad's superintendent has sixty-five laborers aboard the boat," Captain Manning said, nodding agreement. "I'll tell him it's time to put them to work."

On the morning of January 28, the trains stalled at Hood River and The Dalles were ordered to try to reach Dodson's Fish Wheel Landing. Working feverishly in the bitter cold, the sixty-five husky axemen, whose usual task was clearing brush for right-of-way, slashed a path through the tangle of bushes and trees from the riverbank where the side-wheeler lay to the railroad track. By ten o'clock that morning, 175 grateful passengers, along with mail and freight, had been transferred to the *Olympian.*

Taking on food and drink in the toasty-warm comfort of the dining room and bar, the men and women rescued from the snowbound train vied with one another in telling blizzard and ice stories that in time to come would take their place among the legends of the river. Along the quiet stretches of the Columbia between Hood River and

The Dalles, one passenger said, the ice had been eleven feet thick, capable of supporting heavily laden wagons and teams of horses as they crossed back and forth between Oregon and Washington Territory.

In the heart of the Gorge, another traveler related, Bridal Veil, Horse Tail, and Multnomah Falls, whose two-thousand-foot drop off the sheer lava bluffs lining the Oregon side of the river never before had been stilled, had become unmoving, massive icicles. Even the oldest of the local Indians, the passenger claimed, had never seen that sight before.

Adding spice to an experience none of the passengers would ever forget was the fact that they had been rescued by and now were completing their journey on one of the most luxurious riverboats they had ever seen, courtesy of the O.R.&N. Company.

Now that a channel through the ice floes had been broken by the iron-hulled *Olympian*, enough open water ran in the center of the river to let the boat steam at flank speed down to the mouth of the Willamette, then back upstream to Portland. Pulling in to the Ash Street dock at 3:40 P.M., Captain Kenneth Manning discharged the boat's grateful passengers, then, accompanied by his guest pilot, Captain Tommy Warren, got into a rowboat and circled the craft to see how much damage had been done to it during the rescue venture. So far as either of them could see, the *Olympian* had lost a little paint during its ordeal, nothing more.

The next day, with Tommy still aboard, the iron-hulled craft returned upriver with passengers and mail for the East. On January 30, the weather moderated, snowplows cleared the tracks through the Gorge, and normal rail service was resumed. When the boat docked at the Portland wharf this time, Tommy was surprised to see his younger brother, Emil Warren, standing at the gangplank exit with a pleased smile on his face as he handed out a printed flyer to each and every passenger debarking.

"Hi, Tommy!" Emil exclaimed, handing both him and Captain Manning a flyer as they stepped ashore. "Behold how I've made you famous!"

Facing each other in three-quarter profile shots at the top of the flyer were photo likenesses of Captain Manning and Captain Warren, with a picture of the *Olympian* between them. Below this was a sketch of a snowbound train trapped in the depths of the Gorge near the base of a frozen waterfall. Following a few lines of standard-sized print describing the rescue effort just concluded, several big black words declared:

NEXT TRIP, TAKE A BOAT!

Valiant though Emil Warren's effort to promote travel on Mr. Villard's white elephant had been, it generated more praise than profit. Anxious to make something out of the *Olympian*, Villard chartered her out to a company in the Alaska trade, where her experience as an ice-breaker might be of some value. Again a money-loser, she soon was back in his hands. Having no other use for her, he sent her to the Portland boneyard for abandoned ships, where she languished for several years. Finally, the bedraggled old queen was sold for a meager sum to a company which decided to take her back around the Horn and put her in service as a resort boat on the East Coast.

Exactly what happened to her during the trip, Emil Warren never learned. But in some manner or other she ran aground in the Straits of Magellan, the land of perpetual snow and ice, and was heard from no more.

17.

Ever since *Speelyi*, the Coyote Spirit who had created this part of the world ten thousand snows ago, laid out the course of what Alex Conley's people called the *Chiawana* and the whites the Columbia, the 1,250-mile-long river had flowed without hindrance from its source high in the Canadian Rockies to its 4-mile-wide mouth between the states of Oregon and Washington, where it melded its waters with those of the Pacific Ocean. Although the natives of this vast watershed would never have dreamed of altering the flow of the great river, the brash white newcomers to the Pacific Northwest had no compunctions whatsoever against changing what *Speelyi* had wrought.

Washington became a state in 1889, joining the Union of which Oregon had been a member for thirty years. Flexing their joint political muscles, the two states immediately set in motion measures aimed at improving on what until then the natives of the region had accepted as a perfectly satisfactory river. During the next few years, Lars Warren learned, three major projects aimed at enhancing what *Speelyi* had designed got under way: an improved ship channel across the bar outside the mouth of the river; locks and a ship canal in the Columbia Gorge; a river shortcut near the headwaters.

Of the three projects, Lars, like most river captains, approved the first and second, which were being funded by the federal government, while he and they considered the third one, which was being undertaken by private capital, a piece of utter nonsense.

Near the headwaters of the Columbia at the base of the spectacular Selkirk Mountains up in Canada, proponents of the third project claimed *Speelyi* had made a horrendous mistake by having the Columbia flow north, then west, and then south again in an elongated oval three hundred miles long. The river's only reason for doing this was that its waters were obeying the law of gravity, the improvers said, but they could correct that. By cutting directly west across a mile-and-a-half-wide hump of land, the river could save itself three hundred miles of pointless travel through useless, uninhabited mountain wilderness, which would allow it to reach the United States much sooner than it did now.

"What the company plans to do," Lars told Alex, "is dig a canal that will connect the Kootenai River east of the divide with Columbia Lake west of the mountains. Once the project is finished, they say, boats can operate on whichever sector of river offers the most freight traffic."

"How many boats are running up there now?"

"So far as I can tell, the number fluctuates between two and none. But the developers say that if they dig the canal, traffic will come."

As time passed, tales drifting down from Canada ranged from odd to incredible. During the next few years, two steamboats—the *Duchess* and the *Clive*—were built at Golden, British Columbia, on the east side of the divide, Lars heard, though neither was worthy of the name. Put together out of scraps left over from an abandoned Canadian Pacific Railway sawmill, no two boards in the *Duchess* were the same thickness, travelers who saw the vessel reported. Her cabin looked like an enlarged privy, with the captain and steering apparatus of the boat sitting in a small penthouse on top. Propulsion was supplied by an undersized paddle wheel turned by an engine salvaged from a St. Lawrence River ferryboat originally built in 1840.

But ugly as she was, the *Duchess* reigned alone on the upper Columbia for two years until the even less handsome *Clive* arrived to provide competition. Originally built as a pile-driving scow, the *Clive*'s hull was a square, flat-bottomed barge which had been abandoned by the railroad. The same sawmill that had provided parts for the *Duchess* had been picked over for equipment installed in the engine room. Steam was produced by an upright boiler from a Manitoba corncob-fired steam plough, while the engine had been salvaged from a long-defunct river tug.

"So far as the paddle wheel goes," one critic commented, "it's more useful in identifying the stern of the boat than in driving it through the water. On one trip, I was told, the *Clive* took twenty-three days to travel one hundred miles between Golden and Columbia Lake—a lot of it sideways before a strong wind."

Nevertheless, the Canal Flats Company managed to obtain the necessary government permits, form a syndicate in England, sell stock, and raise enough money to start moving dirt. Completed in 1889, what was called the Baillie-Grohman Canal, in honor of its builder, was 6,700 feet long and 45 feet wide, with a 10-foot-high wooden lift lock 100 by 30 feet. But for four years following the canal's completion, the only thing that moved between the two sectors of now-connected river was a small amount of seepage water.

Finally, in 1893, a boat named the *Gwendoline* did use the canal, though from what Lars heard of its first trip it was truly a "dry run." Built on the Kootenai River on the east side of the divide, the boat steamed to Canal Flats, found the locks in such a state of disrepair that they could not be used, then decided to cross the isthmus anyway, even if by traveling on dry land. After being partially dismantled, the boat was put on rollers and dragged over an improvised road to the lower sector of the Columbia. This feat impressed the Canadian government so favorably that it agreed to spend enough money to put the canal and locks back in working condition. When this task had been done, the *Gwendoline* fired up her boilers, entered the west end of the canal, and then steamed triumphantly through to the east end, thus theoretically saving herself a journey of two hundred miles.

Dramatic though the two-way trip had been, it did not stimulate steamboat travel on the upper Columbia or increase use of the canal. In fact, eight years passed before the canal carried a steamboat on its surface again. But that passage was a spectacular one.

Built in Jennings, Montana, in 1897 for the Kootenai River trade, the *North Star* was purchased by Captain Frank Armstrong, who planned to put her in service on the Columbia near Trail, British Columbia, as an ore-hauling boat. With good and sufficient reasons to try the shortcut, he decided to take the canal. But when he and his boat reached its eastern entrance, he was chagrined to find it badly silted in. Going ashore and pacing off the length of the old wooden locks, he found them to be thirty feet shorter than his boat. As a further complication to his using the canal, he discovered that a low-level bridge with no draw span had been built across the midpoint of the canal at Dutch Creek for the benefit of local road travel.

No matter. He would use the canal anyway.

"What Captain Armstrong did," a steamboat man who had witnessed the incredible operation told Lars, "was dig out the entrance to the canal and work his boat in as far as the locks. Since the wood was pretty rotten anyway, he had no trouble tearing out the lower gates, which he replaced with enough sand-filled ore sacks to create a pond that would float the North Star.

"Getting up a good head of steam, Captain Armstrong had his crew fire off a dynamite charge just before the boat reached the dam, letting it dive through on the crest. At Dutch Creek, a little farther on, he rigged a derrick on the bow of the boat, hoisted the bridge out of the way, passed through, then carefully replaced it."

Sad to say, despite all his ingenuity and labor, Captain Armstrong saw his plans come to naught, for the *North Star* had too deep a draft to operate on the lower sector of the Columbia except in high water. Furthermore, Canadian Customs officials decreed that since the boat had been built in the United States and no duty had been paid on its importation, it must be laid up until the appropriate taxes were paid. Feeling no taxes were due on a boat producing no revenue, Captain Armstrong took it out of service. For some years thereafter, when the would-be tax collectors were not looking, he stripped it of usable parts which he transferred to his other boats. Eventually, nothing remained of the original *North Star* except its hull, which was converted into two nameless, untaxed barges.

Though the silt- and weed-filled scar across what came to be known as Canal Flats would remain for many years as physical evidence of man's efforts to correct a mistake made by *Speelyi*, the upper Columbia boat canal would be used no more …

So far as the locks and canal now being built in the Columbia Gorge were concerned, Captain Lars Warren could date the ebb and flow of interest in that project by the birth date of his oldest daughter, Lily, in 1875, and her present age in 1891, sixteen. Pressured by upriver shippers who had long resented the extra freight charges they must pay to have their products portaged fourteen miles at Celilo Falls and six miles at the Cascades, the Corps of Engineers in 1875 had surveyed the rapids in the Gorge and recommended that a canal be built around the upper section.

Soon thereafter, Congress approved ninety thousand dollars to get the work started. When it was discovered that this amount would not be nearly enough to complete the project, the federal funding was slowed, but enough money was added each year to keep hopes up and crews digging for the next ten years.

When the south bank railroad was completed by the O.R.&N.

Company in 1883, interest in the canal dwindled to almost nothing. A further blow was struck against shippers when stern-wheelers working the middle river were taken over the Cascades Rapids during high-water periods and put into service on the lower river, leaving shippers no choice except to use the railroads. Not surprisingly, rail rates went up. But the outraged cries raised by aggrieved wheat men in eastern Oregon and Washington rose to such a pitch that they soon were heard in the halls of Congress.

As a result, Lars read in the *Oregonian*, an appropriation of $1,239,000 probably would be approved in the next session of Congress as an earnest payment against whatever amount might be required to complete the project, whose cost likely would run in the neighborhood of $8 million.

Meanwhile, Lars's family was growing, with a third daughter, Dora Ann Warren, born in 1887, as a younger sister to Sara Jane, who by then was six years old, and to Lily Frieda, who was sixteen. Though Lars had never given Daphne the slightest indication that he was disappointed by the fact that she continued to bear daughters rather than sons, she was quite vocal in her exasperation.

"Grandmother Lolanee used to tell me that if I concentrated hard enough on having a boy, I'd have one. But I didn't. What am I doing wrong?"

"Nothing, so far as I'm concerned, darling. I'll take whatever you give me."

"Well, I won't give up yet. Next time I'll have a boy—or quit trying. I know you want a steamboat captain in the family."

Truth was, Lars admitted wryly, sixteen-year-old Lily, who now was employed as purser aboard the *Inland Queen*, already was well enough qualified in riverboat skills to be licensed as a second or even a first mate, though such a thing was unheard of in this part of the country. As he and his uncle, Emil Warren, who was still chief operations officer for the O.R.&N. Company, had told Lily time and again, ladies were not accepted as pilots in the riverboat profession—and never would be.

"It just won't happen, Lily!" Emil declared firmly. "Why, the very idea is as outlandish and unladylike as the notion of giving women the vote!"

"Which has happened in Wyoming, in case you haven't heard," Lily answered tartly. "Wyoming even has a lady judge."

"But no steamboat captains?"

"Not yet. But I bet they would have if they had as much river traffic as the Columbia does."

As he usually did when he appeared to be on the losing side of an argument, Emil tried a diversionary tactic. "Pretty and charming as you are, Lily, you could save yourself a lot of trouble by marrying a riverboat captain instead of trying to be one. The Company has a lot of handsome young bachelor officers who would be only too happy to take orders from you."

Lily's bright blue eyes flashed in sudden anger, then she relaxed and gave him a sunny smile. "That wouldn't be the same as having a captain's license of my own, Uncle Emil. But I will give it some thought. Meanwhile, I'll offer you a compromise."

"What sort of compromise?" Emil asked warily.

"Father fired his second mate two weeks ago when he showed up drunk for the third time this year. I've been doing both his work and mine ever since."

"I'm sure you do it well, Lily."

"Slow as business is these days, we don't need both a second mate and a purser aboard the *Inland Queen*. I'll keep on doing both jobs if you'll raise me to a second mate's pay."

"Will your father agree to that?"

"Ask him."

When questioned on the matter, Captain Lars Warren admitted that his daughter could handle both positions easily enough. Since railroads had been built along the banks, passenger traffic had dwindled; most of the freight being hauled was in the form of sacked wheat, a bulk product requiring little paperwork. So far as the second mate's duties were concerned, all that was required from that officer was an occasional turn at the wheel and ordering deckhands to secure or cast off a line, both of which Lily could handle as efficiently as any person onboard.

"As a licensed riverboat, we are required to carry a minimum number of officers each trip," Lars said. "But I'm sure you're aware of that."

"I am, indeed. But in an emergency such as this one, no maritime inspector will object to our employing the most competent person available for the job."

"Which in this case happens to be Lily."

"Why, so it does, Captain Warren. Until informed otherwise, carry on with your present staff."

❧

After the peak of the mid-June runoff had passed, Lars told Daphne that this might be a good time to accept the standing invitation from his father and mother that they come downriver to Rooster Rock for a visit. While Daphne and Freda went shopping in Portland for a couple of days, Lars and Tommy could take a busmans' holiday and check out the river improvements now under way at the Cascades Rapids and the river's mouth.

As always, Lili deBeauchamp, a doting grandmother if ever there was one, would be delighted to come down from Walla Walla and look after four-year-old Dora Ann and ten-year-old Sara Jane in the Crow's Nest in Wallula. During most of her stay, sixteen-year-old Lily Frieda would be coming and going on her twice-weekly runs between Celilo and Lewiston on the *Inland Queen*, which would be in the capable hands of First Mate Herb Blalock and Chief Engineer Alex Conley.

Since both men had accepted Acting Second Mate Lily Warren into the privileged realm of steamboat officers, even though she was not licensed, Lars told Daphne he would not be in the least surprised if on their return they found that she had taken over as captain and now was being addressed as "Sir."

After taking the portage cars from Celilo Landing to The Dalles, traveling aboard the boat with his father Captain Tommy Warren for the half-day's journey to the Upper Cascades, then taking the portage cars again to the Lower Cascades, around which the ship canal and locks were in the process of being built, Lars listened with interest as his father explained what was going on.

"As I understand it," Tommy said as the portage train moved slowly past the clutter of scrapers, digging equipment, piles of dark volcanic rock, timbers, and lumber being placed as concrete forms by a swarm of laborers, masons, and carpenters, "the locks will be in two steps. The lower chamber will have a lift of 20 feet and a length of 490, while the upper chamber has a lift of 18 feet and is 402 feet long. In between the two locks, a 90-foot-wide ship channel approximately six miles long will be able to handle any boat now on the river, as well as oceangoing ships in time to come."

"What are all those piles of rocks for?"

"The sides of the ship channel are being laid by stonemasons brought over from Italy, I'm told. They're so skilled in their trade, they can lay a drywall twenty-five feet high without mortar or sealer of any kind, which they guarantee will stand for a thousand years without leaking a drop of water."

After doing a bit of mental arithmetic, Lars said, "With lifts of twenty-four and eighteen feet, that means raising boats forty-two vertical feet between the lower and middle river in a six-mile-long stretch. No wonder the Cascades have been such an obstacle to navigation. That's a lot of drop in a such a short stretch of river. When do they plan on finishing the job?"

"My Corps of Engineers friends say the project should be done in late summer, 1896—if they don't run out of money."

"Is there any danger of that?"

"Not much," Tommy answered, shaking his head. "About the only thing congressmen and engineers agree on is that an unfinished project is a black eye for them both. Come the fall of '96, we'll see boats passing through the locks to the middle river, I'm guessing."

Spending the night at Tommy and Freda's Rooster Rock home, Lars and Daphne took the downriver boat with them to Portland the next morning. Met there by Emil and Dolores Warren, the two women disembarked with plans to go shopping in Portland for a couple of days, while Lars and Tommy took the noon luxury boat, *Wide West*, on down to Astoria, where they intended to have themselves a look at what the Corps of Engineers was doing to improve navigation at the mouth of the river.

Visible through the trees high above the level of the river in the early evening haze as the *Wide West* moved into its Astoria wharf was the imposing Hilltop House, long a landmark on the lower river. Built by Captain Ben Warren when still a bachelor back in 1817, two years before he had gone to the Sandwich Islands and taken Lolanee as a bride, the property no longer belonged to the Warren family, for both Ben and Lolanee were gone now, laid to rest in the green, misty land they both loved.

For Tommy Warren, who had been born in Hilltop House, and for Lars, who had spent many happy days as a child visiting his grandparents there, the two-story house, with its roofed observatory from which a 360-degree view of the lower river and the four-mile-wide Columbia River Bar could be seen, held many memories.

Following the deaths of Ben and Lolanee, Hilltop House had been sold to a seafaring man named Captain Kristen Steffanson, who now was a top-ranked bar pilot with the George Flavel Company, which since 1850 had made a business of guiding ships in and out across the bar. Gazing up through the gray mists of late afternoon, Tommy chuckled softly, keeping his reflections to himself until Lars spoke.

"Long thoughts, Dad?"

"Long and pleasant thoughts, Son. Right now, I'm remembering the time I brought your mother to Hilltop House for a visit when we were thinking about getting married. Dad was still active as a bar pilot then. There were a lot of sailing ships coming into the lower river—both British and American."

"This was before the boundary settlement?"

"Just before—in the autumn of 1845. By then, I was first mate aboard the *Beaver*, a steamer brought out from England in '36. I hadn't worked much aboard sailing ships, so when Dad asked me if I'd like to go out on some piloting jobs with him, I jumped at the chance."

"He was one of the best bar pilots in the business, I've been told."

"That he was, Lars. While Freda and Lolanee had woman talk at home, Dad and I made three trips over the bar in four days' time. The last one was an adventure I'll never forget."

Picking up a big, three-masted American merchant ship named the *Sea Lark* in late afternoon several miles outside the mouth of the Columbia River, Tommy told Lars, his father found the ship to be a clumsy handler, whose best sailing point was running directly before the wind. Because of the ineptitude of its master, Captain Gerald Prudhouse, its position before a building gale moving in from the southwest made taking it in through the deep channel below Cape Disappointment at the northern entrance to the river too risky to attempt. As an alternative, the ship could beat out to sea and lay off the mouth of the river until the storm subsided, which might be a couple of days. Rather than do that, Captain Ben Warren decided to take an all-or-nothing gamble by piloting the ship into the mouth of the river through the seldom-used South Passage just beyond Clatsop Spit—an area long known as a graveyard for ships because of the constantly shifting sands of its many channels.

"Competent as Captain Prudhouse may have been as a deep-water man," Tommy told Lars, "he was a real 'Nervous Nelly' crossing the bar. In fact, before we got into the lower river, I suspect he wet his pants—or worse. But Dad was as steady as a rock."

Standing beside his father and the ship's anxious captain as Ben peered ahead for his landmarks through the driving rain and failing light, Tommy saw that his father's face was rigid with cold concentration as he called up thirty years of experience in piloting ships across the world's most dangerous bar in order to bring the vessel through safely. By now, the seas had become so rough and the wheel so hard to handle that Captain Prudhouse had detailed two husky sailors to man it, one on each side, with orders to maintain their grip on the spokes no matter what happened.

Even under the stress of those tense minutes, Tommy told Lars, his father did not forget that it was experience that made pilots, that he was still a teacher, and that his most apt apprentice pupil stood on the quarter deck beside him. After giving the helmsmen an occasional terse correction in course and making sure it was executed precisely, Ben beckoned Tommy closer, shouting in his ear to make himself heard over the thunder of breaking surf and howling wind.

"We've got a thirty-knot gale astern and a near-record flood tide moving in behind us, Tommy!" he yelled. "Otherwise, I'd never have attempted to use this channel!"

"It looks mighty treacherous to me!"

"Under most conditions, it is. But today it's a good gamble. I'm sure we'll make it through."

"What's the bottom like?"

"Nothing but loose, shifting sand. Given our sailing speed and powerful thrust from the incoming tide, if we do go aground we'll have a hundred yards of dry spit under our keel before we stop. We can walk inland from there without getting our feet wet." Giving the alarmed captain a sidelong glance and a quick grin, Ben added, "I'm not planning to go aground, of course. I mean to keep enough water under our bottom to carry us all the way into the lower river."

Twice during the ten-minute passage through the worst of the violently tossing breakers, the fore-and-aft pitching of the *Sea Lark* made her bow strike so hard when she slammed down into the water that one of the sailors at the wheel shouted, "We've struck!" to which the white-faced Captain Prudhouse cried, "Stay with the wheel, sailor! Stay with the wheel!"

In both instances, Ben did not flinch, merely shaking his head like a street-fighter shrugging off a glancing blow. But just as Tommy was beginning to breathe easier and conclude that the worst of the passage was behind them, the ship rose and fell again, this time slamming its bow down so solidly that there was no doubt she had struck sand, not water. Almost toppled off their feet by the ship's sudden lurch, the two sailors at the wheel were too surprised even to complain, saving all their strength and energy to hold on.

"Come around, damn you! Come around!" Ben pleaded grimly. "You can't cross the bar sideways! Come around!"

Even as it appeared that the *Sea Lark* was going to hang up so badly on the sandbar that the wind and tide would roll her over on her side, she shuddered, turned, came free, and suddenly was moving straight ahead bow-on into calmer, deeper water.

"Good girl!" Ben breathed. Turning, he gave the ashen-faced captain a casually triumphant salute, then smiled at Tommy. "We'll be home for supper tonight after all, Son. I hope you're hungry."

Although Tommy and Lars had declined an invitation from Captain Kristen Steffanson to spend the night at Hilltop House, saying they were to eat supper and spend the evening with fellow O.R.&N. Company employees aboard the *Wide West*, they did accept his offer of a guided tour the next morning of the Corps of Engineers river mouth improvement project on his pilot boat. As might be expected, he and all the other George Flavel Company pilots were keeping a close eye on every aspect of the job, for its successful conclusion would be vital to their work.

From the time of its discovery by Captain William Gray in 1792 to the present day, Lars knew, the Columbia River sandbar had been a graveyard for ships. According to records he had examined in his grandfather's extensive library, the number of vessels lost or destroyed in the area—fishing boats, harbor craft, and seagoing ships—during the past one hundred years exceeded two thousand. As a result of these wrecks, marine historians estimated, at least fifteen hundred lives had been lost.

Because winds, tides, and currents brought air and water of varying temperatures and velocities into constant conflict, changes in the weather near the river's mouth could be sudden and extreme. From April until August, the prevailing winds in the vicinity of Astoria blew from the northwest; for the rest of the year, southwesterly winds dominated. On the coast during the summer months, northwest winds now and then became gales, which sometimes lasted for several days. In winter, southerly winds could rage at any time, bringing with them heavy southwest swells and monstrous seas.

Fog frequently shrouded the mouth of the Columbia during July, August, and September, but it could roll in at any time. Often extending many miles out to sea, it could be very dense and last for days, stopping all traffic in and out of the river. The average annual rainfall at Astoria was seventy-seven inches; the velocity of the current at the entrance to the river was two-and-a-half knots at its peak; and the range between high and low tides was seven and a half feet.

"Vot de Engineers t'ink dey are going to do," Captain Kristen Steffanson explained in his thick Swedish accent, "is narrow de channels of de river down from several into only one. Dis vill hurry it up, dey t'ink, so dot de single channel vill flow fast and deep."

"Do you think it will work?" Lars asked.

"Dey say it vorked at de mouth of the Mississippi," Captain Steffanson said with a skeptical shrug. "But here, who knows?"

Though the Swedish captain had been a licensed bar pilot for twenty years, Tommy Warren's knowledge of the history of the lower Columbia River went back much further, for he could remember when Lieutenant Charles Wilkes of the United States Navy made his disastrous attempt to survey the river's mouth in 1841. Complaining that the bar's constantly shifting sands made it difficult to draw reliable charts, he proved his point the hard way when a unit of his squadron, the USS *Peacock*, grounded on the north shore of the river entrance and became a total loss. In remembrance of that unhappy event, the spot had been christened "Peacock Spit," a name it still bore.

Lieutenant Wilkes expressed puzzlement that so knowledgeable a navigator and explorer as George Vancouver had failed to discover the mouth of the River of the West. "I found breakers extending from Cape Disappointment to Point Adams in one unbroken line," he wrote in 1845. "I am at a loss to conceive how any doubt should have ever existed that here was the mouth of the mighty river, whose existence was reported so long."

From an early time, Tommy knew, responsible ship captains accepted the necessity of employing local pilots with knowledge of the sandbar's changing channels before attempting to take their vessels into or out of the river. Impatient captains wishing to save money or time often took chances piloting their own ships—then regretted doing so. In 1849, for example, four ships were wrecked on the bar: the *Aurora*, the *Morning Star*, the *Sylvia de Grasse*, and the *Josephine*. In 1852, five ships were wrecked: the *Dolphin*, the *General Warren*, the *Machigone*, the *Marie*, and the *Potomac*.

After Captain George Flavel established his bar pilot association in 1850 and the State of Oregon began issuing licenses to Columbia River pilots, wrecks became less frequent. But recently, Captain Steffanson said, a surprising number of sailing ships that had seen their day and no longer were able to compete with steam-propelled craft were attempting to enter the river without going to the expense of employing a pilot—and coming to grief. Part of this could be ascribed to the fact that the sailing ships were being staffed by inexperienced or over-the-hill officers and crews. A more important cause for the wrecks may have been the fact that, if a master wanted to ground his ship for the insurance money, the sand spit guarding the south entrance to the Columbia River was an ideal place to do it.

"Dis is de only coast vhere a captain and his crew can walk ashore from a shipwreck," Captain Steffanson said cynically. "Dese days, a lot of dem do."

As aids to navigation, a lighthouse had been built in 1856 atop Cape Disappointment 220 feet above the sea on the north side of the river, shooting its 700,000 candlepower on the white flash and 160,000 candlepower on the red twenty-one miles out to sea. On the south side, the Point Adams Lighthouse with similar beams had been built in 1875. As a further aid to navigation beginning in 1892, a lightship equipped with a foghorn would go on station five miles at sea outside the entrance to the Columbia, where it would be manned year-round by a Coast Guard crew. Since the vessel stationed there would be out of touch with land and must endure all extremes of wind and weather, the sailors forced to live aboard for six-week stints without relief would suffer the worst kind of sea duty imaginable.

But whatever price must be paid in boredom and discomfort by men tendering warnings to oceangoing craft, it paled to insignificance when compared to the terrible loss of life by those who made their living going to sea in small boats. Legendary among the disasters that had occurred between Tillamook Head to the south and Willapa Bay to the north was the unexpected storm that struck on May 4, 1880.

On that bright, sunny, mild spring morning, Captain Steffanson told Tommy and Lars, virtually every boat in the area was at sea trolling for salmon or dragging for bottom fish. Unknown to the fishermen in the 250 vessels working offshore, a phenomenal freak of weather was in the making. A local historian later wrote:

> Without forewarning, a powerful wind of hurricane force suddenly came out of nowhere, changing the peaceful ocean waves into massive, seething billows. Showing no mercy, winds of more than one hundred miles per hour contorted the sea's face and made playthings of the small fishboats. Pummeled, tossed, turned, capsized, and swamped, one by one they disappeared from view, the terrified fishermen thinking the end of the world had come. Thrown into the mass of liquid fury to fend for themselves, death to most came quickly.

The uncommon local squall, which roared in from the northwest, lasted only thirty minutes. By the time it ended, more than 240 vessels had been destroyed and over three hundred lives were lost.

A year earlier, a spectacular wreck of a large steamship with many lives at risk took place just inside the mouth of the river in perfectly calm weather. With a licensed, experienced pilot aboard, the *Great Republic* grounded the night of April 18, 1879. Built in 1866 at Greenport, Long Island, New York, she had served in the China trade for several years, then in the late 1870s began carrying freight and passengers between San Francisco and Portland. A big side-wheeler measuring 378 feet in length, she was registered at 4,750 tons. She was also fast, once making the hundred-mile run from Portland to Astoria in five hours and fifteen minutes.

Departing San Francisco in the spring of 1879, she was carrying 896 passengers and over a hundred crew members when she arrived at the mouth of the Columbia at midnight on April 18. The pilot boat was waiting for her, Captain Steffanson said, and pulled alongside to put Pilot Thomas Doig aboard.

"He vas a goot man," Captain Steffanson said, "and not one to make mistakes. But dot night, according to de Court of Inquiry vhich vas held later, he made a bad vun."

> There was not a ripple on the water, (Captain James Carroll, the ship's master, told the Court of Inquiry), and we came over the bar under a slow bell all the way, crossing safely and reaching the inside

buoy. The first and third officers were on the lookout with me. I had a pair of glasses and was the first to discover Sand Island, and found the bearings all right. I reported to the pilot, who had not yet seen it. We ran along probably two minutes, and I then told the pilot I thought we were getting too close to the island and that he had better haul her up. He replied, "I do not think we are in far enough." A minute later I said, "Port your helm and put it hard over, as I think you are getting too near the island." He made no reply, but ran along for about five minutes and then put the helm hard aport, and the vessel swung up, heading toward Astoria. But the ebb tide caught her on the starboard bow, and being so near the island sent her on the spit.

Grounding so lightly that few of the people aboard knew she had struck, the *Great Republic* found herself stranded, for the tide was ebbing and she had no chance to get off the sandbar that night. Aware of the fact that the barometer was falling, indicating an impending storm, Captain Carroll appealed to Fort Canby for assistance. The tugs *Benham* and *Canby* soon arrived, followed by the *Shubrick* and the *Columbia*. With the aid of these and a number of small boats, the passengers were taken off the ship and transported to Astoria, while the crew remained onboard to off-load cargo and coal in an attempt to lighten ship and float her off the sandbar on the next high tide.

At 8 P.M. a southwest gale started in, (Captain Carroll told the Court of Inquiry), making a heavy sea, chopping to the southeast about midnight. Up to this time the ship was lying easy and taking no water, but the heavy sea prevented the tugs from rendering assistance and also drove her higher on the spit, and shortly after midnight she began to work, breaking the steampipes and disabling the engines. A few remaining passengers were put ashore on Sand Island at 6 A.M. on Sunday and were followed by the crew, the ship beginning to break up so that it was dangerous to remain aboard. The last boat left the ship at 10:30 A.M., and in getting away, the steering oar broke and the boat capsized, drowning eleven of the fourteen men it contained.

At about this time a heavy sea boarded the ship and carried away the staterooms on the starboard side, gutted the dining room, broke up the floor of the social hall, and carried away the piano. Several seas afterward boarded her forward and carried away the starboard guard, officers' room and steerage deck, also a number of horses. I remained aboard until 5:00 P.M., when the pilot and I lowered a lifeboat and came ashore.

Despite the efforts to save her, Captain Steffanson said, the *Great Republic* was destined never to get off the bar intact. After the underwriters had settled with her owners, a salvage firm paid $3,780 for the stranded vessel and its cargo and went to work reclaiming what it could, which wasn't much. A month later the hull aft of the walking beam crumbled into the sea and the fore and aft mainmasts went over the side. In another ten days the walking beam and the two large paddle wheels alone remained intact. Part of the wreckage could be seen at low tide even today, in 1891, with the steamer's grave now marked on the charts as "Republic Spit."

"Many stories vhich may or may not be true still are told about dis wreck," Captain Steffanson said. "De vun I like best is aboot de fat Chinese cook who didn't float. Have you ever heard it?"

When both Tommy and Lars said they hadn't, Captain Steffanson told the tale with relish. Among the crew members leaving the ship before the seas became too rough was a plump, jolly, round-faced Chinese cook named Ah Ling. The rope ladder down which the other crew members had climbed had become dislodged and fallen into the sea by the time Ah Ling came on deck. But that posed no problem. All he needed to do, his shipmates called up from the lifeboat being held in quiet water in the ship's lee, was jump into the water and be picked up after he came to the surface. The fact that he could not swim was of no concern, for, wearing a voluminous, black quilted jacket and being as fat as he was, there would be enough air pockets in the jacket and enough fat in his body to make him pop to the surface like a cork.

Though it took a lot of back-and-forth jabbering between him and several of his Chinese assistants who were already in the boat to convince him to jump, Ah Ling finally did so, splashing into the water only a few feet from the boat. Moving to the spot, his shipmates waited for his corpulent body to come up, as they knew it must do.

And waited … and waited … and waited …

But Ah Ling never came to the surface.

Not until weeks later, when an unusually high tide washed his body ashore, did his shipmates learn why Ah Ling's body had been far less buoyant than they had thought it would be.

"Before leaving de kitchen and coming to de side of de boat," Captain Steffanson said, "he had filled de pockets of his jacket vith de ship's silverware … Dot vas vhy he did not float."

As four generations of captains in the Warren family had learned since the storm-tossed *Tonquin* had been driven over the bar in 1811, the first and most dangerous obstacle to navigation encountered by ships entering the Columbia was at the mouth of the river itself—the Columbia River sandbar. Contrary to what poets and creators of geographical legends had written, the Great River of the West did not "flow tranquilly into the Western Sea." Many early seafaring explorers had learned to their sorrow that the four-mile-wide juncture of the mighty river with the mightier ocean was one of nature's elemental battlegrounds, where currents, tides, and winds met in constant conflict.

Crossing the bar and entering the river had been a high-risk adventure during the age of sail, Tommy knew, when his father, Ben, and the Chinook Indian, Conco, had begun their pilot service for arriving and departing ships. With the advent of steamboats, it became only slightly less dangerous. At low tide, the river meandered through channels cut in the constantly shifting sand. A pilot coming through deep water one day was never sure what he might find there the next.

"Two problems face the Corps of Engineers," a report written in 1875 stated. "First, to find a way to make the channel deep enough at low tide to permit ships of ordinary draft to enter; second, to keep a channel open once it has been dredged."

In their search for a solution to the river's sandbar problem, the Corps called on Colonel James Eads, who had encountered a similar difficulty at the mouth of the Mississippi.

> On first glance there seemed to be little similarity between the clear Columbia and the muddy Mississippi endlessly dumping silt into the Gulf, (the report continued), but the effect was the same. The ocean kept pushing sand up toward the mouth of the Columbia and building bars that the river had to cut through. Surveys in 1878 showed that an application of the methods Eads had used just below New Orleans would be effective. In 1884 the first appropriation for construction was made. Soon thereafter, work on the project began.

In principle, the solution was simple enough, though as Tommy and Lars saw during their day-long tour with Captain Steffanson aboard the pilot boat, its accomplishment was going to be expensive and prolonged. The river mouth must be compressed between two dikes or jetties of stone. One would be built out from the north shore, Cape Disappointment, and the other from the south, where there was a low projection called Clatsop Spit. Narrowing the passage between the two jetties would increase the river's velocity naturally, scouring the channel in a continual process, thus maintaining a safe depth for oceangoing ships.

As a beginning, railroad tracks were being built atop both jetties where piledrivers were pounding timbers into the sand to form trestles for extending more rails toward the Columbia's central channel. Engines were pushing strings of cars loaded with rocks, which were being dumped into the water. Gradually, as more and more rocks went into the sea beside the trestles, they packed and merged as long ridges or dams against which the waves piled sand to make the whole thing an extension of the spit or jetty itself. Where the bottom seemed unstable, trainloads of brush or small trees with their branches left on were dumped to form a mat that held the rock in place until the waves did their work of scooping sand.

Much of the rock came from over a hundred miles upriver, Tommy knew, for he had seen crews at work excavating and loading rock all the way up to the Lower Cascades. From there, it was being transported downriver on a specially built stern-wheeler, the *Cascades*, a large vessel which could push or pull alongside five barges filled with tons of rock. By the time the engineers finished their work, they estimated, the river would have gouged out a permanent thirty-foot-deep channel.

Building out from the south shore, this jetty would extend seven miles from its beginning at Fort Stevens. Toward it from Cape Disappointment, the north jetty would stretch four-and-one-half miles, ending behind a shoal on an enlarged Peacock Spit, the bar where Lieutenant Charles Wilkes's river-mouth survey had come to grief in 1841.

As Tommy, Lars, and their host headed back to Astoria on the pilot boat after a long day's tour, all three captains were in a pensive mood. Now that the river-modifying process had begun, they wondered, how far would it go before the people demanding the changes would be content with the improvements they had made on the Columbia? In truth, all three men knew, altering the channel of a large river was a process that never ended. As long as water ran downhill, tides rose and ebbed, and winds moved waves toward and away from the shore, the nature of the river bottom would change and the depths of the ship channel would have to be closely monitored and controlled.

"Call it progress, if you like," Tommy said finally. "But the idea of changing the nature of the Columbia by building jetties here, locks and canals there, and blasting rock hazards somewhere else makes me uneasy."

"Why?" Lars asked. "Don't you think the engineers know what they're doing?"

"Maybe they do, son," Tommy said grumpily. "If they don't, it'll be your problem, not mine. Meanwhile, I think we should thank Captain Steffanson for a fine day's boat ride by buying him a couple of drinks and a thick, juicy steak at the best eating house in Astoria, which I've been told is called Pier Eleven."

18.

During his long career as an attorney and chief operating officer for the Oregon Rail & Navigation Company, Emil Warren had dealt with a number of steamboat accidents and lawsuits stemming from them. But the accident and lawsuit detailed in the brief laid on his desk in early December 1891 was the strangest he had yet seen. After reading several pages of "whereases" and "did causes," he shook his head in bewilderment; looked up at his secretary, a prim, spare, maiden lady named Beulah Peters; and said, "Have you read this, Beulah?"

"Yes Sir, I have."

"What do you make of it?"

"As I understand it, Sir, a streetcar operated by the Portland City Trolley system ran through an open drawspan on the Madison Street bridge and fell into the Willamette River, barely missing an O.R.&N. Company boat."

"That's how I read it, too. But by what stretch of the imagination does that make our company liable? Can you tell me that?"

"No Sir, I can't. But as the company attorney, I suspect you'll have to come up with an answer to the charge."

"Was the accident reported in the *Oregonian?*"

"Yes Sir, it was. Since I expected you would ask for it, I brought in the file."

"Thank you, Beulah. You're a gem."

After his secretary had left the office, Emil lighted a cigar, leaned back in his chair, put his feet up on the desk, and began to read the florid, overdramatized newspaper account of the accident, which had occurred on a frosty November morning two weeks ago:

> Groping her way up the Willamette River toward Portland's Madison Street Bridge through a heavy, peasoup fog at 8:15 yesterday morning, the little steamer *Elwood* was making its usual run to Oregon

City. Shivering against the morning frost, the pilot pulled the whistle cord, blowing a long and three shorts for the drawspan, at the same time ringing down to the engine room for a full stop.

In response, the bridge tender acknowledged the whistle, swung the bridge gate shut against electric streetcar and horse-drawn vehicle traffic, then opened the span to let the *Elwood* through.

At the throttle of the town-bound Hawthorne trolley, the motorman eased back a few notches to check the speed his car had picked up on the downgrade to the bridge. As he peered through the fog, he saw the barrier and the open draw. He pushed the control lever to full off and wound on the hand brake to stop the car. The wheels locked, then slid like sled runners on the frosty rails.

The barrier's wood snapped into slivers as the streetcar struck it; for an instant of time the car hung on the edge, then it slipped slowly over into the river. It barely missed the steamer.

There was nothing the pilot of the *Elwood* could do as his boat drifted over the circle of bubbles where the streetcar had fallen in. He could not start his engines, for the paddle wheel would strike survivors struggling in the water. He could only wait until he was clear of the bridge before he could turn back to help. By then, rowboats had been launched, rescuing twenty survivors who had struggled free from the sunken streetcar. Seven people did not make it.

Tragic though the accident had been, Emil Warren could see no reason why the O.R.&N. Company should be held at fault, simply because the drawbridge had been opened to permit the *Elwood* to pass through on its scheduled run up the river. A light draft boat built specifically for the Portland–to–Oregon City run so that she could pass over the rapids at the mouth of the Clackamas River, the *Elwood* had been carrying a maximum load of passengers that morning. If the streetcar had slid through the barrier a few seconds later, it would have dropped squarely on top of the stern-wheeler, causing a much greater loss of life.

Therefore, Emil's recommendation to the Board of Directors of the O.R.&N. Company was that they make a token payment of insurance money to the heirs of the drowned victims in the same amount as they would have done if the unfortunate people had been passengers on an O.R.&N. Company boat, without acknowledging any responsibility for the tragedy. Deemed fair by all parties concerned, the offer was accepted and the case was closed.

By an odd coincidence, the attorney for the streetcar company with whom Emil Warren arranged the settlement was a colorful ex–Army officer who fourteen years earlier had achieved a measure of national fame as an aide to General Oliver Otis Howard, whose long pursuit of Chief Joseph and his fleeing band of Nez Perces had finally resulted in the defeat and surrender of the exhausted Indians on the snow-covered Bear's Paw Mountains battlefield in Montana.

A brilliant man and a born rebel at heart, Lieutenant Charles Erskine Scott Wood had become Chief Joseph's best white friend, Emil knew. After serving with Howard through the Bannock War in 1878, Lieutenant Wood had gone east with him when Howard was appointed superintendent at West Point; then, having long been interested in law, had studied at nearby Columbia and earned a degree. Although he was a West Point graduate, a decade of military discipline and two Indian wars had given him his fill of the army, so in 1883 he resigned his commission, came west to Portland, and began practicing law.

Following the surrender at Bear's Paw, Lieutenant Wood had been assigned the task of watching over Chief Joseph, seeing to his creature comforts, and protecting him from the curious. It had been Wood who recorded Chief Joseph's surrender speech. Although he respected Howard as a man, he had been sharply critical of the general for his failure to return the Nez Perces to Idaho as promised, and done everything he could to persuade the government to return the exiles from Indian Territory to the Pacific Northwest.

Emil Warren had first met Charles Wood two years ago, when the attorney had invited him to lunch, then asked him for a favor.

"I've commissioned the well-known New York sculptor, Olin Warner, to do a series of large medallions of famous Indian chiefs," he told Emil over after-lunch brandy and cigars. "One of them will be of Chief Joseph, who now lives on the Colville Reservation on the upper Columbia."

"I know," Emil said, nodding. "My nephew, Captain Lars Warren, transported the Lapwai band of Nez Perces from Wallula to Lewiston when they were repatriated a few years ago."

"Chief Joseph has accepted my invitation to come down to Portland and sit as a model for the medallion next month," Wood went on. "Whether he travels by boat or train, he'll be using O.R.&N. Company facilities. I'm willing to pay his transportation costs. But he's a very proud man, Mr. Warren, who has been greatly abused by the public and press. On this trip, I hope you can assure me he will be well treated."

"He will be," Emil said. "You have my word for that. Furthermore, he will travel first-class without charge as our guest."

Though the favor was no more than one attorney trying to cultivate goodwill with another would do, Charles Wood did not forget it. Two years later, when he brought both Chief Joseph and Chief Moses down to Portland as his guests during the 1891 Exposition of Progress, he invited Emil to join the visiting and local dignitaries at a formal dinner at his showplace home in the hills overlooking the west side of the Willamette River.

Asking the chiefs to share the limelight of the Exposition, which would give them national publicity as two of the best-known Indians of the day, was an attempt to heal the rift that had developed between them, Charles Wood told Emil.

"During the past couple of years, the friendship between Joseph and Moses has cooled considerably," Wood said. "Joseph, who's a temperance man, blames Moses for encouraging the local whiskey trade, while Moses, who drinks quite a bit, blames Joseph for his people's aversion to work. I'm hoping to bring them together, for they need each other."

During the evening, Wood's diplomatic efforts appeared to work, for both chiefs seemed to enjoy the food, talk, and attention. When wine was served during the course of the dinner, Joseph did not touch his glass, Emil noticed. But Moses kept the vintage wine from going to waste by emptying first his own glass, then the one placed in front of his abstemious friend.

One curious result of the visit of the two chiefs was an adventure all boys interested in outdoor life would envy. Wood's twelve-year-old son, Erskine, a slim, dark-haired, handsome boy who loved hunting, fishing, and horses, had become so fascinated by Chief Joseph that his father asked Joseph if young Erskine could come for a visit next summer. Joseph graciously invited him to do so.

In July 1892 young Erskine went to Nespelem and was taken into Chief Joseph's tepee as a member of the family. He liked it so well, and was so well liked in return, that he did not go home until Christmas. The following year, 1893, he returned for a second visit during the fall, this one shortened to a mere three months. Later asked how Chief Joseph had treated him, he told a reporter:

> He was the kindest of fathers to me, looking after me, providing for me, caring for me, and, it must be said, sometimes gently rebuking me when necessary ... I have been asked whether he was somber. No, he was not. Neither was he merry or boisterous or prone to loud laughter. But he was not morose, nor overwhelmed by his misfortunes. He bore them like the great man he was. Within the limits of the reservation he lived his life quietly with a calm and dignified acceptance of his fate.

So far as Lars Warren was concerned, the spring of 1893 would always be remembered for two important events, one tragic, the other happy. The tragic one was the explosion of the Snake River stern-wheeler, *Annie Faxon*, just as she was pulling into Wade's Bar fifty miles below Lewiston on April 14; the other, the birth of his first son, Douglas Thomas Warren, on April 28, just two weeks later.

"At last we'll have a steamboat captain candidate in the family," Daphne said with a tired smile as she held the red-faced, howling baby close to her breast. "Can I quit trying now?"

What neither of them said, though they both knew it to be true, was that Acting Purser–Second Mate Lily Warren, now eighteen, was giving Uncle Emil Warren all kinds of trouble as she insisted that she be allowed to take the examination for a first mate's license. Given an eighteen-year head start on little Douglas Thomas Warren, if she were allowed to take the test, there was little doubt that she would have obtained her captain's license before he was old enough to toddle.

As for the explosion of the *Annie Faxon*, none of the steamboat men acquainted with the history of the stern-wheeler had an explanation for it. One of four boats built at Celilo in 1878, she was the best of the grain and passenger haulers on the upper river, a vessel whose engines and propulsion machinery always had been scrupulously maintained. Captain Harry Baughman, her master, was an experienced senior pilot in the O.R.&N. Company; her officers were well qualified for their jobs. For this trip, the likable, handsome young purser, Harold Tappan, was celebrating his marriage in Lewiston the afternoon before by bringing his beautiful bride, Susan, along on a Company-approved honeymoon voyage downriver to Celilo, The Dalles, and Portland.

After slowing the engines at Wade's Bar, Captain Baughman pulled the whistle cord and eased the boat in toward the landing, where a lone passenger and a few packages of freight were waiting to be taken aboard. Leaving his wife in the office cabin, Purser Tappan came out on deck to collect the dollar fare from the passengers and check the manifest for the freight. As the *Annie Faxon* neared the dock, Captain Baughman rang down to the engine room for a full stop.

Suddenly, from below decks, there was a low rumble, followed immediately by a terrific explosion. The force was so great that the steamboat literally was blown to bits.

Turning to speak to a deckhand standing nearby, Purser Tappan was stunned to see the man's body sailing over the railing, while just beyond him, flying debris decapitated another crew member. Thrown overboard by the force of the explosion as the boat was reduced to splinters, both Purser Tappan and Captain Baughman survived. Eight crew members and passengers did not. Among the casualties was Susan Tappan, the purser's bride of less than twenty-four hours, whose body was never found.

Inexplicable as the destruction of the *Annie Faxon* had been, an event related to it could only be described as a miracle. Good Catholic though she was, even Daphne Warren admitted that the Lord must have ordered a Presbyterian saint to come down to earth and rescue the lifetime work of two lady missionaries from the deep, cold waters of the Snake River.

As Lars later heard the story, the carefully wrapped package entrusted to the express company and shipped aboard the *Annie Faxon* by Miss Kate McBeth had been addressed to the Indian Office of the Smithsonian Institution in Washington, D.C. Contained in the box, which had a waterproof, red oilskin wrapper, was the most complete dictionary of the Nez Perce language ever compiled. Painstakingly assembled word by word during the twenty years in which Sue McBeth, who had died a month ago, and her younger sister, Kate, had lived with the Nez Perces, the 15,000-word dictionary of Nez Perce words and their English meanings was a one-of-a-kind volume so precious that, when it was offered as a gift to the Smithsonian, the director of that esteemed repository of national treasures had been so delighted that he had given detailed instructions as to how the package should be wrapped and shipped.

No matter what local white people might think of missionaries in general and spinster ladies in particular, Captain Lars Warren knew that to the Christianized Nez Perces living on the reservation near Lapwai and Kamiah, the McBeth sisters were holy people. Devastated by the death of her older sister, Sue, the slightly younger sister, Kate, was ending her mission and returning to her home in Indiana. Deeply religious Indians, such as Elder Billy Williams, took some consolation in the fact that the words they had spoken in their own tongue, which the McBeth sisters had translated into English, were being sent east to a repository maintained by the Great White Father.

"Are you traveling on the *Annie Faxon*, too, Miss Kate?" the express agent for the O.R.&N. Company in Lewiston asked as he accepted and registered the package.

"No, I'm not," Kate McBeth answered, shaking her head. "The half-price vouchers sent me by the Missionary Society call for transportation by stagecoach north to Spokane, then east on the Northern Pacific through Butte, Bismarck, and Chicago, with a change there to the Ohio and Eastern."

"You've got a long ride ahead of you, Ma'am. Do you have a sleeper berth?"

"Heavens, no! A half-fare ticket in day coach is all the Missionary Society can afford. But I won't mind. Are you sure the package for the Smithsonian will go through without difficulty?"

"Don't worry about it, Miss Kate. It's registered for special handling."

Thanks to the telegraph lines paralleling the Northern Pacific tracks, Kate McBeth read a newspaper account of the *Annie Faxon* disaster when her train stopped in Butte, Montana, late the next afternoon. Concerned about her precious package, she wired an inquiry to the express company agent in Lewiston, asking if it had survived. Yes, he replied, it had been recovered and sent on to the Smithsonian, but he did not know how much damage had been done to it. After reaching her home in Indiana a few days later, Kate learned the details.

> All the time I had lived at Fort Lapwai, the clerk at the sutler's store there, with his young wife, had been on the best of terms with me (Kate wrote later). Two years before, he had bought a farm on Snake River, but moved to it only last spring. He understands and talks Nez Perce quite well. His home was some miles below where the boat was blown up.
>
> That morning he was on the shore of the river and saw much stuff

> floating down. His eye was caught by a red box. He mounted his horse and waded out as far as he could. He had a long rope tied to the saddle. He made a noose upon it—threw it out just as the box was going over some rapids, and caught it. He drew it to shore, opened it, and recognized the Nez Perce script. He said at once, "This must be Miss Kate's writing."

Despite its protective wrapping, the pages of the notebook were soaking wet, so the young clerk—whose name was King—opened it up and stood it on end to dry. A couple of days later an agent from the express company arrived and took it back to Portland, where the drying process was completed before the dictionary was forwarded to the Smithsonian, whose experts were pleased to find the entries so painstakingly recorded by Sue and Kate McBeth still perfectly legible.

Elder Billy Williams, a Christianized Nez Perce who had become a preacher, called the recovery of the dictionary a miracle, saying, "It seems as if that box were a living thing, and that the Lord was caring for it."

19.

SINCE TURNING EIGHTEEN, Lily Warren had become the prettiest unlicensed first mate currently employed by the Oregon Rail & Navigation Company. Because she was always at the top of the list when a steamboat captain needed an officer to fill a vacancy, Emil Warren was used to turning down requests for her services on the grounds that she did not have a first mate's ticket.

But when he received a demand from Captain George Williams, who had quit the O.R.&N. Company a year ago after building a steamboat of his own, for Lily Warren as both a first mate and a bride, Emil was forced to give it serious consideration. Summoning the two young people into his Portland office, he fixed them with what he meant to be a stern, business-like glare.

"Let me make sure I understand you, George. You've quit the Company and built a steamboat of your own, which you intend to operate as an independent carrier on the lower river. Right?"

"Yes Sir. It's a small stern-wheeler rebuilt from pieces of three other boats. It's rated at one hundred tons. Lily and I named it the *Lady Duck*."

"George wanted to call it the *Mud Hen*," Lily said, her blue eyes glowing with suppressed excitement. "But that sounded ugly to me. We plan to go poking into a lot of shallow river landings where bigger boats can't go. We think we'll pick up a lot of revenue there."

"I'm sure you will, Lily. But do you have to be married and get a first mate's license before you go into business?"

"No," Lily answered. "But since we'll be working and sleeping together, it would be nice if we did. We were sure you would help us because you're so good at fixing things."

"I'm not your father, Lily. Nor do I have any standing with the Maritime Examining Board."

"Oh, pooh!" Lily exclaimed, lifting and dropping her shapely shoulders in a way that vividly reminded Emil of the Swedish stubbornness of her paternal grandmother, Freda Warren, and the French charm of her maternal grandmother, Lili deBeauchamp. "When you talk sweet, Uncle Emil, everybody does whatever you ask them to do. You're the smoothest diplomat of the family."

If she had expected the compliment to disarm him, she was right. It did. Even so, he made one final effort to be firm.

"Have you talked to your father and mother about this?"

"We have, Sir," Captain George Williams put in, making it clear that he wanted to be included in the discussion. "They both say they approve—if you do."

Recalling that two years ago he had tried to divert sixteen-year-old Lily's ambitions away from getting a captain's license by suggesting that she marry a captain, rather than attempt to become one, Emil wondered fleetingly if she were carrying out that advice now. No, he decided, she surely would not do that. From the way she and George Williams smiled at each other, it was plain to see that they were in love. A few months ago, Lars had told Emil that Lily was becoming increasingly discontented with the monotony of the Celilo-Lewiston run, expressing a growing desire to work on other boats in other sectors of the river. Because of her experience as both a purser and a first mate, she would team up very well with Captain George Williams in a business based on picking up passengers and freight at river landings where the larger boats could not afford to go. Hell, with her charm, Emil conceded, she could persuade men with nothing to ship and no place to go to give the *Lady Duck* some patronage just so they could have the pleasure of talking to her.

"Well, you certainly have my approval, so far as getting married and starting a nonscheduled steamboat service is concerned," Emil said. "But I really can't see why you need a first mate's license, Lily."

"Then I'll give you three good reasons," Lily snapped, her voice suddenly indignant. "First, because it's illegal to operate a boat the size of the *Lady Duck* without two licensed officers aboard. Second, because I'm qualified. Third, because there's no law against it."

"But it's never been done, Lily!" Emil said desperately. "There's no precedent for it in the O.R.&N. Company!"

"Pooh on precedent, Uncle Emil! I'm talking about law. Just to make sure I was right, I went through all the maritime law books in your library. Nowhere is there a word or a phrase that says a woman can't be a licensed officer aboard a steamboat."

It was on the tip of Emil's tongue to ask Lily how she had managed to get access to his maritime law library; but before he wasted his breath, he knew the answer to that question. Like all O.R.&N. Company employees who had known Lily from childhood, Beulah Peters, his secretary, had never been able to deny her anything she asked. He decided to offer a compromise.

"Since neither you nor George are working for the O.R.&N. Company now, I suppose I could persuade the members of the Examining Board, most of whom are retired Company officers, to let you take the test. That way, if you do pass, you won't be setting a precedent for the Company."

"I'll pass," Lily said grimly. "You can bet your boots on that."

"As I understand it," Emil went on, "the test has three parts: written, oral, and physical. If the Maritime Examining Board chooses to do so, it can make the physical part very demanding—such as handling a boat under extremely dangerous conditions."

"Lily will pass that part, too," George Williams said loyally. "She's as capable as I am in all aspects of handling a steamboat."

Since he already had conceded the argument, Emil tried to save a little face by teasing them a bit. "I'm tempted to ask the Examining Board to make you demonstrate your skills by piloting a boat called the *Norma* through a bit of white water on the upper Snake. Could you handle that?"

"Of course we could. Where is the *Norma* now?"

"On the Snake River above Hell's Canyon. Since she's making no money for us where she is, I've been thinking of bringing her downriver through the canyon. That's what your father did, Lily, when he was first mate aboard the *Shoshone* back in '69. Did he ever tell you about that?"

Lily shook her head. "No. But if he did it then, George and I can do it now."

Emil laughed and got to his feet. "I'm sure you could, Lily. But I'm not going to ask you to. Captain William Polk Gray has already been given the job."

Showing them to the door, he shook hands with George Williams, put an arm around Lily Warren, and then kissed her on the cheek. "Blessings on you both. May all your landings be happy ones."

Like the *Shoshone* back in the 1860s, which had been built and launched in the Idaho desert near Farewell Bend by the Oregon Steam Navigation Company in an attempt to make money out of the gold and silver boom in southwestern Idaho Territory, the stern-wheeler *Norma* had been built and launched in the same area in hopes of bringing in revenue from a copper discovery in Hell's Canyon in 1891. Called the Seven Devils boom because of its proximity to the Idaho mountain range nearby, the flurry of mining excitement was said to be the "biggest ever," with fortunes to be made by all parties concerned.

Rails had moved into the Snake River country by then, the Union Pacific having built what was called the Short Line to Portland along the route of the Oregon Trail. The run of the *Norma*, which was built on the banks of the Snake near Huntington, Oregon, was to be from the railroad connection downriver to Seven Devils Landing, a distance of sixty miles. If traffic warranted, she would also run upriver to Weiser or beyond—providing draws were put into the three bridges which the Union Pacific had built across the Snake without stopping to consider that steamboats might wish to use the river.

The *Norma* was 160 feet long, 32 feet wide, 6 feet deep in the hold, and drew forty inches of water under her normal load of two hundred tons. Soon after her launching in the spring of 1891, she proved she could run downriver to Seven Devils Landing and back by making a successful trip. But when she attempted to steam upriver, neither pleas, threats, nor lawsuits aimed at the Union Pacific, the War Department, or anyone else Emil Warren could think of to sue could remove the inconsiderately built bridges. After several years of unprofitable traffic on a limited stretch of river, he decided to do as he done earlier with the *Shoshone*—bring her downriver.

The man he chose to accomplish the feat was Captain William Polk Gray, now fifty years old, with most of those years spent on Pacific Northwest rivers. When Willie Gray finally got around to writing his story of the trip, his prose was as colorful and vivid as his firsthand verbal account.

We left the Union Pacific bridge across Snake River near Huntington at 2:00 p.m., May 17, 1895. At Bay Horse Rapids, three miles down, while drifting in a channel improved by Government engineers, we touched on what afterward proved to be a piece of two-inch steel drill which had been broken off and left when the engineers were working there some years before. The drill ripped several holes through the bottom and the boat swung around and damaged the stern-wheel badly. Working the boat clear with spars and lines we went down to J. A. Gray's Landing and repaired the wheel and patched the holes in the bottom.

Left Gray's Landing on the 19th, no wind. I was steering, my brother, the mate, watching the Government chart. I saw indications of reefs or shoals and remarked: "It don't look good, what does the chart say?" He replied: "All clear—there is a black rock marked on the shore." But I was not satisfied and rung the bell to stop. Almost immediately she struck the starboard knuckle, making a hole forty feet long and four feet wide. I grabbed the chart and flung it out the window and we touched no reefs or rocks afterwards except at Copper Creek Falls. We had struck the edge of a reef about a foot under the muddy water which the Snake carries while in flood.

We were drifting while the mate inspected the damages. I knew they were bad but the crew had been discouraged at the Bay Horse trouble and I was afraid they would jump the job if we landed above Sturgill Rapids, three miles below us. From where we were the boat could easily steam back to the Bridge. I heard that Sturgill Rapids were very swift and it would be almost impossible to bring the boat back over them with our damaged side, so I kept on down slowly. The men gathered on the forward deck and one man asked if I was going to land. I made no reply and soon we were below the rapids, where we landed. There was some talk and I told them we would repair damages as much as possible. We had plenty of lumber and forty cords of wood in the hull. The boat had bulkheads all through her. We built a bulkhead as close as we could to the hole in her side and pumped out the six bulkheads that had been flooded. The men had understood that we would go back over the rapids and the evening before we were ready to start I had sounded the men out as to going on or going back. Every man wanted to go back.

Approaching the engineer, I said: "Charlie, this boat is worthless up here. What do you think of going back?" He replied: "We came up to get her. I say go on or put her where they can't find her." I replied: "Charlie, you're my man. The boys think I'm going to make a short trip down a few miles to test our new bulkhead. But we will forget to come back."

We left Sturgill May 21st, and after we had gone downstream about ten miles the boys accepted their fate. About 5:00 p.m. we came around a short point and there was a steel ferry cable across the river and less than eight feet above the water. I stopped and backed the boat instantly. A strong current was carrying us down to certain decapitation of everything above the main deck, but the boat was a good backer and Charlie answered nobly. I managed to land her, head down, against a rocky cliff and the men wound several ropes around rocks enough to hold her with the engines working.

I whistled several times for the ferryman to lower the wire, but no one moved, so I sent the mate and two men across the river to lower the wire. When the mate asked the ferryman, whose name was Brownlee, why he had delayed lowering the wire, Brownlee replied: "I am doing it to prolong your lives. You have a bullheaded fool running that boat and not a soul will live to go through that canyon. I have been on top of those cliffs and I could jump across that canyon. I saw a drift log a hundred feet long up-end under one cliff and it never came up."

The ferryman was slow in lowering the wire and it was dark when we hunted a landing below. I wonder if you can imagine the strain on a pilot on a strange river known to be swift and treacherous, on a dark night, over-shadowing mountains throwing impenetrable gloom over all, and no searchlight.

About noon the next day we reached the landing above Copper Creek Falls and everyone walked down on the Oregon side to see them. They are more of a pour than a fall. From the brink of a cliff which jutted out into the still water at the foot of the cliff I measured the drop at eighteen feet. For an hour I watched and studied the currents, eddies, and back-lash of the water, and decided that the least damage to the boat would be done by dropping over the fall on the Idaho side and let the back-lash hold me from the cliff as much as possible. The water pours over the fall and the current at about three hundred feet below the summit of the fall. The underside of the point of this cliff has been worn away until the over-hang extends over the water a good many feet and a considerable amount of the current passed under the cliff.

When I returned to the boat I called the carpenter, who had been foreman on Construction for years with the Oregon Steam Navigation Company and had asked to go with me for the excitement of this trip. Putting my foot on the starboard guard about ten feet abaft of the stem, I said: "She will strike about here. I want you to run in a bulkhead six feet back of that to the midship keelson, then have the mate back it up with cordwood in case the water should rush in hard enough to tear away your bulkhead."

He examined the falls and replied: "You ain't intending to go over that place, are you? You will drown us all." I looked at him a moment and then asked: "Tom, you never had much notoriety, did you?" "No, why?" "They have all our names that are on this boat, and if you should be drowned your name would be in every paper in the United States and Europe."

His reply: "Oh, go to hell!" sounded like the decree of fate. I replied: "Put in the bulkhead, Tom, and we'll chance the other place." An hour later the sounds of his hammer ceased and I heard a mumbling. Walking softly to the bulkhead hatch, I heard: "Damned old fool going to be drowned for excitement because a damned fool wants notoriety." But the bulkhead went in good.

The next morning I made the only quarter-deck speech of my life. Calling the crew together, I said: "Boys, you have persuaded yourselves that there is danger to your lives in going over those falls, but there is not a particle of danger to your lives. This boat is built of wood enough to float her machinery and there is forty cords of wood in the hold. We could knock her bow and side in and while the wreck is floating we have boats enough to carry us all ashore. There are life preservers enough for three apiece if you want them, but don't get excited and jump overboard. Snake River never gives up her dead. Now get ready to go."

When we dropped over the fall we seemed to be facing certain destruction on the cliff below, but I knew my engineer was "all there" and would answer promptly. We backed slowly and within ten feet of the rocks to starboard her bow passed the mouth of Copper Creek, where an eddy emptying gave her a slight swing out and I backed strong with helm hard to starboard—the bow must take its chances now, the stern must not.

Almost before one could speak the bow touched the point of the cliff just hard enough to break those guard timbers without touching the hull, and we bounded into the still water below. The carpenter who had stationed himself on the hurricane deck outside of the pilot house with two life preservers around him stepped in front of the pilot house and shouted: "Hurrah, Cap! You start her for hell and I'll go with you from this on!"

A little below Copper Creek Falls we entered the canyon and although a bright sun was shining outside, in the canyon it was twilight. I was too busy watching the surface of the river but the men on deck said they saw stars through the gloom. Shortly after coming out of the canyon we passed down a slight cataract that has cut its way through a plateau of blue clay and granite boulders. The channel was not over sixty feet wide and a mile or two long, with a drop estimated as one hundred feet to the mile. We tied up on account of wind the rest of the day and all night at Johnson Creek, which is now the head of navigation, and reached Lewiston May 24th …

From time to time in years to come, small stern-wheelers and screw-propeller boats would venture upriver into the white-water rapids of Hell's Canyon, assisted through the rapids by ringbolts buried in the rocks of the cliff walls from which a quarter-mile of stranded steel cable would be carried downstream into quiet water below the rapid in a waterproof barrel. There, an ascending boat would pick up the cable, detach the barrel, then hook the cable onto a power winch aboard, following which it would literally haul itself up through the rapid by tightening the bow winch foot by foot while the stern-wheel or screw-propeller pushed the craft from behind.

But the creek at Johnson Bar would remain the head of navigation, just as it was in the days of the Snake River's veteran pilot, Captain William Polk Gray.

20.

Though in their mid-seventies now, Tommy and Freda Warren were still in good health that crisp, clear, November 15, 1896, morning at Cascades Locks to celebrate the opening of the ship canal. Even so, Tommy had decided that this would be a good time to retire as a senior captain for the O.R.&N. Company. Where time had gone, he did not know. But sixty years had passed since he'd signed on as third mate aboard the little Hudson's Bay Company ship, the *Beaver*, which had been the first steam-propelled vessel to operate on the Columbia River. When Freda jokingly suggested that his retirement was a protest against what was being done to the river he loved, he admitted that she was partly right.

"When it comes to accepting change, I'm like my father, I suppose. Till the day he died, he felt that steam was a poor substitute for sail and would never last. Sure, it's going to be convenient to take a boat from the mouth of the Columbia all the way upriver to The Dalles. But for old-timers like me, something has been lost."

"What, dear? Tell me exactly what you feel has been lost."

"Youth and freedom, I suppose. Both the river and I are getting older and more wrinkled."

"Not to me, darling. I think you're both still very handsome."

Today in the depths of the Columbia Gorge, the river certainly was demonstrating how beautiful it could be, Tommy agreed. Usually at this time of year clouds hung low, skies were gray, and strong, rain-laden winds lifted whitecaps that river people called "smoke" off the churning, choppy waves. But as the lock and canal dedication ceremonies got under way at high noon, the sky was cloudless and brilliantly blue, not a breath of wind stirred, and the early autumn air was as sweet as sparkling wine.

Though Tommy might not look or feel his age, he could not help being aware of it, for he was the oldest of three generations of Warren family Columbia River captains present at the dedication ceremonies.

Coming down from Wallula with his still beautiful black-haired wife, Daphne, was Captain Lars Warren, who had been given command of the *Inland Queen* just before the anniversary cruise back in 1871. Also here was Captain Lily Warren Williams, as blue-eyed, golden-haired, and lovely as Freda had been at her age. Lily had earned her captain's license at the age of twenty-one, just as her father Lars had done twenty-five years ago. Emil Warren had seen it coming.

"Hell, I knew when she blackmailed me into letting her take the first mate's examination, she'd be a captain within three years. A month after she got her mate's ticket, she took command of the *Lady Duck*, with George going below decks as chief engineer. Then six months ago, she did something real sneaky."

"What was that?"

"You've heard of Taylor's Nautical School down in San Francisco?"

"Sure," Tommy said. "That's where seamen and rivermen go to bone up for examinations for their mate's and master's licenses."

"Right. Lily applied for admission to the school. When they told her they didn't accept women, she said that unless they could show her a maritime law against admitting females, she would get a federal court order insisting that their school take her in. So they did."

"And she passed?"

"With flying colors, as you might expect. When she took the examination for her master's license later, she passed it, too, so they had to give her a captain's rating. At first, she was restricted to piloting the *Lady Duck* between Portland and Astoria. But when she and George bought more boats and expanded their operations, the maritime commissioners threw up their hands and gave her a captain's license good on any waters in the Pacific Northwest."

"That's our Lily," Tommy said with a smile. "Is her company making money?"

"In ways you wouldn't believe. The *Lady Duck* can go anywhere there's a light dew. Fully loaded, she draws only a foot of water."

"Sounds like just the right kind of boat for the lower river."

"It is. Lily showed me a picture she took several miles up the Cowlitz of a farmer who'd driven his wagon into the river where there was no dock, parking it in six inches of water while he transferred sacks of potatoes directly from his wagon to the freight deck of the boat. Accommodating as we used to be, Tommy, the O.S.N. Company never gave service like that."

"She seems to have found a market we overlooked."

"Here's another market she developed. While she was in San Francisco, she made the rounds of the ladies' wear stores and bought a stock of hats, dresses, and coats she was sure she could sell to women living along the river. If the ladies wanted to see what the clothes looked like on a live model, Lily would put them on and parade around in them. Pretty as she is, she sold her whole stock in a hurry at a nice profit. Some days, George says, she sold the clothes right off her back and had to borrow a pair of his coveralls to wear home."

"Lars is proud of her, I know, and so am I," Tommy said. "But having a granddaughter as a licensed river captain makes me feel mighty old."

"If it will make you feel any better, brother, you can look backward and say your father and grandfather were captains on the Columbia, too. Lars pointed that out to us when we went on the anniversary cruise back in '72. That puts you in the middle of five generations of Columbia River captains."

By now, the days of "benevolent monopoly," first by the O.S.N. Company and then by its successor the O.R.&N. Company, had passed. Thanks to Emil Warren's behind-the-scenes manipulations, the era of "accommodation" had come. Which was a nice way of saying it was better to achieve corporate peace among transportation companies by paying a rival not to duplicate services in an area whose potential revenue could make money for only one carrier.

Operating on the river now were the boats of three companies: Shaver Transportation; the O.R.&N.; and The Dalles, Portland & Astoria Navigation Company. As the oldest pilot on the middle river, Captain Tommy Warren had been invited to be an honored guest aboard the first boat to enter the locks, the *Sarah Dixon*, which was commanded by the owner of the company, Captain James W. Shaver. Standing beside Captain Shaver in the pilot house as the lower lock gates were closed, the lock flooded, and the boat smoothly lifted twenty-four feet, Tommy felt distinctly uncomfortable as he gazed out at the white-water rapids rolling past. Floating serenely around a rapid by diverting a portion of the river's own water to defy the law of gravity seemed like cheating, in a way. Sooner or later, he suspected, the law of gravity would take revenge.

Directly behind the *Sarah Dixon* in the 490-foot-long lock was the *Regulator*, while behind it was the *Dalles City*, each vessel loaded to capacity with dignitaries and deck passengers going along for the historic ride. Aboard all three boats, the dining saloons and bars had been open for the past two hours, with bands playing dance music and patriotic airs as the boats moved up the six-mile-long ship canal. When the *Sarah Dixon* reached the upper lock and sat waiting for its 18-foot lift to fill, Captain James Shaver gave Tommy a sidelong look and a sly grin.

"I suppose you plan to be onboard the first boat to reach The Dalles?"

"Why, yes, Jim, I do. Since the dedication committee turned down the three-boat-race idea as too dangerous and settled for a coin flip, I understand it's agreed that your boat will be the first one through the locks, the *Dalles City* second, and the *Regulator* third. After all three boats pass through the locks, there will be a few more speeches and toasts, I'm told, then the *Regulator* will lead the way on upriver to The Dalles."

"That was the order decided by the coin flip, yes. But while the coin was in the air, I put my hands behind my back and crossed my fingers—"

"—so Freda and I have accepted the invitation of Captain Walter Snow to transfer to the *Regulator* above Cascade Locks—" What Jim Shaver had just said suddenly registered on Tommy. "Crossed your fingers, you say? Why did you do that?"

"Because I believe in free competition, Captain Warren. If things work out the way I've planned, the *Regulator* will be wallowing in the *Sarah Dixon*'s wake all the way to The Dalles. I advise you to stay aboard."

How the matter had been arranged, Tommy never knew, but somehow during the speeches and festivities at the Upper Cascades several attractive, friendly young ladies lured Captain Walter Snow into the ladies' saloon, where champagne was flowing freely amid song, laughter, and high-spirited conversation around the piano. Meanwhile, Captain James Shaver instructed his chief engineer to stoke the fire under the boilers with pitch-filled wood. When the speeches were finished and the three boats headed upriver at what was supposed to be a safe, sane pace, the safety valve aboard the *Sarah Dixon* somehow got stuck in the closed position, with the result that both the *Regulator* and the *Dalles City* were left far behind, while the *Sarah Dixon* and Captain James Shaver's guest, Captain Tommy Warren, arrived in The Dalles a full half-hour ahead of the two other boats.

Though the owners of the losing steamboats were irate and threatened dire revenge against the captain who had crossed his fingers and showed them his heels, all parties concerned were soon mollified when agreements were made to divide potential revenue on the middle and lower river.

"As I understand it," Emil told Tommy, "The Dalles, Portland & Astoria Company will pay Shaver two hundred and fifty dollars a month to stay off the middle river. The O.R.&N. Company has offered Shaver the same amount if his company will quit competing with our fast night boat, the *T. J. Potter*, on the Portland-Astoria run. In return, we'll let the *Sarah Dixon* have a monopoly on the Clatskanie and short-haul routes on the lower river for as long as he wants it. That way, we can all stay alive."

Truth was, Tommy noted with an odd detachment now that he had retired, "staying alive" was about all the steamboat companies managed to do for the next few years, despite the expensive improvements that had been made to river navigation. The chief competitor was the railroad, for long-haul shippers preferred rail because of its speed and convenience. So far as passenger traffic was concerned, most people living along the banks of the Columbia and the Snake favored traveling the leisurely, comfortable, scenic way—by boat—despite the fact that it took them longer to get where they wanted to go. Since passenger traffic alone could not pay a profit to steamboat companies, more and more boats were taken out of service, brought downriver, or junked. Left with little or no competition in the freight-carrying field, the railroad companies raised their rates higher and higher.

In response, grain growers and bulk shippers living east of the Cascades screamed their demands for government lock-and-canal projects that would give them the "open river" they felt they needed to bring down exorbitant rail freight rates. As one of the few captains still working the Celilo-Lewiston run on a regular schedule, Lars Warren watched developments with considerable interest.

The last great barrier to free and open navigation of the Columbia River now lay between The Dalles and Celilo Falls. For more than eight miles the river churned and boiled through one impassable rapid after another. As far back as 1858, a nineteen-mile-long wagon road had been scraped through the sagebrush, over which freight bound for the interior could be hauled. In 1863, this was replaced by an O.S.N. Company portage railroad, whose cost had been $650,000.

After operating until 1882, this south bank line became a link in what would eventually become the Union Pacific to Portland.

In an attempt to quiet the increasingly angry demands of shippers for river improvements at Celilo, the Corps of Engineers set forth a number of ingenious proposals. The most imaginative of these was an elaborate boat-railway that would hydraulically hoist steamboats from the river at the foot of Five Mile Rapids and transport them eight miles to the head of Celilo Falls.

As Lars understood it, the way this would work was that a steamboat would pull into a partially filled lock with flatcars parked below. Draining the lock would lower the vessel onto the cars, which then would be towed by four locomotives pulling side by side to another lock above the rapids, where the process would be reversed. Though Congress appropriated $250,000 for planning and right-of-way purchase in 1896, only $30,000 had been spent by the end of the 1900 fiscal year. By then, the folly of the scheme had become clear, so Congress ordered all work halted while a study was made of the feasibility and cost of a more conventional ship canal.

"Which is a shame in a way," Lars told his father. "Now we'll always wonder if such a cockamamie scheme would have worked. I've seen trains ride on ferryboats, but never a boat on a train."

An 1879 survey recommended a canal on the Washington side of the river at a cost of $7.6 million, but nothing came of it. In 1888, another called for one on the Oregon shore at a cost of $3.7 million. Again, the idea was shelved. By 1900 a new plan was ready, suggesting two locks and a three-thousand-foot canal around Celilo Falls; a thirty-three-foot lift lock; a nine-thousand-foot canal around Five Mile Rapids, with a submerged dam at the head of these rapids; and navigational improvements at Three Mile Rapids. The whole project was estimated to cost around $4 million. By fits and starts, the work progressed as administrations and economic conditions changed from year to year, but it never totally stopped. The completion date, Lars was informed by one of his Corps of Engineer friends, was estimated to be ten to fifteen years away.

Meanwhile, a mining boom in the lower portion of Hell's Canyon drew Lars's attention to the area when the promoters of what was called the Eureka mine came to him and asked if the O.R.&N. Company could give them boat service for hauling mining equipment in and precious metal out of the remote, inaccessible district, which had few roads or trails. Making an exploratory trip upriver from Lewiston on a small company stern-wheeler with the veteran riverman, Captain Harry Baughman, Lars told the managers of the Eureka Mining and Smelting Company that, while the O.R.&N. Company did not own the kind of boat required to navigate the fifty-five miles of rapids and white water between Lewiston and the site of the mine, it would be glad to help design and build one to fill the needs of the Eureka Mining & Smelting Company. Furthermore, the O.R.&N. Company would give Captain Baughman a leave of absence so that he could operate it, as well as contract to transship the refined ore produced by the mine downriver from Lewiston at favorable rates. The mining company agreed to the terms.

"Since you've been so helpful in this matter, Captain Warren," a plump, well-dressed, red-faced Eureka Mining Company executive named Jeremiah Waddingham confided in Lars, "I'm going to let you in on a closely held secret."

"Oh? What's that?"

"According to the assay reports returned from the tunnel we're drilling at the mouth of the Imnaha, there's ten million dollars' worth of copper deposits in that area alone. Furthermore, there's enough recoverable gold and silver to pay the cost of the entire operation. So the copper will be pure profit."

"Sounds like you've got a winner, Mr. Waddingham."

"Already we've sold five thousand dollars' worth of stock in New York and San Francisco. We plan to offer another five thousand dollars' worth of shares in Portland next month. If you'd like to invest in a sure thing, I can let you in on the ground floor."

"Thank you, Mr. Waddingham. I'll give it some thought."

As a matter of fact, Lars Warren knew a great deal more about the history of mining in the Hell's Canyon region of the Snake than Jeremiah Waddingham did, for the walls on either side of the river had been riddled with "gopher hole" mines ever since the Idaho boom days of the 1860s. So far as he was aware, nobody had struck a bonanza yet. Because each spring's flood in the high country to the east and south washed down deposits of "flour" gold that settled along the sandbars as the river level subsided, a prospector working with a shovel, pan, rocker, or sluice box could recover eight to ten dollars' worth of gold a day, if he worked hard enough. But only a handful of Chinese miners willing to move in and take the white man's leavings were industrious enough to do that.

Back in 1886, there had been a scandal that reached international levels when thirty-three Chinamen working a sandbar sixty miles above Lewiston had been brutally murdered and their bodies thrown into the river by half a dozen white roughs who had seen them working and thought they had made a big strike. In the newspaper accounts Lars had read, the amount of gold allegedly stolen ranged from five thousand dollars to fifty-thousand dollars, according to whose story you believed. Eventually, four of the suspected murderers were brought to trial, but were acquitted because of "lack of evidence." None of the stolen gold was ever found.

As for the copper deposits now being worked by the Eureka Mining & Smelting Company, they were real enough, Lars knew, for he was personally acquainted with Martin Hibbs, the man who had made the original strike. Having filed a homestead claim in the depths of Hell's Canyon, where he could raise cattle "without hearing a church bell or a train whistle"—both indications of civilization that ranchers disliked—Martin Hibbs long had made a hobby of chipping off intriguing-looking rock samples, then taking them to his cousin, Bas Hibbs, who was a mining engineer, for evaluation.

Poking around with friend named Luke Barton one day near the steep canyon where the Imnaha River joined the Snake, the two men knocked off a few pieces of grayish-green rock, put them in their saddlebags, then showed them to Bas Hibbs when they paid him a visit at his cabin a few miles up the valley. After making a few simple tests, he said, "Boys, if this stuff assays as well as I think it will, you've got it made. My advice to you is, hump yourselves back down the Imnaha, stake out your claims, then make tracks into town and register them."

This Martin Hibbs and Luke Barton did. Being complete amateurs in the mining game and having no idea of how to go about developing a copper claim, they shopped around until they found an interested buyer, sold their claims to what soon became the Eureka Mining & Smelting Company for fifteen-thousand dollars, then, rich beyond their wildest dreams, went back to ranching in the depths of Hell's Canyon where they could raise cattle away from the sound of church bells and train whistles.

Cynic that he was, Lars suspected that the money the two men had received for their claims might very well be the only treasure ever recovered from the mine, whose optimistic name *Eureka!* was Greek for "I've found it!"

Developing a mine in this area offered many problems, Lars knew. No wagon roads came within twenty-five miles of the site, and the pack trails were steep and dangerous. At river level, no trees grew—a serious handicap in the days when it was axiomatic that "it takes a forest to support a mine." Lumber was needed for buildings and for shoring tunnels, while a great deal of firewood was required to stoke the steam boilers in the stamp mills and the smelter.

For forty years, Lewiston, Idaho, fifty-five miles down the Snake River, had been the supply center for north-central Idaho mines. Waterways normally offered the natural and logical avenues for transportation, but the Snake ran downhill in such a hurry in this area that no regular boat service had ever been established on its turbulent, surging course. In this stretch of river, no less than thirty-two rapids were distinctive enough to have names—and several of them were killers.

But the lure of precious metal in Hell's Canyon prompted the Eureka Mining & Smelting Company, with the help of Captain Lars Warren and the O.R.&N. Company, to build a boat suitable for transporting men, animals, and supplies between Lewiston and the site on a regular schedule. It would be called the *Imnaha.* While its keel was laid and its hull began to take shape in Lewiston, work went on at a feverish pace upriver. On February 27, 1903, a reporter for the Lewiston *Tribune* wrote:

> At their Imnaha camp, a force of thirty men are now driving extensive tunnels into the bowels of the mountains. Forty more are working on a wagon road leading to the timber supply, where a sawmill will operate. W. E. Adams, the engineer, is now engaged in surveying a townsite at the mouth of Deer Creek, about a mile and a half from the smelter. Eureka has been selected as the name of the new town, which ought to become a place of considerable importance in the near future.

Far from being a homemade boat, the *Imnaha*'s boilers came from Portland, her engines from Wisconsin, and some of the machine parts from Pennsylvania. Several special features enabled her to cope with the wildest river in the Pacific Northwest. Sturdily built and heavily cross-braced in the bow, she stretched 125 feet with a 26-foot beam.

Able to carry one hundred passengers and a large cargo of freight, she drew only twelve inches of water when fully loaded. It was estimated that on trips upriver she could handle 50 tons of freight; coming downriver, 125 tons. To breast the heavy current of the Snake, her steam boiler operated at pressures up to 250 pounds per square inch.

If the power of her engines proved unequal to the task of driving the boat through the rapids, she carried fifteen hundred feet of steel cable wound around a power capstan in her bow with which she could pull herself through the white water. After making a trial run downriver to Riparia, seventy miles below Lewiston, Captain Harry Baughman pronounced the *Imnaha* ready to tackle the job for which she had been built.

"Would you like to come along for the ride?" he asked Lars, who, with his ten-year-old son, Douglas Thomas Warren, was picking up Celilo-bound cargo at Riparia that day on the regular run of the *Inland Queen*. "As the first man to chart that stretch of river, you know it better than anyone else."

"Sorry, I'll have to pass this time," Lars said, shaking his head. "Maybe on a later trip—"

Much to Lars's surprise, Douglas, who was standing beside him on the dock when Captain Baughman extended the invitation, tugged at his father's sleeve and said urgently, "Could I go in your place, Dad? Would Captain Baughman mind?"

"Of course you can go!" Captain Baughman said with a hearty laugh. "You can be my cabin boy, Douglas, just like your father was aboard the *Colonel Wright* when he was your age."

Giving his son a puzzled look, Lars asked, "Why this sudden interest in a riverboat trip, Doug? You've never liked boats before. In fact, you wouldn't have come along with me on this trip if you hadn't wanted to see the Indian pictographs I'd told you about on the rocks at the mouth of the Palouse River."

Turning red and looking embarrassed, Douglas Warren lowered his eyes, shook his head, then mumbled, "It's not the boat trip I'm interested in, Dad. It's the mine. I want to see it. Is there anything wrong with that?"

From the time Douglas Thomas Warren had begun to toddle, the boy's lack of interest in boats and the river had baffled Daphne, who more than once had exclaimed in exasperation, "Considering all we went through to have a son after producing three daughters, you'd think he would take *some* interest in the Warren family tradition of being sea or river captains. But no. All he cares about is making mud pies, collecting Indian arrowheads, and picking up pretty rocks."

"Now and then a male member of the Warren clan does prefer dry land to water, dear," Lars said placatingly. "Like Uncle Emil, for instance, who turned out to be a pretty sharp lawyer."

"Weren't you counting on Doug becoming a riverboat captain?"

"We've already got a riverboat captain in the family, Daphne. Her name is Lily, in case you've forgotten."

"I haven't forgotten, darling. I'm as proud of her as you are. But I thought you had your heart set on Doug following in your footsteps."

"Times change. Riverboat traffic is not what it once was. We'll have to let Doug be whatever he wants to be."

A tall, slim, quiet boy with rust-colored hair and brown eyes, Doug Warren had always been something of a loner, taking more pleasure in solitary hikes into the sage-covered desert or climbs over the basaltic cliffs bordering the river than he did in associating with white and Indian boys his age who preferred to hang around the boat landing or the railroad station, watching boats and trains. Like all members of the Warren family, he loved to read, but the books he perused so avidly dealt with land rather than water subjects.

As Lars hesitated, Captain Baughman, a big, good-natured, solid man in his mid-fifties, put a hand on the boy's shoulder and smiled.

"Let him come along, Lars. I'll take good care of him."

"Well, if he won't be a nuisance—"

"If he misbehaves, I'll just strap a life preserver on him, toss him into the river, and tell him to swim back to Wallula. You can fish him out as he floats by."

Carrying only its crew, a few passengers, and a reporter for the Lewiston *Tribune*, the new stern-wheeler left its dock Tuesday afternoon, June 30, 1903, cheered on by several hundred spectators. Though everyone else onboard was interested in the white-water rapids through which the *Imnaha* must fight its way, Doug Warren's gaze for the next fifty-five miles was riveted on the fascinating spectacle of the rising canyon walls, for to him this trip into the deepest canyon in North America was the adventure of a lifetime.

For the first twenty miles, the rapids were mild, the *Tribune* reporter wrote later, giving the boat little trouble. Reaching what was known as the Earl Place a mile below Buffalo Rock, the *Imnaha* tied up for the night.

The next day, she resumed her journey, passing through rapids every mile or so as the riverside bluffs rose higher and higher above either shore. Pulling in to the mouth of the Grande Ronde on the Washington side of the river, the boat paused long enough to take on a supply of fuel and water, then made ready for the three-mile run to the foot of Wild Goose Rapids, long regarded as a major obstacle to navigation upriver. The *Tribune* reporter gave a graphic description of its nature:

> The rocks in fact unnaturally force an immense volume of water against the natural flow of the river and a wall of seething, swirling water results. At the right of this channel the bluff extends almost perpendicular to the waterline and a boat is forced to the left and into the face of the steep, rough climb. The *Imnaha* crept along the right bank of the island slowly and then plunged into the rapid.
>
> The steam gauge showed 210 pounds and the boat steadily crowded forward, while the water dashed in roils to the rim of the lower deck. In two minutes the crest of the rapid had been reached. Cheers were heard above the rush of the waters and the din of the heavy engines. Then the steam gauge began to fall, and slowly, inch by inch, the boat was carried back. Bad coal had defeated the noble craft, and when she drifted into the lee of the island the gauge registered but 160 pounds.
>
> The bells in an instant rang ahead, the boat was pointed to the left channel, and in just three minutes Wild Goose had been conquered and the boat nestled calmly under a bluff in peaceful waters above.

When questioned about the loss of power, Captain Baughman told the reporter: "The coal is inferior and the boiler fouled. With a few more pounds of steam, we could run the main channel. In fact with good fuel, the *Imnaha* could climb a tree."

Poor or scarce fuel long had been the curse of steamboat operations on Snake River, Captain Baughman said, both below and above Hell's Canyon. Pitch-filled wood burned better than low-grade coal, but no pine forests grew at river level. Cordwood cut at higher elevations, as it would have to be at the Eureka mine site, and then hauled by wagon eight or more miles down to the river over narrow, twisting roads, was both expensive and scarce.

Leaving her moorings above Wild Goose, the *Imnaha* spent more than three hours fighting her way twelve miles upstream to the mouth of the Salmon River. Two strong rapids—Cougar and Coon Hollow—were negotiated with no more than 182 pounds of steam pressure. Above the Salmon the craft entered waters traveled only once before by an upriver-bound steamboat. Placing a hand on Douglas Warren's shoulder, Captain Baughman raised his voice to make himself heard above the roar of the engines and the rapids as he yelled at the reporter, "This boy's father, Lars Warren, was aboard the *Colonel Wright* back in 1864 when it went twenty-five miles on upriver in the first trip ever. He was just a fourteen-year-old cabin boy and second mate then, but smart enough to chart and name every rapid in the upper river. Be sure and put that in your story."

"I suppose you plan to be a riverboat captain, too," the reporter yelled at Doug Warren. "Just like your father?"

After giving the question a moment of serious thought, Doug shook his head, then gave it a serious answer. "No Sir, I don't. I'd rather be a geologist or a mining engineer. That's why I'm making this trip—to see which I like best."

Being preoccupied with the spectacular scenery in this section of river, neither the reporter nor Captain Baughman reacted to what Doug realized was an overly serious reply to a casually asked question. Feeling a little foolish, he turned his attention back to the narrowing canyon walls, which here pinched the river's channel in so tightly that it was less than a hundred feet wide. Directly ahead lay Mountain Sheep Rapid, Captain Baughman said, with the Eureka mine site just two miles beyond. But in those next two miles, the *Imnaha* would encounter serious problems. The reporter explained them to *Tribune* readers:

> On the right hand bank for a distance of several hundred feet, huge boulders have rolled into the channel, forming innumerable cross-currents and swirls. Then the roils from the upper rapids are met, which leads to "The Narrows." The latter, as the name suggests, comprises a chute of water that pours down with a steep fall between a long ledge of rocks and an immense rock that has fallen from the mountains above into the stream.
>
> Directly back of the rock lies an eddy which forms a back current of perhaps five miles an hour. The water presented an innocent appearance to the passengers. But Captain Baughman saw trouble ahead. A driving rainstorm with a strong wind was prevailing when the boat shot into the race of the narrows. The *Imnaha* made a game fight for

a minute and poked her nose beyond the point of rock to the left. But a swirl from the current veered her to the right and she was crowded back. Captain Baughman rang to go ahead, but like a flash the stern-wheel was caught in the back current and the boat shot to the opposite shore, turning completely around. She then faced downstream and a landing was made beneath the right bank.

It was decided to put out a line and the cable was strung for a distance of a quarter of a mile along the right hand shore. The boat again shot out into the stream and tackled the strong current, but she had approached to a point within only ten feet of the rock when the heavy current of the eddy again caught her.

Straight toward the bluffs on the right bank she darted, and as the bow turned with the current the cable "deadman" gave way. Captain Baughman signaled for a back wheel, but the bow grazed the bluff. The bow then swung back across the stream and the hull slid on a sloping rock, where the craft was temporarily lodged. She was soon, however, backed off the rock and the run to the opposite bank was made, where the craft was tied up for the night.

When Captain Baughman directed a deckhand to take a two-mile hike along the narrow right-hand shore to the Eureka mine site, requesting that a crew and explosives to blast away the obstructing rock be sent downriver, Doug Warren asked eagerly, "Can I go along?"

"Sorry, Son," the captain answered, shaking his head. "When you're aboard the boat, I can look after you—as I promised your father I'd do. But along the shore, the canyon is full of rock slides, rattlesnakes, and all kinds of hazards I can't protect you from. You'll have to stay aboard the boat."

It was on the tip of Doug's tongue to tell Captain Baughman that rock slides, rattlesnakes, and hazards ashore did not scare him a bit. Then he remembered his father's warning not to make a nuisance of himself, so he stayed silent.

In response to the captain's request, mining engineer W. C. Adams came down to the spot where the *Imnaha* was moored, examined the rock, and estimated that the task of removing it would take several days. After a full day of drilling, setting charges, and blasting out ledges on the Oregon side of the canyon, he decided that the big rock on the Idaho side of the channel must be pulverized, too. Impatient with the delay, Captain Baughman went ashore—this time letting Doug go with him—and hiked up to the head of the Mountain Sheep Rapid to give it a closer evaluation. After contemplating the wild, tumbling, tossing water for a few minutes, he clapped Doug on the shoulder and exclaimed, "If your father could run it, so can I. Tomorrow is the Fourth of July. We'll celebrate it, Doug, by running Mountain Sheep without waiting for the rock to be blasted. How does that sound to you?"

"Fine, Sir. I'm sure you can do it."

Shortly after daylight the next morning, a six-man crew went ashore on the Oregon side of the river, dragging with them the fifteen hundred feet of steel cable carried aboard the boat, managing to manhandle it over the rocks, through the shallows, and past several projecting lava bluffs to a spot above the Mountain Sheep Rapid, where they secured a loop in its upper end around the base of a massive granite boulder. Because the downstream end of the cable did not quite reach the spot where the *Imnaha* was moored, a three-quarter-inch-thick rope line was tied to the lower end of the cable, with a workman taking a station atop a flat rock, prepared to heave the rope end aboard the boat when and if the *Imnaha* managed to churn her way that far into the surging white water. The *Tribune* reporter detailed what followed:

> At exactly 10 o'clock the *Imnaha* left the bank and tackled the current for the fourth time. She "walked" up to the crest between the two rocks where she was held for fully three minutes. The man on the rock made an unsuccessful throw with the light line; there followed two unsuccessful casts by deckhands on the boat, and then Mate Bluhn shot out a line that reached the goal.
>
> In a minute the cable was pulled aboard, the line tightened, and the wiry craft crept inch by inch over the top of the torrent to smooth waters. From the time the *Imnaha* left the rapid until the cable was slacked and taken aboard, only fifteen minutes had elapsed. The run to Eureka was then made in forty-five minutes and the boat tied up at exactly 11 o'clock. She had made the run from Lewiston to Mountain Sheep Rapid in ten hours.
>
> A wild demonstration occurred at Eureka when the boat was seen in the canyon below. On the highest peaks, the miners could be seen waving their hats with enthusiasm, and loud blasts resounded through the valley.

As the boat pulled into the sandbar on the Oregon side of the river, where the dock which would serve the new town of Eureka soon would be built, Captain Baughman explained to the newspaper reporter and to Doug that the continuing explosions echoing and re-echoing off the three-thousand-foot-high walls of the canyon were the hardrock miners and "powder monkeys" exuberantly celebrating both the arrival of the *Imnaha* and the Fourth of July by "shooting off anvils."

"What they do," the captain said, "is cap a stick of dynamite and lay it on an anvil or some other hard surface, then put a big empty tin or iron can on top and light the fuse. It makes the loudest firecracker you ever heard."

"Well, you certainly deserve a twenty-one-anvil salute yourself, Captain Baughman!" the reporter exclaimed. "Your feat in establishing the first boat service between Lewiston and Eureka is an event that will be long remembered."

"Thank you, Sir. But I wasn't the first man to come this far upriver. Doug's father was. Be sure to mention that."

"I certainly will, Captain." The reporter smiled down at Doug. "What are your feelings, young man? Don't you agree that this is a day to remember?"

"Yes Sir, I do," Doug answered politely.

Lifting his eyes to the dark brown canyon wall looming above the sandbar where the boat was being moored, he stared in fascination at the mouth of a horizontal tunnel, into and out of which ore cars pulled by mules were moving. As the boat's lines were being secured, he blurted eagerly, "May I go ashore now, Captain Baughman? I can't wait to see the mine."

21.

IF CAPTAIN LARS WARREN had expected his son, Douglas, to give him a detailed report of the maiden trip of the *Imnaha* up Snake River from Lewiston to Eureka, he was doomed to disappointment. When asked about it on his return to Wallula, Doug said casually, "Oh, it was all right."

"No trouble getting through the rapids?"

"Some of them were kind of rough. Captain Baughman had to rig a line a couple of times. But we made it up and back."

"Judging from the four gunnysacks of rock specimens you brought home, I gather you explored the mine?"

"Oh, boy, I sure did!" Doug exclaimed. "And I learned an awful lot—"

What Doug had learned during a long afternoon of being taken on a tour of the developing Eureka mine by the chief mining engineer, W. C. Adams, was that a lot of drilling, blasting, moving, and crushing of massive amounts of "country rock" must be done before any precious metal could be extracted. Dragging his father out to what Daphne laughingly called the "Rock Bin"—an unused carriage house where he stored all his treasures—Doug showed his father the amazing collection of mineral samples gathered during his tour of the mine, which he had unpacked, sorted, labeled, and laid out on shelves, benches, and tables.

"Mr. Adams told me his company is now working six of its claims," Doug said with an enthusiasm that would brook no interruption. "He says they're developing two mines at the same time, the Mountain Chief and the Delta. That's so they can keep the smelter running night and day, once they get it in operation. Before they can do that, they've got to drive a tunnel through the base of the mountain ridge separating the Imnaha and Snake Rivers."

"Sounds like a lot of work," Lars said. "When do they think it will pay off?"

"When the tunnel is finished, it will be seven hundred forty feet long," Doug continued, ignoring his father's question. "It will have good ventilation, Mr. Adams says, because there will be an opening at both ends. Bad air is always a problem in hardrock mining, he says."

"I should think it would be," Lars murmured.

"The reason there's so much bad air in a mine, Mr. Adams says, is that mineral-bearing rocks such as quartzite, hydrosulfuric pyrite, and cuprous-carbonate contain acids and gases which are harmless when they're locked up inside the rocks, but become deadly when released in confined spaces underground. When he took me into the tunnel, he made sure we both carried miners' safety lamps, which flicker and give you a warning when the air starts turning bad."

"Sounds like Mr. Adams is a careful sort of man."

"He is. Some miners carry caged canaries, he says, which turn on their backs and faint when the air gets bad. But he thinks safety lamps are much better. Besides, canaries are expensive and require special feeding and care."

"Yes, I suppose they do."

"Right now, the tunnel is in one hundred ninety feet on the Snake River side and sixty-five feet on the Imnaha side. All of it is in good smelting ore, Mr. Adams says. When it's done, they plan to sink a shaft below water level, then drift both ways. They've crosscut the pay streak on the hanging wall in six places, Mr. Adams says, and they figure that when they finish it in about six more weeks, the rock they've excavated will furnish the smelter with one hundred tons of ore every day. By then, they'll have a four-stamp crushing mill built—"

There was more, much more, for once Doug started showing his samples and talking about his tour of the mine, Lars could find no way to stop him even if he had wanted to—which he certainly did not. When Doug finally ran down, Lars asked him a question.

"Would you like to become a mining engineer, Doug? When you're a little older, we could send you off to school."

As he always did when asked a serious question, Doug was silent for a time, picking up and intently studying first one rock sample and then another, as if seeking an answer in their multifaceted exteriors.

Finally, he shook his head and said quietly, "I've always liked rocks, you know that, Dad. I don't know why."

"You don't need to have a reason for liking something, Son. Or for disliking it, either. For instance, I've always liked water and boats. But I've never given a hoot for rocks. All I want to know about rocks is how much water is between them and my boat's bottom."

"One reason I'm interested in rocks," Doug said, raising his eyes and gazing off into the distance through the dust-streaked glass of the carriage house window, "is I wonder how they got where they are. How long have they been there? What natural forces created them? Sure, going into a mine and taking samples of all the minerals that are there is real interesting. But learning how they got there would be even more interesting, I think. As I understand it, studying geology would teach me that. So I'd rather become a geologist than a mining engineer."

"Well, whatever you want to be, your mother and I will support you, Doug, you know that," Lars said gently. "Right now, though, it's supper time. Let's go into the house and see what's cooking."

For a more detailed report on the *Imnaha's* first trip to the Eureka mine site, Lars talked to Captain Harry Baughman a few days later in Lewiston, when both the *Inland Queen* and the new boat were there at the same time.

"We suffered some minor hull damage when we scraped against a couple of rock ledges," Captain Baughman said. "But overall, the first trip worked out fine. Even after lining a couple of rapids, we made the upriver trip in ten hours. Coming downriver took just three-and-a-half hours."

"You've asked the Corps of Engineers to do some channel work upriver, I understand, before you establish a regular run to Eureka."

"That's right. The mine manager tells me that it'll be a couple of months before the smelter can produce enough refined ore to give us a load coming downriver. The Corps plans to lease the *Imnaha* as a work boat while they blast out the hazards I've marked on their charts. They've also agreed to set ringbolts in the cliff walls above two rapids."

"Which two?"

"Wild Goose and Mountain Sheep. In both places, the Corps

plans to embed heavy iron rings in the rock walls on the Oregon side of the river, with fifteen hundred feet of steel cable and a waterproof barrel that we can fish out of the water below the rapid, bring the cable aboard, hook it to the steam-powered capstan in the bow, then pull ourselves up through the rapid while the stern-wheel pushes from behind."

"Sounds like a time-saver to me."

"It will be, Lars. Since we won't have to send a crew of deckhands ashore to do our own cable-stringing each trip, it'll be a labor-saver, too."

After completing her channel improvement work with the Corps of Engineers during the next two months, the *Imnaha* began regular runs upriver in September. In early October, she suffered her first serious accident when the current threw her against a rock that punched a hole in her hull. Dropping downriver to Riparia, she was patched up and declared as good as new. Returning to Eureka with a load of half a dozen horses for the mine, she then carried forty tons of granite from the newly opened Lime Point quarry back downriver to Lewiston.

Because the flow of the Snake had become so low downstream from the mouth of the Salmon that navigation was dangerous, additional trips in late October were postponed until autumn rains raised the level of the river. By that time, thirteen trips had been made to and from the rapidly developing mining town of Eureka. The businessmen of Lewiston and the editor of the *Tribune* seemed justified in boasting that the hazards of the Snake River had been overcome.

By November 8, 1903, the rains had come, the Snake began to rise, and the *Imnaha* embarked on her fourteenth trip to Eureka.

It proved to be her last one.

Leaving the Lewiston dock Sunday morning, the first part of the stern-wheeler's trip went smoothly. But only a few minutes before pulling into the landing at Eureka, disaster struck without warning. Captain Baughman later told what happened:

> We had successfully ascended the rapid and cast off the line when in some manner the wheel picked up the bight of the line, which caught in the eccentric rods. As a result, the rods were bent, the rock shaft broken, and the engines rendered useless. At the time this

> occurred, the boat was about four hundred yards above Mountain Sheep Rapids, and the helpless steamer drifted stern-on onto the sharp rock that has been a menace to navigation since the boat was first placed in commission.
>
> The wheel struck the rock squarely and was doubled back over the boat. The bow then swung to the Oregon shore where it remained but a moment when the stern slipped from the rock and swung to the Oregon side while the bow turned against the big rock, completely filling the channel.

The Snake River was only 62 feet wide at that point, Lars knew, so the 125-foot-long boat now was turned broadside to the tremendous force of the current. Fortunately, it hung there long enough for the fifteen crew members and twenty-five passengers to scramble ashore. Quick thinking by Chief Engineer L.H. Campbell prevented what could have been a murderous explosion. He later said:

> Knowing that great danger existed from escaping steam in case the boat was badly injured by striking the rock, my first move was to start the pumps and open the siphons. By the time the boat commenced to go to pieces the steam was so reduced that no danger of an explosion existed. As the boat struck the rock, I swung out of the engine room at the side door, but as the jar was not sufficient to break the pipes the dangerous period had passed and I returned to the engine room to find that the entire stern had been stove in and that the abandonment of the boat was sure to follow.

Only seconds after the last of the crew and passengers got safely ashore, the bow of the disabled boat dipped. The *Imnaha* slipped off the rock upon which she had lodged and drifted into deep water downstream. In an eddy there, she spun around several times. Taking water rapidly now, the hull tilted and the boiler tore loose from its supports and rolled into the water, carrying a large portion of the pilot house with it.

The *Imnaha* was finished.

Though no human lives were lost, several horses tied to stanchions on the freight deck were forgotten by the crewmen scurrying ashore. Their whinnies of terror as the boat sank were pathetic to hear, said the survivors, but nothing could be done to save them.

As in all such disasters on the river, rumors, guesses, and attempts to place blame lasted for months, with no conclusive results. Had an inexperienced deckhand thrown the barrel attached to the slack cable into the river on the wrong side of the boat? Had the helmsman turned the boat the wrong way, making the stern-wheel hook into rather than avoid the looped winching line? Had an order been carelessly given, not heard, or recklessly disobeyed? No one could say.

Ultimately, the blame was placed on Captain Baughman, of course, for the *Imnaha* was under his command. But knowing the man as he did, Lars could not believe that the accident had been entirely his fault. He explained his reasoning to Doug, who was indignant because his captain friend had been charged with negligence.

"When a boat is running a white-water rapid, things can happen awfully fast," he told his son. "A crew member gets distracted and forgets what he's doing, an unexpected swirl passes under the boat, a back-eddy caused by an underwater slide lifts the stern-wheel out of the water for a few seconds—and *wham!*—you're in big trouble. But whatever happens, the captain has to accept the blame."

"Did the O.R.&N. Company have insurance on the boat?"

"It wasn't our boat, Doug. All we did was advise in its design and construction. But no, it wasn't insured. From what I've heard, the Eureka Mining and Smelting Company is writing off its thirty-five thousand dollar cost as a total loss. And as well capitalized as they're supposed to be, they're refusing to build a boat to replace it."

"How will they get their refined ore downriver if they don't have a boat?"

"That's a good question, Doug. Talk is that the Lewiston merchants are raising funds to build a new boat themselves. They're going to call it the *Mountain Gem.*"

"Will Captain Baughman run it?"

"Afraid not. The merchants plan to hire an old friend of mine, William Polk Gray, to be its skipper. If any man knows the Snake River, he does."

The talk proved to be correct. After the Lewiston businessmen had subscribed twenty-two thousand dollars to pay for the building of a new stern-wheeler to ply the upper river, the *Mountain Gem* was launched in September 1904, with Willie Gray as its skipper. But by then the Hell's Canyon mining-boom bubble had burst.

Angry investors who had purchased an estimated two million dollars' worth of stock began filing lawsuits against the corporation directors because their money was going into the ground with no profits coming out. The digging stopped.

With no ore to bring downriver, the *Mountain Gem* ceased runs to Eureka and began hauling freight and passengers on the Snake River below Lewiston. Eventually smaller boats would be built to carry mail, groceries, farm and ranch supplies, fishermen, hunters, and sightseers to remote cabins and camps in the upper reaches of Hell's Canyon.

Prospectors would continue to pan for gold on the sandbars of the Snake, occasionally exposing a vein that merited drilling, blasting, and excavating in "gopher hole" mines. But the bonanza promised at Eureka never was realized. The tunnel between the mouth of the Imnaha and the Snake would remain there for years to come to be explored by the curious and eventually examined by mining experts who would reassess its mineral potential more scientifically than its discoverers and promoters had done.

Not surprisingly, their verdict was that the copper vein's width should have been measured in inches, not feet, and that the potential wealth of the mines in the area should have been stated in thousands rather than in millions of dollars. Like so many boom-and-bust mines, Eureka's real value, Lars suspected, may well have been more in its paper stock certificates than in its copper, silver, or gold.

Fortunately, he had no certificates to burn or to be shown as evidence in lawsuits.

22.

On their way down the Columbia to the Pacific in the fall of 1805, the Lewis and Clark party had missed seeing the future site of Portland because the mouth of the Willamette River had been hidden behind fog, rain, and a tree-covered island. Traveling east the next spring, they would have missed it again if a "Cashook" Indian had not escorted Captain Clark and a party of seven men back to the lower valley of what the local Indians called the Multnomah River for a brief look around, accepting the payment of "a birning glass" for his services.

But on the 100th birthday of the Lewis and Clark Expedition in 1905, the movers and shakers of Portland had no intention of having their city overlooked again. Though Emil Warren by now was seventy-five years old and no longer played an active role in the affairs of the Oregon Rail & Navigation Company, he was delighted with the way his younger mover-and-shaker friends went about calling the attention of the nation and the world to their growing metropolis by putting on a Centennial Exposition.

"It's the kind of con game I always liked to play!" he declared. "More power to them!"

Plans for the "Great Extravaganza," as the celebration came to be called, began before the turn of the century. By then, world's fairs were widely accepted as "schools of progress," attracting investors and newcomers to the host city. It would be, boosters claimed, the greatest exposition ever staged on the West Coast, one that would put the city of Portland on the national map once and for all. If one of the two cities bearing the Portland name should be called a backwoods hamlet, the backers asserted, it must be the one in Maine.

Pointing out that Americans had flocked to the Centennial Exposition at Philadelphia in 1876, to the Columbian Exposition at Chicago in 1893, and to Omaha's Trans Mississippi Exposition in 1898, the local exposition promoters noted that St. Louis was planning a real humdinger for its Louisiana Purchase Exposition in 1904 to celebrate the centennial of the beginning of the Lewis and Clark journey west. Therefore, would it not be eminently fitting, proper, and rewarding for the great state of Oregon in general and for Portland in particular to tell the nation and the world about the Promised Land lying at the end of the Lewis and Clark Trail?

Upon its first proposal in 1895, the idea met with little enthusiasm, for a national depression was two years old and hanging on. Because federal assistance would be required to stage the show, Portland businessmen preferred that any funds appropriated by Congress be spent improving navigation across the bar at the mouth of the Columbia. But by 1900 the mood of the community leaders had turned more optimistic. A committee began exploring the possibilities of putting on the tentatively named "Lewis and Clark Centennial and American Pacific and Oriental Fair."

Though Portland's population was barely one hundred thousand, Emil Warren was glad to see that the city's movers and shakers were thinking big. Businessmen asked to put up $300,000 to get the project rolling pledged that amount within ten days. Dispatching five special agents to stalk the corridors of western capitols and cadge votes in the nearby barrooms, the exposition committee's "con" men showed Emil that they were excellent salesmen. By the end of 1903, sixteen states came through with appropriations for exhibits; ten would construct special buildings. Prompted by the fact that the exhibition would promote and benefit the entire state, the legislature authorized $450,000 for exhibits emphasizing "the development of our material resources and manufacturing interests."

In lobbying for money in Washington, D.C., the Portland promoters soon found out that nobody in Congress cared about historical heroes and their two-thousand-mile trek. But they did share the same vision of the Pacific trade that had motivated the exploration and settlement of the Oregon Country.

With congressional delegations from California and Washington supporting the claim that the exposition was a Pacific Coast enterprise supported by chambers of commerce from San Diego to Spokane, it was not difficult to sell the slogan: "The railroads opened the door and laid the region's resources open for development. The only remaining need is for enough people to break the soil and fell the trees."

When Emil quietly pointed out to his young mover-and-shaker

friends that oceangoing sailing ships and river-plying steamboats had played an important role in laying the region's resources open for development too, the promoters wisely added shipping and the potential of Pacific Rim markets to the region's assets. After Emil did some simple arithmetic and worked out the figures for him, one inspired publicist declared, "China alone offers a tremendous market for American grain. Why, if every Chinaman would eat one pancake a month, it would require all the flour ground from all the wheat raised west of the Mississippi to satisfy the demand. And that flour would have to be carried in ships sailing from West Coast ports."

How the wheat-raisers west of the Mississippi would go about teaching the Chinese to like, let alone pay for, a pancake a month, was a question neither asked nor answered.

From the beginning, President Theodore Roosevelt strongly supported the exposition. But even with his help, a thrifty Congress reduced the requested allocation of $2 million to $475,000. The last step was to settle on a location for the fairgrounds. The site finally chosen was in northwest Portland between the Willamette and Columbia Rivers, an area which contained a grove of trees, 180 acres of pasture, and 220 acres of waist-deep, stagnant water. Still thinking big, the fair commissioners hired Massachusetts landscape architect John Olmstead, whose father had designed New York City's Central Park, to lay out and design the exposition grounds.

Because all the newspapers in the Pacific Northwest were full of stories about the upcoming fair, Lars, Daphne, and two of their children had gladly accepted an invitation from Uncle Emil Warren and his wife Dolores to come down to Portland and stay at their home for a week while attending the show. While there, they would see their oldest daughter, Lily Warren Williams, who, with her husband, George, now owned and ran a successful tug-and-barge business headquartered in Vancouver. Staying home with her rancher husband in the Walla Walla Valley would be their twenty-four-year-old daughter, Sara Jane, who already had a two-year-old son, with another baby due in late summer.

Traveling with Lars and Daphne would be their eighteen-year-old daughter, Dora Ann, who had just finished her final year at the same Catholic school her mother had attended in Walla Walla, and their twelve-year-old son, Douglas Thomas, who next term would be attending Whitman Seminary, which was beginning to make itself a reputation as both a quality upper-grades high school and a liberal arts college.

"What I want to see," Dora Ann declared after reading a brochure on the fair's attractions, "is the million-dollar Japanese 'Gateway to the Orient' pavilion, which is supposed to be the most impressive foreign building on the grounds."

"I'd like to see the 'Carnival of Venice' concession," Daphne mused, "which the brochure says has a four-hundred-foot-long stage and a cast of hundreds. 'Gondolas float between the audience and the stage,' the brochure says, 'and the entertainment consists of dances, choruses, solos, marches, specialties, and tableaux, with a touch of comedy running through the performance.' That sounds like a sight worth seeing."

"What's a tableaux?" Dora Ann asked curiously.

"That's where a bunch of people wearing practically no clothes stand around posing like Greek gods and goddesses," Lars said. "If they get frisky and move, the police arrest them."

"Oh, Father, you're teasing me!" Dora Ann looked questioningly at her brother. "What would you like to see, Doug?"

"The Forestry Building sounds interesting to me. The big lumberman, Simon Benson, is having it built out of the biggest, thickest, most perfect trees to be found in the Pacific Northwest, the brochure says. It's going to be 105 feet wide, 209 feet long, and will look like an Oregon Gothic church. They're calling it 'The Largest Log Cabin in the World.' " He looked at his father. "What do you want to see at the Fair, Dad?"

"Oh, I suppose I'll take in high-toned exhibits—like Professor Barnes and His Educated Animals. I want to see his two trained elk dive off a forty-foot-high platform into a tank of water. Also, Princess Trixie, the intellectual horse, demonstrates her mastery of the English language and arithmetic by whinnying her ABCs and counting up to ten." After a thoughtful pause, Lars added, "Of course, all that walking and gawking will probably make me mighty hungry and thirsty. So I may join Uncle Emil at the end of the day and take in a place he says he likes in downtown Portland."

"Knowing how you and Uncle Emil behave at the end of the day," Daphne said caustically, "I'll bet it's a bar."

"As a matter of fact, it's a block-long eating place called the Oyster House," Lars answered calmly. "Uncle Emil tells me it serves the best oysters, clams, chowder, and seafood in the Pacific Northwest."

"If it's a block long, it must serve beer and whiskey, too."

"Perhaps it does, dear. If so, I'll be a good nephew and join Uncle Emil in a libation or two."

The agreed-upon style of architecture for the buildings on the exposition grounds was Spanish Renaissance, the advance publicity said, which leaned heavily to domes, cupolas, arched doorways, and roofs covered with red tile. One notable exception was the Oregon Forestry Building, which a delighted newspaper critic from New York described: "Standing out like a logger at a toney party, scrubbed and shaved but still wearing a wool jacket in a room full of tails and starched shirts, the Forestry Building is a huge log cabin of the sort no pioneer ever built."

The promotional campaign preceding the exposition began two years in advance, Emil observed, and despite its modest budget, was awesome in scope. More than 250,000 columns of newspaper space were obtained nationwide. Ten thousand newspapers were on the mailing list by the midpoint of the fair. More than six thousand received a weekly packet of features and photographs on western history.

One of the best chunks of money spent on publicity, Emil gathered, was the fifty thousand dollars appropriated by the Oregon Legislature in 1903 for the state's participation in the St. Louis Lewis and Clark Centennial Exposition in 1904. Among many other products donated, displayed, or given away at St. Louis were six tons—a freight car load—of Oregon prunes.

From the moment the exposition opened, June 1, 1905, to the day it closed, October 15, it was clear that Portland had done a superb job of planning to handle its visitors, despite the fact that it was the smallest city ever to put on a world's fair. Because the midsummer flow of the Snake River between its mouth and Lewiston was so low that the *Inland Queen* could not negotiate some of the rapids, Lars, Daphne, Dora Ann, and Douglas Warren chose the first week of July for their visit to Portland. During their stay with Uncle Emil and Aunt Dolores, they spent the days separately or together at the fair, sightseeing and shopping in the city, or traveling up and down the river.

From the central business district, fairgoers could catch the Portland Railway streetcars for a twenty-minute ride for a nickel. For a dime, they could board a steamer for a ride down the Willamette to the U.S. government building on the fairgrounds. For a dollar and fifty cents they could take an eight-hour ride upriver to Cascades Locks and back aboard the newest, fastest, most luxuriously furnished stern-wheeler currently operating on the lower Columbia, the *Bailey Gatzert*, with lunch or supper included according to which of the twice-daily round-trips was taken. Because Lars was a longtime employee and senior captain with the Oregon Rail and Navigation Company, the price of the round-trip ticket for himself and Daphne was even better—free.

Taking the trip twice during the week-long fair, the first time leaving Portland with the eight-thirty morning crowd of excursionists, the second time on the boat departing at five-thirty in the afternoon so that they could enjoy the sights along the river at all times of day, Lars told Daphne that they probably were seeing the best and last of luxury boat travel on the Columbia.

"When the locks and ship canal at Celilo are completed a few years from now, the only traffic moving on the river will be freight. Lily and George are in the right part of the business, I suspect, with their tug and barge company. Old fogeys like me have had their day."

"Oh, pooh! You're only fifty-five years old, Lars. That's not old at all, these days."

"Well, the way they're changing the river with locks, canals, channel-markers, and all the other navigational aids the Corps of Engineers is installing, they're going to make the Columbia so easy to navigate that any twenty-year-old kid can command a riverboat."

"My, my! What *is* the world coming to? You weren't given a boat of your own until you were twenty-one!" Putting an arm through his, Daphne impelled him toward the main saloon of the excursion boat, where the orchestra was tuning up for the after-supper dance scheduled to begin as soon as the vessel cleared the locks, to continue all the way down to Portland through the long summer twilight. "We'll celebrate our approaching old age, dear, by dancing together when the orchestra plays "The Bailey Gatzert March," which was specially written for old fogeys like us."

"How can I dance to a march?" Lars grumbled.

"The same way you danced to a gavotte aboard the *Colonel Wright* forty-five years ago, when you were a love-smitten cabin boy of eleven and I was the nine-year-old girl you adored: by letting me teach you."

"Well, at least this time I won't have your mother's bodyguard, Goliath Samson, watching me like a hawk, ready to toss me overboard if I step on your toes and make you scream."

"As I recall," Daphne said with a giggle, "you did step on my toes, dear. But I managed to keep quiet so that you wouldn't have to be fished out of the river. Even then, I thought you might grow up and amount to something someday."

Neither George nor Lily Williams, who had learned their trade in paddle wheel-propelled boats, were so inconsiderate of Lars' feelings as to relegate him to the role of an "old fogey" quite yet; still, they both had accepted the fact that the day of the stern-wheeler was done, so far as working tugboats were concerned. One possible exception was the radically different, new, steel-hulled stern-wheel tug, the *Jean*, which was built and launched in a Portland shipyard in 1910.

"She's got four diesel engines that can operate independently," Lily told her husband after taking a day off to attend the christening of the new boat. "Her twin stacks are set just aft of the pilot house. She has three rudders and the stern-wheel is in two sections, each one capable of turning backward or forward independently or at the same time."

"Sounds like she'd have good maneuverability."

"Her captain says he can spin the *Jean* in a circle within her own length. Which ought to make her a great harbor tug for tight spots like the Portland docks along the Willamette River."

"How's her fuel consumption?"

"They won't know that till she's been in service for a while," Lily said, shaking her head. "But they think it will be satisfactory."

"Maintaining steam pressure for four engines all the time, while using only two, makes low fuel consumption sound doubtful to me, Lily. But we'll wait and see how she does."

Meanwhile, as traffic increased on the Columbia from Astoria to Portland and on upriver through the Cascades Locks and ship canal to The Dalles, the Williams Tug & Barge Company found its location on the north side of the river in Vancouver, Washington, ideal. By transferring freight carried on seagoing vessels to barges at the Port of Astoria, masters who did not want to navigate the intricacies of channels upriver could save their vessels considerable turnaround time, an important factor these days for increasingly bigger oceangoing ships.

All five tugboats owned by their company were screw-propelled, diesel-fueled craft, highly maneuverable, powerful, low-in-the-water vessels which could pull or push three large barges scaled to fit with only a few inches to spare within the two sets of locks now in operation at the Cascades and those in the process of being built between The Dalles and Celilo.

In national circles these days, New York and San Francisco shipping interests were buzzing with news of two impending events which they were convinced would drastically change the commercial world: completion of the Panama Canal and the probability of another European war. That either happening would affect traffic on the Columbia River was a matter neither Lily nor George took seriously.

"Opening the Panama Canal will lower shipping costs to the West Coast," George conceded. "But I doubt that it will increase our business much. So far as a European war is concerned, that shouldn't affect us at all. Foreign squabbles have never been the concern of the United States in general or the Pacific Northwest in particular—and never will be."

Though the Panama Canal was opened and war did start in Europe in 1914, a much bigger event insofar as the Warren family was concerned was the completion of the Celilo locks and ship canal a year later. Going up to attend the dedication ceremonies on May 10, 1915, Lily was pleased to see her brother, Douglas, with her two sisters, mother, father, and several old family friends there, not the least of whom was William Polk Gray. Though not asked to make a formal speech at the dedication ceremonies, Captain Gray, now in his seventies and looking like an Old Testament prophet with his white hair and beard, had plenty to say to any reporters who cared to listen.

Leading a steamboat fleet that had come downriver from Lewiston, Pasco, Wallula, Umatilla, and Arlington, Captain Gray declared that people who believed that the Columbia and Snake Rivers had only recently been made navigable by the Corps of Engineers were "know-nothings," as far as the history of those rivers was concerned.

"As soon as railroads were built along the banks of the river thirty years ago, the numbskulls started saying the rivers were too dangerous to navigate because of rapids and rocks. This idea was so prevalent that in 1905, when I was preparing to take Idaho Senator Heyburn and a party of excursionists from Lewiston to The Dalles on the *Mountain Gem* for the opening of the portage road, the senator asked me if it would be safe for his wife to make the trip. He was surprised when I told him that the river had been navigated for forty years and at one time carried all the traffic between Portland and Lewiston."

As the climax to a week of festivities which drew an estimated twenty thousand people to Celilo, the official program distributed to the enthusiastic participants declared:

> To the Inland Empire, the Celilo Canal is relatively of as much importance as is the Panama Canal to the nation as a whole. It will reestablish trade lines; it will mean the revision of railroad tariffs; it will bring new development to the great valley of the Columbia, a territory rich with latent possibilities.
>
> This may come about slowly and by gradual degrees, but it will come, and the present celebration commemorating the completion of the Celilo Canal marks the commencement of a new era of commerce and industry for this section of the great Northwest.

To Douglas Warren, now twenty-two years old and soon to graduate from Washington State College with a degree in geology, it was not commerce, industry, or improved river navigation that interested him, so far as completion of the project was concerned. It was the sheer magnitude of the amount of earth that had been moved during the digging of the canal and the construction of the locks. Because only his oldest sister, Lily, seemed interested in the statistics he had learned firsthand, it was to her that he related them.

"Next to the Panama Canal, it's the biggest earth-moving project ever undertaken by the federal government," he said. "One million, four hundred thousand cubic yards of granite had to be excavated, while eight hundred thousand cubic yards of gravel had to be removed. A million pounds of dynamite were used to blast out the channel."

"Did you work on the job?"

"You bet I did! For four straight summers while I was in college, I did grunt work, first with a pick and shovel, then carrying a rod on a survey crew, and finally as a carpenter's helper setting concrete forms. The heaviest labor was on the concrete-pouring crew, when we poured the last of what I was told was two hundred thousand yards of concrete. Believe me, that was real grunt work."

"You look like it agreed with you," Lily said with an affectionate smile as she squeezed his hard-muscled upper right arm. "I've never seen you looking better. You'll be graduating from Washington State College in a few weeks, I hear."

"That's right. With a degree in geology."

"What does a geologist do besides chip off pieces of rocks to see what they're made of?"

"There are several kinds of geologists, Lily. Some look for precious minerals. Some look for oil. Others try to read the history of how the earth was created by the record left in the rocks. Before digging a foundation for any kind of building, bridge, or dam, you've got to know what kind of earth, soil, or rock is underneath. So you hire a geologist to check on it."

"Well, whatever kind of geologist you become, Doug, I know you'll be good at it. But wherever you go, don't forget your big sister, who thinks you're the nicest brother she's got. Come see George and me when you can."

With a final price of $4,850,000, the Celilo Locks and Ship Canal was considered a bargain by the Inland Empire farmers and businessmen who had lobbied for it so long. Eight-and-a-half miles long, sixty-five feet wide, and eight feet deep, the canal had numerous passing turnouts so that traffic would not be delayed. Now that it had been put in service, it allowed the largest steamer operating on the river to travel from Astoria, Oregon, at the mouth of the Columbia, to the Snake River port of Lewiston, Idaho, 470 miles inland without a single portage.

At long last, the advocates of an "Open River" had achieved their dream.

23.

FOLLOWING DOUG WARREN'S graduation from Washington State College in late May, responses to his job-seeking letters were so scant that he began to wonder if he would ever find work.

"Now that I've got a degree saying I'm a geologist," he complained to his father after spending the first three weeks of June loafing around home, "where do I go to get a job?"

"You'll find one, Son. Give it a little time."

"I'm so sick of doing nothing, Dad, I'd even be willing to go to work on the *Inland Queen*. Can you use a deckhand?"

"Coming from you, that's quite a concession," Lars said with a smile. He shook his head. "Right now, I'm laying off rather than hiring help. Low as Snake River is at this time of year, we're making the Lewiston run just every other week, while the Columbia River schedule to Celilo has been trimmed back to weekly."

"I thought the new locks and canal at Celilo were supposed to increase traffic."

"Eventually, they will, I'm sure. But right now, business is slow."

"I feel so damned useless, Dad, not working."

"Be patient, Son. Something will turn up."

A few days later, the downriver mail from Lewiston brought a letter from John Fleming, a geology professor under whom Doug had studied at Washington State College. It read:

Dear Doug:

If you'd care to work with me on a summer job studying the Nespelem Mining District, I can offer you bed, board, and a dollar a day as long as my grant money holds out. I'll be doing some field work on the Colville Reservation for the U.S. Geological Survey under the overall direction of Joseph Pardee, a man I met while at Yale.

In order to clear title to a hundred or so claims white miners have made on what are now Indian lands, the U.S.G.S. is assessing the mineralization and ore-bearing rock formations on the Colville Reservation. Joseph Pardee has asked me to do the Nespelem sector, giving me a small grant which will pay for food, equipment, camping gear, and the rental of horses for a couple of months.

If you can work as my assistant for the rest of the summer, drop me a line by return mail, then plan to meet me at Agency headquarters in Nespelem no later than July 3.

Best Regards,
John Fleming

Running down to the dock to show the letter to his father, who was just about to take the *Inland Queen* on down the Columbia to Celilo Landing, Doug dashed exuberantly up the steps to the pilot house and waved the letter in his father's face.

"A job, Dad! I've been offered a job!"

After reading the letter, Lars looked up questioningly. "Are you going to take it?"

"You bet! Even though the pay isn't much, it'll give me experience and a start in my field. Professor Fleming is one of the finest geologists in the Pacific Northwest."

"The Colville Reservation is a big one, I understand."

"That's right. It runs from the north side of the Columbia clear up to Canada. It's just beyond the Grand Coulee."

"That's a piece of country I've always wanted to see, but never have," Lars said wistfully. "The closest I ever got to it was when Willie Gray and I hired a French-Canadian squawman as a river guide on a survey we were doing of the upper Columbia for the Oregon Steam Navigation Company back in 1873. We didn't have time for exploring the Coulee then. But I told Willie I'd like to come back someday with an expert geologist as a guide who could explain how and when it was formed. Have you seen it?"

Doug nodded. "When I was in college, Professor Fleming took our geology class on a couple of field trips to Grand Coulee. It's a fantastic, awesome place. Maybe when this job is done, I can give you a conducted tour, if you still want to go."

“That would be great, Doug. I never dreamed the expert geologist guide would be my own son.”

A tall, slim, angular man in his late twenties, Professor John Fleming was a graduate of Yale who had come to Washington State College three years ago because of his interest in volcanoes, lava flows, the Columbia River, and what he called the “channeled scablands.” Since the term had been in common usage for many years, Doug doubted that Professor Fleming was the first person to apply it to the layers of basalt that had risen as molten lava from the bowels of the Cascades during their mountain-building period eons ago. But he certainly had been the first to bring it to Doug’s attention in articles published in scientific journals such as those written for the *Journal of Geology* in 1910 by his colleague, Joseph Pardee.

Meeting him in the small, grubby agency town of Nespelem ten miles north of the Columbia, Doug was soon disabused of the notion that this was to be a scholarly scientific expedition.

“As usual, the federal government has gotten itself in trouble by giving with one hand and taking away with the other,” Professor Fleming told Doug as they assembled the camping gear and supplies needed for their trip. “Under the terms of the Mining Act of 1872, white citizens are allowed to prospect anywhere they like on federal lands in search of precious minerals. But the Presidential Executive Order establishing the Colville Indian Reservation that same year clearly states that white men are forbidden to trespass on the reservation without Indian permission.”

“Which they have done?”

“Frequently. So far, the hundred or so white prospectors that have gone poking around inside the reservation boundaries haven’t found any minerals of value. If they should make a strike, the entire United States Army would not be able to prevent them from overrunning Indian lands.”

“In which case, the government would have to redraw the reservation boundaries or face the prospect of an Indian-white war.”

“Exactly. So if our mineralization study shows that no precious metals exist on the Nespelem sector of the Colville Reservation, the federal government can avoid what otherwise might become a major hassle on that portion at least. In essence, what we're being asked to do, Doug, is prove a negative proposition—which, if you'll recall your philosophy courses, cannot be done."

"But we're going to do it anyway?" Doug asked, a bit bewildered.

"Not at all. What we're going to do during the next two months is visit every gopher-hole mine dug by white prospectors inside the reservation boundaries. We'll sample their tailings and then summarize the nature and value of their findings. After we've turned in our report to the U.S.G.S., the Indian Bureau can base their conclusion that there are no precious metals on the reservation on our positive report of what we have found."

"Somewhere along the way, you lost me, Professor Fleming," Doug said ruefully, shaking his head. "But it sounds like it's going to be an interesting summer."

"Let's not waste our breath on dignified titles, Doug," Professor Fleming said grumpily. Refilling and relighting the stumpy black clay pipe, which seldom left his mouth, he favored Doug with a sour smile. "Considering how small my grant is and how little I'm paying you, forget the 'Professor.' Just call me John."

The first problem they ran into was that the Indian agent, a fat, red-faced, often inebriated man named Horace Baber, wanted to charge them two dollars a day for the rental of four horses, a wagon, and the services of an Indian who would act as a guide, camp-tender, and driver. The money must be paid directly to him, Agent Baber said, in advance each week. When John Fleming protested that his grant had not allowed for that expense, the agent shrugged and grunted, "Then I reckon you'll just have to walk."

"On the contrary," Professor Fleming snapped, "what I'll have to do is report your lack of cooperation to your superiors. I do not intend to have my project held up by your greed."

"Them's mighty hard words, Professor Fleming," Agent Baber muttered, turning red. "Tell you what I'll do. I'll make it a dollar-fifty."

"No! According to the terms of my grant, I was not to be charged at all."

Before the argument could go any further, Doug touched John Fleming's elbow, then inclined his head toward the office door. When they got outside, he said, "If you'll let me handle it, Sir, I'm sure I can get what we need much more reasonably."

"How?"

"By dealing directly with the Indians."

"But Agent Baber says they don't speak English and won't deal with white strangers except through him."

"He's a liar, a cheat, and a drunk, John. Let me try it my way."

"As you will."

A short distance beyond the cluster of unpainted, board-and-batten, gray frame buildings that served as agency headquarters, a large open meadow lying below a range of pine-covered hills was dotted with a circle of Indian tepees. Beyond the Indian village, a herd of scrawny cattle and a number of thin, bony horses grazed under the loose guard of a dozen half-naked Indian boys who seemed more interested in their roughhouse wrestling and mock war games than they did in tending the livestock. Seeing the two white men, who wore khakis and Teddy Roosevelt, Rough Ride–style hats, approaching the circle of tepees, a group of smaller boys ranging from five to ten years of age began tagging after them, taking great delight in mimicking their posture and walk.

"*Nika Hyas Tyee Boston man!*"

"*Nika Hyas Tyee Kuitan Pil Pil!*"

"All right, Chief White Man and Chief Red Horse," Doug said with a good-natured laugh as he shooed the boys away. "You've showed off enough. *Klosche Kopet!* Quiet down!"

"*Aieee!*" one of the boys exclaimed, clapping a hand over his mouth in surprise. "*Mika kumtux wa-wa Chinook!*"

"Of course I talk Chinook, you little rascal! *Kla-how-ya-sikhs?* How are you?"

"*Klosche tum-tum, mika chaco!*" several of the boys shouted exuberantly. "*Klosche Kahkwe!* We are fine!"

"What the devil language are you talking?" Professor Fleming demanded.

"Chinook Jargon, Sir. In this part of the country, all the Indians and most of the white settlers speak it like a second tongue. Because of the way we're dressed, the kids thought we were outlanders."

"Your talents amaze me, Doug."

Taking a dime out of his pocket, flipping it in the air, and then catching it in the palm of his hand, Doug grinned down at the youngsters. "*Kumtux okoke?* Know what this is?"

"*Kluckamon!*" one of the boys shouted, with another crying, "*Tenas kwata!*"

"That's right. It's money—a bit, a little quarter. *Kumtux Chako Charley?*"

Because three of the boys immediately started jumping up and down and screaming that they knew where Chako Charley could be found, Doug fished two more dimes out of his pocket, gave one to each boy, then gestured for them to lead the way to the Indian's tepee. As they followed, Professor Fleming muttered, "A catchy name, 'Chako Charley.' What does it mean?"

"Just that his name is Charley. Though I'm not much of a linguist, John, I understand that 'chako' means 'to be' or 'that one is,' just like in Chinese they say 'Ah Fat' or 'Ah Wong,' which translates into 'That man is named Fat' or 'That man is named Wong.'"

"Don't tell me you speak Chinese, too!"

"No, I don't," Doug said with a laugh. "But when you run into a Chinaman in this part of the country, don't be surprised if he speaks Chinook Jargon instead of English. He finds it easier to learn."

"What can this Chako Charley do for us?"

"Well, to begin with, he's chief of Indian Police on the Nespelem part of the reservation. If he'll travel with us as our guide and escort, we'll have authority on our side."

"Do you know him?"

"No. But he's been recommended to me by a mutual friend."

"An Indian?"

"Yes, Sir. Alex Conley, my father's chief engineer on the *Inland Queen*, is half Chinook and half Wanapum. Ever since I was old enough to toddle and dig for artifacts and arrowheads, Alex has looked after me, treating me like a grandson, taking me along to root-digging and first-food festivals along the *Chiawana*—which is what the Wanapums call the Columbia River. When he found out I was going to spend the summer on the Colville Reservation, he told me to be sure and look up his brother, Chako Charley."

"Are they *really* brothers?"

"In Indian parlance, John, they could be fourth or fifth cousins and still call themselves brothers. To them, it's the relationship that counts, not its closeness. By that same standard, Alex is my grandfather or uncle, so I'm sure Chako Charley will treat us well. It's the Indian way."

Outside a tepee at the near end of the village, a farm wagon loaded with fence posts, rolls of barbed wire, and digging and wire-stretching tools was parked. In response to the shouts of the boys, a short, stocky, powerfully built Indian man in his mid-forties came out of the tepee, gave the two white men an appraising look, then grunted, "*Nika Chako Charley.* You come see me?"

Taking off his hat so that the Indian could get a good look at his blonde hair, blue eyes, and family features, Doug said politely, "*Nika Doug Warren, tillicum lagh mika kahpo Alex Conley.*" In an aside to make sure John Fleming understood, he murmured, "I just told him who I am and that I'm a friend of his brother."

"*Ah klosche!*" Chako Charley exclaimed, a twinkle brightening his black eyes. "*Mika tenas tillicum laly. Siah laaa-laaa-ly!*"

"He says, yes, he remembers me as a 'very little friend' of his brother Alex from a long time ago. What he means is that he saw me with Alex at root or first-food festivals when I tagged along as a kid years ago."

"He does remember you favorably. I can see that."

After Doug had shaken hands Indian-style with Chako Charley—gently, barely touching palm to palm without offensive pressure—he introduced John Fleming who, Doug was pleased to note, removed his pipe from his mouth, then shook hands in the same manner.

"*Nika hyas tyee* John Fleming," Doug said. "*Hyas stone mitlite.*"

"You're the college professor who's doing the mineral study on the Colville Reservation, true?" Chako Charley asked, switching to perfectly understandable English. "This is why the Indian Bureau hired you."

"Right!" Professor Fleming exclaimed, obviously glad that the talk now was in a familiar tongue. "I'll inspect the existing claims and make an estimate of their value. In addition, I'll sample enough unexplored areas to make an accurate analysis of the reservation's precious metal possibilities."

"Good! I'll go with you. Helping you make your study will beat building a fence to keep the stock out of my wife's garden by a damn sight."

During the next two months of fieldwork with John Fleming and

Chako Charley, Doug Warren learned a number of things not taught in his geology courses at Washington State College. The first was that a working geologist had to know how to get along with a wide variety of cantankerous, suspicious people, for the white miners trespassing on the reservation were extremely reluctant to disclose the nature of their findings. At the same time, the prospect of a free analysis by a qualified expert of the value of the minerals they had discovered often tempted them to reveal secrets they never would have dreamed of disclosing to a rival.

The second thing Doug learned was that, contrary to the way the textbooks broke geological time into ages such as Archeozoic, Proterozoic, Paleozoic, Mesozoic, and so on (meaning "primitive, former, ancient," and "middle life"), the terms were really very broad, for the duration of each period could vary by a million or more years.

"Geology is a very young science," John Fleming admitted during one of their conversations at an evening campfire after a long day of rock-sampling. "The pages we're just beginning to read are in the very first chapter of the book. This is particularly true in the West, where Major John Wesley Powell first began to read the record in the Grand Canyon of the Colorado River back in the 1870s and, more recently, in the inland Pacific Northwest, where we've just begun to scratch the surface of 100,000 square miles of lava flows in eastern Washington and Oregon, southern Idaho, northern Nevada, and California."

The third thing Doug learned during the summer was that being a trained geologist did not mean that a person must set aside his religious beliefs or his interest in native folklore.

"The Bible says God created the Earth in six days, then rested on the seventh," Professor Fleming said as he refilled his pipe. "It does not say how long those days were. According to some of the regional Indian lore you've told me, the natives think their world was created ten thousand years ago. Yet we know that their ancestors came across a land bridge now covered by the Bering Strait thirty thousand years ago. Do we need to reconcile those figures? I think not."

"According to Wanapum grandfather tales I've heard," Doug said, "*Speelyi*, the Coyote Spirit who made their world, did it in just one moon, ten thousand snows ago. To them, a 'snow' may be longer than a year."

"'Grandfather tales?' What are they?"

"The Indians in this part of the country had no written language until the white man came. So all their history is oral, passed down from the old to the young by means of tales told in the winter lodge."

"Was Chinook Jargon brought to the Indians by the whites?"

"Not according to what I've been told. After they began to trade with the whites around 1770, they did incorporate a few French, Spanish, and English words they found useful into Chinook Jargon. But it existed as a trade language between the Chinooks at the mouth of the Columbia and the Nootkas up by Vancouver Island long before that."

"What did they trade?"

"Slaves and seashells."

After a silence during which he spent an inordinate length of time knocking the dottle out of the bowl of his pipe, refilling, and then relighting it, Professor Fleming raised his eyes to Chako Charley, who was hunkered down on the other side of the campfire.

"Is he pulling my leg, Charley?"

"No. He's telling the truth. In olden times, my people set a great value on a thin, hollow, white seashell called 'haiqua.' They would insert the shells into their pierced noses and ears or string them on long necklaces. The whites called the shells 'dentalium.' "

"Something like the 'wampum' treasured by eastern Indians?"

Chako Charley nodded. "In olden times, I've been told, a three-foot-long necklace of haiqua shells could be traded for a new rifle. Or a new wife."

"Who supplied the slaves?"

"These usually came from the 'round-head' tribes living along the Oregon coast," Doug said, "after the Chinooks, who had slanted heads and were a very war-like tribe, had raided a village and taken enough captives to make a trading trip north to Nootka country worthwhile. You see, diving for haiqua shells was exhausting, tedious work, which the Nootkas hated to do themselves. So they traded shells for slaves, then trained them to dive—"

Raising both hands in a signal of surrender, Professor Fleming got to his feet, grunting caustically, "Enough, gentlemen! I've absorbed all the local lore I can digest for the night. If you don't mind, I'll spread my blanket roll in the wagon bed tonight, where the rattlesnakes won't get me. See you in the morning."

Despite the smallness of his grant from the U.S.G.S., the two-month study made by John Fleming of mineralization on the Nespelem sector of the Colville Reservation was an extensive one, which later would be used to extinguish the claims of trespassing white prospectors who, the study proved, had found nothing of value. Because the Mining Act of 1872 required that a certain amount of work be done each year in order to retain title to a claim, most of the prospectors gave up and left when faced with the U.S.G.S. negative report. Furthermore, the constant surveillance of Chako Charley, whose visits to their gopher-hole mines with John Fleming and Doug Warren gave them the feeling that they were being closely watched, made them very nervous.

"Every time Charley looks at them," Professor Fleming chuckled after still another white prospector said he was pulling up stakes and leaving the reservation, "they think he's planning to lift their scalps. Is that the message you mean to convey, Charley?"

"No, it ain't," Chako Charley grunted, shaking his head. "I hung up my scalping knife years ago. But if they think I want to lift their hair, that's fine with me."

"Actually, scalping was a Plains Indian custom that never caught on among Pacific Northwest Indians," Doug said helpfully. "I tell you this, John, to fill in an obvious gap in your knowledge of Charley's people."

"Thank you, Doug," Professor Fleming answered sarcastically. "You are a veritable fount of local lore."

"Of course," Doug added, "the Haidas along the Northwest Coast of British Columbia did raid their neighbors now and then to take heads—"

"Which they traded for haiqua shell necklaces or pretty young wives, no doubt—"

"The hair was still on the heads, naturally. So you could say the Haidas took scalps, if you wanted to quibble—"

Throwing up his hands in despair, Professor Fleming grimaced at Chako Charley, who was smiling as he enjoyed the exchange. "I could have flunked him as a student, Charley. But he did do well in his geology courses."

"I'm glad you managed to put up with him, John. My people appreciate the way you and Doug got rid of the prospectors."

"All we did, Charley, was prove not enough precious metals have been found on this part of the Colville Reservation to warrant opening it up to the general public. However, as I shall point out in my report, large-scale mining for lower-class minerals might be a possibility your leaders will want to consider at some time in the future."

Though it was of no interest to the Indians at this time, Professor Fleming noted in his report that, in addition to the manganese and silver deposits which he and Doug already knew were there, their study had found molybdenite, quartz, pyrite, fluorite, and chalcopyrite as a filling in northeast-trending fractures. This filling, he wrote, appeared to be associated with a high-temperature prelude to the mineralization along the northwest-trending fissures, although he was in some doubt as to its age.

During the recently completed study, he added, he had found similar quartz-pyrite-fluorite-molybdenite veins extending south from Nespelem to the Columbia River and beyond, perhaps as far as the Grand Coulee, in coarse granite formations, an interesting phenomenon he wanted to investigate further.

"There's no indication of their age or relation to the mineralization we've been studying," he told Doug. "But as long as we're heading south anyway, I'd like to spend a few days in the Coulee, checking them out, if we can persuade Charley to rent us riding and pack-horses."

"You don't need to pay me no rent, John," Charley said. "Use the horses as long as you like. Take the wagon, too, if you want to use it to sleep in. There's some bad rattlesnake country in the Coulee."

"Thank you, Charley. You're very kind. How will we get the wagon and horses back to you?"

"Just turn them over to any Indian you see headed for Nespelem. If you tell him they're mine, he'll bring them back to me." He paused for a moment, then added, "Don't give them to a white man, though. He'd probably steal them."

Parting company with Chako Charley at the Nespelem Indian Agency headquarters the next day, Doug found that he had inherited the Indian's job as camp-tender, wagon-driver, and general flunky. Accepting it grudgingly, he climbed up to the right-hand seat, picked up the reins, and slapped the team of bony horses on their rumps to get them moving.

"Some scientific expedition this turned out to be!" he complained. "Why does a brilliant young geologist like me have to waste his talent and time driving a wagon?"

"Cheer up, Doug. With practice, you may get to be as good at it as Chako Charley."

"I wouldn't mind driving an automobile, John. Have you ever asked Washington State College to buy one for the Geology Department?"

Professor Fleming sighed. "Frequently. But they keep telling me their budget for my department is still in the horse-and-buggy age." After a silence during which he fussed with his pipe, he asked curiously, "How fast would you say we're going?"

"Maybe two miles an hour."

"How fast will a Model T Ford truck go?"

"A well-tuned Model T can do thirty-five miles an hour on a decent dirt road. Fifty on brick or macadam."

"Could you handle one at that speed?"

"Sure."

"What about fixing flats, adjusting the way the engine runs, and all those other things that happen to an automobile? Can you deal with them, too?"

"If I can't, I can darn sure study the driver's manual until I learn how to do what needs to be done," Doug said confidently. "If you'll get the college to buy us a Model T truck, I'll damn sure drive it for you."

"Well, we certainly could cover a lot more ground in a lot less time, Doug," Professor Fleming said thoughtfully. "I'll see what I can do."

24.

By the time Doug Warren had driven the wagon and its slow-moving team the ten dusty miles south from Nespelem, then down the steep, narrow, twisting road which descended the face of the thousand-foot-high bluff to the ferry landing, he had gained a new appreciation of Chako Charley's skill as a driver. He had also come to respect the worth of the pair of bony gray horses pulling the wagon and the two sorrel riding horses trailing behind at the end of halters tied to tailgate. Whether born, reared, or trained to be indifferent to their surroundings, they were the most placid horses he had ever seen; nothing seemed to bother them.

Which was comforting to him, for the only expertise he possessed as a teamster when maneuvering the wagon across difficult terrain was pointing the vehicle in the general direction he wanted it to go, then hoping that the team would take it there.

"As a driver, you do pretty well, Doug," Professor Fleming said as the wagon jolted down toward the north shore landing where the cable ferry was moored. "I'm impressed by the breadth of your talents."

"Thank you, John. But it's Chako Charley you should compliment, not me. The Indians in this part of the country have always trained their horses to behave. It's a matter of survival."

"For the horses or the Indians?"

"Both. If a horse has trouble getting over a rock slide on a mountain trail, its rider whips it unmercifully until it either makes it or falls. If it breaks a leg, he wastes no pity on it. He just leaves it where it lies and hops on another horse."

"I'm sure Charles Darwin would approve of that."

"In earlier times, his warhorse—which was always the best one he owned—was trained so well that when he dropped its rein and hopped off during a battle to fight on foot, the horse would stand and eat grass, paying no attention to the bullets flying around it, until the Indian climbed on again. In contrast, in the United States Cavalry, when troopers dismounted to fight on foot, one out of every four became a noncombatant because he had to hold his and three other horses so that the spooked animals wouldn't run away. That's why the Nez Perces did so well against the Army during the Chief Joseph War."

Having an intense dislike for small ferries in big rivers, Professor Fleming said that hopping off the wagon while Doug drove it aboard the ferry sounded like a sensible idea to him, so he stepped down and watched the procedure from a safe distance ashore. As the leather-faced, lanky, unshaven ferryman took the reins of the team and maneuvered the wagon and the trailing horses aboard the oblong, flat-bottomed, barge-like boat, Professor Fleming shaded his eyes against the brassy glare of the noontime sun, gazing up at the stark, barren, dun-colored hills rising from either side of the river.

From crest to crest, the distance between the thousand-foot-high hilltops here would be about a mile, he guessed. At river level, the greenish-blue waters of the Columbia, which was flowing at its lowest stage now in late August, moved swiftly westward in a quarter-mile-wide channel. Long a crossing point on the trail from the upper reaches of the Grand Coulee country to Nespelem on the Colville Indian Reservation, this spot was unusual in a region of repeated lava flows because of the exposure of an uplifted ridge of white granite, which here thrust skyward like the blunt edge of a gigantic knife on both sides of the river. Part of the massive batholith which underlay the region, the granitic ridge served as solid anchor points for the overhead wire cable towers of the ferry, which depended on current alone for propulsion power.

Though so far he had explored only a small portion of the upper Columbia River watershed, Professor Fleming already had identified several geological mysteries he would like to solve. When and how Grand Coulee had been formed was one. The growth and recession of the Cordilleran ice sheets was another. Still a third—and perhaps the most intriguing of all—was what his mentor, Joseph Pardee, had titled "The Glacial Lake Missoula" in his 1910 *Journal of Geology* paper. Eventually, a relationship would be established between the three subjects, he suspected, but before that could happen a lot of fieldwork by a lot of geologists would have to be done, requiring a great deal of time and money.

Meanwhile, one fact related to this particular spot seemed crystal clear now. At some point in geological time a massive glacier more than two thousand feet thick must have blocked the Columbia at exactly this place, causing the river to alter its course long enough to overflow the high ridge to the south, then gouge out the tremendous fifty-mile-long gash called Grand Coulee, which he and his assistant, Doug Warren, would spend the next week exploring on their way home.

After flowing directly west from the Grand Coulee ferry for fifty miles through dry, treeless, barren country into which it had eroded a sixteen-hundred-foot-deep canyon, the Columbia River turned south past the Okanogan highlands region, toward Wenatchee. Upriver to the east, the river remained deep in its gorge for 30 miles, then swung north past the mouth of the Spokane River, the great Indian fishery of Kettle Falls, then on toward Canada, 150 miles northeast of this spot. Though most of the white settlers living in this part of the country considered the Columbia as belonging to the United States, Professor Fleming knew that 450 miles of its 1,250-mile length, as well as its source, lay in Canada.

For much of that distance, waterfalls and rapids made it unnavigable except on a piecemeal basis. Time and again during his recently completed survey of mineralization of the Nespelem sector of the Colville Reservation, mine owners who had found what they felt were commercially profitable veins of silver, lead, copper, or other relatively valuable metals had complained that freighting costs were prohibitive. A sixty-dollar-a-ton silver vein ordinarily would be worth working, but the nearest railroad was twenty miles away, while on the river, which was ten miles closer, no boats at all were running.

"The damn government," they said plaintively, "ought to do something about making the river navigable. Ain't that what we pay taxes for?"

Though he felt no great sympathy for the miners, he knew it was not politic to tell them they were trespassers on Indian lands, thus deserving no special treatment. What he did tell them was that, following the Oregon Steam Navigation Company's assessment of the feasibility of running boats through Priest Rapids above the mouth of the Yakima and Rock Island Rapids in the Wenatchee area by Captain William Polk Gray's party in 1873, the Corps of Engineers had made a very detailed study of the Columbia from its source down to the mouth of the Snake in 1881, under the leadership of Colonel Thomas W. Symons.

His study had confirmed the conclusion long proclaimed by French-Canadian boatmen for the Hudson's Bay Company, by Captain Leonard White, by Captain William Polk Gray, and by many other rivermen who had tested the navigability of the upper Columbia: Although it could be run in some sectors, making it navigable all the way north to Canada was not feasible.

With the wagon now taken aboard, its wheels chocked, and its horses secured so that they would not be tempted to jump overboard and refresh themselves with a swim in the cold waters of the river, Professor Fleming judged it safe to get aboard himself. Considered from a purely mechanical point of view, he mused as he watched the ferryman go through the routine of getting under way, the operation of the cable ferry was a marvel of efficiency, so far as using the powers of nature was concerned.

Set in a shallow well at one end of the ferry was a wooden wheel six feet high, from which a two-inch-thick rope wound around the wheel ran up to a set of iron trolleys running along a stranded-steel cable hung between towers anchored in granite footings high above either bank. By turning the spokes of the big wheel, the ferry operator could tighten one portion of the rope while loosening the other, which, by an arrangement of smaller pulleys fastened to the bow and stern of the boat, changed the angle at which the strong current of the river struck the side of the flat-bottomed barge. This resulted in making the ferry move directly across the river, while the fore and aft lines running up to the cable strung between the towers on either bank prevented the craft from being carried downstream.

Though he preferred not to think about what would happen to the ferry if the rope or the cable broke, he took some comfort in observing that there was a small rowboat aboard, as well as what appeared to be a gasoline engine attached to a screw-type propeller, both of which might be of some use in an emergency. Fortunately, none occurred during the crossing. When Doug Warren joined him in the bow of the ferry at mid-river, he pointed out a geological feature high up on the cliff to the south that his young assistant might not have noticed.

"Do you see the notch in the hill yonder, Doug?"

"Yes, Sir."

"The head of Grand Coulee lies just beyond, though it can't be seen from here. At some epoch in geological time, a small stream flowed north through that notch from the high basaltic tableland to the south. Eventually, its waters would have eroded a canyon back into the mesa. But before that could happen, an ice sheet more than two thousand feet thick blocked the Columbia just below this spot, pushing the entire flow of the river up and over the bluffs near that notch, which of course destroyed the stream."

"When the ice sheet melted, its waters gouged out the Coulee, right?"

"Apparently that's what happened."

"How many million years did it take to erode the Coulee?"

"That's a question yet to be answered, Doug. Geologists of the 'Uniformitarianism School' maintain that the erosion of the Coulee was similar to that of the Grand Canyon of the Colorado, requiring eons of time. The younger, more radical thinkers of the 'Catastrophic School' accept a growing accumulation of evidence which indicates that the erosional forces at work required far less time to carve out the Coulee than the older geologists say."

"How much less time?"

"Quite a bit less, Doug. Six thousand years, perhaps. Or maybe only sixteen days."

"That's quite a difference, John. Which theory do you subscribe to?"

Taking his time to refill and relight his pipe, Professor Fleming chuckled and shook his head. "As more than one older geologist has told me, Doug, I have not yet reached the age or achieved the stature where I am entitled to subscribe to anything other than the trade journals."

"But you must have some theories of your own. I'd like to know what they are."

"All in good time, Doug," Professor Fleming said, pleased that he had been asked. "As we travel through Grand Coulee during the next week, I'll point out a few pieces of evidence I have observed and explain to you the direction in which I think they point."

From the ferry landing on the south shore of the river to the top of the bluff overlooking the head of the Coulee, the thousand-foot rise of the tortuous, narrow road took five miles and four hours of exhausting effort by the team before the hill could be climbed. Whether the Model T truck Doug hoped would be acquired for the Washington State College Geology Department could have made the ascent without being rested and watered several times, as were the horses, Doug did not know. Probably not, for during rides he had taken with Model T owners during the past year or two, he had learned the wisdom of carrying along a supply of water for the radiator, which invariably boiled over when climbing a hill, and extra oil for the engine bearings, which invariably ran dry when the car moved up a steep slope.

One good trick with a Model T, he had learned, was to turn it around and back it up the hill, for this made sure that the front bearing—which was the one that usually ran dry—stayed lubricated.

In any case, he was not faced with that problem today.

After making camp that evening in the channeled scabland at the northern end of the Coulee, where the scarred, brown, treeless terrain stretched bleakly in all directions, Doug found that his education regarding what one of his geology textbooks called the "Seventh Corrasional Wonder of the World" began in earnest the next morning. He was not long in discovering that he could not have had a better guide, for Professor Fleming's enthusiasm for the Grand Coulee country was boundless, his knowledge encyclopedic.

Extending southwest for fifty miles from the present channel of the Columbia River, the Coulee was divided into two parts, each twenty-five miles long. The northeast end of the Coulee lay deep in a lava-walled canyon whose level floor was six hundred feet above the present surface of the Columbia River. Its vertical walls rose eight hundred feet above either side of the Coulee, while its width ranged from two to five miles. Though completely dry and extremely dusty now, Doug got the uncomfortable feeling as he drove the wagon along the floor of the Coulee that he was trapped in the bed of an immense river, down which a torrent of water might come rolling at any time. When he expressed that feeling to Professor Fleming, the senior geologist laughed and nodded.

"Six thousand years ago, Doug, you'd have been floating on the surface of the biggest river that ever existed. A few miles ahead, you'd be going over the world's greatest waterfall."

Twenty-five miles to the southwest, Professor Fleming said, the steepness of the Coulee was broken by a broad, low valley running from west to east; it was through this opening that the road between Wenatchee and Spokane ran. A few miles beyond the break, the Coulee deepened again; just to the south, the spectacular erosional wonder called "Dry Falls" gave stark testimony that at some point in the geological past, a waterfall many times the size of Niagara once tumbled and roared.

Intrigued by Professor Fleming's statement that a disagreement existed among geologists as to when and how the Coulee had been formed, Doug asked how there could be such a wide divergence in the theories of older and younger geologists.

"After all," he said, "the difference between millions of years, six thousand years, and sixteen days is considerable."

"That's true, Doug. But a number of factors must be considered."

"Such as?"

"Water, wind, and lava flows, to begin with. For example, much of the soil east of the Cascades consists of very fine particles of loess, which over eons of time has been eroded from old lava flows and then brought by prevailing southwesterly winds to eastern Washington, where it eventually becomes extremely fertile soil. The Palouse Hills, for instance, are made up of wind-deposited soil."

"That much I know. But why is it, John, we don't see much of that kind of soil in the channeled scabland country around here?"

"Now you're getting at the heart of the mystery, Doug," Professor Fleming said with a smile. "Would you like to try to answer your own question?"

"Because it's been blown away?" Doug said tentatively.

"Why would the same southwesterly wind that deposited the loessal soil pick it up and blow it away? Furthermore, why would the country west of Grand Coulee have an abundance of that kind of soil, while the channeled scablands east of the Coulee are stripped down to bare basalt?"

"Has the soil on the east side of the Coulee been washed away?"

"There's strong evidence that's exactly what happened," Professor Fleming answered, nodding. "We'll get a good look at a piece of that evidence when we examine Steamboat Rock, which is just ahead."

Looming in the distance a quarter of the way into the Coulee, the massive formation called Steamboat Rock measured two and a half miles in length, half a mile in width, and stood eight hundred feet high, its flat top level with the country on both sides. Technically called an "enisled mesa" or a "monadnock," it once had stood as a divider between two branches of what for a time had been the greatest waterfall on earth, Professor Fleming told Doug.

"Imagine, if you can, a rolling, churning cataract with a gradient of eighty feet to the mile," Professor Fleming said, taking his pipe out of his mouth and using its stem as a pointer as he gestured up at the immense rock face looming above. "Or rather, twin cataracts, each of which was eight hundred feet high, two miles wide, and a hundred or more feet deep. Can you begin to conceive of the tremendous excavating power of so much moving water?"

"No, I can't. But it must have been enormous."

"That doesn't even begin to describe it, Doug. By my calculations, the volume of water flowing over the Steamboat Rock cataracts equaled or exceeded the total flow of all the rivers on earth. Nothing remotely like it has ever existed, before or since."

"This is the sixteen-day catastrophic flood you say may have happened?"

"Yes. This is it."

"Where did so much water come from? And why did it come all at once?"

Now they were getting into the realm of speculation, Professor Fleming said, in which drawing firm conclusions was dangerous. So far, he had not done enough field research to substantiate his catastrophic flood theory, but his colleague, Joseph Pardee, had established a location for the lake in which a massive amount of water could have been stored.

"We know that the Cordilleran ice sheets covered this part of the country at least three times. More than once, a lobe coming down through the Okanogan highlands formed a dam across the Columbia at least two thousand feet high, so it is reasonable to assume that similar ice lobes might have formed dams in the Missoula area a few hundred miles to the east. Are you with me so far, Doug?"

"Yes, Sir, I am."

"In that part of the country, the Selkirks, the Rockies, and the Bitterroot Mountains are all high enough that an ice dam twenty-five-hundred feet high across Clark's Fork River to the west would create a lake that would not overflow the mountain crests. While that ice dam was in place, it would impound a body of water fifty miles long, twenty miles wide, and half a mile deep. If my arithmetic is correct, that totals five hundred cubic miles of water. If such a dam should suddenly collapse—"

"That's a mighty big 'if,' isn't it?" Doug interrupted. "Usually when an ice dam melts, the process is gradual."

"True. But there are two forces an ice dam cannot withstand, Doug. Undercutting and overflowing. When either event happens, the collapse of the dam is both sudden and complete."

"In which case, five hundred cubic miles would be released. It would flow in this direction."

"Exactly—though 'flow' is far too mild a word. Topographically, it would do one hell of a job excavating and rearranging the landscape in a hurry. Conceivably, in sixteen days."

Leaving the wagon, the team of grays, and the supplies in camp beside a shallow lake at the base of Steamboat Rock, the two men saddled the spare horses, packed a lunch, then spent the rest of the day exploring the top of the mesa, which could be reached only by a narrow, twisting trail. Because of its remoteness and lack of water, no white settlers lived on it, nor had it been fenced. Unlike the bare, channeled scabland of the lower country to the north and east, where not even a blade of grass grew, the soil atop the mesa was deep and rich, supporting an abundant growth of bunchgrass, wildflowers, and bitterroot plants, now rarely to be found in the lower country because of cultivation and overgrazing.

Apparently aware of the fact that he had given Doug a great deal to mull over, Professor Fleming did not mention the catastrophic flood hypothesis again for a while. But as they moved on down the Coulee during the next two days, he did point out bits of physical evidence that Doug could interpret however he liked.

One was the fact that the floor of the upper half of the Grand Coulee was flat and its gradient level now, where as at the time of the flood, the estimated slope had ranged from thirty to eighty feet to the mile. This meant that the sand and gravel now filling the canyon floor had been deposited evenly as the force of the current slowed, which it naturally would do toward the end of such a flood.

Another was that along the floor of both the upper and lower reaches of the Coulee, a number of isolated rocks called "erratics" were deposited in unexpected places. Called "haystacks" by the local settlers because of their shape, these granite, argillite, quartzite, coarse-grained limestone, or basaltic boulders ranged from fist-size to as large as a barn. Because the bigger ones were too immense to be moved and too solid to be broken up, they must be farmed around, which was an infernal nuisance to the settlers. Because they bore no relation to local rock formations, it was impossible to say where they had come from or how they had gotten where they were. When one farmer facetiously suggested that the "haystack" in his field "must of floated in on the gully-washer that dug the canyon, then been left high and dry when it went down," he was not talking complete nonsense, Professor Fleming told Doug.

"There are two ways a rock can float, no matter how big it is," he said. "One is when it's carried on the lobe of an ice sheet that eventually melts. The other is when it breaks off and tumbles into a current of water moving in such volume and with so much force that the rocks it carries are made as light as corks. For example, when the rate of current in a stream doubles, its carrying capacity increases sixty-four times. That may have been how the erratics on the floor of the Coulee got where they are."

"Isn't there some way you can tell?"

"Lots of ways. Scratches on the rock's surface. Comparisons with the surrounding soil. Age and color of the lichens on the rocks. But this takes time, Doug, not to mention knowledge. In this part of the country, too few qualified geologists have been gathering rock samples for too short a time to assemble the facts we need to know."

Back in Cretaceous times, a vast inland sea occupied all of central Washington, Professor Fleming said, extending from the Gulf of California to the Arctic Ocean. The old Cascade peneplain formed its western border, while to the east and south the Rockies and the Blue Mountains were washed by its waters. With Miocene times came crustal warpings and continued elevation of the Cascades. Volcanic activity was initiated, and out of thousands of fissures came prodigious lava flows. Flow succeeded flow, as revealed in the Coulee walls, until altogether they covered 100,000 square miles, building the interior plateau to a height of four thousand feet in places.

"There is no record of greater lava flows having appeared anywhere on the face of the earth," Professor Fleming declared. "Rivers were dammed and made to change their courses. The Coulee walls record the history of at least seven floods, separated from one another by long intervals of time. Each time the lava plain must have cooled and weathered into soil."

As impressive as Steamboat Rock and the twin cataracts described by Professor Fleming had been to Doug, Dry Falls in the lower Coulee was far more dramatic, for here the basic structure of the stupendous falls was still intact. Located a few miles south of the low-walled valley which bisected Grand Coulee, Dry Falls gave no advance warning of its presence. Broad, flat, and treeless, the canyon floor was perfectly level until the very brink of the horseshoe-shaped formation was reached. There, quite suddenly, a four-hundred-foot vertical drop-off stretching several miles from end to end marked the place where a torrent a hundred times greater than Niagara once had poured over the brink and cascaded into the plunge pool below, where a sizable lake still existed.

"At a rough guess, the catastrophic flood caused by the breaking of the Lake Missoula glacial dam washed at least a hundred square miles of soil off the northeast side of the scablands," Professor Fleming told Doug. "In the upper part of the Coulee, fully twenty cubic miles of basalt was ground up and pushed over Dry Falls. In the beginning, of course, the brink of the falls was not here. It was seventeen miles to the southwest, in the Quincy Basin."

"Why did it move?"

"Erosion, Doug. At its height, the flood was carrying so much rock and gravel and its underlying bed was so soft that it kept eating its way back to this spot at a fairly rapid rate. By rapid, I mean twenty or so feet a year, taking something like five thousand years to work its way this far."

"But you said the flood may have taken only sixteen days."

"That's just one flood, Doug. There could have been more. We won't know how many more until a great deal of field research has been done. These days, unfortunately, only a few of the younger geologists are doing fieldwork, while the older Uniformitarians sit in their stuffy offices propounding theories that we people in the field think are outdated."

Camping that night on the shore of a beautiful blue lake in the vast canyon just below Dry Falls, Doug again got the uneasy feeling of being in the path of a potentially disastrous flood, even though not a trickle of water was coming over the brink of the falls at the present time. Though he had never found the study of geology dull, his association with Professor John Fleming these past two months, the friendship that had developed between them, and the frank way John had discussed some of the problems of the profession had given Doug a new appreciation of what a living science geology really was.

After supper in the flickering glow of their small campfire, he sought answers to several questions that were troubling him.

"You've referred several times to the 'Uniformitarianism School' of geology, John. But I never heard you mention it in class. Why didn't you?"

"For several reasons, Doug. First, because I'm trying to teach my students geology as it is practiced today. Second, because differing with the elders in my field could be extremely dangerous to my career. Third, because I want to teach my students that before they can prove an existing theory wrong, they must have strong tangible evidence that their theory is right."

"Exactly what is the 'Uniformitarianism School'?"

"Basically, its followers believe that the physical forces which created the world are the same everywhere and every age. One stream bed erodes like another. A lava flow, an eruption, an advancement or recession of a glacier, the growth or shrinking of a sea, the warming or cooling of the earth—all these forces are controlled by immutable physical laws which never vary. It's not quite as simple as that, of course, but those are the basic tenets of their school."

"Where do you differ with them?"

"Chiefly on one point. They regard catastrophe as heresy."

"Why?"

"It goes back to the controversy Charles Darwin raised some years ago, I suppose, when he destroyed the belief that God created the world in six biblical days, which religious scholars declared equaled 4,178 or so of our calendar years." Pausing to relight his pipe, Professor Fleming shook out the flame of the wooden match and tossed it into the fire. "Once the intellectual dust settled on that squabble, scientists began to claim that there were immutable, unchanging, universal laws in all sciences, which never varied. In a word, catastrophes were not allowed."

"How does that apply to Grand Coulee?"

"Because of its size, shape, and the fact that a river once ran through it, the erosion that created it must have been similar to that which created the Grand Canyon of the Colorado over a period of several million years, the Uniformitarians say," Professor Fleming replied. "Never mind that there is solid physical evidence to the contrary. Such a departure from their rules cannot be allowed."

"Have they seen the evidence?"

"Very few of them, Doug. Even some of my esteemed colleagues at the University of Washington in Seattle have never crossed the Cascades and scuffed the toes of their field boots—assuming they have any—on the gritty rocks of the scablands. But they do agree with the pundits back East, who have never seen the scablands either, that it takes millions of years of conventional erosion to create a canyon."

"What about your friend, Joseph Pardee?"

"He's the exception, Doug. He did do some fieldwork several years ago, which resulted in his 1910 article 'Glacial Lake Missoula.' In it, he merely stated that he had found evidence such a lake existed. He did not say that the ice dam suddenly collapsed or speculate on where the water went. These assumptions are my own."

"You think the water came through this part of the country?"

"It had to, Doug. There was no place else it could go."

"Are you going to write a paper connecting Pardee's Lake Missoula with your theory of how the Coulee was formed?"

"Lord no! Before I can do that, I've got to gather a lot more evidence that I know what I'm talking about."

After a silence during which Doug considered how exciting it would be to take part in field research whose eventual result would be to propound a new theory that would astound the senior members of his profession, he smiled and said, "This probably wouldn't qualify as evidence, John, but according to the grandfather tales of the Wanapums, a catastrophic flood did wash over this country long ago. It was caused when *Speelyi*, the Coyote Spirit who made the world, got into an argument with *Takspul*, Beaver, over a beautiful young lady. Out of spite, *Speelyi* hid *Ahn*, the sun, for many moons, making ice cover the land. When they finally settled their argument and the ice melted, a big flood washed over the land."

Professor Fleming chuckled. "Do you know, Doug, the notion of having you relate that grandfather tale to a room full of distinguished geologists during a national symposium in Washington, D.C., appeals to my sense of humor, if not to my better judgment. It would really cause a riot."

He fiddled with his pipe, then shook his head. "No, Doug, what I must do is build a body of evidence piece by piece proving that what I suspect happened did happen, which will make all other hypotheses invalid. That will take time, Doug. Lots and lots of time."

As they neared the small town of Ephrata at the lower end of the Coulee, they began to see some signs of settlement in the form of farms on whose dusty acres efforts at cultivation had been made. By definition, Professor Fleming said, an area receiving less than fifteen inches of moisture a year in this part of the country was desert land on which no crops could be grown without irrigation. Around the turn of the century, a publicist employed by one of the transcontinental railroad lines with a lot of land to sell had propounded the optimistic theory that "Rainfall Follows the Plough," which meant that when land normally receiving less than fifteen inches of moisture a year was broken up and planted to crops, its annual rainfall increased substantially.

Accepting that myth as fact, a number of land-hungry farmers had come west; purchased a quarter-section of dry desert land for next to nothing; planted it to wheat, rye, or barley; then set back and waited for a bountiful harvest. For a few years, the rainfall did increase and the harvest was good. Unfortunately, the farmers soon came to realize that this was not the result of ploughing but of a cyclical pattern old as time. In a region of marginal moisture, some years were wetter than others. Now the obverse proved to be true; some years were drier than others.

At least half of the farms they passed north of Ephrata had been abandoned, Doug noted, their shabby, unpainted, board-and-batten cabins and barns deserted. In a few places where people still lived, the farmers owed their precarious existence to windmill-driven pumps sucking water to the surface from wells drilled ninety or so feet into the bone-dry soil. In most cases, as they were told by a settler who let them water their horses from his half-empty stock tank, the wells produced only enough water for domestic use, with none left over to irrigate the substantial orchard plantings which had been made over the nine thousand acres developed locally during the past few years.

"They been talking about bringing irrigation water down from Lake Wenatchee 'tother side of the Columbia," he said wearily, "but ain't nothing been done about it yet because it would cost upwards of $12 million. Been some pumping out of Soap Lake, but the electric company ain't very dependable. Even when the system is working, the fruit growers who can afford to pay its costs can't get near all the water they need. Way things are going, this country is about to dry up and blow away."

In Ephrata, where they planned to catch a Great Northern train to Spokane, then take the motor stage south to Washington State College at Pullman, Doug found a dependable-looking Indian family consisting of a middle-aged man, his wife, two boys in their teens, and a couple of bright-eyed toddlers. The man said they were headed for Nespelem on the Colville Reservation after a visit to relatives in the Yakima area. Yes, he knew Chako Charley, he said, and would be glad to return the wagon and horses to him.

Consolidating their personal and camping gear into duffel bags they could carry on the train, they learned that the eastbound passenger train came through at two o'clock in the afternoon. Since it now was noon, they left their baggage at the depot and went in search of a place to eat. Walking a block down the street to a building bearing the euphonious name Ephrata Eats Emporium, they were about to "enter and attempt to ingest its edibles" (as Professor Fleming put it) when a dust-streaked Model T Ford touring sedan came chugging along the street, then wheezed to a stop in front of the restaurant whose food the two men were about to sample.

Prominently displayed on the side of the vehicle was a sign which read:

The Wenatchee Daily World

THE WORLD'S GREATEST PAPER
FOR CITIES UNDER 10,000 POPULATION

Rufus Woods • *Publisher*

Behind the steering wheel sat a stocky, muscular man in his late thirties. He wore a dusty derby hat, which he tipped jauntily to greet them, revealing a slicked-down head of black hair above alert dark eyes and a wide, friendly mouth. Resting on the backseat of the car, Doug noticed, was a portable typewriter, two cameras, and what appeared to be a rudimentary dictating machine with an attached speaking phone and recording device, all of which were covered and protected from the dust with a transparent isinglass sheet.

"I'm Rufus Woods," the man said cheerfully, hopping out of the car and extending his hand. "If I'm not mistaken, you are the two Washington State College geologists who have been taking rock samples on the Colville Reservation for the past couple of months."

"You're right, Sir," Professor Fleming said, shaking hands. "I'm John Fleming. This is my assistant, Doug Warren."

"Pleased to meet you both. About to take on some grub, are you?"

"Those were our plans, yes."

"Tell you what I'll do. Give me a good story for my paper and I'll pick up the check. Is that a deal?"

"If a preliminary summary of our findings qualifies as a 'good story,' I'll be happy to oblige," Professor Fleming said. "But I'm afraid it won't be very sensational."

"What the heck! I'll pick up the check anyway. The proprietor can deduct it from the advertising bill he owes me."

To tell the truth, Rufus Woods confessed without rancor during the meal, just about all the advertisers in the north-central Washington area, comprising Grant, Douglas, Chelan, and Okanogan Counties, were behind on their bills, for times had been tough lately. Still, he believed in the region, for its soil was fertile, its climate good, and it raised the finest apples in the world.

"The problem is," he said, "the growers have planted so darn many trees and they've borne so well that they can't get enough railroad cars to ship the apples to market before they go bad. Also, the growers refuse to organize so that they can control quality and limit supply. One year, they get two-fifty a box for their apples and ship nine thousand carloads. The next, they double their harvest, the price drops to twenty-five cents, and they all go broke. It's a boom or bust thing. I keep telling them to diversify, but they don't listen."

"Your newspaper has a wide circulation, I gather," Professor Fleming said.

"You bet it does. It's the only daily in north-central Washington, with two-thirds of its circulation outside Wenatchee. That's why I call it 'The World's Greatest Paper for Cities Under 10,000 Population.'" Pushing aside his plate, which he had cleaned to the last morsel, Rufus Woods leaned back and smiled. "Now it's time to pay for your grub, Professor. Did you find any big gold mines on the Colville Reservation?"

"Our study was limited to the Nespelem part of the reserve," Professor Fleming answered. "We found no claims worth working there."

"That's too bad," Rufus Woods said, scowling. "A rip-snorting gold boom would do wonders for this part of the state. Of course, what we really need is water. Any way you geologist fellows can arrange for the Columbia River to go back to its old bed in Grand Coulee?"

"I'm afraid that would take some doing, Mr. Woods. The floor of the Coulee is six hundred feet above the present level of the river."

"How come the Columbia once did flow through the Coulee?"

"Apparently an ice lobe coming down from the Okanogan country created a dam high enough to block the river, forcing it up and over the hills to the south for a time."

"If we built such a dam now, how high would it have to be?"

"At least eight hundred feet."

"Could it be done?"

"I'm a geologist, not a dam-builder, Mr. Woods—"

"Call me Rufus."

"—but before a dam that high could be built, you would have to get permission from Canada, which would be flooded for at least two hundred miles north of the border."

25.

Back at Washington State College, Professor John Fleming found enough funds in his budget for the following academic year to keep Doug Warren working as his assistant, though the salary was only fifty dollars a month. Having gotten interested in a bright, beautiful, black-haired young lady named Jenny Fraser, who was due to receive her degree in biology the next spring, Doug was pleased to get this chance to stay in the area, for in these uncertain times employment opportunities for young geologists were few and far between.

"Professor Fleming says if Joseph Pardee asks him to do some more work on the Colville Indian Reservation next year, he'll use me as his assistant again," Doug told Jenny. "But federal funds are tight these days. A lot depends on the war situation in Europe, he says, and whether or not Woodrow Wilson gets reelected."

"President Wilson pleased a lot of voters by keeping us out of war during his first term," Jenny said. "If he campaigns on a promise to do it again, he'll be a shoo-in, Dad says. Even though Wilson is a Democrat, Dad plans to vote for him because of his antiwar stand."

"That's quite a concession for your father, Jenny."

"Dad's pretty conservative, I'll admit that. But he likes you, Doug, even though you do have a college degree. If you need a job next summer, he says, he'll be glad to put you to work on the ranch."

Owning five thousand acres of fertile Palouse Hills land near the small town of Dusty twenty miles west of Pullman, Abe Lincoln Fraser was a rock-ribbed Republican who believed that the less government the country had, the better off its people would be. Though his own education had ended with the eighth grade and he derided the "college professors" who were running the country, he was a strong supporter of Washington State insofar as its agricultural department was concerned. As a member of the Board of Regents, he had voted time and again to approve funds for experimental plots of smut free wheat, drought-resistant range grasses, better types of fruit trees, and improved breeds of livestock.

"Kind of a shame Jenny didn't bring home an agronomist instead of a rock hound," Abe Fraser told Doug gruffly upon first meeting him. "But I suppose we need experts in dirt, too, seeing as how that's what our crops grow in."

"Father!" Jenny exclaimed indignantly. "Doug is not a rock hound, he's a geologist."

"Same difference, honey," her father said with an amiable grin. "But if you can put up with him, so can I. How about another beer, Doug?"

Despite the fact that no mines worth working had been found in the Nespelem sector of the Colville Reservation, Doug was surprised to read in the Spokane and Wenatchee papers that the federal government was opening a substantial portion of the reserve to preemption by the whites. According to the newspaper stories, a lottery would be held in late May 1916, with each of the five thousand winners to be given the opportunity to purchase an eighty-acre tract of land for the bargain price of $1.50 per acre.

"This is surplus land which the Indians do not need," declared the newspaper articles. "The upland tracts are covered with stands of prime timber, while the bottom lands are so fertile they will grow anything, when irrigated. This is a fine opportunity for land-hungry families to get a start."

"How can the government do this to the Indians?" Jenny asked Doug indignantly. "I thought the Colvilles signed a treaty with the United States, which could only be abrogated by a two-thirds vote of the Senate, then signed by the President."

Doug shook his head. "The Colville Reservation was established by an Executive Order, Jenny, not by a treaty. By law, an Executive Order can be changed or revoked either by the President or a simple majority vote of Congress."

"Are you sure about that?"

"Very sure. I'm an adopted member of the tribe."

"Well, it doesn't sound fair to me."

"No—and it isn't. But the politicians made it sound fair by passing a law giving the Colvilles first crack at reservation land, permitting every man, woman, and child registered as a member of the tribe to take title to an eighty-acre tract of his choice, with a few square miles at agency headquarters being set aside for schools, churches, and tribal offices. The lands left over are declared 'surplus' and sold to the lottery winners for $1.50 an acre, with the funds received put into the tribal treasury."

"Less Indian Bureau expenses?"

"That I don't know, Jenny. But it seems a reasonable assumption."

With the first drawing scheduled to be held in Wenatchee in late May, "The World's Greatest Daily Paper for Cities Under 10,000 Population" printed a coupon which, when filled out and accompanied by twenty-five cents, would bring the applicant a pamphlet containing instructions on how to become a participant in the lottery. According to publisher Rufus Woods, ninety thousand pamphlets eventually were requested and mailed. On the day of the drawing, the city of Wenatchee, whose normal population was seventy-five hundred, became a jam-packed madhouse, with twenty thousand visitors.

Meanwhile, on the Colville Reservation near Spokane, a politically ambitious young attorney named Clarence Dill posed for a newspaper picture uncomfortably mounted astride a horse with which he obviously was not well acquainted. By a freak of redistricting, Dill had been elected to Congress as a Democrat in what was normally a solidly Republican section of the state. Flushed with success and feeling that he deserved credit for the role he had played in arranging the surplus-lands lottery, he was showing the residents of his district what their votes had bought them. None of his constituents were Indians, of course; Indians could not vote.

At the time of Jenny's graduation in late May, Professor Fleming still had received no word from Joseph Pardee regarding his employment on the Colville Reservation mineralization study. When he said he had no funds for summer work, Doug began to seriously consider Abe Fraser's offer to employ him on the ranch during wheat harvest, which would be starting in a couple of weeks. Calling him into the office one morning, John Fleming waved a letter he was holding in his hand.

"Here's a job offer for you, Doug."

"Who is it from?"

"Rufus Woods, publisher of the *Wenatchee World.* If you'll recall, we met him in Ephrata last summer. He bought us lunch."

"I remember. What does he want?"

"His letter is a bit murky. But what he seems to be after is a young geologist who will work cheap, keep his mouth shut, and spend a month or two poking around the Grand Coulee with a group of Ephrata people led by a lawyer named Billy Clapp."

"Doing what?"

"Rufus Woods is very vague about that. But the best I can make out, this Billy Clapp has a cockamamie notion of developing a big irrigation project whose success will hinge on whether or not the Coulee will hold water."

"He wants me to determine that?"

"What I suspect he wants is an expert's opinion on the irrigation scheme for a bargain-basement price. As you go through life as a professional geologist, Doug, you're going to have to put up with a lot of this sort of thing, if you expect to survive. You don't have to give your valuable professional advice for a ridiculously low fee, but you may want to now and then just to get the job."

"What do you think I should do, John?"

"If you're interested, I suggest you write Rufus Woods and tell him you'll come over to Ephrata if he'll send you a month's salary in advance."

"How much should I ask for?"

"Try fifty dollars a month. But you may have to settle for less. From what we saw of those dryland farms in the lower part of the Coulee last summer, it doesn't look like very prosperous country."

Truth was, Doug mused as he got off the train in Ephrata a week later, the town and the country surrounding it looked even drier, dustier, and bleaker than it had a year ago. Even though the railroad-builder, James J. Hill, had made his fortune persuading settlers to take up claims along the route of the Great Northern through country almost as bleak as this, when he had gone for a walk beside the Ephrata station during a brief stop there, he had shaken his head and said grimly, "Without water, the land around here has no use except to hold the world together."

Following which, he had climbed back into his private railroad car and ordered the engineer to highball it for Puget Sound.

In response to Doug's request for a fifty-dollar salary, Rufus Woods had sent him a *Wenatchee World* check for forty dollars on a take-it-or-leave-it basis, saying that was all the people promoting the project could afford at the moment.

"If you'll give us a month's work," he promised, "I'll see if I can't wangle some preliminary engineering funds out of the county commissioners, though Grant County is low on money, too. We've got to find some way to put water on the land in this part of the state but we're practically broke. We're hoping Washington State College can help with some technical advice."

Choosing between accepting a low-paying job in his profession or spending the summer working in wheat harvest on the Fraser ranch was not too difficult for Doug. Fertile though the loessal soil near Dusty was, many of the wheat fields were on land with slopes up to 20 percent. All too frequently, the big, cumbersome headers used to cut the thick-stemmed wheat took spectacular tumbles, whether drawn by thirty-three-span teams of mules or by one of the new steam- or gas-fueled tractors which progressive farmers like Abe Fraser were beginning to use.

"A bright young fellow like you shouldn't have any trouble learning how to drive a tractor," Abe Fraser told Doug cheerfully. " 'Course, handling a thirty-three-span team of mules ain't something you learn in college. Takes a lot of natural talent for that."

Telling Jenny that he would trust her to explain to her father why he would rather go rock-hounding in Grand Coulee this summer than learn how to drive a tractor, Doug had cashed the forty-dollar check and come to Ephrata. Though the poorly lettered sign outside the small, unpainted, one-story building two blocks from the railroad station read William M. Clapp, Attorney, Doug knew the moment he entered the office and introduced himself to the short, plump, round-faced man who rose to greet him why everyone called him "Billy." Prosperous or broke, sober or mellow with drink, in good luck or bad, William M. Clapp, attorney-at-law, never lost his smile or his cheerful outlook on life. So people naturally called him "Billy."

Rufus Woods had written Doug that he would be busy with newspaper affairs in Wenatchee, sixty miles to the west, when Doug arrived in Ephrata, so the editor was not among the half dozen people waiting in Billy Clapp's office. Though it would be a while before Doug got their identities and positions in the loosely structured irrigation-planning committee straightened out, he soon became aware of the fact that, as a group, they had only a vague idea of what they were doing.

Paul Donaldson, a slim, tanned, quiet-spoken man in his mid-thirties, told Doug that he had just returned from examining several mining claims he had staked out in the upper Coulee, including one he had decided to abandon in the Nespelem sector of the Colville Reservation following the negative report of the U.S.G.S. mineralization study.

A fat, red-faced man named Fred Wolfson was introduced to Doug as a "big man in our dry little puddle" because he owned the local brewery, which was renowned countywide for its superior product. Just last weekend, Billy Clapp said with a chuckle, when he and several other committee members were touring the desert country a few miles east of town and the radiator of his Model T Ford boiled over, the party had been saved from a long, hot walk back to town by the fact that they still had half a keg of Wolfson beer in the rack on the running board. Poured into the radiator instead of drunk, it got them safely back to town.

"Had the best head on it you ever saw," Billy boasted.

In time to come, Doug would be told by several of Billy Clapp's friends that the round-faced little man had been well on his way to becoming the leading attorney in Seattle when his love affair with the bottle spoiled his career. Coming to Ephrata to "dry out," he was sober most of the time now and had acquired a host of supporters for his sometimes visionary schemes.

Dominating the group with his rich, eloquent, spellbinding Irish voice and combative personality, tall, gaunt James O'Sullivan who wore gold-rimmed glasses also had crossed the Cascades from Puget Sound when drawn to the dryland country by the promises of promoters such as James J. Hill. Prodded by Billy Clapp, who seemed to feel that getting to know the local people would make Doug more sympathetic to their cause, O'Sullivan related what had happened to him that chilly, windy November morning in 1909 when he got off the eastbound train. Going to one of the few places open for business, he introduced himself to Bill Terry, the liveryman.

"I'm James O'Sullivan," he said. "If you've got a nice, gentle horse I can rent, I'd like to ride out to look at a piece of land on Moses Lake."

Judging from the appearance of the lanky stranger that he was a city fellow unused to horses, the liveryman saddled and bridled the gentlest mare he had, then, when asked, gave O'Sullivan directions to the Moses Lake land development project he was seeking.

"A few years earlier I'd left a good contracting business back in Michigan and come out to Everett, Washington, looking for new opportunities," O'Sullivan told Doug, "but the rain and fog along Puget Sound depressed me. When I read an advertisement telling what great fruit country there was on this side of the Cascades, where I could purchase a hundred-acre irrigated tract already planted to apples, I bought it sight unseen for twenty-five hundred dollars. This was the Moses Lake property I'd come to see."

Thanks to the accurate directions given him by the liveryman, O'Sullivan did find the piece of property he'd purchased and was given a friendly greeting by the man who still lived on it, who seemed glad to have company. By then, O'Sullivan said, "I'd begun to smell a rat—the real estate agent who'd sold me the property. Without telling the man living on the place that I'd bought it, I let on I was interested in the area, first loosening his tongue with a few drinks from the quart of whiskey I'd brought along."

Everything the Everett real estate agent had told him about the hundred-acre fruit farm was technically true, O'Sullivan learned. There was a well, a windmill, a house, and five thousand apple trees planted on the place. But the well was dry, the windmill broken, the house merely a one-room shack, and most of the apple trees had died from lack of water. The man who lived on the place said he had paid five hundred dollars for it four years ago, and had since invested five hundred more in improvements and fruit trees. But when the well went dry, the windmill broke, and the apple trees began to die, he decided he'd had enough of this godforsaken country. Listing the property with a Puget Sound real estate agent, who had agreed to try to sell the place for a 20 percent commission, he was planning to cut his losses and get the hell out.

"By noon, he was drunk and I was sick," O'Sullivan said gloomily. "Finally I said, 'Looks like you're going to take quite a financial licking on the property.' The guy leered at me and grunted. 'My friend, I'm gonna come out smellin' like rose. The agent just wrote me he's sold the place to a sucker over on Puget Sound for twenty-five hundred dollars cash. Soon as I get his check, I'm gone.' "

Without revealing his identity to the man, Jim O'Sullivan rode the placid mare back to Ephrata, returned to Everett to wind up his affairs, then came back and moved into the now-vacant shack. Repairing the windmill, he discovered that the well was still dry. Digging a mile-long network of canals from Moses Lake, he installed a pump, brought in electricity to run it, pulled out the dead apple trees, and replaced them with seedlings. When two wetter-than-usual years made it appear that alfalfa and wheat would do well, he purchased nine hundred acres of desert land nearby and seeded them. When two drier-than-usual years followed, the crops failed completely, so he took out a $40,000 mortgage against his contracting business back in Michigan to cover his losses, then became a member of the committee which was trying to develop an irrigation project.

"By all the saints," he told Doug fervently, "I swear I'll make this desert country blossom like a rose—even though it takes me the rest of my life to do it."

Observing the steely glint flashing in O'Sullivan's eyes as he repeated the vow, Doug got the feeling that he would do just that.

During the two summer months that Doug spent exploring the Coulee with Billy Clapp and other members of the irrigation project committee, he learned how frustrating establishing productive farms in this desert country had proved to be to the land-hungry settlers. Even though the federal government had organized the Bureau of Reclamation in 1902 for the specific purpose of putting water on the land, getting it there in the Columbia Basin appeared to be a problem too vast for the Bureau to handle.

In a reconnaissance of the area, it was proved that the long growing season and the extremely fertile soil made the land capable of producing crops worth twice the value of what could be grown elsewhere in the United States. Because annual precipitation ranged from five to twelve inches per year, the crops must be irrigated, of course, so the first problem was to find an economical way to bring water to the thirsty land. The so-called Big Bend project, which would have taken water from the Pend Oreille River over in Idaho and delivered it through a series of tunnels and canals to the Grand Coulee by gravity flow, which was briefly studied by Bureau of Reclamation engineers, was declared not economically feasible when its initial cost was estimated to be over $100 million.

A scheme to bring water down from Lake Wenatchee a hundred

miles to the northwest, under the Columbia through a tunnel, then spread across the Quincy Basin by means of canals, laterals, and ditches, also was abandoned because of its excessive initial cost. Because of the substantial lift required for pumping out of the river itself, the capital outlay for pumping equipment and the sizable bill for electricity—which was not presently available—put that alternative out of reach, too.

So Billy Clapp concocted his scheme.

"One hot day last summer, Paul Richardson and I got to talking over a beer," he told Doug. "Paul had just come back from looking over a mine prospect in the Coulee. 'That sure is a whopper of a coulee,' I said. 'Got any notion of how it was made?'

" 'Made by the Columbia, I reckon,' Paul said. 'A long time ago, the whole river ran that way because there was an ice dam across the regular channel right below the head of Grand Coulee. That was millions of years ago, of course, when glaciers were pretty much all over the place.' "

Mopping the sweat off his brow, Paul had grinned, then took another sip of his lukewarm beer. "Could stand a little of that ice around here today, couldn't we?"

"Ice dam," Billy had muttered. "An ice dam. If glaciers could do it, why can't we?"

It was such a wild idea, Billy Clapp told Doug, that for a long time he was afraid even to tell it to Rufus Woods and Jim O'Sullivan, with whom he had attended "a thousand meetings" to discuss ways and means of putting water on the land. Finally deciding to reveal it to them, he found that they both were interested.

"Jim O'Sullivan bought a book on the fundamentals of dam-building," Billy told Doug. "He started reading up on things we'd have to do—like make sure we've got a firm foundation underneath and solid walls on both sides. Rufus Woods asked the Grant County engineering department to do a feasibility study, even though most of the Coulee is outside the county. The commissioners say they'll help all they can, as long as we don't tell anybody."

"Why should that matter?"

"Well, they've got a brick scandal to deal with. The voters authorized a new courthouse, you see, but one of the commissioners bought some bricks at a bargain price from a kiln owned by his wife's brother. With an election coming up, having the voters find out that the commissioners are spending money doing a feasibility study on a hare-brained scheme outside the county might not sit too well with the voters. So Rufus Woods suggested we get Washington State College involved, too. I'm sure you can see the sense of that."

Not at all sure he did, Doug decided not to pursue the matter. "Tell me more about this dam you propose to build, Billy."

"Well, Rufus says you geologist fellows told him the floor of Grand Coulee is six hundred feet higher than the level of the Columbia River. Is that right?"

"Yes, it is."

"The hill on the south side of the river is three hundred feet high, you say. So in order to boost the Columbia up to where it would go back into its old course in Grand Coulee, a dam would have to be at least eight hundred feet high?"

"That's right."

"How far would the reservoir behind it back up water into Canada?"

"I'd have to check a contour map to make sure, Billy, but without looking at one I would guess maybe two hundred miles."

"Suppose we built a lower dam that would back up water just to the border. How high would it be?"

"At a guess, maybe five hundred feet."

"Which means we would have to figure out some way to pump the water up over the hill into the Coulee, right? That would be a lift of roughly three hundred feet."

"Right. Which would require some mighty big pumps and conduits, not to mention a tremendous amount of electricity."

"Oh, electricity will be no problem," Billy Clapp said with a deprecating shrug. "With a dam that high, we can just stick in some generators and produce our own electricity right on the spot. Not only that, we'll have enough left over to sell and pay for the whole reclamation project, which, according to my figures, will irrigate two million acres of land."

Doug stared at Billy Clapp for several moments in stunned silence before he could frame a reply. Then he said, "That will take a lot of doing, Billy."

"I know it will, Doug," Billy Clapp said with a smile. "But as the steer told the farmer who turned him into the barnyard with a herd of cows: 'All I can do is try.' "

26.

EVEN THOUGH THE FORTY-DOLLAR check from Rufus Woods was all the money he received from the irrigation committee that summer, Doug gave the project his time, advice, and best efforts until late August without further pay. His reasons for doing so were that the sheer magnitude of the scheme intrigued him; that he was fascinated by his continuing study of the geology of the Coulee; and that he had developed a liking for the men who facetiously called themselves "Students of the Dam University" because they were getting an education in dam-building, politics, and reclamation as they went along.

Before a proposal of this size could be taken to a state or federal agency, the committee members discovered, a prospectus declaring that it would work if properly engineered and funded must be drawn up and sold to the bureau chiefs and politicians. Having access to contour maps, well-drilling records, and U.S. Geological Survey studies, Doug advised them on the nature of strata underlying the Coulee and the riverbed, predicting with reasonable accuracy how much overburden would have to be removed at the proposed dam site before the granite bedrock on which the base of the dam must set was reached.

He also told them that up until now, the tallest such structure in this part of the country was 348-foot-high Arrowrock Dam on the Boise River twenty miles upstream from Boise, Idaho, which the Bureau of Reclamation had recently completed as a storage reservoir for irrigation water.

"Compared to the Columbia, the Boise River is just a trickle," Billy Clapp said after hearing that. "I imagine we'll need a much bigger, thicker dam. With a hundred and fifty miles of water backed up behind it, our dam will have to be strong enough to resist a lot of pressure."

"As a lawyer you may be pretty sharp, Billy," Jim O'Sullivan said, shaking his head. "But you don't know beans about dams, else you wouldn't have made such an ignorant statement."

"What's ignorant about it?" Billy asked.

"Well, to begin with, water stored behind a dam exercises very little horizontal force against it."

"It doesn't?"

"The only force is the weight of the water next to the dam's face, which is directly downward. That's vertical, Billy, not horizontal. Whether a foot, a mile, or a hundred and fifty miles of water is stored in the pool behind the dam really doesn't matter. As long as the dam blocks the flow of the river, that's all that counts."

"But it will have to be thick, won't it?"

"The book says that the base of a dam should be as thick as the dam is tall. That's to prevent undercutting, which would destroy it. So if our dam is five hundred feet high, it will have to be five hundred feet thick at the base."

"How long will it be?"

"Somewhere between forty-five and fifty-five hundred feet. Roughly, a mile from wall to wall."

"Lord-amighty, Jim! That'll make it the biggest dam ever built!"

"I know. But we're going to build it, Billy. By all the saints, I swear it."

Sympathetic though he was to the people who were making such fantastic plans and dreaming such tremendous dreams, Doug Warren feared that their chances for realizing them were about the same as for a blizzard to rage through Grand Coulee in late August.

The possibility that he would return to Ephrata and continue to donate his services to the irrigation committee was decided negatively by events of the next two years. First, Professor John Fleming managed to persuade Washington State College to give Doug an appointment as an assistant professor in the Geology Department on a permanent basis. Second, he and Jenny Fraser decided to get married and buy a house in Pullman, now that he was assured of a steady job. Third, President Wilson did run for a second term, the strongest plank in his platform being "He kept us out of war!", and got elected by a landslide.

Shortly after his inauguration, Germany threatened to wage unrestricted submarine warfare against American shipping unless the United States quit helping England and France, then did so when Wilson ignored the ultimatum.

Stirred to a patriotic pitch by the sinking of the *Lusitania* and newspaper sketches of German soldiers impaling Belgian babies on bayonets, the pacifist mood prevailing in the United States changed overnight. Wilson asked Congress for a declaration of war and got it with only a few dissenting votes, one of which, Doug noted with surprise, was cast by Representative Clarence Dill.

Though 90 percent of the people and newspaper publishers in the Pacific Northwest became strong supporters of the war effort, Abe Fraser vehemently maintained that educated young men such as his new son-in-law should be exempt from the draft.

"Hell, Doug, the country is full of unskilled young fellows who ought to be glad for a chance to be soldiers," he declared. "But you're a college professor now. The government should let you stay home and teach."

"In my age bracket, Abe, being a college professor doesn't exempt me from registering for the draft."

"You're a married man, Doug."

"That doesn't exempt me, either."

"Well, what if you and Jenny had a couple of babies right away? Wouldn't that do it?"

Even if it would, Doug said, Jenny's cooperation and quite a bit of time would be required for that expedient to work. So even though he had little enthusiasm for becoming a soldier and going off to war, he registered for the draft. Caught in an early round, he refused to request an exemption because of his status as a teacher in a specialized field, though he did permit Washington State College to do so. When the exemption was denied and he was ordered to report to Camp Lewis, just south of Tacoma, for induction and training, he was promised by Professor Fleming and the college that his job would be waiting for him when he was mustered out. Deciding to stay in Pullman and pursue a master's degree in biology, Jenny gave him a parting gift—the news that she was pregnant.

"Not that I took Dad's advice," she said with a wistful smile. "This was strictly my own idea."

After spending two months at Camp Lewis learning such warlike arts as close-order drill and how to wrap wool leggings, Doug was transferred across the continent to Camp Dix, New Jersey. After filling out a form listing his education and special skills, he was assigned to an infantry unit and given a corporal's rating, his training as a geologist being put to good use in designing and supervising the digging of latrines and trenches. Scheduled to be shipped overseas to France in the spring of 1918, he came down with a vicious case of influenza, which was causing more casualties that year than the war did. Unlike too many other young soldiers, he managed to survive. Sending him letters and hometown newspapers during the long weeks of his convalescence, Jenny informed him that he now had a son, who, at her father's insistence, would be christened Theodore Lincoln Warren if that was all right with him—which it was.

She also brought him up-to-date on the latest doings of his "Dam University" friends when she sent him a copy of the *Wenatchee World* dated July 18, 1918. Running entirely across the top of the front page, a banner headline read:

TWO MILLION WILD HORSES!

FORMULATE BRAND NEW IDEA FOR IRRIGATION GRANT, ADAMS, FRANKLIN COUNTIES, COVERING MILLIONS OF ACRES OR MORE

The last, the newest, the most ambitious idea in the way of reclamation and the development of water power ever formulated is now in the process of development. The idea contemplates turning the Columbia River back into its old bed in Grand Coulee, by the construction of a giant dam, the reclamation of between one and two million acres of land in Grant, Adams and Franklin counties and the development of a water power approximating Niagara Falls. It was first conceived by William Clapp of Ephrata who kept it under his hat for several months owing to the fact that it appeared too much at first as an evanescent dream. But as the idea began to develop he talked it over with some of his friends. It so appealed to the Grant County Commissioners that they have sent the County Engineer to look the matter up from an engineer's standpoint.

The figures of the engineer will undoubtedly prove most interesting. Should it develop that the dam could be built at a reasonable cost, there will unfold one of the most interesting development projects ever conceived by man.

> The height of the dam will approximate several hundred feet …
> When the dam has been completed to such a height that the Columbia River will run down Grand Coulee the job will be about completed …

While Doug slowly regained his strength during the next few weeks in the Camp Dix hospital, later copies of the *Wenatchee World* sent to him by Jenny revealed local reaction to the article.

"Don't you nutty people down there think you ought to ask us Canadians how we feel about your crazy scheme?" an indignant resident of Revelstoke, British Columbia, wrote. "Or don't you realize a dam high enough to put water into the Coulee will put us under one hundred and seventy feet of water?"

"Dam the Columbia!" Superior Court Judge R. S. Steiner, a good friend of Rufus Woods, wrote jokingly from the nearby town of Waterville. "Verily, Baron Munchausen, thou art a piker!"

As was his habit after breaking an unusual story with a big splash and then dropping it immediately, Rufus Woods did not mention the project again until nine months later, when he briefly noted a report made by Grant County Engineer Norval Duncan, who had confined his comments on the feasibility of the dam to a single typewritten page.

"Based on a hasty reconnaissance," the report concluded, "we find that a dam across the Columbia at the site of the Nespelem cable ferry is feasible. Since it would have to be something over 550 feet high, it therefore would be without precedent as to height and volume. The benefits which might follow the building of such a dam would seem to justify investigating the merits of the project more thoroughly."

Later, Doug would learn that the Grant County commissioners, who were still involved in the brick courthouse scandal, were so sensitive to adverse voter reaction in case their constituents discovered they had spent money studying a big dam project well outside their district that they ordered the report torn out of the record book and burned.

He would also learn that by a curious coincidence a carpenter named Ole J. Kallsted, who had worked in the Wenatchee area for a time but now was retired and living in Olympia, Washington, had read the "Two Million Wild Horses!" article, had been intrigued by it, and had written a letter to an old friend in

Washington, D.C., Arthur Powell Davis, who now happened to be director of the United States Bureau of Reclamation. In his letter, Ole Kallsted casually mentioned the fact that some of his former friends out here in the *other* Washington had proposed building a dam in the Grand Coulee country, which sounded like a good idea to him. Had the Bureau ever looked into the idea? he wondered.

Replying in due time through Washington State Senator Miles Poindexter, Director Davis wrote on February 15, 1919:

> The Reclamation Service has never made the necessary surveys to pass on such a project but I understand that one feature of it would be a dam of unprecedented height, probably 600 to 700 feet, or in any event the project would require an expenditure far greater than can be considered with the Reclamation Fund with which we are now working.

Not in the least impressed by the objections, Ole Kallsted, who had nothing better to do, wrote back to Senator Poindexter:

> As a matter of fact a dam much lower would perhaps do the work just as well, by excavating somewhat of a canal to let the water through, or again such a dam would develop such a tremendous amount of electric power that it might be as well to raise the water say 350 to 400 feet by the dam and lift the water the balance of the way by large pumps.

Whether or not Ole Kallsted's second letter ever reached the head of the Bureau of Reclamation, let alone became part of the planning process, no one could later say. Certainly, Doug Warren had more important matters on his mind by then, for after being thumped, prodded, and tested by several Army doctors who were displeased with the rate of his recovery, he finally got the diagnosis he'd been hoping for.

"You're not going to get well in this climate, Corporal Warren," the medical officer said brusquely, after completing his examination, "and you certainly won't improve if I send you to France. If you're to recover, you'll need plenty of rest, good food, and tender loving care in a dry, sunny climate."

"Doctor," Doug said earnestly, after his fit of coughing had subsided, "I know just the place ..."

Discharged from the Army and sent home in August 1918, Doug began to feel better the moment the westbound train left St. Paul headed for Spokane. Driven to meet him by her father in a brand-new Model T touring car, Jenny looked even more radiant and beautiful than he remembered her, while the chubby-cheeked, blue-eyed, tow-headed one-year-old boy introduced to him as his son was such a perfect image of Jenny and himself that merely looking at him made tears come to Doug's eyes.

Following the two-hour drive south to Pullman over a rough, narrow, dusty road, with Abe Fraser demonstrating both his skill as a driver and how well he had adapted a mule skinner's vocabulary to the automobile age, they reached the small two-bedroom house near the W.S.C. campus on which Doug and Jenny had started making payments when he had gotten his appointment as an assistant professor. Soon thereafter, ranch foreman Jeet Burrows, a laconic, wrinkled, perpetually squinting man in his early sixties, chugged into the driveway in a battered, prewar truck. After consulting with him briefly, Abe Fraser gulped down the glass of iced tea his daughter had fixed for him, then grunted, "Got to get back to the ranch, honey. See you in a week or two."

"Can't you stay for supper?"

"Like to, but I got things to do." He extended a big, callused hand to Doug. "Welcome home, Son. See you later."

Frowning as his father-in-law climbed into the battered old truck, leaving the new touring car parked in the driveway, Doug asked, "Aren't you taking the new car home?"

"Naw. It's yours. Call it a coming-home present."

"You're *giving* me a new car, Abe? Surely you don't expect me to accept such an expensive present!"

"Why not? You done me a big favor by taking Jenny off my hands."

"Father!" Jenny exclaimed indignantly, but there was no indignation in her smile.

Pulling his hat down over his eyes and resting the rundown heels of his manure-streaked cowboy boots on the dashboard, Abe growled to his foreman, "We're burning daylight, Jeet. Let's hit the road."

When Doug checked with Professor Fleming a few days later to see if he would indeed be given back his teaching position as promised, he received another present.

"I've been offered a post at the University of California in Berkeley, starting the spring semester," John Fleming said. "I've recommended you as my replacement, if your health is up to it. How do you feel?"

"Great, John! But speechless."

"Making speeches is not required of young geology professors, Doug. In fact, the less they say, the better."

What he planned to do, Professor Fleming said, was stay on through the fall semester, helping Doug set up his courses and hire a new assistant of his own from a list of recent graduates whom Fleming would recommend. From the way the war was going in Europe, it likely would end before long with the Allies victorious and the German army crushed, never to rise again. With a million or so young men to be mustered out and thrust back into a civilian economy starving for consumer goods, the country probably would enter a decade of unrivaled prosperity, with a lot of discharged soldiers clamoring for a college education.

"We'll be moving into an exciting new world, Doug, in which anything is possible."

"Jenny's been sending me the Wenatchee and Spokane papers. What's the latest on the Grand Coulee project?"

"It's still in the talking stage. Several new players have gotten into the game—the governor, the mayor of Seattle, the Washington Water Power Company, the Spokane Chamber of Commerce. It's shaping up to be the biggest political free-for-all this part of the state has ever seen."

"Did Joseph Pardee complete his mineralization study on the Colville Reservation?"

"Yes—and I helped him with it. The results will be published by the Geological Survey this fall. As a matter of fact, Joe Pardee was responsible for my getting the appointment to Berkeley, which was the school he graduated from." Filling and lighting his pipe, Professor Fleming stared reflectively at the match as it burned itself out, then tossed it into the ashtray on his desk. "My only regret on leaving this part of the country, Doug, is that I won't be able to finish my work in Grand Coulee. Hopefully, you can carry it on."

"I'll certainly try, John. It intrigues me, too."

"During your field trips into the Coulee, you'll probably run into a geologist named J Harlen Bretz, who's been poking around there for a summer or two. He used to teach in a Seattle high school, then moved east to the University of Chicago. From what I've seen of him, he's a very bright fellow. A bit bullheaded. But bright."

"Did you tell him about your flood theory?"

"Heavens, no! It's far too speculative to be discussed with a newcomer to the field." Professor Fleming sighed. "I'm going to miss the Coulee, Doug. Of course, I'll have the San Andreas Fault as a plaything now ..."

Busy taking over the Geology Department, regaining his health, and getting acquainted with his son, Theodore Lincoln Warren, whose name was soon shortened to Ted, Doug made few field trips into the Coulee during the next two years. From newspaper accounts he read, it had become as lively a battlefield as any that recently existed in France, though the missiles flying through the air here were words instead of shells.

In November 1918, Washington State Governor Ernest Lister, speaking in Spokane, proposed that the Big Bend canal project, which the Reclamation Service had found not feasible fifteen years ago, be developed to irrigate up to three million acres of land, even though its cost would be in the neighborhood of $250 million.

Dr. Henry Landes, the state geologist, quickly endorsed the idea. So did the mayor of Seattle, Ole Hanson. Telling the people of Spokane that the voters in the western part of the state would support and help finance the project, Governor Lister instructed the chairman of the State Public Service Commission, E. F. Blaine, who was an expert on irrigation matters, to come up with what came to be called the "gravity flow" plan, which he and his fellow politicians could take to Washington, D.C., with a request for funding.

It took Doug Warren and his former friends from the "Dam University" a while to realize the consequences of the "gravity flow" plan, as opposed to their scheme to pump water into the Coulee using electricity generated by the dam. When they did, the battle lines between the "gravity flow" advocates and the "pumpers" was drawn.

It would rage for fifteen years.

Following the appearance of the original story in the *Wenatchee World*, Rufus Woods had become the victim of ridicule by people who thought the proposal the craziest scheme they ever had heard. The only engineer Woods knew was James O'Sullivan, who still stubbornly hung onto his nine hundred dry, dusty acres near Ephrata, while at the same time trying to keep his contracting business back in Michigan going in order to stay afloat financially.

"Jim, you're the only construction man I know," Woods told his friend one day. "I need an expert's opinion I can publish in the paper to support our project. If you think the dam can be built, write me an article saying so."

While browsing through a bookstore in Seattle a few years earlier, O'Sullivan had found and purchased a book titled *Principles of Irrigation Engineering* by F. H. Newell and Daniel William Murphy. It was Newell, he learned later, who, as chief of the Division of Hydrography and Reclamation of the United States Geological Survey, had looked over the Columbia Basin lands in 1903. Murphy, too, was a Reclamation Service engineer. Over the years, the volume became the well-worn, heavily penciled Holy Writ of the Pumpers—the only book in the Dam University's library. It would be inscribed in its owner's hand, "This book was purchased by Jas. O'Sullivan so that he could study Grand Coulee Dam intelligently."

Among other things, he learned:

> The heights of masonry dams have been steadily increased and larger structures each year are being designed on the basis of experience attained in building and operating the previously finished works. As in the case of ships or other structures each decade appears to see the limit of size, but this is quickly surpassed by the next design. Theoretically, there is no limit to size, as a masonry dam is an artificial reproduction of a hill or dike, such as those built by nature to heights of thousands of feet. It is merely a question of using enough material properly put together, the size being governed by the relation between the cost and the value of the result.

"What I learned from this book," O'Sullivan told Rufus Woods in the office of the *Wenatchee World*, as he showed it to the publisher, "was that if you have good rock foundations and sidewalls, you can build a dam as high as you want—if you have the money."

"That's a great lead, Jim. Fill in some facts and figures, and I'll publish the article."

After driving up to the proposed dam site with County Engineer Norval Duncan and confirming by triangulation that the length of the dam would be approximately a mile, that the six hundred-foot-high hills on either side would be solid anchor points, and guessing that bedrock could be found a hundred or so feet below the gravel overburden filling the riverbed, O'Sullivan returned to Ephrata and used the typewriter in Billy Clapp's law office to peck out an article for the *Wenatchee World.* First stressing the strong points of the Pumpers' proposal, he then attacked the weak spots of the gravity flow plan.

> "The revenue from the sale of electricity alone," he wrote, "would surely pay all upkeep, interest on the investment, and provide a sinking fund for the liquidation of the project itself." Comparing the dam with the gravity flow proposal, which advocated building a reservoir in the Idaho Panhandle east of Spokane, then bringing the water to the Coulee country through a series of canals and tunnels, he pointed out the advantage of "... using the great canal that nature has already blasted for us."

By nature a dynamic, compelling speaker when addressing a live audience, O'Sullivan proved to be just as eloquent with the written word. Not only did he present an impassioned, well-reasoned argument for the Pumpers' cause, but his political instincts were good, in that he knew exactly which bureaucratic buttons to punch in order to achieve results. As article followed article, he mailed weekly sets of clippings to Director Davis of the Reclamation Service in Washington, D.C., one of the great engineers in the nation, the man who had built such high dams as Roosevelt in Arizona, Elephant Butte in New Mexico, and Arrowrock in Idaho. The mailings got results.

"Some damn fool named O'Sullivan has written some articles and sent them to Washington, D.C.," complained an irritated state engineer in the Spokane office of the Columbia Basin Survey Commission one afternoon, waving a telegram he had just received from Director Davis. "Now we've got to spend ten thousand dollars making a survey of a ridiculous proposition."

Engaged in a state survey of the gravity flow project, the commission had not intended to spend any money examining the Grand Coulee Dam idea, but since the Bureau of Reclamation must be appealed to for federal funds, the request by Director Davis could not be ignored.

Down in Ephrata a few days later, O'Sullivan received a telephone call from the commission office, saying they were going to look at the

Grand Coulee dam site and asking him to join the party. As he stood with the engineers on the hill overlooking the river, he was questioned closely by Professor William Waller, secretary of the commission.

"Where would you build that dam of yours, O'Sullivan?"

"Right across there," O'Sullivan answered, pointing.

"How thick would it be across the base?"

"The book says a dam should be as thick as it is high. So if we build it high enough to divert the flow of the river without pumping, it would have to be 850 feet thick."

"Why, that would mean a base a quarter of a mile thick!" Waller exclaimed. "That's unheard of!"

"There's an alternative," O'Sullivan said. "With a lower dam and plenty of cheap electricity, we could pump water into the Coulee."

"How much lift are you talking about?"

"Two or three hundred feet."

"How much water would you be pumping?"

"Enough to irrigate two million acres."

"How big would your pipes be?"

"We'd need a dozen or so conduits ten or twelve feet in diameter."

"How much electricity would your pumps require?"

"Around sixty-five thousand horsepower apiece. But with plenty of electricity being generated by five hundred feet of fall at the dam, that would be no problem."

Professor Waller snorted. "No problem, you say? That's a damn-fool statement, if ever I heard one, Mr. O'Sullivan. The project you propose is impossible!"

Satisfied that they had seen all they needed to see and rejecting the dam idea out of hand, the members of the commission kidded Jim O'Sullivan unmercifully as they left the site and returned to Ephrata, which they reached in time for a late supper at the Ephrata Eats Emporium. The only member of the party who did not join in the general ribbing was Arthur Turner, chief engineer for the Columbia Basin Survey Commission, a man whose good opinion O'Sullivan greatly coveted. In an effort to soothe O'Sullivan's hurt feelings, Professor Waller said, "Come on in and eat with us, Jim. It's my treat."

Remaining seated in his car, O'Sullivan shook his head, muttering that he would be in shortly. After the party had gone inside, he pulled the well-thumbed Newell and Murphy reference book out of the jockey box, opened it, and began studying it under the dash light. A figure moved in the dusk outside the car, then a voice asked quietly, "What are you doing, Jim?"

"Trying to see whether I'm a damn fool," O'Sullivan grunted, not bothering to look up from the cone of light falling on the pages of the book, even though he recognized the voice as that of the commission engineer, Arthur Turner.

"I don't need a book to answer that," Turner said firmly. "You're not a damn fool, Jim. Far from it."

Looking up in surprise, O'Sullivan stared at the commission engineer. "I'm not?"

"For whatever it may be worth to you, Jim, I'd rather build that dam than anything else in the world."

27.

On two occasions the next summer, Doug ran into J Harlen Bretz in Grand Coulee when both geologists were camping with their wives and children in the area. Driving out from Chicago in a Dodge four-door sedan carrying a family-size umbrella tent, jointed poles, a three-burner kerosene cook stove, a grub box, ice chest, and his rock-sampling tools, Bretz was more interested in relating his adventures fixing flats and driving the "Yellowstone Road" through the national park, across southern Montana, and the Idaho Panhandle than in sharing trade talk about the Coulee.

Ten years older than Doug and very much his senior so far as his standing as a geologist was concerned, J Harlen Bretz (who never explained what the "J" stood for or why it was not followed with a period), appeared to be a man so intent on pursuing his own theories and documenting them in his own way that Doug would not dream of asking questions or volunteering information unless asked to do so, which he never was. Because the two Bretz children, a boy ten and a girl eight, were much older than three-year-old Ted, who required constant watching lest he pick up a night-chilled baby rattlesnake and bring it to his mother for identification along with the other biology specimens she was collecting, the two families had no reason to associate much with one another.

Because Chako Charley and his Indian relatives on the Nespelem sector of the Colville Reservation were always glad to loan Doug horses whenever he needed them, Doug frequently rode into the rougher sections of the Coulee, where the Model T Ford touring car could not go. Noticing that J Harlen Bretz often had his wife drive him in the Dodge to the edge of broken, lava-strewn country too rugged to be traversed by car early in the morning, then come back and pick him up after he had spent a long day hiking afoot, Doug offered to lend the older geologist a horse borrowed from Chako Charley. But Bretz politely declined.

"Shanks' mare does fine for me, Doug. A horse would just slow me down."

For Bretz, Doug learned, a hike of twenty, thirty, or even forty miles a day over the roughest kind of terrain was considered a normal outing. When Bretz later complained about armchair geologists who had never explored the Coulee step by step as he had done, his criticism was justified.

In June 1920 the *Wenatchee World* published a long letter from Jim O'Sullivan to Billy Clapp giving preliminary engineering figures on the cost of building Grand Coulee Dam and its power-producing units. An editorial by Rufus Woods called the project "the most unique, the most interesting, and the most remarkable development of both irrigation and power in this age of industrial and scientific miracles."

Later that same month, two local Dam University members, Nat Washington and Frank Bell, went down to San Francisco to attend the Democratic National Convention. The Ephrata delegates managed to get a plank in the platform urging the construction of the dam and the development of the irrigation project. Little notice was given to the fact that the vice-presidential candidate chosen to run on the ticket with James M. Cox was a handsome young New Yorker named Franklin Roosevelt, whose highest government office to date had been that of assistant secretary of the Navy. When Clarence Dill, one of the few members of Congress to vote against the declaration of war requested by President Wilson, volunteered his services on the campaign trail in Washington State to the Democratic candidates, the offer was accepted, though it was to be doubted that the Cox-Roosevelt ticket would win in either the nation or the state.

In July, a serious blow fell on the Grand Coulee Dam project when the Columbia Basin Survey Commission submitted its report to the governor of Washington State. Endorsing the gravity flow system without qualification, the commission recommended a reservoir in Idaho that would back water into Montana, a 130-mile-long main canal, a system of concrete, earth- and rock-filled lower dams, tunnels, artificial lakes, and siphons, costing in all $300 million, which eventually would deliver water from the Pend Oreille River to thirsty Columbia Basin lands.

Under Appendix H of the commission's report, a dam at Grand

Coulee was briefly considered. The proposal analyzed was for a dam 180 feet high, which would afford just enough head to supply power for pumping water up over the hill and into the Coulee. Since there would be no excess power to sell, all the costs of the dam and the pumping would have to be charged to the lands to be irrigated, which contained a much smaller acreage than what was contemplated under the gravity flow system, making reclamation costs prohibitive.

"Judging from the outcrops of granite on the sides of the valley at opposite ends of the dam," the report stated critically, "the maximum depth to bedrock in the center of the channel is estimated to be between 150 feet and 250 feet. The probabilities are that the depth will be in excess of 200 feet, rather than less. Every probability points to the site being not suitable for a dam of sufficient height to develop the power required."

For most members of the Dam University, the commission report came as a crushing blow. But all it did for Jim O'Sullivan was make him mad. When O'Sullivan phoned Pullman, his voice was so harsh and belligerent that Doug had to hold the receiver six inches away from his head to prevent having an eardrum punctured.

"What kind of crackpot statement is that, saying 'the probabilities are that the depth will be in excess of 200 feet, rather than less'?" O'Sullivan demanded. "How in the name of all the saints can they say such a stupid thing?"

"They're guessing, Jim. They admit that."

"What would your guess be?"

"A hundred feet would be more likely."

"Can I quote you on that?"

"I'd rather you didn't, Jim. Without core-drilling at the site, there's no way any geologist can be sure."

"We can't afford core-drilling, Doug. They can—but they didn't do it."

In what was obviously a prejudiced report, the commission noted "the impracticability, and perhaps the impossibility, of building a dam in the Columbia River near Grand Coulee or of securing sufficient power for pumping from any outside source. Every consideration indicates the superiority of the Pend Oreille gravity supply over the Columbia River pumping supply."

As a final crushing argument against the dam, the report cited the Bulwer-Lytton Treaty of 1846 between the United States and Great

Britain which declared that the Columbia River from the international boundary to the Pacific Ocean "shall be free and open to the Hudson's Bay Company and to all British subjects trading with the same ..."

Disregarding the fact that natural rapids and waterfalls long had made that portion of the river unnavigable for craft of any kind, the commission claimed that the cost of locks and lifts designed to make the river suitable for large vessels would make building Grand Coulee completely impractical.

What was curious about that argument, as Jim O'Sullivan pointed out to both Rufus Woods and Doug Warren, was that the Washington Water Power Company, a private utility, had recently applied to the Federal Power Commission for a license to build a dam on the Columbia at Kettle Falls a hundred miles upstream from the Grand Coulee site, making no mention of facilities for navigation by Hudson's Bay Company boats. Furthermore, it had now become clear that the extra water dispatched to the Columbia Basin Irrigation project would be channeled into the Spokane River, in which the Washington Water Power Company just happened to have some hydroelectric turbines whose output would be greatly enhanced by the augmented flow.

If the Washington Water Power Company had any plans to reduce customer rates or pay for the increased supply of water, neither fact was mentioned in the commission report.

In addition to this bit of skullduggery, O'Sullivan told his Dam University friends, an F.P.C. license for the Kettle Falls dam and hydroelectric plant would mean that the five-hundred-foot height of the proposed Grand Coulee Dam would have to be reduced by at least a third, effectively killing the whole plan.

"Gentlemen, I smell a rat," O'Sullivan declared vehemently. "It's spelled 'W.W.P.C.' "

Any way you chose to spell the names of the formidable forces now arrayed against the Pumpers, the combined resources of the Washington Water Power Company, the state-financed Columbia Basin Irrigation Study Commission, the Spokane Chamber of Commerce, and the *Spokesman-Review* were so great that Jim O'Sullivan, whose own finances were strained to the breaking point, came very close to giving up the fight and going back to his contracting business in Wisconsin.

In fact, several times during the next ten years, he did go back to his hometown, where his wife and children maintained the family residence and kept the family contracting business alive, long enough to submit successful bids on enough profitable jobs to stay solvent. Still owning the dry nine hundred acres near Ephrata upon which he hoped to put water someday, he refused to abandon his dream and his vow that someday he would make this country "blossom like a rose."

Scrounging money from whatever private and public sources they could tap, the Pumpers managed to raise enough funds to do extensive core-drilling at the proposed dam site. Their findings, they gleefully announced, were that solid granite not only underlay the river bed at a depth of less than fifty feet, but it also was available in the canyon walls as anchors for the ends of the dam. Loftily ignoring the pronouncement of the Pumpers, the Gravity Flow people said the granite was "rotten" to a depth of at least two hundred feet, and thus was useless as a base for the dam.

"How can you tell when granite is rotten?" a student asked Doug after reading the report. "By its smell?"

Doug had to admit that he did not know.

To the argument of the Pumpers that income from the sale of electricity produced by the dam would pay for the development of irrigable lands, the Gravity Flows replied that since excess crops were being grown in other parts of the country, more irrigated land was not needed at this time. Furthermore, no market presently existed for more electricity in the region; when and if such a market did develop, the private utilities could supply it.

Each group brought in outside experts to make studies and voice opinions supporting its side of the argument. One of the most prestigious of those imported by the Gravity Flow people was General George Goethals, who eight years earlier had been in charge of building the Panama Canal. At the suggestion of Clarence Dill, who, though a Democrat in a normally Republican district, had managed to get elected to Congress, the Pumpers imported Colonel Hugh L. Cooper who, Dill claimed, "was known to be the greatest dam builder in the world," having built the Niagara Falls, the Keokuk, and other dams.

As a rock-ribbed Republican, Rufus Woods ordinarily would have been suspicious of any expert Clarence Dill endorsed, but in this case he had good reason to believe that Dill was sincere in backing the cause of the Pumpers.

"He's mad at the Gravity Flows because the people at the *Spokesman-Review*, the Washington Water Power Company, and the

Columbia Basin Survey Commission are all Republicans and campaigned against him when he ran for Congress," Woods told O'Sullivan. "So for now, at least, he's on our side."

"Faith and I'd sleep with the Devil himself," O'Sullivan said, "if he'd endorse the dam."

Managing to raise only enough cash to pay Colonel Cooper's expenses for a one-day tour of the dam site, the Pumpers got their money's worth when he pronounced their plan for a 550-foot-high dam which would back a 150-mile-long reservoir to the Canadian border as "perfectly feasible."

Having been granted fifty thousand dollars in state funds, of which amount twenty thousand dollars still remained, the Gravity Flow people were able to authorize a study of their plan in more detail and depth. Bringing General Goethals out from New York, they wined, dined, and entertained him for a week in a plush suite at the Davenport Hotel, showed him their blueprints and plans, then, accompanied by an escort of Spokane dignitaries worthy of his exalted position in the engineering world, gave him a day-long tour of the Pumpers' Grand Coulee Dam site just to show the general public how fair-minded they were.

In a remarkable mixture of factual writing and mind reading, the reporter who covered the story for the *Spokesman-Review* wrote:

> General Goethals made no remarks as he studied this great challenge, but his face admitted the magnitude of the task. He gazed at the Columbia River today rolling along placidly and visualized the river at high water time, when the mountain snows would melt, realized huge flows would crash into the superdam which might stand as a threatening menace to life and property on the flat lands below.

Though General Goethals's final report expressed approval for the gravity flow proposal, he also was quoted by the Pumpers as having said, "Given the time and the money, the dam can be built," which the Pumpers took to mean he was on *their* side. Though he left behind a bunch of cost estimates related to developing the irrigated land under the gravity flow plan, they were so ridiculously low when compared to known sums spent for reclamation projects elsewhere in the West that even his sponsors were too embarrassed to publicize them.

But on one cost estimate he was right on the money—his twenty thousand dollar fee. After collecting it, he returned to New York City and was heard from no more.

At about this same time, the personable young assistant secretary of the Navy, Franklin Delano Roosevelt, toured Washington State in his campaign for vice-president on the James M. Cox ticket. True to his promise, Clarence Dill accompanied him as one of the few sympathetic Democrats to be found in the state at that time. It was then, Dill later claimed, that he and Roosevelt became friends, with FDR saying at the end of the tour, "I'm an easterner, Clarence, and not much of a politician. But I really appreciate what you've done. If ever I can return the favor, let me know."

Meanwhile, the Gravity Flow advocates seemed to have everything going their way—except for a few minor details. One of these was the fact that neither the state nor the federal government cared to invest $300 million in a project to irrigate a million or two acres of desert land in eastern Washington. Another was that citizens living in the states of Idaho and Montana objected so vehemently to having their homes drowned out under storage reservoirs built to benefit Columbia Basin lands that their legislatures passed laws prohibiting such projects.

When the peace-and-prosperity boom of the Republican Harding-Coolidge era collapsed with the crash of '29, then was followed with the Hoover Depression of the early '30s, Democrats nationwide rode into office on the coattails of the now-crippled but still-personable Franklin Delano Roosevelt. With so many unemployed men and so much excess food in the country, putting water on desert land in order to grow still more crops became a useless endeavor. When an unprecedented drought struck eastern Washington and the powder-dry land itself got up and started moving away, the long-cherished dream of Jim O'Sullivan and his Dam University friends seemed about to blow away, too.

But the tall, gaunt "Prophet in the Wilderness," James O'Sullivan, who, because of his frequent trips east seeking funds, became known as "The Poorest Lobbyist in Washington," somehow managed to keep the dream alive.

With the moral backing of Rufus Woods, Billy Clapp, and other Pumper friends, O'Sullivan established an organization called the "Columbia River Development League" whose avowed purpose was to collect funds for the promotion of the Grand Coulee Dam project. Starting off with a fifty-dollar contribution from the *Wenatchee World*, the size of the contributions diminished sharply thereafter, with five dollars here, two dollars there, on down to promises by Billy Clapp and small-town merchants who had joined the league to donate a few bucks the next time *their* creditors made a payment on *their* bills.

More than once when important legislation was being debated in Congress, O'Sullivan barely managed to scrape up train fare and board-and-room money at dollar-a-day houses of friendly widows in Washington, D.C., whom he charmed into giving him special rates. Between 1931, when the first serious efforts to obtain federal backing for the Grand Coulee project were made, and 1948, when the first water was put on the land, O'Sullivan made twelve trips to Washington, D.C., as an advocate and expert witness for the project.

Despite his lack of funds, he had no equal in the extent and quality of his knowledge regarding the project, his enduring belief in it, and the political know-how with which he steered enabling and appropriation bills through often hostile committees, executive-branch offices, and the halls of Congress.

During one of his trips home following several unusually dry years, he experienced the worst dust storm he had ever seen in this part of the country. For eons of time, prevailing winds from the southwest had eroded the Cascades bringing in the extremely fertile loessal soil which covered the Palouse Hills and the Columbia Basin lands. Now, through a freak of climate change, the hot summer wind reversed itself, blowing from east to west day after day, as if determined to take the powdery brown soil back where it came from. In Portland, the *Oregonian* reported:

> Six hundred miles at sea, en route from Seattle to Honolulu, passengers aboard the Matson liner *Maui* were surprised to see the sun suddenly obscured by a great black cloud and then to see, feel, and taste descending gritty particles which could only be soil blown from the mainland. The Pacific Northwest was having the most spectacular dust storm in its history.

Much of that soil was being blown from the waterless lands of the Grand Coulee country, O'Sullivan knew. Joining the county agent from Wenatchee for a drive over the Columbia Basin during the storm, he was appalled when he saw a stretch of beautiful farmland containing some of the finest soil in the country now turned to drifts of worthless sand.

Still, his dream did not die …

Devout Catholic though he was, Jim O'Sullivan was always willing to do a favor for a friend, even if that meant preaching a sermon in a Protestant church. When a member of the Columbia River Development League, who happened to be a Presbyterian pastor, asked Jim to fill in for him by giving a Thanksgiving Day sermon in his church, O'Sullivan was happy to oblige. His sermon began:

> Who shall say that he is not thankful for having been born into a paradise of freedom of religion, of politics, of economic opportunity, of power harnessed to do the work of man, of surpluses instead of famines, of love instead of brutality, of bewildering advances in science and invention? And we can be thankful for living not only in this great republic, but in that part that is still undiscovered—the new West—the West of opportunity and a future …
>
> It seems that at last the star of destiny points toward the Northwest. All factors point this way—the President's waterway development, the growing use of electric power, the shortage on the Sound, the Boulder Canyon precedent, the crash on Wall Street, the very atmosphere seems to be charged with hope and faith. Grand Coulee is next …

How many people joined the Presbyterian church following the service is not known. But it is a matter of record that the next day five members of the congregation joined the Columbia River Development League.

Whatever the sermon lacked in spirituality, it more than made up for in its reference to topics of the times. After many years of pleading with the federal government to make a comprehensive study of the Columbia River, President Hoover, an engineer himself, had authorized and Congress had funded a Corps of Engineers study titled the "308 Report." It would be made by Major John S. Butler, a man known to be incorruptible in his principles and unbiased in his judgments. When finished in two or three years, the report would outline an orderly plan of development for the second greatest river in the United States during the next fifty years.

The Boulder Canyon project referred to was the dam now being built on the lower Colorado River between Arizona and Nevada. A single-arch structure 726 feet high, it and the hundreds of thousands of acres of land its waters would irrigate, plus the tremendous amount of electricity its generators would provide for Los Angeles and Phoenix, was the biggest project the Bureau of Reclamation had ever undertaken. As visualized by O'Sullivan, the Grand Coulee project would be even bigger, which did not bother him at all, though in these economically troubled times it made the Bureau of Reclamation nervous.

As to the "growing use of electric power and the shortage on the Sound" mentioned in his sermon, what he referred to here was the surprising fact that, contrary to assurances from private utilities that they had plenty of generating capacity to serve electric needs for some time to come, use had so outgrown supply in the Puget Sound region that the City of Tacoma, on the verge of an imposed blackout, had been forced to use all the political clout its representatives in Washington, D.C., possessed in order to compel the secretary of the Navy to order the new aircraft carrier *Lexington*, which had a huge electrical generator onboard, to sail from its base in Bremerton to Tacoma, where it anchored in Commencement Bay, then hooked onto the municipal power system in order to supply electricity for essential city services.

Learning of this, Jim O'Sullivan immediately put together a statement syndicated in thirty-four of the nation's newspapers, adding the footnote, "As a source of year-round power, Grand Coulee Dam could be built for the cost of a single aircraft carrier."

By now, a dam built to the full height of 550 feet on the Grand Coulee site, with all its generating and pumping facilities, was estimated at $450 million. First called Hoover, then Boulder, and finally Hoover again, the dam on the Colorado River had been authorized for a mind-boggling $165 million. With the national debt now approaching the $3 billion level and the Depression paralyzing the economy, the chances of the federal government committing $450 million to the Grand Coulee project were near zero.

Still, there was the Corps of Engineers 308 Report to look forward to. And with Franklin Roosevelt and the New Deal taking over, some pretty wild things were starting to happen.

Answering the question of if, how, or when Clarence Dill may have persuaded Franklin Roosevelt to endorse the Grand Coulee Dam project depends on whose memory could be trusted. So far as

Dill was concerned, it happened in this fashion: After being out of a Republican-dominated Congress for a term, Dill went back as a Democratic senator in the late 1920s and was serving as chairman of the newly created Federal Communications Commission when the General Electric Company invited him to come up to their plant in Schenectady, New York, to take a look at a new gadget they had just produced, a television set. By then, Franklin D. Roosevelt had been elected to his second term as governor of New York. Albany, the state capital, was only eighteen miles away, so Dill wrote a note asking for an appointment on January 3, 1931, "to discuss a public question." In response, FDR phoned and invited Dill to have dinner with him at the executive mansion, saying, "My missus will be away and we can talk politics all evening."

At one point during the evening, Dill wrote later, Gus, FDR's private aide, came into the room and Roosevelt asked Dill, "You don't mind if I don't put on my braces? It's much more comfortable without them." When Dill replied that he certainly did not mind, "Gus picked up this tall, broad-shouldered, healthy-looking man and placed him in a wheelchair as though he were a child. It was the first time I had ever seen anything like that."

For several hours during and after dinner, the two men discussed the Depression, unemployment, the farm problem, the deficit, and world peace. Dill did not drink or smoke; Roosevelt did. They both liked to talk, but, as Dill wrote later, "Anybody who ever spent much time with Roosevelt learned how difficult it was to interrupt him with a new subject."

During a lull in the conversation, Dill finally managed to break in. "Governor, I have a Northwest problem I came to discuss with you."

"Oh? What is it?"

As Clarence Dill later remembered the conversation, when he mentioned the Columbia River, FDR discoursed at length on the fact that Thomas Jefferson, a Democrat, had made the Louisiana Purchase, and had sent Lewis and Clark to explore the newly acquired territory; that James J. Polk, another Democrat, had brought the British to their knees with his "54–40 or Fight" threat; and that he himself had always liked the Pacific Northwest. After listening to Dill's detailed explanation of the size of the dam and its accompanying reclamation project, Roosevelt asked, "How do you propose to pay for the project?"

"That's the remarkable part of our plan," Dill answered. "Our engineers figure the dam will produce power for the cost of one mill per kilowatt hour. Selling it at two mills, we'll be able to pay off the entire cost in forty years at 3 percent interest. After that, the public will own the dam free and clear."

"I agree with your thinking," Roosevelt said, nodding in approval. "You don't want private power profiteers to exploit this wonderful resource for low-cost electricity as they're doing with our gas and oil."

When asked what President Hoover's attitude was toward the project, Dill said he was against it because of the deficit and other economic reasons. After a silence, Roosevelt said thoughtfully, "I don't suppose I'll ever be President, Clarence. But if I am, I'll build that dam."

"That's what I came here to get you to say!" Dill exclaimed. "But we'll have a long, hard fight to get Congress to authorize it."

Quick as a flash, Dill said later, FDR thrust out his jaw, turned on his brilliant smile, and replied, "Ah, if I were President, I'd start it and Congress would have to finish it."

"If you stick to that promise," Dill said exuberantly, "I'm going to help nominate and elect you President."

And he did …

During the boom years of the 1920s, Doug Warren had been offered a number of jobs as a geologist with mining or oil companies that would have paid much better than his position as a faculty member at Washington State College. But tempting though the jobs were financially and challenging as they were professionally, he had turned them down. His main reason for doing so was that he did not want to leave Jenny and the children—there were four of them now, two boys and two girls—at home or force them to lead the gypsy life of a traveling geologist in the rough oil or mining towns to which such jobs would take him. Now and then he did take on limited work in Idaho, Montana, or Wyoming, if the job were interesting or happened to be near a national park or wilderness area where Jenny and the children could camp out, which they loved to do.

Still giving moral support to the Pumpers and his friends at the Dam University, Doug and his family joined them one hot, dry, dusty weekend in Grand Coulee in what was billed as a fund-raising event featuring a mass picnic and rides in a Ford Tri-motor. Having taken his first plane ride at the age of eight in a barnstorming biplane that had landed in a cow pasture near Pullman, Ted Warren, who now was twelve, considered himself a veteran air traveler. Following Charles Lindbergh's New York–to–Paris solo flight two years ago, Ted had announced that he, too, was going to be an aviator, with his first solo flight to be across the Pacific.

Well, why not? Doug mused. So far in the Warren family there had been an unbroken line of sea and river captains until he came along; even then, his older sister Lily had kept the chain intact by getting a captain's license herself. After he had broken the pattern by becoming an earth scientist instead of a riverman, the next logical step for his son was into the air.

In a dramatic show of support for the Columbia River Development League, eight thousand people attended the Sunday afternoon picnic in Coulee Park. Taking off from an eighteen hundred-foot dirt runway scraped through the sagebrush of the flat Coulee floor, the big, noisy Ford Tri-motor made flight after flight with capacity loads all morning and afternoon at a dollar a head, half that sum going to the crew of the plane, the other half into the league coffers. With lots of home-cooked food and speeches by Rufus Woods, Jim O'Sullivan, and Clarence Dill, the assembly could have been called a show of grassroots support for the project had it not been for the fact that neither grass nor roots were visible under the ankle-deep dust. One newsman covering the event quoted a farmer who told him, "It's so dry around here we have to prime our cows before we can milk them."

After long months of waiting and speculation, Major John S. Butler's 308 Report was finally released. Because both the Gravity Flow people and the Pumpers had said that they would abide by its findings, they perused it with eager eyes. To their mutual surprise, they found its conclusions to be far more sweeping than they ever had dreamed they would be.

Covering the entire drainage area of the Columbia and its tributaries in both the United States and Canada, the report analyzed dam sites, power, irrigation, and navigation possibilities, proposing potential development that would require the expenditure of billions of dollars over a period of fifty to seventy-five years.

Beginning 145 miles upriver from the mouth of the Columbia at a dam site called Bonneville, it identified a dozen more sites up the Columbia to Grand Coulee and beyond into Canada. Yes, Grand Coulee was feasible, the report said, as was the irrigation proposal of the Pumpers. But since each dam located on the upper reaches of the river would store water to be reused and produce electricity by the next dam downstream, the total energy in the river would be doubled dam by dam; therefore, this factor should be considered before any dams at all were built.

Being an engineer, Major Butler stressed the fact that his report stated only what *could* be done. Privately, he admitted to Jim O'Sullivan that what *would* be done lay in the realm of politics and economics, which he was happy to say were outside his field of expertise.

By this time, President Roosevelt had been elected by a landslide vote and was being besieged with proposals to spend money and put people back to work. Boulder Dam was already under way and would be carried through to completion. In the Mississippi watershed, Muscle Shoals on the Tennessee River—the first step in a massive public power system that would develop into TVA (Tennessee Valley Authority)—would be approved and funded. While on a campaign tour through the Pacific Northwest, FDR had responded to Oregon Senator Charles McNary's plea that the federal government build a dam east of the Cascades with a vague promise to site a dam on the Columbia somewhere in Oregon. Portland, which was west of the Cascades, took that to mean that the proposed dam would be built in *their* area.

Astute politician that he was, FDR favored the region with the most unemployment and the most votes, dipping into Public Works Administration (P.W.A.) funds to authorize the building of Bonneville Dam forty-five miles east of Portland for a modest $43 million as the first dam to be built on the Columbia River under the 308 Report.

As might be expected, Senator Clarence Dill wasted no time in calling on President Roosevelt and reminding him of his promise to build Grand Coulee Dam if he were elected. Senator Dill later reported that their conversation went something like this:

FDR: How much will it cost?

DILL: $450 million.

FDR: Out of the question. Money is tight and the government already has taken on a lot of Public Works projects.

DILL: You promised to build it.

FDR: I know I did and I will. But can't it wait for a while?

DILL: We need it now.

FDR: Would you settle for a low dam now, with a high dam to be built later on?

DILL: How low?

FDR: Say a hundred feet or so—just high enough to generate a little power we could sell to get the project going, with a high dam to come.

DILL: How much money will you commit?

FDR: Say $40 million.

DILL: Why, that won't even get concrete poured across the river, let alone build a dam. How about $100 million?

Eventually, they settled for $60 million and a 145-foot-high dam, which Dill admitted was probably what the President had in mind in the first place.

Typical of his behavior once he had made a commitment, President Roosevelt plunged full speed ahead. In late March 1933, Senator Dill introduced a bill requesting the appropriation of $60 million; a permit was applied for on May 19; FDR tapped already-approved P.W.A. funds to get the project started immediately; job applications poured in at the rate of 150 a day; and on July 16, 1933, a ground-breaking ceremony was held at the dam site with five thousand people in attendance.

In the East, politicians and newspaper editors howled in protest. The *Washington Post* editorialized:

> "Muscle Shoals, Hoover Dam, and the Columbia River projects are all misuses of federal authority, and now Roosevelt adds the immensely costly Grand Coulee Dam project to the list of squanderings …"
>
> "The Bureau of Reclamation is public enemy No. 1," declared New York Representative Francis D. Culkin. "Not a single reclamation project has been sound. The proposition of the Grand Coulee in my judgment is the most colossal fraud in the history of America."
>
> "Of all the outrages on agriculture not stumbled into by accident but deliberately to be riveted on our necks," screamed the *Farm*

Journal, which was published in Philadelphia, "we are beginning to think the Columbia Basin project takes the cake. Who wants it? Nobody. Well, perhaps not quite nobody, but nobody whose wishes have the slightest weight with Congress and the nation."

As the cofferdams to divert the flow of the river were built and the foundation was excavated to bedrock, Senator Dill and advocates of the project grew concerned that completion of the low dam would preclude the building of a high dam later on. From an engineering and financial standpoint, it certainly would be a waste of money to pour a foundation for a 550-foot-high dam and build only a 145-foot dam on its base. Installing penstocks, gates, and generators that would be used for only a few years on a low dam, then would have to be removed and replaced by those for a high dam, would be a blatant squandering of money, while problems involved with making concrete sections poured for a low dam bond with those later poured for a high dam would be difficult to overcome.

But as President Roosevelt often did during his long administration, he overcame the problem with ease. When Senator Dill told him of his concern, FDR flashed his famous smile and said calmly, "Don't worry, Clarence. The important thing is that we have our foot in the door."

Shortly thereafter, the President asked Secretary of Interior Harold Ickes to come over to the White House. When Ickes arrived, FDR told him that Grand Coulee was to be approved and completed as a high dam.

"If that is what you want," Ickes replied, "it will be done."

It was.

As a staunch Democrat in a solidly Republican district, Senator Dill had never been much of a hero in Spokane. But he certainly got a hero's welcome when he came home a few days later after telegraphing the good news. A band was there to greet him at the Great Northern station when his train pulled in. A radio network carried his words not only to people in and around Spokane but across the state to Seattle, Tacoma, Aberdeen, and to Portland, Astoria, and other lower Columbia River cities in Oregon.

“The first Sunday after the big news was announced,” the *Spokesman-Review* reported, “more than one thousand people drove to the dam site to see what it was all about. One of the beneficial aspects of the mass visitation was that the rattlesnakes have retreated from the area. A party from Spokane on a rattlesnake hunt succeeded only in taking one small one after an all-day search.”

28.

IF EVER A GEOLOGIST lived by the dictum of the nineteenth-century scientist Louis Agassiz—"Study nature, not books!"—it was J Harlen Bretz. The year after he finished graduate school, he had accepted a position as an assistant professor of geology at the University of Washington, he told Doug Warren, feeling that teaching in the Seattle area would give him an opportunity to continue his field studies of the eastern Washington scablands and the Grand Coulee. But after a year during which he failed to find a single colleague who shared his enthusiasm for field trips to the hot, dusty, dry country east of the Cascades, he quit in disgust, accepting a position at the University of Chicago.

"A lot of my desk-bound friends at East Coast universities call it 'that trade school out in Chicago,' " Bretz snorted in derision. "But no matter what they say, it has a fine geology department. Every summer since I've been there, my field trips have been funded, sometimes to the extent that I can bring half a dozen students along."

Like Doug's former professor at Washington State College, John Fleming, Bretz was an inveterate pipe-smoker, packing a big-bowled Kaywoodie briar with Edgeworth tobacco and keeping it going from morning till night during his long hikes over the rough terrain of the scablands. He took it out of his mouth only to eat, talk, and sleep, being scrupulously careful each time he lit it to extinguish the wooden match, rub the charred head between a callused thumb and forefinger to make sure it was out, then put the match away in a pants pocket so that it would not litter the landscape.

Like Professor Fleming, Bretz was impressed by the number and size of the misfit rocks called "erratics" to be found scattered over a wide distance from their probable point of origin.

"So far as I can determine, they occur from Lake Pend Oreille in Idaho near the headwaters of the Columbia to Eugene, Oregon, in the Willamette Valley. Some of them are monsters, weighing over a hundred tons. How did they get there?"

"Carried by glaciers, maybe?"

"Glaciers never got as far south as the Willamette Valley, Doug. But I suspect ice was involved. My guess is that they floated on the surface of icebergs carried down the Columbia by unusually high floods."

The largest erratic he had found, Bretz said, was an argillite boulder, lying at 306 feet of elevation on the top of a low spur of hills near McMinnville, Oregon, in the Willamette Valley southwest of Portland. It weighed around 160 tons, he estimated, though at the rate souvenir hunters were chipping off pieces and carrying them home, it was being diminished rapidly. The iceberg that floated it there must have measured at least thirty-five feet on a side, he judged. Wherever the black volcanic rock came from, it must have been carried on the first wave of a tremendous flood.

Treasured by Northwest Coast Indians because it could be carved into such beautiful replicas of bears, seals, and whales, argillite possessed the curious quality of always feeling cold to the touch, no matter how hot the day. Doug had often demonstrated this fact to his students by blindfolding them and placing a piece of the shiny black rock in their hand. Though there was no scientific basis for the feeling of coldness, it was as if the rock remembered its carrier and still retained some of the iceberg's chill.

Bretz was not the first geologist to suggest that vast amounts of water had once inundated the inland Pacific Northwest, Doug knew. As far back as 1871, Thomas Condon, Oregon's pioneer geologist, had proposed a Pleistocene flood in the Willamette Valley that had put it underwater as far south as Eugene. How to account for the volume of water needed to float icebergs carrying erratics of such an immense size was the question that concerned Bretz most, he told Doug. His hypothesis demanded not just a moderate raising of the water level but an inexplicable and extraordinary flooding, a quantity of water that reason told him was not possible.

When Doug started to tell him about Professor John Fleming's ice-lobe dam theory, Bretz cut him off impatiently. "Ah, yes, the 'Catastrophic Flood' theory! Other geologists have mentioned that. But in today's geological community, all you will do when you voice *that* theory is raise the hackles of the desk-bound pundits. They sneer and consider you wrong-minded to the point of heresy—unless you show them documented proof."

"Isn't it the duty of science to be open-minded?"

"Not where Catastrophism is concerned. Here's why ..."

In the beginning, Bretz explained, Catastrophism was not at odds with traditional religious beliefs. It was a theory that remained compatible with Judeo-Christian doctrine, which maintained that time was restricted to the biblical six thousand years since Genesis. Within this relatively short time period, all the geological developments on earth were supposed to have occurred.

Being omnipresent, God could do anything he wanted to, and usually did it in a catastrophic way. He could divide or close up the Red Sea at will; call up a pillar of fire to consume sinners among the Israelites; or produce a forty-day flood during which all human and earthly creatures except Noah and passengers on the Ark would be drowned.

"The first clear inroad against Catastrophism came in 1788," Bretz told Doug, "when James Hutton published his *Theory of the Earth*. It was Hutton who pointed out that sedimentary rocks had not been created by a forty-day flood. Instead, they had been deposited layer by layer in seas that had repeatedly covered the land over a long period of time. From that day on, Catastrophic thinking began to crumble."

"Giving way to Uniformitarianism," Doug said, nodding.

"Exactly. One dogma replaced another. If I were to get up in a scientific meeting and lay out my catastrophic flood theory, I would be committing as heinous a crime as if I were to propose returning to Noah, the Ark, and the fifteen-cubit deep flood which drowned out the world in biblical days, citing as my authority Genesis 7:20. It would be considered a giant step backward, a betrayal of all that geological science has fought to gain."

"That I can understand."

Knocking the dottle out of the bowl of his pipe, refilling it with Edgeworth, lighting it, and then carefully extinguishing the match and putting it in his pocket, Bretz squinted off into the distance for a time, chuckled, and murmured, "But one of these days, I may do it, Doug. I just may."

"If and when you do," Doug said, "I hope I'm there to hear you. It should be a lively session."

As matters turned out, Doug was there, attending a 1923 meeting of the United States Geological Survey in Washington, D.C., when Bretz made his first modest effort to present his flood theory. The paper he read, *Washington's Channeled Scabland*, was not nearly as explosive as Doug had expected it to be, though its language was strong, vigorous, and direct, like the man himself. In it, the closest Bretz came to mentioning what he privately had called the "Spokane Flood" was to suggest that the scabland's excessive channel erosion would seem to have required excessive amounts of water. Since the idea was given such a low-key presentation, it did not attract much attention.

Before the year was out, however, Bretz published a second scabland paper in which he took such a long leap forward in the same direction that his conclusions could not be ignored by the scientific community. One by one he ran through his arguments, explaining how "approved" geological concepts failed to account for many of the scabland's aberrant features. What other than colossal flooding could have placed the immense erratic boulders, with their unmistakable signs of being ice-borne, three or four hundred feet above the present-day Coulee floor? he asked bluntly, saying in essence, "If I'm wrong, prove it."

That the sharp, vigorous, earthy wording of the Bretz paper should offend many of his colleagues did not surprise Doug Warren. Having met and worked with nationally known geologists such as Joseph Pardee on both the Pumpers and the Gravity Flow side of the Columbia Basin project, Doug had learned that the politics of the U.S.G.S. office were as intricate and involved as those of state universities and colleges. For example, the middle initial of one of the leading geologists in the Survey, W. C. Alden, was said by his associates to stand for "Cautious" because his carefully phrased reports so often used terms such as "it would seem," "perhaps," and "not yet well enough understood."

To further complicate the situation, a number of now-prominent geologists had dealt with Bretz in situations where they were subordinate to him. James Gilluly had been a student in Seattle's Franklin High School when Bretz taught there. O. E. Meinzer had been examined by Bretz during his Ph.D. finals at the University of Chicago. W. C. Alden was Joseph Pardee's superior in the U.S.G.S. office. When the conflict finally erupted during the 1927 meeting, Gilluly and Meinzer were openly hostile to Bretz; Alden expressed his disapproval in milder terms, urging "further consideration"; while Joseph Pardee remained discreetly silent except for one notable exception, which Doug Warren happened to overhear.

Born in Salt Lake City and raised in Philipsburg, Montana, Pardee was no armchair geologist, having engaged in mining, run an assay office, and done considerable work in the field before attending college first in Deer Lodge, then at the University of California in Berkeley. Taking a position with the U.S.G.S. in 1909, he had worked out of the Washington, D.C., office ever since, frequently going into the field to conduct studies in the Pacific Northwest. In his paper, "The Glacial Lake Missoula," published in the *Journal of Geology* in 1910, his opening paragraph had stated quietly, "The object of this paper is to show that in comparatively recent time an ice-dammed lake filled a large part of the drainage basin of the Clark Fork in northwestern Montana."

Though it had been twelve years since Doug had heard Professor Fleming expound on his theory of the collapse of a huge ice dam below Glacial Lake Missoula as the cause of the catastrophic flood which had carved out Grand Coulee, he did recall that Joseph Pardee had said nothing in his paper about the collapse of such a dam or where its released waters had gone. But now, sitting in the row just ahead of him in the meeting hall, Joe Pardee leaned toward a geologist friend seated beside him, Kirk Bryan, and murmured, "I know where Bretz's flood came from."

In view of the heated controversy that began soon after J Harlen Bretz finished reading his paper and that would rage for years, Doug found it curious that Joseph Pardee made no public statement lending support to the Bretz theory. Later, he learned that Pardee did correspond with Bretz on the matter, but years would pass before Pardee finally rose in a scientific meeting and presented the piece of evidence that proved beyond all possible doubt that Bretz was right and his enemies wrong.

Meanwhile, reading his paper now, Bretz was making his case point by point. In essence, he was saying that as many as seven times in the recent geological past, ice dams two or three thousand feet high had blocked the Clark Fork River, backing up lakes twenty miles or so wide and fifty miles or more long, containing at least five hundred cubic miles of water. When these dams of ice suddenly collapsed, he maintained, the surges of water flowing southwest had possessed such incredible erosive power that coulees, canyons, potholes, and now-dry waterfalls had been created not as the work of millions of years, as the Uniformitarians claimed, but in a matter of days.

One of the most striking parts of the Bretz paper, so far as Doug was concerned, was his description of what must have happened at Wallula Gap, just across from where Doug himself had been born and raised. Here, eleven miles below the mouth of the Snake River, eight-hundred-foot high lava bluffs confined the westward-flowing Columbia in a narrow bottleneck which would have acted like a stopper in a bathtub to the five hundred cubic miles of water rushing toward it at an estimated rate of fifty-eight miles per hour.

"The water by then would have eroded loessal cover one hundred to two hundred feet deep from over a wide area," Bretz read. "Striking the bottleneck of Wallula Gap, the flood would have ponded back into the lower reaches of the Snake, Tucannon, and Walla Rivers as much as fifty miles, carrying massive erratics on its crest."

How long would the obstruction at Wallula Gap have lasted? Probably only a matter of days, Bretz suggested, then the surging water would have widened the Gap and poured through, carrying with it such huge erratics as the one found at the three-hundred-foot level in the Willamette Valley. Though he did not quote Genesis 7:20 as his authority, as he had facetiously told Doug he might do, the reaction from the geologists present at the meeting was as violent as if he had.

Some of them belittled him to the point of insult. James Gilluly claimed Bretz's hypothesis was "wholly inadequate," "preposterous," and "incompetent." The most critical comment came from O. E. Meinzer, whom Doug had heard called "the father of modern hydrology." It was Meinzer's belief that a glacier-swollen Pleistocene Columbia could easily have produced Dry Falls, and that the scabland's puzzling high terraces had been created by the river simply cutting them down to lower levels. He wrote:

> The Columbia River is a very large stream, especially in its flood stages, and it was undoubtedly still larger in the Pleistocene epoch … Having seen only the Dry Falls part of the region, I am naturally loath to accept a theory of an abnormal flood for the scablands farther east. Before a theory that requires a seemingly impossible quantity of water is fully accepted, every effort should be made to account for the existing features without employing so violent an assumption.

This unquestioning loyalty to the Uniformitarian party line was not the only similarity Bretz's opponents shared, Doug noted. None of the opposition seemed to feel that firsthand exposure to the scablands was necessary for a solid defeat of the Bretz hypothesis. As the controversy raged on, Doug sympathized with Bretz's frustration, though, as a geology professor in a relatively obscure state college, nothing he could say or write in scholarly journals could have much influence on the scientific debate.

Even Bretz admitted that "a bedside practitioner may err." But he deeply resented the criticism of those who believed "history can be diagnosed readily at a distance." Confronted by some of the best geological minds of the era, each of which was holding on tightly to his own untested opinion, Bretz firmly stated his personal fixed and unalterable truth: "I believe that my interpretation of the channeled scabland should stand or fall on the scabland phenomenon itself. If there are other explanations, let them be tested in the field."

Between 1932 and 1940, the period during which Grand Coulee Dam was being proposed and built, a great deal of attention was paid to the area as core-drillings were made and footings for structures were tested, with Doug Warren, Joseph Pardee, J Harlen Bretz, and a number of geologist members of the U.S.G.S. involved. In 1933, the International Geological Congress scheduled a field trip through the region, which Bretz planned to lead. Though he wrote a guidebook for the excursion, pressing business elsewhere prevented him from taking part in the tour, which, in his absence, was conducted by Ira S. Allison, from Oregon State College.

Taking part in it himself, Doug realized that this was no ordinary, run-of-the-mill field trip. Given the nature of the scablands, there was no way driving or hiking over it mile after mile and observing its wonders day after day could be called "ordinary." But even more important, the participants were not credulous souls, willing to trot at the heels of their guide. Several were internationally famous geologists, men who insisted upon looking for their own evidence and applying their own reasoning to what they saw.

Expeditions such as this one, Doug became aware, were creating an open season on scabland speculation. Throughout the 1930s, a rush for new hypotheses was on. Most were still reinterpretations that attempted to avoid Bretz's Catastrophism theory; but among the new "see-for-myself" geologists were a number who began to suspect that Bretz may not have been entirely wrong.

Just as he had been present at the 1927 meeting when J Harlen Bretz first proposed his heretical theory, so was Doug Warren in the audience when at last it was confirmed. The occasion was a 1940 session of the American Association for the Advancement of Science, which was held that year in Seattle. Judging from the titles of the papers being read during the geological section of the program, it was heavily loaded with opponents of the Bretz hypothesis. But scheduled as the eighth geologist to read a paper that day was Joseph Pardee, the man who had whispered to Kirk Braun during the 1927 debate that he knew where Bretz's water had come from.

Seventy years old now and about to retire after thirty-two years in the U.S.G.S., Pardee was as tall, whip-lean, and quiet-spoken as ever, one of the most highly respected men in the Service, particularly where fieldwork in the Pacific Northwest was concerned. The title of his paper, "Unusual Currents in Lake Missoula," was not very exciting, giving no hint of what was to come. Like many other members of the audience toward the end of the long day, Doug's primary interest in liquid matters inclined more toward thoughts of a cold beer than toward newly discovered facts about ancient glacial lakes.

Speaking first of the prehistoric body of water itself, Pardee mentioned the lobe of the Cordilleran glacier which plugged the drainage of the Clark Fork River, then described certain basic, measurable facts about the lake. Its elevation had reached a maximum of 4,150 feet, he said; its depth had been about 2,000 feet. This was tame enough. Then came the unexpected bombshell.

"The ice dam is thought to have failed," he said, "permitting a sudden large outflow."

Most members of the audience, Doug included, failed to recognize the significance of the statement at first. Then, as Pardee read on, the full meaning of what he had said began to dawn on the listening geologists.

An ice dam two thousand feet high? Thought to have failed? A sudden large outflow?

According to his calculations, Pardee continued, the velocity of the out-rushing water "reached a maximum of 9.46 cubic miles an hour." By comparison, as all the hydrologists present knew, the Mississippi

River flood of 1937 had reached a measured peak flow at Natchez of only .05 cubic mile an hour.

All this was impressive enough to make the audience sit up and take notice. But where was Pardee's proof? In scientific meetings such as this, no one would be so rude as to jump to his feet and demand proof. But every geologist present knew that a man of Joseph Pardee's standing would follow up his astounding statement with unassailable evidence that it was true.

Pardee did so. Put simply, he said, he had discovered ripple marks left on the floor sediments of Lake Missoula.

Ripple marks?

As every geologist and most laymen know, ripple marks are nothing more than those little wavy configurations that show up along the shorelines of lakes, rivers, and oceans, wherever the water has retreated a bit. At the beach, they are found in the shallow, sandy hollows that appear at low tide: lumpy, washboard-like formations, strange to walk on and pleasing in their smooth, patterned regularity. And what creates ripple marks? Currents flowing over the bottom and warping the sediments into smooth, parallel ridge rows.

These were the "unusual currents" mentioned in the title of Pardee's paper. In the valley where the ancient Lake Missoula ice dams had stood, he had discovered ripple marks to end all ripple marks, spaced so far apart that they could only have been formed by currents of an inconceivable size. They had been there since the Pleistocene era, of course, but no one before Pardee had recognized them for what they were. They had been walked upon, measured, and described, but because they had disguised themselves as hills up to fifty feet high and five hundred feet apart, no geologist before Pardee had given them their proper name. True, a geologist named Flint had referred to them as "mamillary undulatory topography," but the tongue-twisting name had never caught on or even been understood.

In geology, as Doug later pointed out to his students as he tried to explain why it had taken so long for the Bretz "Catastrophic Flood" theory to be verified, viewpoint is everything. Scale is deceiving. Seen from the air—which was the way Pardee finally had seen the Lake Missoula terrain during his recent years of research—symmetry and form take shapes that cannot be seen at ground level. For something so large, the term "ripple mark" simply was not appropriate. But once he had applied it, all the pieces fell into place …

Although the primary purpose for building Grand Coulee Dam had been to put water on the land, Jim O'Sullivan's dream of making the desert "blossom like a rose" was the last objective achieved following the dam's completion. There were several reasons for this:

First, the nation's farmers already were producing more food than could be consumed, so new farmland was a low priority. Second, the liberals in the administration were trying to break the grip of the private electric monopolies with cheap public power supplied by entities such as TVA. Third, while events in Europe foreshadowed a world war for which the country was ill-prepared, insofar as armaments and the capacity to produce them were concerned.

On the private-public power issue, Senator Clarence Dill reported traveling in February 1933 with President Roosevelt and a group of southern senators to Muscle Shoals, a key area in the developing TVA project. He wrote:

> Muscle Shoals was built during the first world war to make war munitions, but the war ended too soon. Instead the War Department sold the power to private power utilities for distribution in surrounding towns. As I stood with Roosevelt looking out over the dam, he said, "You see all those church spires of Florence?" pointing to the town. "The private power company buys this power from the War Department for eight mills per kilowatt hour and then sells it for eight cents a kilowatt hour to the people of Florence, Sheffield and other towns near here. That must be stopped."

Despite the strong protests of private utilities in the Pacific Northwest, the federal government established a new agency, Bonneville Power Administration, to distribute and sell power generated by Bonneville, Grand Coulee, and all other dams to be built in the Columbia River watershed. The high-voltage transmission lines connecting the power plants installed at these dams would be built and controlled by BPA, with public power companies and rural electric co-ops given first preference as energy purchasers, while the rest would be sold to private utilities.

For a time, Doug Warren and his colleagues at Washington State College engaged in a lively debate as to how speculation could be controlled when relatively worthless, arid desert lands were made extremely valuable with abundant irrigation water and cheap electrical power. For example, it was estimated that farms purchased under the Desert Lands Act for a dollar-fifty per acre would be worth at least five hundred dollars an acre when irrigated. By the time all the generating facilities were installed in Grand Coulee Dam, projections indicated that the cost of electricity would be less than two mills a kilowatt hour, which meant that if three or four mills was charged to big users such as the aluminum- and steel-fabricating plants and the shipbuilding yards now under construction in the Portland area, the cost of the entire project would be paid off with interest in very little time.

When the dam was first proposed, newspaper editors and politicians in the East had ridiculed the project as a boondoggle of the worst kind, asking, "Who's going to use all that electricity, the jackrabbits?", and suggesting that as soon as the dam was finished, it should be torn down, "since it's only use is to put men to work." But with the nation now gearing up for war and the need for electricity growing, the question had changed to whether the "bus bar" or the "postage stamp" scale of billing should be used.

As Doug understood it, charging the "bus bar" rate meant that the closer the user was to the source, the less he would pay, while the "postage stamp" rate meant that the kilowatt-hour charge would be the same over the entire distribution area. This meant that an aluminum plant or a shipyard located on the outskirts of Portland could buy electricity generated at Grand Coulee three hundred miles away just as cheaply as it could be purchased at the dam site itself. Despite the protests from Wenatchee and Spokane, the "postage stamp" scale was adopted, though the upriver communities were later appeased by having a couple of aluminum plants built in their area.

Interested and involved though Doug and Jenny Warren had been in the building of Grand Coulee Dam and the development of the irrigation project, family concerns in the spring of 1941 were so disturbing that completion of the project became a minor matter in comparison. War shadows were darkening. Both Theodore Lincoln Warren, now twenty-four, and Jefferson Thomas Warren, now twenty, were prime candidates for military service. Ted, a senior, and Jeff, a freshman, were members of the Reserve Officers Training Corps at Washington State College, while daughters Gayle, eighteen, and Linda, fifteen, attended Pullman High School.

Like all young people these days, the war now raging so fiercely in

Europe was never far from their thoughts. Since the ROTC at Washington State gave its enrollees only a choice between serving in the Infantry or the Engineers, which neither of them wanted to do, Ted had enlisted in the Naval Air Corps, Jeff in the Coast Guard, and they were staying in school only until they received their call. Having taken enough private flying lessons to solo and obtain a license, Ted had applied to and been accepted by Naval Flight School at San Diego, where he expected to go into training as a fighter pilot on an aircraft carrier. Having enlisted in the Coast Guard, Jeff presently would report to Sheepshead Bay in Brooklyn for training on some sort of seagoing vessel, thus resuming a Warren family tradition going back many generations to the ancestor for whom he had been named, Captain Thomas Warren, who had been drowned guiding the Astor ship *Tonquin* into the mouth of the Columbia over the storm-tossed bar in 1811.

Despite its tremendous size and the unique problems arising during its construction, Grand Coulee Dam was completed on schedule, producing its first power on March 22, 1941. That day, formal ceremonies were held at the dam when two small generating units came on the line for the first time. Much bigger generators were soon to come, with a 108,000 kilowatt unit scheduled for completion in October 1941, a second the same size in February 1942, and a third due to start spinning in June 1942. Whether commendable vision, remarkable foresight, or typical Roosevelt good luck was responsible, no one could say, but for once the nation's energy planners had made wise decisions before a crisis came.

"Without the completion of Bonneville and Grand Coulee Dams," Oregon Representative Homer Angell declared with justifiable pride, "the national aviation program would have been retarded eighteen months to two years."

Because of the availability of cheap energy, shipbuilding, aircraft manufacturing, aluminum- and steel-fabricating, munitions making, and other war industries were being established in the Pacific Northwest. Early in 1941, Dr. Raver, BPA director, told an Appropriations subcommittee that the entire output of Bonneville and Grand Coulee Dams for the next year had been spoken for. When installations at both dams had been completed, BPA would have a total installed capacity of 2,138,400 kilowatts, most of it at Grand Coulee.

By the end of 1941, Grand Coulee was 90 percent complete, except for its irrigation facilities, which had been suspended for the duration of the war. A total of $138 million had been spent. The labor had entailed 150 million man-hours. Wages had totaled $52 million. In all, seventy-five men had lost their lives during the building of the dam, not a single one of which was a workman buried in a concrete pour, despite wild rumors that such things had happened, for, by the very nature of the pours, such an accident was an impossibility.

In July 1937, when employment peaked, 7,445 men were working at the dam. The force had dwindled as the work neared completion; in October 1941, there were only 2,079 workers applying final touches to the biggest construction project ever undertaken in the United States. By then, the fame of Grand Coulee Dam had spread so far and wide that it had become the greatest tourist attraction in the West, with1,651,699 visitors by the end of 1941.

Following the Japanese attack on Pearl Harbor on December 7, 1941, the nature of Grand Coulee Dam changed from the greatest sight-seeing attraction in the West to the country's mightiest weapon.

By then, Ted Warren was in San Diego training to be a carrier pilot, while Jeff was in Brooklyn, learning to be a signalman on an LST. Why the Coast Guard should train young men to relay signals between ships engaged in disgorging tanks on far-off beaches held by enemy troops in Africa, Italy, France, or South Pacific Islands was a question Doug could not answer for himself, let alone explain to Jenny.

"At least he won't be digging trenches or latrines, like I did in World War I," Doug told Jenny lamely. "All I did for my country was catch the flu."

"I don't care what they catch or do for their country," Jenny murmured, tight-lipped, "so long as they both come home."

Before the day longed for by so many millions of mothers, fathers, sweethearts, and wives arrived four years later, the country endured many traumatic times and events that made little sense. To Doug, one of these was the internment of American citizens of Japanese descent.

Among the minority-race students enrolled at Washington State College were a few young men whose parents had immigrated to the United States a generation ago from Japan, established roots, become citizens, had children, and accumulated enough property and money that they could afford to send their sons to college. Names such as Shima, Araki, Hamada, and Nishi indicated their Japanese ancestry, though more often than not, first names such as Joe, Harry, Roy, and Johnny preceded them. Invariably, these young men were good students, spoke the same slang-tainted English their classmates did, participated enthusiastically in all college social activities, made little trouble, and earned excellent grades.

Yet two months after Pearl Harbor, President Roosevelt issued an Executive Order declaring all West Coast Japanese residents to be potential subversives. Despite the fact that they were American citizens, their property was to be confiscated and they were to be rounded up and placed in barbed-wire-surrounded inland camps where they could be closely watched and prevented from performing any hostile acts.

Before leaving for Yakima, where he planned to join his father, mother, and nine younger brothers and sisters who were being escorted under guard to an internment camp near Ontario, Oregon, a nineteen-year-old student named Roy Hamada, who had been a close friend of Jeff Warren's, came into Doug's office with tears in his eyes to tell Doug he was leaving.

"Why are they doing this to us?" he pleaded. "Why, Professor Warren—why, why, why?"

"God knows, Roy. Because there's a war on, they say."

"And because our parents are Japanese?"

"That's the excuse they give, yes."

"But my father and mother became naturalized citizens years ago, Professor Warren. All their children were born in the United States. None of us has ever been to Japan or can speak Japanese. We love America. This is our country. How can they call us subversives?"

"Legally, they can't," Doug said, shaking his head. "But under the Wartime Powers Act, my colleagues in the Law School tell me, the federal government can do anything it wants to do, whether it's constitutional or not."

For whatever comfort it may have been to the American citizens of Japanese ancestry interned for the duration, not a single instance of sabotage or subversion was attributed to them during the war on either the West Coast or in Hawaii, where, for some inexplicable reason, the Japanese-Americans were not placed in camps. After living with his parents in the Ontario, Oregon, camp only a few months, Doug heard later, Roy Hamada and a number of other Japanese-American boys were given an opportunity to enlist as infantrymen in the United States Army and did so, serving with great distinction and suffering heavy casualties with the 440th Infantry Division in Italy during some of the bloodiest battles of the war.

Still later, Doug heard that Roy Hamada, following his honorable discharge at the end of the war, went to U.C.L.A. on the GI Bill, got a degree in electrical engineering, and returned to Portland, where he went to work for the Bonneville Power Administration in a well-paid, responsible position.

With both sons somewhere on the wartime high seas, Doug and Jenny used a few precious A-ration gas coupons to drive their relatively new 1939 Chevrolet four-door to Grand Coulee Dam with daughters Gayle and Linda for a milestone in the history of the project. On June 1, 1942, with the 151-mile-long reservoir behind the dam completely filled for the first time, the eleven huge gates of the 550-foot-high structure were lowered, forcing a vast sheet of water stretching just under a mile from bank to bank to pour over the dam's spillways.

> With a crowd of more than ten thousand witnessing the spectacle, (the *Spokesman-Review* reported) forty Bureau of Reclamation engineers simultaneously closed the gates on forty outlet tubes which until that prearranged instant had permitted water to pour through the dam. Suddenly the torrent was forced over the crest instead.
>
> The crystal green water cascaded over in a single sheet five city blocks wide and the full height of a thirty-story building. Every second, 1,500,000 gallons of water weighing 6,256 tons fell in this manner. The volume of the waterfall was such that it would have filled a tank having the dimensions of a city block to the height of a thirteen-story building every minute.

Finding new ways to arrange facts and figures into newspaper accounts showing the size of the Grand Coulee project had long been a problem for reporters. But none of them wrote a single word on the most dramatic story of all, so far as the project was concerned. Responding to requests from the federal government, their silence was self-imposed, for most people living east of the Cascades were aware of the fact that something big was going on in the arid, thinly populated region between Wenatchee and Wallula Gap.

Acting with great speed and secrecy in late summer 1942, the federal government preempted 200,000 acres of desert land and created a new scientific manufacturing community for which an immense amount of electrical energy and water would be needed. Hiring thousands of workers to build the facility, the government fenced the land so tightly that not even a jackrabbit could slip past the perimeter sensors without triggering an alarm.

Security on the project was so complete that only a few of the people working on it knew its purpose. Even speculating upon the type of object being fabricated at the facility was frowned on, with the least sort of leak sure to bring a swarm of FBI investigators to the household of the offending person. Inevitably, leaks did occur—one of them by a fourth-grade child who, in this period of wartime shortages, blurted in class one day despite his teacher's effort to stop him, "I know what they're making. Daddy brings some of it home in his lunch pail every day—lightbulbs and toilet paper."

With President Roosevelt about to run for an unprecedented fourth term, a disgruntled Republican ventured the sour opinion that the item being manufactured at the Hanford plant was "FDR campaign buttons."

If Doug had been inclined to speculate, which he certainly was not, he probably could have come closer to guessing the real product of the Hanford Project, for he and his colleagues at W.S.C. long had been aware of how many professors in the field of physics, chemistry, and engineering were leaving the school for classified jobs inside the barbed wire. Some kind of new weapon was being produced, he guessed, whose use hopefully would help end the war.

By now, the Allies had landed in Italy and France; the Russians had turned back the Germans at Stalingrad; and wave after wave of American bombers were reducing the German war machine to impotence. In the Kaiser shipyards in Portland, ten-thousand-ton freighters called "Liberty ships" were being built with such incredible speed that Winston Churchill, when told by President Roosevelt that he had recently attended the launching of the freighter *Joseph N. Teal*—whose construction had required less than fourteen days—had declared the feat "almost unbelievable."

Though it now seemed inevitable that the war in Europe would be brought to an end in the spring of 1945, the outcome of the conflict with Japan was far less certain. Both Ted and Jeff had been in the Pacific theater for two years now. Ted had fought in the Battles of the Midway and Coral Sea, twice being fished out of the water when his plane was shot down. Jeff and the LST on which he served had come under intense fire at the Okinawa landing, where the Japanese troops defending the island literally fought on to the last man. Though the censors would not permit either son to tell his parents where he was stationed now, clues they dropped in their letters home made Doug and Jenny suspect that in late July 1945, Ted's carrier and Jeff's LST were in staging areas preparing for the final attack on the Japanese homeland itself. Judging from the ferocity with which Japanese troops had fought on Okinawa and elsewhere, conquest of the mainland likely would cost a million lives on each side, President Truman estimated.

Both Ted and Jeff had been wounded, their parents knew, but neither seriously enough to be sent home.

"Oh, God!" Jenny cried after reading yet another news story speculating on when, where, and how the invasion of the Japanese mainland might take place. "Haven't our sons done enough for their country? When is it all going to end?"

On August 6, 1945, an airplane whose wings and body had been fabricated out of aluminum smelted in potlines fired by electrical power generated at Bonneville Dam flew over Hiroshima, Japan, and dropped an atomic bomb assembled at the Hanford Project, using Grand Coulee power and cooling water from the Columbia River. Three days later, a second bomb was dropped on Nagasaki.

Within a week, Japan surrendered. The invasion would not be necessary after all. When the news was announced on the radio in the Warren living room at four o'clock in the afternoon on a hot mid-August day, Gayle and Linda, both of whom had boyfriends in the service, snatched Jenny to her feet and began dancing her around the room, crying, laughing, and shouting at the same time, "Oh boy! Oh boy! Oh boy!"

Doug could not have said it better himself.

29.

With the war over now and Grand Coulee about to begin the irrigation phase of the project, many changes had come to the Columbia River basin and to the lives of the Warren family. After a few months' rest at home, Ted Warren had gone to work as a test pilot for the Boeing Company in Seattle, which was in the process of adapting skills learned building wartime bombers to fabricating peacetime airliners. Though still enthused about flying, Ted told his parents he had had his fill of being a jockey for "hot" fighter planes and would be quite content to accept a job flying passengers and mail for a civilian airline company.

"At the rate that sector of the aircraft industry is growing," he told his father, "railroads will be out of the passenger and mail-carrying business in ten years. I want to get in on the ground floor."

Jeff Warren planned to give up the dullness of the high seas as he had experienced it in slow, tedious LST voyages across both the Atlantic and the Pacific for more interesting Columbia River trips as captain of a tug-and-barge with the Williams & Sons Transportation Company, which had been founded by his Aunt Lily and her husband George forty years ago in Vancouver, Washington, and now was being carried on by their two sons.

"We're going to be lobbying for improved locks, navigation markers, and river improvements," he told Doug. "Once we get them, we'll set rates on bulk cargo so low we'll put the railroads out of business."

Though he was glad to see his sons so enthusiastic about their civilian careers, Doug refrained from saying that the railroads had been in business for a long time and, he suspected, would be around for a while longer.

As had happened following the First World War, returning veterans now were taking a serious interest in getting a college education. So serious, in fact, that many of them preferred living in family housing with their wives and children to single dormitories, sports, and fraternity hijinks. This was particularly true in Portland, where a war-built community first called Kaiserville, then Vanport City, then Vanport, and finally Veterans' Village, was now inhabited by ex-GIs seeking a college education.

Built as living quarters for workers at the nearby shipyard by that master of planning and getting things done, Henry J. Kaiser, the housing was so rudimentary that it was called "Wartime Box." Announcing that ten thousand homes were needed within walking distance of the Oregon Shipbuilding Corporation, Kaiser had bought 650 acres of low-lying land in northwest Portland in February 1942; surrounded it with dikes; and, with a minimum of red tape, spent $26 million building a company city that at its peak housed forty-two thousand people.

Architecturally, the design of the units fitted the "Wartime Box" name. Each two-story building measured 38 by 108 feet and contained fourteen apartments, each with a living-room/kitchen area, a bathroom with a shower stall, a closet, and a bedroom in the rear. The walls were thin, insulation nonexistent, coal-heating furnaces poor, and all other amenities the bare minimum. Zoning, local housing, and waste disposal laws posed no problem, for the city of Portland, Multnomah County, and the State of Oregon were never consulted. Sewage, for example, was simply pumped up and over the dike into the Columbia River and sent downstream toward Astoria and the Pacific Ocean.

For the people recruited to work in the shipyards from the Dust Bowl of western Oklahoma, Kansas, and the Texas Panhandle, who now were earning the highest wages of their lives, the housing was a dream come true. As one weary young "Okie" housewife said, "It sure beats living in a tourist court." To the six thousand ex-GI families, it sure beat living in foxholes or being separated from loved ones.

Admittedly, the psychological effects of living on the bottom of a relatively small area diked on all sides to a height of fifteen to twenty-five feet were disturbing. The earlier response to any complaint— "Well, there's a war on" —now was replaced by the comment "Well, it's cheap." By March 1947, the number of occupied housing units in Vanport had stabilized at about two-thirds of capacity.

The returning veterans, mostly married and raising children, were beginning to change the nature of the community; they wanted an education, a home, and a decent neighborhood. Pressure from these serious-minded veterans helped establish Vanport City College. Gradually, Vanport's identity changed from a company town of shipyard workers to a colony proudly calling itself Veterans' Village.

Meanwhile, upriver in the Columbia Basin area, veterans more interested in becoming farmers than in getting college degrees were taking steps to acquire tracts of soon-to-be-irrigated land. At the insistence of President Roosevelt several years earlier, the Bureau of Reclamation had drawn up rules which Congress had passed as laws making sure that speculators would not make money on project land. Though the immense pumps and conduits needed to lift water into the Coulee itself would not be completed for several years, a strong supporter of Jim O'Sullivan, who had worked so long to make the plan a reality, wrote the *Spokesman-Review* a letter in June 1947, proposing that the reservoir to be built in the lower Coulee where irrigation water would be stored be named "O'Sullivan" rather than "Potholes."

In honor of the man who had sworn back in 1909 to "make the desert blossom like a rose" if it took him the rest of his life to do it, which it almost did, the suggestion was followed to the extent that the two-mile-long earth-fill dam creating the reservoir would be called "O'Sullivan Dam," while the "Potholes" name would be retained for the huge body of irrigation water itself. Furthermore, it was agreed that a smaller reservoir to be built as part of the project in the upper Coulee would be called "Billy Clapp Lake."

In August 1947, when Michael Straus, the new commissioner of reclamation, visited the region and took part in a Columbia Basin Jubilee celebrated in Ephrata, he was hailed into a kangaroo court on the charge of conspiring to put water on the land. Even though he was given a spirited defense by Jim O'Sullivan, he was found guilty and sentenced to be dunked in a nearby pool, with a pretty young Ephrata housewife volunteering to suffer the penalty in his place.

What had been predicted as an excess of electrical power in the postwar years was turning out to be a shortage. In the year ending June 30, 1947, the ten generators at Bonneville and the six at Grand Coulee produced just under nine million kilowatt hours of electricity. Predicting that the dams would earn $270 million in revenue during the next ten years, BPA Director Dr. Raver declared that the system was well ahead of its repayment schedule, then warned that planning should begin for more hydroelectric dams on the Columbia and its tributaries in order to meet growing power needs.

A fabulous boom was taking place on the Pacific Coast, *Kiplinger's* magazine reported, noting that the coast states had acquired four million new residents in the past ten years and that the region now had the highest per capita income of any section of the United States. The Bureau of Reclamation was anticipating several epochal events in the history of the project. Looking ahead several years, it announced it would begin pumping at Grand Coulee in the spring of 1951 to "season" the equalizing reservoir and the rest of the system in preparation for delivery of water in the spring of 1952, when 216,000 acres of desert land were scheduled to be irrigated.

Having celebrated his fifty-fifth birthday on March 20, 1948, Doug Warren wryly told Jenny he was not sure how much more growth and prosperity he could stand, but since there was nothing he could do to stop it, he supposed he might as well sit back and watch it happen. As usual, the "highest per capita income in the United States" had not yet reached the state college level of the economy, but he did have tenure, a reasonably well-funded department, and could look forward to a retirement pension in ten or fifteen years that he hopes would equal half his present salary.

"What's more important," he told Jenny, "is that we've got our health, our children are doing well, and the country is at peace. Still, there are times when I miss the excitement of the old days."

"Which ones, dear?"

"Like the summer before we got married, when Rufus Woods offered me forty dollars a month to work for his Dam University friends on a survey of Grand Coulee whose main purpose, Professor Fleming said, was to tell them if the Coulee would hold water."

"What was your verdict?"

"As I recall, I told them there was no way of knowing until they pumped water into it. Which it appears they're about to do."

Jenny giggled. "What if it leaks?"

"Why, I guess they'll just have to hire another geologist who can find them a better location. But it won't be me. They still owe me my second month's salary."

By the end of March 1948, the biggest local stories in the Grand Coulee project area were that that upward air currents below the face of the dam were causing rainbow colored "snowrises"—waterfalls that rose upward and turned to ice crystals in the freezing air—and that the accumulated snowpack in the mountains where the Columbia and its principal tributary, the Snake, were born, had been measured at 42 percent above normal. This was good news for downstream power-users, irrigators, and tug-and-barge companies, for an above-average snowpack meant an above-normal water supply, which was money in the bank for them.

That it might also mean Mother Nature was preparing a dramatic demonstration of her power did not occur to anyone for a while. But that was exactly what she had in mind.

By late April, the 151-mile-long reservoir backed up by Grand Coulee Dam to the Canadian border, which had been named Lake Roosevelt, had reached the 1,286-foot level. This meant it could go no higher without flooding Canadian land, which by treaty the reservoir was not permitted to do. Therefore, all eleven gates of the 1,600-foot-long spillway were opened, letting water cascade down the face of the 550-foot dam. Measured first at 65,000 cubic feet per second, the flow of the great river a week later increased to 146,000 cubic feet per second, and then, by May 10, to 202,000 cubic feet per second. In six weeks' time, the river's rate of flow had increased five times.

Still, the unprecedented rate of the river's flow continued to increase. On May 17, it was 222,000 feet per second; on May 18, 224,700; on May 29, 441,000. Alarmed hydrologists predicted the river's peak would probably reach an all-time high of 700,000 cubic feet per second, the rate achieved in 1894 during the maximum flood of record on the Columbia. At Grand Coulee Dam itself, the engineers were not worried about the safety of the structure, for the dam had been built to withstand a flow of a million feet per second.

But people living downriver had plenty to worry about.

Unusual weather conditions over the entire watershed had combined during the past two months to bring on a record flood. In the Selkirk Mountains of Canada, the Bitterroots of Idaho, the Rockies of Montana, and the Tetons of Wyoming, day after day of blazing sunshine had started the deep snowdrifts melting at a rapid rate. Warm, steady rains were followed with sudden cloudbursts that sent torrents racing down the gullies and canyons.

On May 11, Elmer Fisher, the river forecaster for the Weather Bureau in Portland, noted that the Snake River, which generally had its heaviest runoff two or three weeks ahead of the more northerly headwaters of the Columbia, was late this year and probably would peak at the same time as the larger river.

On May 10, a cloudburst sent a wall of water two feet deep rushing through the little town of Oakesdale, thirty-five miles north of Pullman, to which emergency Washington State College responded by sending Doug Warren in charge of three trucks loaded with ROTC students, sandbags, and shovels in a mostly vain attempt to prevent the flooding of homes and business establishments. Two days later, rising waters were reported in the tributaries of several rivers—the Kootenai, the St. Joe, the Spokane, the Clearwater, and the Snake itself, which had overflowed its banks in the Lewiston area.

By May 21, many tributaries were rising fast in western Montana, northern Idaho, and British Columbia. The next day, the Clark Fork rose six inches to flood parts of Missoula and St. Regis, Montana.

On May 23, the Kootenai broke the first of many dikes outside of Bonners Ferry, Idaho; a dam washed out at Lardner, British Columbia; and rivers were running wild all over northeastern Washington. Upstream, the Pend Oreille River was surging with such fury that where it met the Columbia below "Z" Canyon, it sliced its way clear across to the west bank of the much bigger river even though at that point the Columbia itself was flowing at the rate of seventeen miles an hour.

Below Bonneville Dam on the lower Columbia, where all the water was going, the flooding was even worse. Backed-up water reduced the amount of fall from sixty to forty feet, causing a 30 percent loss of generating power. This was more than made up for at Grand Coulee, where the record flow through the turbines had them all spinning at capacity. Water covered most of the Vancouver, Washington, airport. Five area sawmills were forced to close because of high water. With the Willamette nine feet above flood stage in Portland, buildings near the river, Union Station, and many other low-lying places were endangered.

But it was at Vanport that the worst disaster struck.

Despite the fact that the community had been expected to go out of existence when the war ended, the veterans who had kept it alive as a college town were proud of their community. When the federal government withdrew its support and discontinued the summer school program, seventy adults volunteered as recreation supervisors, and the community raised its own money for supplies and equipment. Though some conservative politicians and writers accused the Housing Authority of Portland (HAP) of encouraging socialism in its management of Vanport, its low-cost housing was 50 percent cheaper than that of any other urban area in the United States, with even New York City running a distant second.

Even though Vanport lay fifteen feet lower than the Columbia River, there had never been any real concern for its safety. So-called impervious dikes surrounded the entire project. At that time, only three dams—Grand Coulee, Rock Island, and Bonneville—existed on the river, and their function was generating electricity, not controlling floods.

In May 1948, six thousand families lived in Vanport, an estimated 18,700 people. Because of the combination of heavy snowpack, unusually hot weather, and a great deal of rain, it was expected that the most water since 1894 would flow past Portland to the mouth of the Columbia River that summer; it appeared that the crest would come early. But no one was worried.

On Tuesday, May 25, routine patrols of the north and south dikes went on twenty-four hours a day. Two men in an automobile equipped with a spotlight drove the roads at the base of the dikes, looking for seepage, boils, or blisters. Two years earlier, when the water reached a relatively high level, the auto patrols had been increased, another man watched the west dike (which was railroad fill), and a foot patrol was added, but no problems had occurred. This time, Housing Authority officials had decided to rely on the advice of the U.S. Army Corps of Engineers, which had completed the diking system and had experience in flood control. They assured HAP they had nothing to worry about.

Continuing its rapid rise, the river now appeared more ominous. The possibility of evacuation was discussed, but the problems involved in moving, housing, and feeding eighteen thousand people made postponing a decision for a day or two seem the logical thing to do—particularly when there appeared to be no imminent danger.

Memorial Day, May 30, dawned fair and clear, with a promise of more warm, sunny weather. At 4 A.M. that Sunday morning, a sheet of paper bearing a message from HAP was shoved under each door by the furnace firemen. It stated:

> ... the flood situation has not changed. Barring unforeseen developments Vanport is safe. However, if it should be necessary to evacuate, the Housing Authority will give warning at the earliest possible moment.

A siren and air horn would blow, the message promised, and sound trucks would broadcast instructions. If the warning came, residents were told not to panic, to pack personal goods and a change of clothes, to turn off lights and stoves, to close windows, and to lock doors. Sick, elderly, or disabled persons were encouraged to leave for a few days. The message concluded:

REMEMBER:
THE DIKES ARE SAFE AT PRESENT; YOU WILL BE WARNED IF NECESSARY; YOU WILL HAVE TIME TO LEAVE; DON'T GET EXCITED!

At 4:00 P.M. that afternoon, the river gauge on the north bank at Vancouver read 28.3 feet, 13 feet above flood stage. Near what was regarded as the strongest link in the chain of dikes protecting Vanport—the railroad fill to the west—the water level was still 17 feet below the top. This dike, 125 feet wide at its base and 75 feet wide at its top, was considered indestructible. But deep within its seemingly solid exterior lay a fatal weak spot.

At 4:17 P.M., without warning, the railroad fill gave way. Calvin Hulbert, who was flying a seaplane above the tracks when the roadbed washed out, saw it happen. Suddenly the break was six feet, then sixty, then five hundred feet wide. A ten-foot-high wall of water flattened some buildings; others crumpled or split open.

As the surging waves moved in, they struck the sides of the flimsy buildings with stunning impact, sending showers of spray fifty feet into the air. Because water is heavy and cannot be compressed, its destructive power is enormous. Rolling back and forth across the confined area inside the dikes, it tossed the buildings about like models made of balsa wood or cork.

Cars were sent careening; houses were torn apart. For half an hour, waves moved back and forth as the great river spread out over what once had been a densely populated city. All electric power went off at 4:50 P.M. Buildings floated like slow-moving giants, turning in whirlpools. Now and then a man, woman, or child was seen clinging to the side of a building until it again turned over, after which they were seen no more.

The fact that the area flooded on a warm Sunday afternoon greatly reduced the number of fatalities from drowning that would have surely occurred if the dike had broken during the night as people slept in their beds. Despite the promise made that morning in the bulletin, the warning siren either sounded too late, could not be heard, or did not sound at all.

The sheriff issued an emergency call for boats, which brought a quick response in this river city. As the rescue boats picked their way through the floating debris, people crawled through windows to get into the boats or waited on rooftops to be rescued. The compactness of the project and its proximity to city thoroughfares proved invaluable so far as rescue efforts were concerned. Buses, taxis, ambulances, and private cars lined the streets, with sightseers who had come to gawk often being put to work at more useful tasks.

The sudden flood made headlines all over the United States as the worst disaster of its kind since the Johnstown flood of May 31, 1899. It took months to compile the official death toll. Although over two thousand names were on the missing list, Sheriff Martin T. Pratt predicted the death count would total no more than twenty-five persons. He proved to be right. Though only eighteen bodies were found and identified, seven other people known to have been living in Vanport at the time of the flood remained lost and unaccounted for, so they were assumed to be victims.

From the day of the disaster it was clear that the question of liability was going to be important and difficult. The lack of warning and poor evacuation plans upset many people. No one seemed to know why this city that had once housed forty-two thousand had only one exit. Most residents felt that either HAP or the Corps of Engineers should be held accountable. HAP looked to the Corps, and the Corps recounted the history of diking in the area. The railroad fill had survived a similar situation in 1933, it was pointed out. In 1941, the whole system was completed and turned over to Peninsula Diking District Number 1. The most likely theory of the dike failure, the experts said, was that the fill had been dumped around an existing trestle. As the covered timbers rotted, they left the roadbed weak, and that was where the dike broke.

By the time the lawsuits reached the state courts, over seven hundred cases involving 2,993 claimants and ninety-one attorneys were registered. It was consolidated into a twenty-case class-action suit, which finally went to a federal court; the final ruling was that an "honest mistake" had been made, freeing both HAP and the Corps of Engineers of liability. By then, the former residents of Veterans' Village had either left the area or found other housing.

Vanport disappeared into oblivion.

But the results of the disastrous flood of 1948 were far-reaching. When the damage was totaled up, it was found that even though the peak flow of 1,050,000 cubic feet per second at the river's mouth had been slightly lower than the 1,174,000 cubic feet per second registered in 1894, the resulting damage was much higher, for many more people, cities, and expensive facilities existed now compared to those of fifty-four years ago, making the flood the worst in history.

The flood claimed thirty-five lives, drove an estimated sixty thousand people from their homes, and cost over $100 million in property damage. From the mouth of the Columbia River just below Astoria to its headwaters in Canada, stricken, angry people were demanding answers to two questions:

Why did it happen?

How can we keep it from happening again?

As Doug Warren and his fellow science professors at Washington State College were acutely aware, this was no time for simplistic answers such as "As long as water runs downhill, there will be floods." Nor were government officials or elected officeholders so foolish as to attempt to pass the blame to poor management or bad decisions by members of a rival bureau or political party. One by one as each question was asked, it had to be answered by a responsible expert.

Why didn't Grand Coulee Dam hold back the flood?

"Because a power-generating dam must be full in order to provide a maximum head to spin the turbines," a Bureau of Reclamation official replied. "The 151-mile-long reservoir behind the dam holds only five million acre-feet of water. Even if it had been completely drained in anticipation of the flood, it would have filled to overflowing in only five days at the rate the river was running."

What about the other dams in the system?

"Rock Island and Bonneville on the Columbia are power dams, with very little storage capacity," a BPA engineer pointed out. "On the Snake, Arrowrock, American Falls, and Jackson Lake store a relatively small amount of irrigation water, but if they had been empty too, they would have taken only a few inches off the crest of the flood for a few hours."

How much storage capacity would be needed to control a flood this size?

"In an average year, the Columbia pours 198 million acre-feet of water into the Pacific," a hydrologist answered, "of which 36 million acre-feet comes from its principal tributary, the Snake. The flow this year was much greater. The Corps of Engineers estimates that in order to control a potentially damaging flood on the Columbia River system, 40 million acre-feet of storage capacity would be needed."

Where would these storage dams be located?

"All over the system. The Corps of Engineers 308 Report made by Major John Butler back in 1931 lists a number of sites."

How would these dams be paid for?

"Mostly by income from the sale of electricity. They would be multipurpose dams, of course, providing navigation and recreational benefits, as well as irrigation water for arid lands—all of which would be charged a portion of the cost. Certainly, the flood-control benefits would be substantial and should be included in the cost-benefit formula ..."

Already, the facts and figures that would become part of that formula were being assembled, Doug Warren knew, and as a geologist at a state college he would be involved in the process. What was being contemplated, he soon realized, was nothing less than bringing the second largest river system in the United States completely under human control. As one Idaho senator put it, "We must put the Columbia and Snake Rivers to useful work. No longer can we permit their wild, destructive waters to run unharnessed to the sea. We must have a fully plumbed river system."

If some of his fellow science professors winced—as Doug did—at the thought of a river system that could be flushed like a toilet, they were careful not to voice their objections openly. After the major disaster that had occurred, the concept of a controlled river system was too appealing to be denigrated. Not only had the Grand Coulee Dam project proved itself worthwhile by providing the cheap hydroelectric power needed to win the war and manufacture the atomic bomb, it soon would be pumping water into the Coulee itself, eventually turning a million acres of dry, useless desert into green, productive land capable of supporting a large population.

If the recommendations of the 308 Report were followed, eight more dams would be built on the mainstem Columbia to supplement the three already in existence, turning the once-mighty river into a series of slackwater pools from Bonneville Dam at River Mile 145 to the Canadian border at River Mile 747. Because much of the river's water originated in Canada, it was hoped that by negotiations with the traditionally friendly neighbor, plans could be made to build dams and create large reservoirs north of the border. Not only would these dams hold back potentially damaging floodwaters, they also would augment downriver flow through the power-producing turbines of dams in the United States in accordance with the principle that each upriver dam doubled the efficiency of the one just below it.

"Canada doesn't need the power now, of course," a prominent BPA engineer said, "so we may have to build the dams ourselves, then reimburse Canada by giving them half the revenue from its sale."

When it was pointed out that the Pacific Northwest might not need all the power either, it was suggested that a high-voltage transmission line be built to Southern California, which was enduring a brownout at the moment, with the power being sold there.

On the Snake River, the principal tributary of the Columbia, a dozen or so more dams were planned too, whose slackwater pools and navigation locks would make the Snake navigable from its mouth to Lewiston, Idaho, 470 miles inland. Doug knew that his son, Jeff, was all for the idea because it would greatly expand the business of the Williams & Sons Tug and Barge Company.

The questions asked by Jenny, as a biologist, and by Doug, as a friend of the Wanapum Indians and an adopted member of the Priest Rapids band, were not answered by the river development advocates as clearly as they both would have liked them to be.

"What will be done to preserve the fish runs?" Jenny asked.

Well, the Corps of Engineers, BPA, and the Fish and Wildlife Service were consulting on the design of fish-ladders, the experts replied rather vaguely. They were sure some satisfactory means of getting anadromous fish around the dams would be worked out.

"What will happen to traditional Indian fishing places such as Celilo Falls and Priest Rapids?" Doug asked, "which were guaranteed to them by the Treaty of 1855?"

Well, the federal government will probably negotiate on that, just as they did when they made the treaty a hundred years ago.

In anticipation of what most people regarded as a dynamic era of river development that would benefit all residents of the Pacific Northwest, political entities called "port districts," which until now had existed only in cities accessible to seagoing ships, came into existence. Established in every county along the Columbia and Snake Rivers that hoped to become ports for bulk shippers, the districts were empowered to collect taxes, build docks, and engage in lobbying activity at the state and federal levels.

Recalling the early days of the Grand Coulee project, when Rufus Woods, Billy Clapp, and his Dam University friends had been so strapped for funds that they had forced Jim O'Sullivan to earn the title of the "poorest lobbyist in Washington," Doug had to admit that times had changed.

"I guess we'll have to go along with the changes," he told his wife sadly. "But I'm not sure I approve of what they're doing to our river, Jenny. It's been a member of the Warren family for six generations. We liked it the way it was."

30.
Epilogue

DURING THE FIFTY YEARS that have passed since the great flood which ends this novel, more changes have come to the Columbia River than occurred between the establishment of Fort Astoria in 1811 and the completion of Grand Coulee Dam in 1941. In 1948, only three dams existed on the Columbia River; three more had been built on its principal tributary, the Snake.

Now there are 161 dams on the watershed as a whole, ranging in size from large to small.

On the 1,250-mile length of the Columbia, the mainstem dams and their completion dates are:

River Mile	*Name*	*Completed*
145	Bonneville	1938
196	The Dalles	1957
230	John Day	1968
307	McNary	1953
412	Priest Rapids	1959
430	Wanapum	1963
483	Rock Island	1933
526	Wells	1967
552	Chief Joseph	1965
596	Grand Coulee	1941

Because a substantial portion of Columbia River water originates in Canada, it was necessary to bring that nation into the planning process. Since Grand Coulee blocked the return of anadromous fish to Canadian waters and electric energy benefits would help the economy of the United States more than that of Canada, some touchy negotiations were required before all the problems could be solved. But eventually they were, with the treaty being signed by President Lyndon Johnson and Canadian Prime Minister Lester Pearson on September 16, 1964.

Appropriately enough, the signing ceremony took place beneath the Peace Arch near Blaine, Washington, where a bronze plaque on the Canadian side states: BROTHERS DWELLING TOGETHER IN UNITY, while another on the American side says: CHILDREN OF A COMMON MOTHER.

Beneficial to both nations, the pact provides 14 million acre-feet of water storage behind five Canadian dams, with Canada entitled to 50 percent of the extra power generated downriver for the next fifty years. Added to the capacity of other dams in Montana, Idaho, and the Snake River in eastern Washington, this makes a total of 40 million acre-feet of storage capacity on the watershed as a whole, thus ensuring that devastating floods such as the one in 1948 can never happen again.

Like all projects that drastically alter the natural environment, the end-effects of having what engineers call "a fully plumbed river system" do not please everybody. Ironically enough, it was Idaho Senator Len Jordan who first used that phrase during a debate on whether a high dam should be built in the depths of Hells Canyon on the Snake River, near where he and his wife, Grace, long had owned a sheep ranch. Her nonfiction book, *Home Below Hells Canyon*, incidentally, is a classic in its field.

Stating that it was high time the wild, free-flowing Snake River be put to work, Senator Jordan said that the Colorado River in the thirsty Southwest already had enough storage dams in its length to contain four years of the river's flow, thus making the Colorado "a fully plumbed river" whose example should be emulated. The fact that this did not happen hinged on a landmark Supreme Court decision written by Justice William O. Douglas, who would become a patron saint of the environmental movement.

While most of the dams on the Columbia River were built by the Bureau of Reclamation, the Corps of Engineers, or taxpayer-supported public utility districts, many of those on the upper and middle reaches of the Snake had been built by the Idaho Power Company, a private utility. On the lower Snake beginning at its juncture with the Columbia near Pasco, the Corps of Engineers during the 1960s was building Ice Harbor, Lower Monumental, Little Goose, and Lower Granite Dams. Joined by the Bureau of Reclamation and a number of public utility districts, the Corps of Engineers applied for a federal license to build the biggest dam of all, High Mountain Sheep, in the heart of Hells Canyon. Joining Idaho Power in an attempt to secure an FPC license for the same site was a combine of private utilities called Pacific Northwest Power.

At issue was whether the ninety-eight-mile stretch of wild river upstream from Lewiston would be "put to work" by public or private power. But even as these two adversaries prepared for their Battle of Armageddon in the depths of Hells Canyon, a third party entered the contest.

The environmentalist.

He had been around for a long while in many guises: the Indian inarticulately protesting the flooding of his traditional fishing grounds; the bird-watcher concerned over the loss of nesting areas for migratory waterfowl; the sports fisherman worried about the future of steelhead and salmon; the Sierra Club member in love with wilderness areas; the white-water boatman bent on preserving a few challenging rapids; the naturalist, the antiquarian, the maiden lady in tennis shoes, and other assorted "little" people who for obscure reasons insisted on throwing their fragile bodies before the juggernaut of Progress.

The question was not *who* should build the next dam, they quietly insisted, but whether *any* dam should be built. For a long while, private power advocates, public power boosters, the Federal Power Commission, and the courts, which were being called upon to referee the frequent quarrels, paid them little heed.

But the mouse had roared.

Eventually, the complicated dispute reached the United States Supreme Court, which was asked to rule on a two-part question:

(1) Should the FPC reconsider its order licensing Pacific Northwest Power to build the High Mountain Sheep Dam?

(2) Did the association of public utilities have a preference claim on the site?

The Court ruled on neither question. Instead, in a 6–2 decision dated June 5, 1967, with Justice William O. Douglas writing the majority opinion, it decreed: "The test is whether the project will be in the public interest. And that determination can be made only after an exploration of all issues relevant ..."

One highly relevant issue, the opinion stated, was "the public interest in preserving reaches of rivers and wilderness areas, the preservation of anadromous fish for commercial and recreation purposes, and the protection of wildlife ..."

From that day on, the controversy between people who wanted to put the river to work and those who wished to preserve portions of it in its natural state began—and has continued down to the present day.

By the mid-1970s, the dam-building era had ended, with most of the licensed dams completed and a few of the more dubious ones canceled. After years of hearings and volumes of reports, ninety-one miles of the Snake River upstream from Lewiston was declared a National Recreation Area in which the building of dams was prohibited, with recreational activities such as river-running, hunting, fishing, hiking, and sightseeing to be supervised by the National Forest Service.

Ten miles of the headwaters of the Snake in Jackson Hole still ran free, as did twenty-five miles of scenic river below the town of Jackson, Wyoming. All the rest of the 1,036-mile length of the Snake River waters had been stilled by a total of forty-eight large, medium, and small dams.

On the mainstem Columbia, the 145 miles of river between Bonneville and the Pacific remained undammed, with a forty-foot-deep ship channel to Portland and a twenty-four-foot-deep tug-and-barge channel to Bonneville being maintained by the Corps of Engineers.

Upriver from Bonneville, the Columbia had been turned into a series of slackwater pools all the way to the Canadian border except for a 51-mile stretch of river called the "Hanford Reach" just upstream from Pasco. Though at one time plans had been drawn to dam this section of river, they were postponed because of the wartime Hanford atomic bomb project when public access was forbidden. Later, the project was canceled because only thirty-seven feet of vertical fall existed in the area, making the proposed Ben Franklin Dam impractical.

At Grand Coulee in the early 1950s, the long-delayed irrigation part of the project finally got under way with the completion of pumping facilities to lift water up and over the ridge and into the upper portion of the Coulee, from which it could be distributed by gravity flow to the thirsty lands downslope. Sucking water up through twelve fourteen-foot diameter pipes, each pump is rated at 65,000 horsepower, with a lift of 280 feet. Discharging the water into the Coulee (which does *not* leak), the twelve pumps create an instant river, which already has irrigated 500,000 acres of desert land and eventually will irrigate half a million more. Two of the pumps contain reversible turbines capable of generating electricity with water drained back into Lake Roosevelt, if the need should ever arise.

That a shortage of electricity will ever occur at Grand Coulee is highly unlikely; following completion of the third powerhouse, the dam now generates 9.2 million kilowatts of electricity and is North America's leader in that field.

As a means of distributing energy through the Bonneville Power Administration system, a high-tech center situated atop a bluff near The Dalles, Oregon, serves a function unlike any other on the continent. Called the Celilo Converter Station, the purpose of the center is to analyze the power needs of the western third of the United States and Canada, then instantly dispatch all the electric power being produced by the thirty major dams on the Columbia River system, plus that being produced by coal, oil, nuclear, wind, sun, and other facilities in the Pacific Northwest to wherever it is needed.

Through the Celilo Converter Station flows an incredible amount of electricity generated by at least 150 units as far north as British Columbia, as far east as Montana, as far west as the lower Columbia, and as far south as Los Angeles.

The station's single million-volt direct current line (DC), for instance, can carry enough electricity to supply the needs of Los Angeles. In addition to this high-capacity transmission line, which runs uninterrupted across 846 miles of high desert and mountain country to the Sylmar Station near Los Angeles, there are three 500,000-volt alternating current (AC) lines that run parallel to it for a ways before heading west toward Oregon and California population centers.

Collectively, these transmission lines are called the "Intertie." Its purpose is to carry electricity from a region that produces it in abundance to regions where it is in short supply.

Eighty percent of the electricity generated in the Pacific Northwest is hydropower, while that generated in the South is mostly thermal power. Each relies on spinning turbines, but one uses the weight of falling water while the other uses the force of steam created by burning gas, oil, coal, or nuclear fuel. Since falling water is a renewable resource, hydro generation is cheaper, costing only a cent or two per kilowatt hour. Thermal generation, which uses nonrenewable resources, is more expensive, costing five or six cents per kilowatt hour. An exchange rate of three or so cents per kilowatt hour between an area with a surplus and one with a deficit benefits everybody.

Of the thirty major dams on the Columbia River system, only a few have any significant storage capacity. This means that during periods of high runoff, the water must be "spilled," or allowed to leave the reservoir without making electricity. Usually this happens during the late spring and summer months, when Southern California's needs for air-conditioning are great. By sending the cheaper hydropower south, that region can avoid generating expensive thermal energy. During the winter, when river water in the Pacific Northwest is locked up as snow and ice but electric needs for heating and light intensify, the South can send thermal power north over the two-way Intertie.

In practice, the exchange is not quite that simple, of course; in fact, the energy exchange may turn around hourly, depending on sophisticated computer calculations to monitor who owes whom how much and whether the debt will be paid in energy or cash. But the exchange is beneficial to all who participate.

A different kind of exchange between the water-rich North and the desert South, which became a controversial issue during the 1970s, was not settled so amicably. This was the proposal to divert water from the Snake or Columbia River to the metropolitan centers of Los Angeles, Las Vegas, and Phoenix, whose rate of population growth was rising while their supply of water diminished. Instead of letting all that 198 million-acre feet of clean, fresh, cold Columbia River water flow wasted to the sea, the thirsty southland wondered, why not have the federal government develop a project to send some of it our way?

For a time, it appeared that the water-diversion question would lead to serious trouble. The root of the problem, so far as the Pacific

Northwest was concerned, was that while it had the water, California had the votes. But by a series of delaying tactics (such as a ten-year moratorium on even permitting the question to be studied), the politicians of the states drained by the Columbia River system managed to stall long enough to let Southern California's problems with smog, traffic, and excess population become so acute that instead of water being sent south, Californians came north, inundating Oregon, Washington, and Idaho with a flood of people whose influx was thought in some quarters to be far less of a bargain than if water *had* been sent south …

Finally, one of the major unanticipated results of the dam-building era was the damage done to the fish runs. To ensure passage around Bonneville Dam, the first one built on the Columbia River in 1938, a "ladder," was designed to provide white-water pools resembling rapids surmounted by anadromous fish during their once-in-a-lifetime return to the mountain streams of their birth. Drawn by a concentrated spill of "attraction water" flowing at the foot of the ladder, 85 percent of the fish reaching the dam climbed a series of pools rising a foot at a time from the base of the dam to the quiet water above. The 15 percent that failed to climb the ladder would be replaced by a hatchery built just below Bonneville Dam, the experts said.

When McNary, The Dalles, and John Day dams were built, fish ladders were included in their designs. There, too, 15 percent of the fish reaching the foot of each dam failed to solve the ladder obstacle; but the experts overcame the loss by raising and releasing more hatchery fish.

Fish ladders are impractical when the height of a dam exceeds 100 feet, so the 550-foot-high Grand Coulee Dam has no such facilities. As a result, all anadromous fish runs upstream from it—including the entire upper Columbia River watershed in Canada—ended. Canada did not protest unduly. After all, theirs was a big country with many rivers filled with fish.

The Indians who traditionally fished at Celilo Falls did protest the building of The Dalles Dam. This stretch of white water was being smoothed out forever, they knew, and they could not gaff or net salmon in still water. Back in 1855, the federal government had made treaties with all the Indian tribes in the Pacific Northwest, requiring them to give up most of their ancestral lands in exchange for relatively small amounts of money and goods, plus guarantees that the government would take care of them on designated reservations.

In addition, the Great White Father promised that they would be permitted "to fish and take game in your usual and accustomed places forever ..."

The obliteration of Celilo Falls, the most important fishing place on the Columbia River for many tribes, required monetary compensation for its loss. The Yakima Nation, the Nez Perce Tribe, the Umatilla Confederation, and the Warm Springs Tribe were awarded cash sums ranging from $3 million to $10 million, according to how much value could be placed on their loss of the Celilo fishery.

As the dam-building era came to an end during the mid-1970s, the fish experts were surprised to discover that despite the tender loving care they thought had been given to migrating salmon, steelhead, and sturgeon, fish in the Columbia River system were dying in alarming numbers.

The killer, they soon learned, was nitrogen, defined by *Webster's* dictionary as "a colorless, tasteless, odorless gaseous chemical forming nearly four-fifths of the atmosphere and a component of all living things." In normal amounts, it is harmless. In excessive amounts, it is lethal.

Whether natural or man-made, all waterfalls pick up nitrogen and carry it into the pools in which they plunge. The process causes the water in these pools to become "supersaturated" with up to half again the normal nitrogen level. When fish absorb excessive nitrogen into their bloodstream through respiration, they sicken and die—like a diver with the "bends."

Below a natural waterfall, river water gives up its nitrogen when it strikes shallows and rapids, resuming a normal balance of the elements. But below each man-made dam on the Columbia and the Snake, there is typically only a quarter-mile or so of free-flowing river before another still, deep pool up to fifty miles long is encountered. In these pools, the nitrogen content reaches a level far above the 110 percent that anadromous fish can tolerate for a brief period of time.

To ensure propagation of the species, at least 22,500 adult steelhead must pass through the counting station at Lower Granite Dam on the Snake River. It is the eighth dam pool (following Bonneville,

The Dalles, John Day, and McNary on the Columbia; Ice Harbor, Lower Monumental, and Little Goose on the Snake) that the fish must swim through before they reach their spawning beds. So the nitrogen supersaturation problem—added to the stress of negotiating eight sets of fish ladders—proved deadly to the fish runs.

In the autumn of 1974, only ten thousand steelhead made their way through the counting station at Lower Granite Dam. Faced with the stark prospect that this seagoing trout most prized by fishermen would vanish forever from the upriver streams, the Fish and Game Departments of Idaho, Oregon, and Washington closed the season to all sportsmen in early October that year. For three years, the season remained closed while fish experts and the Corps of Engineers took desperate measures to restore the runs.

The Corps experimented with several devices intended to reduce the amount of nitrogen absorbed by the falling water—perforated gates, flip-lips, and others—but none worked very well. Because the loss of a few adult fish could be tolerated, while the preservation of the young smolt was vital, the fish experts concentrated on saving the young fish, which would be the breeding stock of the future.

Several unique methods of transporting the steelhead smolt around the downstream hazards were tried. A few made the trip down the Snake and Columbia in deluxe style—by air, in a specially equipped tanker plane. Others were transported around the dam pools by tanker trucks whose refrigerated, oxygen-enriched water kept the fish in the best possible environment during the long ride from eastern Washington to western Oregon.

Soon after the completion of Lower Granite Dam in 1975, another method of transporting smolt downstream was tried: hauling them by tug and barge. Since two million smolt can fit into a barge filled with specially conditioned water, this has proved to be the most efficient and successful of all the methods tried to date.

By September 1977, the steelhead count at Lower Granite had increased to forty-five thousand and so, after three closed seasons, sports fishing in the three states resumed. The problem seemed solved. But during the late 1980s, Mother Nature taught us another lesson regarding what happens when we make drastic alterations in the natural environment.

Hatchery-raised fish, the biologists learned, did not possess the natural immunity to disease that wild fish whose ancestors had lived in the Pacific Northwest for millennia did. Consequently, when a virus or germ that would not affect a wild fish got into a batch of hatchery-bred fish, they all sickened and died.

The solution to that problem, the fish experts realized, was to increase the number of wild fish spawning and going to sea from Pacific Northwest rivers. But this was not happening. Instead, one species—the sockeye salmon—which for eons had migrated from the mouth of the Columbia River almost a thousand miles to the white-graveled beds of Redfish Lake at the foot of the Sawtooth Mountains in Idaho—had dwindled almost to the vanishing point.

The shocking discovery in 1991 that only five sockeye salmon—that's right, five—had returned to spawn in Redfish Lake caused the species immediately to be put on the endangered list.

Since that time, state and federal Fish and Game officials have become aware of the fact that the most valuable anadromous fish of all, the Chinook salmon, is also in trouble. Whether blame for the diminishing runs should be placed on the increased number of dams, industrial pollution, the siltation of spawning beds by poor logging practices, or a combination of all these factors remains to be seen.

But the situation is so serious that in 1995, all commercial and most sports fishing off the coasts of Oregon and Washington was closed down completely. What is involved here is the shutdown of a food and sports industry that generates a billion dollars annually.

Though none of the experts have come up with a solution for this massive problem, one school of biologists has suggested that if a way could be found to move downriver-migrating smolt to the sea more quickly, a larger number of them might survive the hazards of the dam pools. At present, it takes fifty-three days for the smolt to travel from the Lower Granite Dam pool to saltwater, biologists say. By releasing more water from each dam pool, the Corps of Engineers suggested, they could imitate the seasonal flooding of the rivers that existed before the dams were built, reducing the fifty-three-day period by half.

After a great deal of discussion and controversy, a month-long experiment called a "drawdown" was tried in March 1992, and may be repeated in years to come. Its overall results cannot become known until that particular batch of salmon returns to the river several years from now. But the screams of the people affected by the drawdown—

which in the Lewiston-Clarkston sector of the Snake was twenty-eight feet—were immediate and loud.

Port district and tug-and-barge companies whose shipping was suspended for thirty days felt they were being badly abused. Private marina operators whose docks were damaged and whose users now found several hundred feet of mudflats where deep water used to flow were outraged. Because the large releases of water could not be used to generate electricity, the Bonneville Power Administration said it might have to raise electric rates, which displeased all their customers. Even though the irrigation season had not yet come, farmers pumping out of the dam pools feared they might have to add to the length of their intakes, install new pumps, or pay higher pumping costs.

For a time, threats were made by a number of interests to sue somebody for damages—though exactly who should be sued for what was not clear. Now that the first experiment has ended and the Snake and Columbia have been raised to their normal levels, the complaints have subsided. But they illustrate how complicated the regulation of a great river system has become.

So far as we know, not even the most radical environmentalist has suggested that the sure way to renew the anadromous fish runs in the Columbia River system would be to remove *all* the dams and let *all* the water run unharnessed to the sea. The people of the region and the nation have far too much invested in the facilities that have been installed during the past century to deliberately destroy them for the benefit of even a billion-dollar-a-year fishing industry.

The dams could never be destroyed by a natural calamity, of course. Unless …

Unless, instead of warming, the earth should turn cold again, as it did in the several ice ages that occurred not too many thousands of years ago, with an ice lobe moving south to form a dam across the Clark Fork River half a mile high, backing up a lake twenty miles wide and fifty miles long, containing five hundred cubic miles of water, which, when the dam collapsed, would send a catastrophic flood racing down the Columbia River at fifty-eight miles an hour, destroying everything in its path.

In an early paper, J Harlen Bretz said he had found evidence that such a flood had taken place at least seven times in the fairly recent geological past. By the time he died, he had revised that estimate upward to say such a flood may have taken place at least forty-one times.

So, for the true lover of a free-flowing river, there still is something to look forward to …

End of Book Three